The Tenor Man's Story

Carole Strachan

Cinnamon Press
:: small miracles from distinctive voices ::

Published by Cinnamon Press,
Office 49019, PO Box 15113, Birmingham, B2 2NJ
www.cinnamonpress.com

Designed and typeset in Adobe Caslon Pro by Cinnamon Press.
Cover design by Adam Craig © Adam Craig. Image: DMP/iStock.
Cinnamon Press is represented by Inpress

Permissions

Author biography

Carole Strachan grew up in Merthyr Tydfil and studied History at St Hugh's College, Oxford. In a working life that took her from the Potteries to Manchester, from Cardiff to Llandeilo and back to Oxford, in 2001 she returned to live permanently in South Wales. This is her third novel for Cinnamon Press and like *The Truth in Masquerade* (2016) and *A Song of Thyme and Willow* (2019), its characters inhabit the world of classical music, reflecting the twenty-three years Carole spent working in opera.

Also by Carole Strachan

The Truth in Masquerade

An unusual story of love, loss and the possibility of second chances, *The Truth in Masquerade* follows Anna Maxwell, struggling to understand the abrupt ending of her marriage. Haunted by memories of her husband, Edwyn, and of another man who once loved her, she returns to Oxford to sing the role of the Governess in Benjamin Britten's spine-chilling opera, *The Turn of the Screw*. Caught up in a world of secrets and uncertainties, Anna has to confront the reasons her marriage unravelled. Meanwhile, Edwyn, is haunted by his own ghosts, and a mystery of identity is revealed that Anna must resolve for both of them, if either is to move on with life.

A Song of Thyme & Willow

At the heart of the story is the mystery of Isabel Grey, a successful opera singer who disappeared in the late 1970s. Two musicians, facing life-changing crises of their own, decide to look for her. Steven Bennett's career as an orchestral bassoonist has been ended by a violent mugging; singer Alice Wade is suffering serious vocal problems and trying to move on from the latest in a long line of failed relationships.

When Steven takes a job as archivist for Hope Street Theatre and Alice takes refuge in the house she's inherited from her godmother, Imogen, finding that Imogen had a sister she never spoke of, their discoveries become woven into Isabel's gradually unfolding story. As Isabel emerges from the shadows, Alice faces her own loss and, not wanting her life to become a sad echo of Isabel's, must look to the future with courage and acceptance.

For there is no despair so absolute as that which comes with the first moments of our first great sorrow, when we have not yet known what it is to have suffered and be healed, to have despaired and to have recovered hope.

George Eliot *Adam Bede*

In the dark times
Will there also be singing?
Yes, there will be singing.
About the dark times.

Bertolt Brecht *The Svendborg Poems*

The Tenor Man's Story

The Choirmaster's Burial—'The Tenor Man's Story'
by Thomas Hardy

He often would ask us
That, when he died,
After playing so many
To their last rest,
If out of us any
Should here abide,
And it would not task us,
We would with our lutes
Play over him
By his grave-brim
The psalm he liked best—
The one whose sense suits
"Mount Ephraim"—
And perhaps we should seem
To him, in death's dream,
Like the seraphim.

As soon as I knew
That his spirit was gone
I thought this his due,
And spoke thereupon.
"I think," said the vicar,
"A read service quicker
Than viols out-of-doors
In these frosts and hoars.
That old-fashioned way
Requires a fine day,
And it seems to me
It had better not be."

Hence, that afternoon,
Though never knew he
That his wish could not be,
To get through it faster
They buried the master
Without any tune.

But 'twas said that, when
At the dead of next night
The vicar looked out,
There struck on his ken
Thronged roundabout,
Where the frost was graying
The headstoned grass,
A band all in white
Like the saints in church-glass,
Singing and playing
The ancient stave
By the choirmaster's grave.

Such the tenor man told
When he had grown old.

PART 1
Winter 1983 to Spring 1987

6 December 1983

Fog smothered the city like a blanket—a winter visitation both sinister and beautiful. In the parks and meadows, ice sheaths had appeared on the trees and hedgerows and the streetlights were so faint and blurred as to be of little use. Even the showy Christmas decorations were no more than glowing smears in the mist, with one side of the street barely visible from the other.

Near the church of St Giles, two cyclists, trying to avoid a bus that bore down on them out of the darkness, found themselves sprawled on the icy pavement in a tangle of wheels and spilt saddle bags. Bruised but unhurt, they picked up their bikes and their bags and pedalled away into the night. In the distance behind them, the clock at Carfax Tower chimed the half hour, its bells sounding muffled and mysterious. A mile away, the Holywell Music Room resounded with applause for a song recital just ending, the audience unaware they would soon emerge into a world robbed of all its familiar markers.

People were standing, demanding more. When Johnny smiled and went back to the piano, there were grateful murmurs of anticipation and soon everyone was once again seated. Though I was tired and my left leg was aching, I hoped our final gesture would be as potent as the last sentence of a book or the closing frames of a film—a delicate postscript the audience would take out into the world with them. I waited for the last ripples of applause to die away, and as I smiled at the faces looking up at me from the lower part of the hall, in my mind's eye, I saw my parents, Jane and George, in a row near the front almost forty years ago. They'd ventured out alone to hear a concert in Freshers' Week and prophetically found themselves sitting next to each other.

'Thank you,' I said at last. 'Thank you for being such an appreciative audience. I know you'd like something else, and if you'll allow me, I'll sing two more songs to close the evening.'

I felt my breathing quicken and I took a moment to shift my weight and steady myself. 'First of all, a simple little song that has particular significance for me, and I'd like to tell you why it's so special.'

I paused again and some of the audience leaned forward, as if willing me to go on. 'In 1956, I spent several months in hospital in Cork. It was the most frightening time of my life. I'd never been away from my parents before and for several weeks, they weren't allowed to visit me. I was very scared, but I was lucky, because one of the nurses took me under her wing and looked after me. Everyone called her "Jeanie with the light brown hair". She was very pretty and very kind and like all the young doctors on the ward, I wanted to marry her.' I shook my head and smiled. 'I was five years old.'

Some of the audience laughed. 'Whenever she had time, at the end of a day shift, Jeanie would carry me downstairs and push me in a wheelchair into a quiet corner of the grounds. And once there, she'd tell me stories and sing to me, and in those dark months, I learnt to love words and music and singing.'

I faltered as I recalled the sweet voice that had consoled and delighted me all those years ago. 'I didn't marry Jeanie, but we stayed in touch and became good friends. She married one of those young doctors and sadly, he rang me this morning to tell me she died in her sleep last night.'

Someone in the audience gasped audibly and I felt my heart skip a beat. 'She'd been ill for many months, but her death came sooner than expected.'

There was a whisper of sighs around the room, and before I continued, I somehow summoned a smile.

'Jeanie loved ballads and folk songs and one of her favourites was *Simple Gifts*. It's well-known and popular now, but until 1944 it was a little-known Shaker song and then the American composer Aaron Copland made its haunting melody the central musical idea for his ballet, *Appalachian Spring*. A few years later, in 1950, at the request of Benjamin Britten, Copland arranged it for piano and singer as part of his set of *Old American Songs*, and it was given its first performance at the Aldeburgh Festival that summer by Peter Pears accompanied by Britten. It appears to be a simple Shaker dancing song, incorporating the dance instructions into the lyrics. But listen to the words, and you'll see that the song relates to much more than a dance between two people.'

I spoke the words aloud:

'Tis the gift to be simple, 'tis the gift to be free,
'Tis the gift to come down where we ought to be,
And when we find ourselves in the place just right,
'Twill be in the valley of love and delight.

When true simplicity is gain'd,
To bow and to bend we shan't be asham'd,

To turn, turn will be our delight,
Till by turning, turning we come round right.

'As you see, it's about the dance we perform every day of our lives, and it advocates a way of living lightly in the world—simple and free. Copland was once asked what he thought his music would be remembered for and he said he hoped it would be seen as an affirmation of life, so I'd like to sing this song as an affirmation of Jeanie's life.'

I didn't want to break the mood, so I didn't move back to my earlier position near the piano, but sang from where I stood, at the edge of the platform. After two short bars of piano introduction, we began. By devising an accompaniment placed squarely on the weak beats, Copland gave the song a recitative-like quality, ensuring it would be sung without a regular rhythmic pulse, but I knew Johnny would follow me, however freely I took it, and I relaxed into focussing on the intention behind the words.

At the end, I closed my eyes briefly and smiled. After a short silence, there was warm applause and I stepped back to acknowledge Johnny and signal for him to stand. When the clapping died away, Johnny sat down, and I moved forward once again.

'My final song tonight is—in my view—a miraculous masterpiece. It's by one of the greatest ever song composers, Franz Schubert, and was written when he knew that time was running out for him. He completed this song not long before he died, a couple of months short of his 32nd birthday.' I paused. 'The age I am today. It's called *Der Winterabend—The Winter Evening*—and it conveys the pleasure of being indoors on a long winter evening, with the narrator enjoying the tranquillity of his moonlit room in a small town. He tells us that the tradesmen have stopped work and gone home, and the street noises are deadened by a blanket of snow. In the beautiful, aching melody Schubert captures both the contentment of the man and the pain, as he remembers his wife, lost to him in person, but still very much alive in his heart.'

I stopped and clasped my hands together. 'Ill as he was, Schubert could still write music of extraordinary serenity and joy and I'd like to dedicate this exquisite song to Jeanie's husband, Eamon.'

In the small, elegant music room, I knew I could lower my voice as if I was crooning a lullaby to a sleepy child and I'd still be heard by people sitting in the tiers of crimson benches at the back. Immediately, I lost myself in the narrator's musings and memories, imagining myself sitting alone in the darkness, gazing up at the clouds and stars, my only visitor the silent moonlight. In the song's final lines, when the narrator looks back to a vanished past, I saw, immediately in my line of vision, an elderly man reach for his wife's hand, while along the row from them, a young woman in a bright red jumper closed her eyes and held her hands on her chest. On her right hand, a ring clustered with diamonds sparkled in the light of the gilded chandelier above her head.

When it was over there was a long silence before the audience allowed themselves to applaud. Johnny stepped forward and took my hand, squeezing it hard as we smiled and bowed. The woman in the red jumper was dabbing her eyes and, when she smiled up at us, I saw that her cheeks were glistening with tears.

Later, when everyone had gone and we were ready to leave, a subtle pang of loneliness tugged at my heart. I needed companionship and was glad that Johnny wasn't rushing back to London. We stepped into the street to discover the city had been taken over by a gothic-like miasma. We edged our way down Bath Place, a cobbled lane off Holywell Street, at the end of which the Turf Tavern awaited. Its two small bars were usually crammed and noisy with drinkers, but tonight it was easy to find a table in a quiet corner. The atmosphere was convivial enough, with the mainly student clientele refusing to allow the weather to spoil their end of term festivities.

While Johnny waited at the bar to be served, I hunted in my music bag for the small torch I kept there in case of gloomy church lighting or ill-timed power cuts, and which tonight, I'd be glad of on the walk home. As I retrieved the torch from among the music and pencils and put it in my coat pocket, my mind was a jumble of disjointed memories, and I was relieved when Johnny sat down with two pints of real ale and some crisps.

'Cheers,' he said. 'Well done tonight. I know that was tough for you.'

My shoulders sagged and as I looked into my pint, I let out a long sigh. 'It was, but I think it went alright.'

'More than alright,' he assured me. 'The audience seemed to particularly enjoy the direct connection you made with them when you introduced the pieces, especially the encores. I do love that Schubert—the accompaniment almost as much as the vocal line. All those pattering semi-quavers give it a wonderful hypnotic restfulness.'

'I fear the audience will be roused out of any restfulness by having to find their way home through this filthy fog,' I said with a grimace.

'How will you get home?' he asked.

'If there's a taxi on the rank in St Giles, I'll take it. If not, I'll brave my way northwards.'

We settled into companionable silence, before Johnny asked me about Jeanie.

'I met her a few weeks after I was transferred from St Finbarr's Fever Hospital to St Mary's, the rehabilitation unit. It was on a steep hill overlooking the centre of Cork.' I frowned and shook my head. 'I hated the place and if it hadn't been for Jeanie, I think I might have died there.'

Johnny's eyes widened in alarm.

'St Finbarr's was pretty old, but the nuns who were in charge were lovely. Perhaps understandably, the Irish health authorities concentrated the best doctors and nurses in St Finbarr's, and they let the staff of St Mary's run it like a barracks, with threats and shouting the default modus operandi.'

'Sounds grim,' said Johnny, offering me a crisp.

'It was brutal. Jeanie was new and by the time she arrived, I'd retreated into silent misery, but in the midst of harridans, she was an angel of mercy. She was a trained nurse—unlike most of the others—and she had an interest in rehabilitation, which was why she was there and not at St Finbarr's.'

I chewed a mouthful of crisps and washed them down with a gulp of beer. 'One night, she found me crying in the dark. I'd wet the bed and was terrified of the wrath of the Matron. Without any fuss, Jeanie sorted me out and then brought me a glass of milk and a chocolate biscuit.'

'Bless her. How long were you there?'

'Three weeks at St Finbarr's, which is where you went for the acute stage of the virus. Almost four months in St Mary's.'

For a moment, I fell silent. I'd learned endurance from a young age and part of that involved filtering out unhappy memories, but Jeanie's death made it feel necessary to face those parts of my childhood experience that were not completely lost to conscious memory. Johnny was a kind and patient listener, and I knew I could open up to him.

'Did I ever tell you about Bobby?' I asked.

Johnny shook his head and frowned, as if trying to recall the name.

'He and I were admitted to St Finbarr's on the same day, and we were in beds next to each other. He was a Londoner, too, and like me he was visiting Ireland for the summer. He was staying with his grandmother—the first time he'd been away from home without his parents and his younger brother. He was missing them.'

I ran my fingers across the rim of my glass. 'When the pain was bad for one of us, we'd ask the nurses to push our beds together so we could hold hands.' I smiled. 'I always thought he was very brave. Even though he was so ill, he was a live wire.'

'How old was he?'

'He was nine but he seemed so much older than me. He couldn't wait to go home for the start of the football season. He and his dad went to West Ham matches together.'

I turned to look at Johnny and his steady goodness encouraged me to go on. 'When I was feeling especially miserable, he'd do his best to cheer me up.' I laughed. 'He had a good line in funny faces.'

To my horror, I could feel my eyes fill with tears, but Johnny, completely unperturbed, simply touched my hand and without saying anything, waited for me to go on.

'At first, we had mostly the same symptoms—terrible headaches, raging fever, unbearable muscle ache—but Bobby developed a cough and was soon having difficulty breathing. They moved him to another part of the ward where I couldn't see him. The next morning, his bed was still empty. The nurses were busy, and it was lunchtime before one of the nuns came to tell me that he had died in the early hours.'

Johnny gasped and then sighed.

'I couldn't grasp what she was saying or what it meant, but the loss of him knocked the stuffing out of me, so by the time I was transferred to St Mary's I was very low. That first time Jeanie looked after me, I told her about Bobby and I'm sure it was her gentle care at that traumatic time in my life that put me back on the road to recovery.'

'Thanks be,' said Johnny, quietly.

I nodded.

'I owe her so much. I'm relieved I can get to her funeral on Saturday.'

We finished our beers and agreed it would be wise to make a move. I pulled on my duffle coat and my claret and blue striped gloves.

'How are they doing?' Johnny asked, nodding in the direction of my hands as I held the door open for him.

'Well, they lost in the cup on Saturday, but they're in a good position in the league.'

Outside, thick fog still clung to everything, and it felt frightening and yet thrilling to be venturing into a world so utterly transformed by the elements. The illuminated window displays of Blackwell's briefly gave us guidance, but as we passed the Sheldonian and headed further up Broad Street, the fog was so dense it was like walking through a cloud. It was a relief when the Martyrs' Memorial gradually emerged from the mist.

'What time are you leaving tomorrow?' I asked, before we went our separate ways and Johnny set off towards Worcester College, where he was staying the night.

'I'm having coffee with one of my old room mates who has a Junior Fellowship at Worcester. I'll get a train after that. What about you?'

'A train to Manchester mid-afternoon.'

He moved forward to embrace me in a bear hug. 'All the best,' he said. 'See you soon.'

I stood outside the Randolph Hotel and watched him go. I'd only gone a short distance when he called after me. 'Alex, I almost forgot. I promised to serenade you.'

I smiled and pressed on towards St Giles, with the strains of *Happy Birthday* growing ever fainter as my friend disappeared down the noiseless street.

Park Town

I was not surprised to find there were no taxis on the rank. The beam of my torch was no match for the enveloping mist, but it helped me navigate my way across the broadest point of St Giles to join the Banbury Road. In the distance I heard a dog barking, but the streets were eerily empty of people and traffic. The graveyard of St Giles loomed to the left and as I walked alongside the churchyard wall, I heard a woman's voice calling out from somewhere ahead of me.

'Please, will you help me?'

I stopped and listened.

'I'm down here, on the path.'

I shone the torch downwards and saw a woman, no more than a couple of feet away from me, leaning her back against the wall.

'Are you hurt?' I asked, bending down beside her.

She held up something that in the light of the torch I could see was a bicycle pump.

'I didn't see it,' she explained, handing it to me, 'and I stepped on it and slipped over. I think I've sprained my ankle.'

'Oh, poor you. Where are you trying to get to?'

'Home, to Park Town.'

'Do you think you could walk that far if you lean on me? I'm going to Bardwell Road, so it's on my way.'

'Thank you, yes,' she said, with obvious relief. 'I'm so grateful to you for stopping.'

I helped her to her feet and as she smoothed out her crumpled coat, I placed the bicycle pump on top of the wall.

'How long have you been here?'

'About an hour,' she said, shivering. 'The clock at Carfax struck ten o'clock when I passed the Martyrs' Memorial.'

'It's almost eleven now. You must be freezing,' I said, noticing her bare hands.

'Thank goodness for my hat,' she said, looking up at me with a smile.

'Have my gloves,' I said, peeling them off and handing them to her.

As she eased them over her stiffened fingers, there was a momentary sparkle of diamonds. 'They feel good,' she said. 'As warm as toast. Thank you.'

I nodded. She took my arm and we set off, tentatively at first as she tested how much weight her ankle could tolerate. She was slightly built but I saw her glance quizzically at me and assumed she was concerned she was leaning against me too heavily.

'Don't worry,' I said, laughing. 'I can manage.'

But that was not it. She stopped at a lamp post and under its hazy glow she looked up into my face. 'You're Alexander Ingram, aren't you? I thought I recognised your voice.'

'Were you at the recital?'

She nodded and I realised she was the young woman in the red jumper.

'I loved it,' she said, as we set off again, 'especially the Schubert. It's so wistful, yet somehow very soothing.'

'It's one of my favourites, and it seemed right to sing it tonight.'

She squeezed my arm gently. 'My mother died when she was thirty-two, and as you were singing it, I imagined my father sitting alone by the fire, remembering their life together. The time they had was very brief—only twelve years.'

This frank disclosure took me off guard but before I could come up with an appropriate response, she spoke again.

'I'm Emily, by the way. Emily Fairfax. Perhaps you know my father?'

'Freddie?' I said with surprise.

She nodded.

'We've never met, but I enjoy his broadcasts. I love the way he talks about what happens when words meet music.'

'That's one of his great interests.'

'Mine, too.'

I'd often wondered about the man behind the radio programmes. I knew he was a respected academic and musicologist, so it was no wonder he spoke with intelligence and authority. But it was his sincerity and empathy that most impressed me when I listened to his rich, mellow voice discussing the power of music to move and uplift, to comfort and console.

'I'm sorry about your mother,' I said at last. 'You must have been very young when she died?'

'I was ten. Old enough to remember her.'

Our progress was slow because although she was making light of her injury, her ankle was clearly very painful. At last, to my relief, I could make out the illuminated red, green, and blue carboys in the window of the pharmacy on the corner of North Parade.

'Let's cross over. It's not far now.'

I had only ever been to Park Town once before, as a student over twelve years earlier, and it had been a nerve-wracking experience.

'I had a tutor who lived in one of the odd numbered houses on the north side,' I said. 'He was a Fellow at Balliol and he taught one of my specialist subjects—Thomas Hardy—but he wouldn't take me on until he'd met me first.'

'Sounds like an entrance interview,' she said with a laugh.

'It was worse than that. I had to undergo his version of the Spanish Inquisition to show I could pass muster.'

She laughed again.

At the entrance to Park Town were a number of detached Italianate villas set in large gardens. Beyond them, to the right and left, were a pair of matched curving terraces which faced one another across an elliptical, ornamental garden. Emily led us to a house in the terrace on the south side, a row of three-storeyed houses with basements and recessed front doors up a small flight of steps. As we got to the top step, her ankle gave way and fearing she would fall, I grabbed her clumsily and she stumbled against me, laughing and flinching at the same time. She had no sooner gathered herself and begun to look for her key when the door opened.

'There you are! I was getting worried.'

'Hello, Dad. I'm the walking wounded, I'm afraid, and had to be rescued. This is Alexander.'

Freddie Fairfax looked at me with a mix of uncertainty and amusement.

'Alexander Ingram,' she clarified.

'Come in and get warm,' he said at last, standing aside to let us pass into the hall.

Not expecting to be up close to this distinguished academic, I felt disconcertingly nervous, as if I'd been whisked back in time and was once again a callow student about to meet a fearsome professor. I stood awkwardly in the long, narrow hallway, feeling I had stepped into a Victorian time-capsule. Highly decorated tiles covered the hallway floor, from which a wide, handsome staircase ascended. On my left was a huge ornate mirror while the wall up the stairs was hung with Japanese embossed wallpaper and lined with close-hung prints and photographs. Here and there, wall lights with shiny brass fittings added a restful glow.

'It's Alex, actually,' I said, recovering myself and holding out my hand. 'I'm very pleased to meet you.'

Emily was heading for the stairs.

'What happened,' Freddie asked, looking from one to the other of us.

'Someone must have dropped a bicycle pump,' Emily said, 'but I didn't see it in the fog. I stepped on it and twisted my ankle when I tripped. I don't think it's anything serious, but I'll give it some anti-inflammatory gel and strap it up. Will you stay for a drink, Alex? I won't be long.'

I looked at her father and, as he was smiling, I sensed I was not unwelcome. Emily inched her way up the stairs and Freddie ushered me into the third of three rooms off the hallway. It was surprisingly large, having obviously been extended, with a modern kitchen area at the far end overlooking the garden and a slightly old-fashioned sitting area with a fireplace at the other. A faded, patterned carpet was surrounded by a border of polished floorboards and the walls were a rich, calming green and I began to feel more relaxed.

Freddie signalled for me to sit on a small sofa near the fire while he went to a low bookcase on which stood a tray of drinks.

'What can I get you?' he asked.

'Whiskey, please.'

I watched as he unstopped a glass decanter and poured two tumblers of what looked like liquid golden syrup. On the end of the bookcase nearest the hearth was a large, framed black and white photograph of a young woman in her wedding dress with the Eiffel Tower in the background. The dress was ballerina-like, with a low neckline, short sleeves, and a full skirt. The woman was holding aloft a small nosegay of flowers as if in triumph, her face alight with a dazzling smile, the photo capturing a moment of joyful exuberance. I guessed this was Emily's mother—the likeness was unmistakable. As Freddie turned towards me, I saw that even in his slippers and baggy cardigan he was still a good-looking man, with his ruddy, handsome face offset by tousled grey hair. Two decades earlier, he and his young wife must have made a handsome couple.

'These are magnificent houses,' I said as Freddie handed me a glass and sat down in an armchair on the other side of the fire. 'How long have you lived here?'

He laughed. 'My great-grandparents moved into the house in 1875 and it's been in the family ever since.'

I shook my head in astonishment.

'I never lived here as a child—though I visited of course—because my mother didn't inherit it until 1945, when I was mainly away at school. My late wife and I moved in when we married in 1958, the year I took up a Fellowship at Pembroke College. My mother was still alive then, but she died in 1959. There's been modernisation and some reconfiguration, but much of the house is unchanged. Some of the rooms—the downstairs cloakroom for instance—still have the William Morris wallpaper my great-grandmother chose in the 1870s. It's faded and rather shabby now, but I'd be loath to part with it.'

'How old is the house?'

'Park Town was the first part of North Oxford to be developed in the early 1850s. These curved Classical-style terraces are unusual for Oxford. John Betjeman described them as "a kind of last gasp of Bath" and they certainly have more in common with the terraces and crescents of Bath or Cheltenham than with the gothic creations you see so much of in Oxford.'

He swirled his whiskey around his glass and smiled.

'The family's taste, however, as you may have noticed in the hallway, was for high Victoriana rather than Classical.'

I looked up as Emily appeared in the doorway.

'Dad, are you boring Alex with the history of Park Town?'

Her right ankle was bandaged, and she limped a little as she eased her way into the room.

'How's your foot?' I asked.

'It's a bit painful, but I think the gel will help.'

'Where's your bike?' Freddie asked.

'When I was leaving for work this morning, I discovered I'd got a puncture, so it's in the shed in the garden.'

She came to stand beside me.

'Thank you,' she said, handing me my gloves.

I nodded and watched as she walked to the back of her father's chair and put her arms around his shoulders.

'Here's a copy of the concert programme,' she said, moving to sit in a chair next to him.

'Ah, thanks. Before I look at it, let me get you a drink. I'm sure you need one.'

'A very small brandy, please.' She indicated with her fingers how little she wanted.

'Medicinal,' I said with approval, as the glass her father produced held rather more than a little.

He sat down again and opened the programme.

'I'd like to have come, but there was an event at college I couldn't get out of. How did it go?'

'It was wonderful,' Emily said, before I could answer more circumspectly.

'Interesting combination of Vaughan Williams' *Songs of Travel* in the first half, with Britten's *Winter Words* in the second.'

'Two of my favourite composers matched with two of my favourite poets. I studied Thomas Hardy as part of my degree and Robert Louis Stevenson's poetry was the first I ever heard or read as a child.'

'I enjoyed the way you introduced the pieces,' Emily said.

'I'm glad. I love the way poetry and music together can communicate so powerfully and I like to share that with audiences.'

'You have an excellent accompanist, too,' Freddie said. 'Even as a student, he was exceptional.'

'He is,' I agreed. 'We met when I was doing finals and he was in his first year. We hit it off immediately and I love working with him.'

''So, you read English?' Freddie said, looking up from the programme. 'Why didn't you do music?'

'It was a tough choice, and I would love to have done music, but in the end I had the best of both worlds, because as a choral scholar at Christ Church, I was immersed in music anyway, and the English degree enabled me to explore my love of literature and poetry.' I hesitated. 'It was actually one of your lectures that ignited my love of song and opened my mind and my ears to the alchemy of poetry and music.'

As soon as I'd spoken, I feared he would think I was trying to suck up to him, so I quickly turned to Emily and asked what she did for a living.

'I'm an Assistant Librarian at Lincoln College. I went to Aberystwyth University to study librarianship and did a postgraduate qualification there in archives. In one of my summer vacations, I helped in the library at Lincoln. The vacancy for a part-time Assistant came up just before I finished my final year, so I went there straight from university.' She looked over at her father. 'I was very lucky. I could afford to take something part-time to begin with because I can live at home. And in January, I'll start working part-time on Dad's song collection.'

I turned to Freddie in surprise. 'You have a song collection?'

'Well, I will have,' he laughed, 'when Emily has turned chaos into order.'

'Perhaps, you'd like to see it sometime?' she suggested.

'I would, thank you, but I should be going now. I'm off to Manchester tomorrow for a *Messiah* on Thursday.'

I finished my whiskey and stood up.

'I hope you don't have far to go?' Freddie asked.

'No, not far. I have a flat in Bardwell Road.'

'How long have you lived there?' Emily asked.

'About three years. It was my aunt's. She left it to me when she died. I'd been sharing a dingy flat in Earl's Court with another singer and I was very happy to come back to live in Oxford.'

'You must have been a much-favoured nephew,' Freddie said with a smile.

'I was. When my parents moved to Cairo, I was sent to school at St Edward's, partly so that my mother's sister, Ruth, could keep an eye on me. She was an administrator at the Ashmolean and sometimes I stayed with her in the school holidays. We were very close. She never married or had children and she regarded me as more of a son than a nephew.'

All the while I was talking, I felt Freddie and Emily studying me intently and, feeling self-conscious, I moved towards the door. Father and daughter followed me into the hall.

'Would you like to come for supper next week?' Freddie said. 'We could show you the collection after we've eaten. How's Tuesday?'

I turned in surprise. 'I'd love to. Thank you.'

'Good. Let's say seven o'clock. It'll only be Spag Bol but it's my speciality.'

'Then I'll bring a suitable bottle of red wine to go with it,' I said as I made my way down the steps.

When I turned to say a final goodnight, Emily was standing on the doorstep slightly in front of her father. 'Thank you for looking after me tonight.'

I waved and her face lit up with a smile as luminous as her mother's in the wedding day photograph on the bookcase.

Return to Cork

The morning of the funeral was cold and sunny, but it was raining heavily as the plane began the short flight to Heathrow. The lights of the city sparkled below us in the darkness and as I turned away from the window, I felt a sinking sense of loss and emptiness. Though Cork remained haunted by dark memories, it was where Jeanie had lived and, on my visits to see her, I could shut away those feelings and enjoy spending time with the woman who had set me on my life's path.

The summer of 1956 was long remembered in Ireland because it was extremely hot. Instead of the typically uncertain Irish weather, the sun shone day after day. But that summer was also remembered for what was sometimes called the 'summer plague'. The epidemic in Cork that year was one of the last major outbreaks of polio anywhere in Western Europe. Its peak came in August and September, and it was on the last day of August, a few days before we were due to go back to London, that I woke up with a headache and a sore throat and with my bed sheets damp with sweat. The epidemic had begun in July, so the local doctor had no doubt what was wrong with me.

I closed my eyes, feeling suddenly weary, just as a steward leaned across the empty aisle seat to offer me a drink. With quiet efficiency, he lowered the tray rest, poured the contents of a miniature bottle of whiskey into a plastic beaker and placed it on the tray along with a small bag of nuts. I felt myself relax and as I sipped the warming spirit, I thought back on the events of the day.

The church had been packed with friends and colleagues of Jeanie and Eamon, both of whom had lived and worked in Cork all their adult lives. Eamon gave the eulogy, full of sweet reminiscences of their life together, his narrative telling of lasting contentment, despite the lack of children they had both hoped for. He spoke without notes and his gentle voice remained steady throughout, but in his pale, tired face there was no mistaking the intensity of his pain. When it was time to introduce me, his tone lightened.

'Alex Ingram was one of Jeanie's first patients at St Mary's, and he was always very special. During the months when she was caring for him, I'd already got my eye on her, and I was relieved that the chap she spent so much time with was just a poorly little lad because I could see he was as smitten with her as I was.'

The congregation laughed and I blushed.

'When he grew up and pursued a career in music, we heard him sing in London on several occasions.' He paused and indicated where I was sitting at the end of a row halfway back. 'Alex,' he said, 'Jeanie was very proud of your achievements. But back then, in the 1950s, when you were a boy, her favourite singer was a handsome and flamboyantly roguish Irish tenor called Josef Locke. She especially loved his version of *I'll walk beside you*, a song that had been popular since the second world war when Vera Lynn sang it. I'm delighted that Alex has travelled over from England to sing it for us today.'

As I walked up the aisle to the front of the church, I decided that though I hadn't prepared anything, I would share the story of my friendship with Jeanie. Donal, the middle-aged man who was to accompany me, sat down at the piano with a flourish, but when I whispered that I wanted to say a few words before I sang, he nodded his head and folded his hands in his lap.

'I met Jeanie when I was five years old. My parents and I were staying in a village on the coast, thirty miles from Cork, and for six idyllic weeks I played on the beach and in the orchard behind the house. Like most five-year old boys, I was full of energy. I loved kicking a ball about or doing somersaults across the lawn. I could even stand on my head and count to ten. When we were almost at the end of our holiday, I contracted polio. On the thirtieth of August, I was on the beach building sandcastles and collecting seashells. By the following afternoon, my left leg was floppy and I was too weak to stand. Months of physiotherapy and later, in London, an operation, meant that in time I could walk again, albeit with a limp, but eventually without needing a calliper or a crutch.'

I paused and looked around and my eye was caught by an elderly woman, sitting near the front, who was nodding her head vigorously. It took me a moment to recognise her as Brigid, one of the senior physiotherapists who had worked on me before I went back to London. I smiled at her and she beamed back.

'I'm grateful to Jeanie and Brigid and all the other therapists who worked so tirelessly to mend my body and just as importantly, my spirit.' I paused and considered what to say next. 'It was when I eventually went back to school and mixed with 'normal' boys again that I realised I'd been changed by my illness. It was then I knew I would have to abandon dreams of being an athlete or a footballer. But Jeanie had opened up a different world to me—a wondrous world of books and music. She read me *A Child's*

Garden of Verse by Robert Louis Stevenson and told me that though Stevenson suffered badly from ill health and came close to death many times, he was always incredibly optimistic and positive with a great love of life. I've never forgotten that.'

I looked over at Eamon in his seat at the front and said, 'I owe Jeanie more than I can say.' I held his gaze and saw his eyes fill with tears of pride. I turned back to the congregation. 'Jeanie often talked about her love of music. Many times, when we were sitting together in the garden at St Mary's, she sang *I'll walk beside you*. It's a lovely song, and I'll do my best, but I doubt I can match the incomparable Josef Locke!'

I turned to Donal, who was now ready to begin. We'd been introduced outside the church, and he'd assured me he'd been playing the song since he was a teenager.

'Don't you worry,' he said. 'I'll not get in your way.'

And he didn't. He played it with great sensitivity and a genuine feel for the idiom. The melody was sweet and simple, and I had learnt the words from memory in the days before the funeral. Now as the plane bumped its way through a patch of turbulence, I closed my eyes and sang it silently in my head, imagining myself singing along with Jeanie in the hospital garden.

> *I'll walk beside you through the world today*
> *While dreams and songs and flowers bless your way*
> *I'll look into your eyes and hold your hand*
> *I'll walk beside you through the golden land*

It was a sentimental love song, but Jeanie loved it and I understood why Eamon had chosen it.

> *I'll walk beside you through the world tonight*
> *Beneath the starry skies ablaze with light*
> *Within your soul love's tender words I'll hide*
> *I'll walk beside you through the eventide*

By now I was feeling sleepy, and images of Jeanie and Ruth as young women blurred in my mind's eye—two women who had nurtured and encouraged me, both taken too soon by the same cruel cancer.

The words of the third verse presented a challenge and it took all my self-control and technique to deliver the last line in the pianissimo falsetto called for in the score, and to sustain the long last note without my voice cracking.

I'll walk beside you through the passing years
Through days of cloud and sunshine, joys, and tears
And when the great call comes, the sunset gleams
I'll walk beside you to the land of dreams

At the end, as I walked back to my seat, Brigid reached out and squeezed my hand and I felt the tears come.

I opened my eyes and looked out into the darkness and the tears came again. I blew my nose and somehow I found myself wondering what music Freddie had chosen for his wife's funeral. I was cheered by the thought of dinner the following week and as I finished my whiskey and closed my eyes, Emily's smile was the last thing I remembered before I fell asleep.

A Life in Books

We ate supper in the dining room, the middle of the three rooms off the hallway, the walls of which were windowless and lined with bookshelves.

'I lived in books for a long time,' Emily said. 'I found I could lose myself for hours in a good story and for a while, at least, I could forget how much I missed my mum.'

I nodded in recognition. I had turned to books for enjoyment and distraction, too, but also because studying hard became a necessary compensation for my lack of physical agility.

'If you look around the house,' she said, 'you'll see there are books everywhere, even on the landings and in the downstairs loo. The school I went to had a fantastic library so I grew up surrounded by books. All through my teens I was a compulsive reader and even before I left school, I knew I wanted to work in books. It was wonderful getting to know the National Library of Wales, and as part of my degree, we sometimes visited other libraries—I particularly loved Gladstone's Library in North Wales and the Duke of Northumberland's Library at Alnwick Castle. Books piled high in rooms aglow with buttery lamplight.'

She came alive as she spoke, and I was charmed by her enthusiasm.

'Lincoln's library is one of Oxford's most beautiful, and that's saying something because the city is full of magnificent libraries. You'll have walked past it many times on the High Street; it was formerly All Saints Church.'

'Ah, yes, I can picture it,' I said. 'What are you reading at the moment?'

'*The Song of the Lark* by Willa Cather. I've been reading novels by American writers, and Dad recommended this one.'

'What's it about?'

'It's the life story of Thea Kronborg, from her hometown in Colorado to international success as a Wagnerian soprano.'

'Is it good? Are you enjoying it?'

'I'm loving it, though Thea isn't always an easy person to spend time with.'

'Why's that?'

'She's intelligent and ambitious, but she can be pig-headed and crude. I find it sad that her artistic life is the only one in which she's truly happy.'

'Yes,' said Freddie. 'As her artistic life grew fuller and richer, it became more interesting to her than her own life.'

'I think that may be true for many opera singers,' I said.

Freddie nodded and poured each of us a glass of the Chianti I'd contributed.

'What are you reading?' Emily asked me.

'Like you, I'm focussing on one type of work—novels set in modern-day Egypt. I'm currently working my way through the six books that make up *The Fortunes of War* by Olivia Manning. It's about a young married couple who at the outbreak of the second world war, are forced to leave Romania and flee to Greece, then Palestine, and then Egypt. I've reached the spring of 1941 when they arrive in Egypt just as Rommel's forces are approaching Cairo. European refugees and well-heeled Anglo-Egyptians are preparing to pack their bags and escape, but at night, they flock to the seedy cabarets, looking for one last dance before the tanks roll in.'

'It sounds amazing,' Emily said.

'It's fascinating. It captures the uncertainty and excitement of civilian life at a time of political and military crisis.'

Emily passed me a small dish of grated parmesan.

'I was introduced to books when I was in hospital in Cork, and from then on, all through my childhood and teens, I loved reading. Sometimes, I wondered if I might become a writer, but I soon realised I wanted to be a singer and use songs to tell stories.'

'Did you sing as a boy?' Emily asked.

'Not seriously. My treble voice was sweet enough but nothing remarkable. I was sixteen when people began to say I might have a decent tenor voice.'

'What were your first experiences of reading?' Freddie asked.

'Robert Louis Stevenson,' I replied. 'Jeanie, a nurse who looked after me in the rehabilitation hospital, introduced me to him, first with *A Child's Garden of Verse* which I loved for the sheer delight of the way the poems sound when they're read aloud. And later, when I was in hospital in London, she sent me *Treasure Island* which I loved because it's the classic, exciting tale of a young boy's search for buried treasure, pirates and all.'

We laughed, and I felt myself flushing.

'Stevenson was an only child who like me suffered a serious attack of illness when he was very young. I admired the fact that despite his life-long ill health, he travelled widely, wrote prolifically, and above all, relished life, despite its problems and disappointments.'

I pondered for a moment.

'I suppose I felt a sense of kinship with him. He gave me hope that one day I would be well enough to lead such a life.'

'Jeanie sounds very special,' Emily said.

'Oh, she was. I sang at her funeral in Cork on Saturday and the church was full of people whose life she'd touched. When I was leaving, two sisters stopped me and told me that they, too, caught polio that summer and it was Jeanie's encouragement that led them both into careers in medicine.'

'Were you born in Cork?' Emily asked.

'No, in London. My father worked in the civil service there. In July 1956, we went to Ireland to spend the summer at Cedar Lodge, a house owned by a colleague of his. It was in a lovely spot near the coast, not far from Cork. My mother had suffered a series of miscarriages and my father hoped that an extended vacation would restore her health and her spirits. We unwittingly arrived in the midst of the polio epidemic, but my parents believed that the isolation of the house would give us protection.'

'So, how did you catch it?' Freddie asked.

'My father made regular visits to London, and it's likely he contracted a mild case during his train journeys to Dublin. I caught it much more seriously and had to go through years of rehabilitation, first in Cork and then in London.'

'You were very unlucky,' Freddie said with a frown, 'because surely, around that time a vaccination was being rolled out?'

'That's right. It was being used experimentally in small quantities in Britain at the time I contracted the disease, but there were delays in implementing a mass vaccination programme. A year later, by the summer of 1957, people in Britain could look forward to the miracle of prevention.'

Freddie shared the remainder of the wine between the three of us.

'I *was* unlucky,' I said, 'but at least I survived. I made friends in hospital with a boy who died, and I've often thought how wretched it must have been for his family to know that there was a vaccine that came too late for him.'

All three of us fell silent.

'But in 1961, I threw away my calliper and my crutches and tried to live as normally as possible. That year, my parents moved to Cairo, and I came to board at St Edward's. I spent Christmases with my aunt in Oxford and most of the other holidays in Cairo.'

'Are your parents still there?' Freddie asked, as he stood up to clear away the empty plates.

'They are. They live in a quiet, leafy district where many expats live. They love it there.'

Emily got up to help Freddie take the dishes through to the kitchen and when they reappeared, she was carrying three glass dishes.

'Lemon Posset,' she said. 'It's very simple. Just cream, sugar, and lemons.'

'It looks delicious. Thank you.'

I watched as she took her seat at the table and saw she was still struggling with her right foot.

'Are you still in pain?' I asked.

'It's much better, but it's tightened up now so it's a different sort of discomfort. The college nurse had a look at it and assured me it's just a sprain.'

She smiled at me as she sat down, and to my horror, I blushed. She was younger than me, but she seemed remarkably at ease with herself and with me.

'Can I tempt you to a glass of sweet red wine to wash down your posset?' asked Freddie, going over to a small side table. 'It's Greek and totally delicious.'

'Sounds good,' I replied, thinking it was worth a try.

He poured three small glasses and carried them over to the table.

'Cheers,' he said. 'Good health.'

I breathed in a rich aroma of dried fruits.

'What are you getting?' Freddie asked.

I took a cautious sip and then another more confident one.

'Could it be dates? Raisins?'

'It could. It's a Mavrodaphne, which means black laurel. It's particularly good with desserts, but it also works well with something strong flavoured like game stew.'

I liked it, though sensed it might be deceptively alcoholic.

'What are your plans, short-term and further ahead?' Freddie asked. 'How do you see your career developing?'

'Well, for the last few years, December has become the month of *Messiah* and I'm currently in the middle of a run of performances. I've done two since I saw you last week and I have three coming up before Christmas. It's a work I owe a huge debt of gratitude to because it gave me my first big break as a professional soloist.'

'Ah yes,' Freddie said. 'I was there at that concert on the South Bank. Quite a drama, but mercifully no lasting harm to the tenor you stepped in for.'

'No, thankfully.'

'What happened?' Emily asked, bemused that her father and I had shared an experience of which she knew nothing.

'It was sheer serendipity. One of those occasions when you find yourself in the right place at the right time.'

Freddie nodded in agreement, and I took another sip of the dark red wine.

'On the morning of the concert, I had a singing lesson during which we were working on *Messiah*. The chap who played for my lesson was playing harpsichord for the *Messiah* that night and as I had a ticket for the concert, we agreed to meet up for a drink afterwards. In the break between the afternoon rehearsal and the performance, the tenor soloist left the building to get some fresh air but didn't reappear. After some frantic phoning around nearby hospitals, the Company Manager discovered that he'd collapsed in the street near Waterloo station and gashed his head badly. A concerned passer-by called an ambulance and at the time the concert was due to start, he was flat out on a stretcher in A&E. The harpsichord player knew I would be somewhere in the building so suggested I could step in if I could be located. They put out calls on the public address system in the foyers, but by this time, I had just struggled to my seat in the middle of a row. I hadn't even sat down when the Company Manager went on stage and said if Alexander Ingram was in the auditorium, would he please go to the pass door immediately.'

Freddie was relishing the description of an event to which he'd been witness, whereas Emily looked increasingly wide-eyed and aghast.

'I felt very self-conscious because before I could find my way to the pass door, I had to struggle back along the row—clutching my music case which fortunately held my copy of *Messiah*.'

'What a drama,' Emily said. 'Did you guess what was happening?'

'Well, mishaps like these happen, so I had a strong suspicion about what was coming.'

'And how did you feel when they asked you to step in?'

'I was excited and nervous, but to be honest, I was more concerned about how scruffy I would look alongside the other soloists who would be dolled up in their finest concert attire.'

I laughed.

'In retrospect, that was probably a good thing because it distracted me from the sheer terror I might have felt if I'd focussed entirely on what I was getting myself into.'

'At least your white sneakers were clean, and your jumper was reasonably sober,' said Freddie with a smile. 'Seriously though, you did brilliantly. I think the entire audience was holding its breath throughout the overture, knowing that the first voice they would hear was the tenor, but as soon as you sang the opening line of "Comfort Ye" everyone knew we were in safe hands. It was a triumph.'

Emily beamed and I flushed with surprise and pleasure.

'Thank you. After that performance, I was offered concert work with good conductors and good orchestras and that helped me secure an agent. The oratorio work enables me to make a reasonable living while I build my repertoire as a recitalist, which is where my true interests lie.'

'How do you go about planning your recitals?' Freddie asked.

'I try to devise programmes that will be enjoyable to perform and to hear. For me, that means that the contents of the programme need to cohere, perhaps around a theme or a period or a group of poets or composers, so that the whole event, not just individual items, will resonate.'

Freddie raised an eyebrow and nodded, which I took to mean he agreed.

'I also have to consider what my voice is ready for. It will be a few years yet until I tackle the two Schubert song cycles, for instance.'

'What about opera?' Emily asked.

I hesitated to answer, knowing I was avoiding opera for fear that my uneven gait would be an impediment for many roles for which my voice might be suited. I hated the thought that my limp would be an ungainly distraction.

'I would like to do some opera,' I said at last, 'but I think I need to choose what I do with care. There are roles in some of Britten's operas that interest me, and I've already agreed to do Quint in *The Turn of the Screw*.'

'Perhaps, in time,' Freddie suggested, 'the Madwoman in *Curlew River* and Aschenbach in *Death in Venice*?'

'Maybe,' I said, with a smile. 'We'll see.'

By now we had finished our dessert and as if he had read my mind, Freddie got to his feet.

'Are you ready to have a look at the collection?'

I followed him and Emily out into the hall towards a door at the back of the stairs which led down to the basement.

'Am I right in thinking you do your broadcasts from the house?' I asked, as we made our way downstairs.

'I do. The BBC installed the necessary recording equipment so I've no need to go to London unless there are guests who can't get to Oxford. It suits me very well, given my teaching commitments. We converted one of the two guest rooms on the first floor. It doubles as my study and I sometimes teach in there.'

At the bottom of the stairs, another door opened into a large open space.

'When the house was built,' Emily explained, 'the kitchen, scullery and pantry were down here.'

Freddie was standing in front of a desk under a window high up on the wall that fronted onto the street.

'My late wife, Marie-Odile, was training to be an Alexander teacher and she'd planned to use this space for one-to-one teaching and occasional group sessions, but she fell ill not long after we started the building work.' He paused. 'It lay untouched for over ten years until we cleaned it up a few months ago, ahead of taking delivery of all the packing cases you see around you. We had to make sure it was free from damp and mould and we're using manual hygrometers to measure the humidity and temperature levels each day.'

I had been taking it all in while he was speaking and wondering how many songs the boxes might contain and how long it would take to organise and catalogue them.

'Have a look,' he said. 'Open any of the boxes at random and see what you find.'

I went to a box which was sealed tight with wide, brown parcel tape. I peeled this away carefully and opened the flaps to reveal a box full of sheet music. On the top was a song for tenor and piano: *Music, when soft voices die* by Roger Quilter to words by Shelley. I picked it up and showed it to Freddie.

'Do you know it?' he asked.

'I don't, but when I was a choral scholar, the choir sang a setting by Frank Bridge of the same poem at the funeral of an undergraduate who died of meningitis.'

'Yes, the poem and its various musical settings are often performed at funerals. It's saying that even if something dies, it doesn't necessarily disappear forever. It lives on, sleeping, in the memories of those who have loved it.'

I looked at the song more closely.

Music, when soft voices die
Vibrates in the memory;
Odours, when sweet violets sicken
Live within the sense they quicken
Rose leaves, when the rose is dead

Are heaped for the beloved's bed;
And so my thoughts, when thou art gone
Love itself shall slumber on.

'You should sing this setting,' Freddie said. 'It's a little gem and I think it would suit you—but make sure you don't take it too slowly or it can sound rather lugubrious.'

'I'll look it out,' I said, returning the copy to the top of the box.

'Please—borrow that copy. See if you like it.'

'Thank you, I will. Are all the boxes full of music like this?'

'We think so. The collector estimated there could be between eight and ten thousand songs. He wanted me to take the whole collection in the hope I would organise and catalogue it, with a view to it eventually ending up somewhere like the Bodleian.'

'Who was the collector?' I asked.

'Let's go upstairs and I'll tell you about him.'

April 1949: Mortuos Plango, Vivos Voco

Philip Nash was Freddie's piano teacher, but Freddie remembered him most of all as a wise and compassionate friend. A man who understood, as George Eliot wrote in *Adam Bede*, that 'there is no despair so absolute as that which comes with the first moments of our first great sorrow.'

Laura's death on Freddie's twentieth birthday seemed likely to condemn him to a life of stoic singleness. His guilt and remorse were so profound he believed he could atone only by eschewing the romantic intimacy that might have been, learning instead to be content with the consolation he found in music.

He and Laura were students of Philip's at Chetham's School of Music in Manchester and remained close friends when Freddie left to go to Cambridge and Laura continued her studies at what became the Royal Northern College of Music. On Easter Sunday 1949 they cried off going to church with the rest of Laura's family, choosing instead to walk on the gritstone moors near Laura's home in Flash, a windswept village in the Peak district, a few miles from Buxton. Winter came early to Flash and lingered long after spring had arrived in more sheltered places. On that April Sunday, the wind was bitter and blustery when they set off towards a point from where there were views in all directions over the Staffordshire moorland, the Derbyshire hills and the Cheshire plain. They'd not gone far when the skies darkened, and the rain came. Laura grew uneasy, convinced she could hear thunder.

'We should take shelter in that barn we saw back there,' she called out, pointing in the direction from which they'd come, but struggling to make herself heard above the elements.

Freddie, exhilarated to be out in the wild, open countryside and to be alone with Laura, dismissed her concerns and urged her to keep going. He pressed on ahead of her but when the first flash of lightning lit up the sky, she cried out again.

'That was less than thirty seconds. The lightning could be six miles away or closer. We need to run for cover.'

'Where to?' he laughed and spun round holding his arms out wide. 'We're in the middle of nowhere. I don't remember seeing a barn.'

As he turned, the wind knocked him off balance and he tumbled awkwardly to the ground and lay sprawled on his front in the rough grass.

'Get up,' she shouted. 'We need to run, now.'

She swung away from him, just as the sky was lit up by a spectacular bolt of lightning. Struggling to get back on his feet, Freddie could only watch in horror as she dropped to the ground as if felled by a bullet. Doctors told them she had suffered cardiac arrest and deep, internal thermal burns. In contrast, Freddie was dazed and dizzy with a piercing headache, but otherwise he was physically unharmed.

Not so, his heart and spirit, which felt broken. On the day of Laura's funeral, as the bells summoned the mourners to church, he imagined their baleful clangour tolling across the pitiless moors. He dreaded the prospect of seeing Laura's devastated family, fearing they would blame his recklessness for her death. He hung back alone, watching from among the gravestones as friends and teachers from School and College arrived. When at last it was time to go in, he saw that Philip was standing at the church door, waiting for him. The older man took his arm and led him gently to a pew near the back of the church.

Freddie guessed that Laura's family and teachers would have devised a funeral service which put music at its heart. Music to hymn the dead loved one and console the living. At the end of the service, members of the College chamber choir gathered at the front of the church to sing the final movement of the *Requiem* by Fauré: *In Paradisum*, Fauré's musical evocation of the eternal peace he believed awaits us all. As the music moved towards its transcendental climax, its serene vocal lines and ethereal organ arpeggios induced an atmosphere of quiet calm among the grieving listeners. Though Freddie longed for a miraculous intervention that could exorcise his trauma and salve his pain, he yielded to neither the words spoken nor the words sung,

Afterwards, outside in the chilly sunshine, surrounded by former school mates, Freddie forced himself to engage with reminiscences about Laura, to acknowledge people's concern for his welfare and accept their sympathy and words of support. But all the time, out of the corner of his eye, he was aware of Laura's ashen-faced parents and her stricken younger sister. He knew he had to face them and when at last they stood alone in the church porch, he seized the moment. To his surprise, Laura's mother—a tall, wiry woman with startling, pale blue eyes—took him in her arms and hugged him. And to his shame, he wept uncontrollably into her shoulder, wanting to be held and comforted and forgiven.

'It wasn't your fault,' she said, quietly. 'The storm came up very fast. You were simply in the wrong place at the wrong time.'

'We should have turned back sooner,' he began.

'Listen,' she said firmly. 'Grieve for Laura, remember her, but don't let misplaced guilt ruin your life.'

She pushed him gently away from her so she could look him square in the face. Then she squeezed his shoulders and let him go, into the care of Philip, who had been standing nearby.

'Come on,' he said. 'We need a cup of tea.'

They went into the hall behind the church and having queued at a long trestle table laden with sandwiches and cake, Philip led them to a quiet corner, where they could sit and talk in private.

'I loved my lessons with Laura,' Philip said. 'They were always fun and yet she worked hard. I was pleased she stayed in Manchester because it meant we could keep in touch. She even came for the occasional lesson if she was struggling with something she found problematic.'

He drank his tea, all the while studying Freddie closely.

'She often spoke about you and her visits to Cambridge.'

He laughed.

'She assured me she wasn't allowing you to become any sort of Oxbridge toff (her word).'

'As if,' Freddie said, managing a watery smile.

'Were you two a couple?' Philip asked. 'I began to wonder…'

'I think we might have been,' Freddie said ruefully. 'I'd cared for her for a long time, but she was in a torrid-sounding relationship with a junior doctor. When he took up a post in Edinburgh at Christmas, he called it off and she was utterly lost.'

He hesitated, finding it almost too sad to speak about what might have been.

'I suppose she turned to me for comfort and gradually realised she had feelings for me, too.'

He put his cup down and fumbled for a handkerchief.

'I've never met anyone who engaged so intensely with life as she did,' he said at last. 'The way she committed so passionately to everything she tackled. I found that incredibly attractive—inspiring even.'

He paused.

'She made me believe that anything was possible if you were single-minded enough.'

'And you can't imagine how to keep going without her, how to recover the belief that life is worth living.'

Freddie nodded despondently.

'Right now, I can't even face going back to Cambridge. The thought of trying to pick up the life I left just a few weeks ago at the end of term seems inconceivable.'

He turned to face Philip, his eyes filling with tears.

'What's the point?'

Philip shook his head and sighed.

'The challenge for you now is to endure this senseless tragedy—and others that may come your way—and to continue living in hope.'

'You don't get it,' Freddie said, his voice rising in frustration.

'Oh, I do,' Philip said. 'Trust me, I do.'

'But I feel this awful guilt,' Freddie cried, thumping his chest, the tears now flowing freely.

Philip took his arm and led him outside.

'If you give up on life now,' he said quietly, 'you forgo any possibility that it could be different. And in time it will be. You will find a way to hold out hope for what the future might bring.'

Freddie sniffed and bowed his head.

'You heard Laura's mother. She doesn't hold you responsible or blame you. Accept that and believe it. Take the gift she's offered you, that despite everything, this need not haunt your future and blight your life.'

Freddie shuddered and forced himself to straighten up.

'In time, you will be able to move on, and you owe it to Laura to commit to life, as she did, and to seize every opportunity it offers you to start again.'

Freddie nodded but remained silent. They were walking towards the lych-gate when the church bell chimed the hour, twelve times.

'There's an inscription written around the great tenor bell at Winchester Cathedral,' Philip said. '*Mortuos Plango, Vivos Voco*. I lament the dead, I call the living.'

Philip Nash

'Let's have coffee,' said Freddie as we headed back upstairs.

He had picked up a manuscript from the desk under the window and placed it on one of the work surfaces in the kitchen. He invited me to sit by the fire while he made coffee and Emily started on the washing up. I watched the ease with which they worked alongside each other and was struck by how comfortable they were in each other's company.

They joined me round the hearth, where without realising, I had stretched out my legs towards the fire. I quickly altered my position but Freddie had noticed and smiled.

'You like the fire?'

'I do—it's very cosy.'

'Marie-Odile loved a fire and in winter we still always light fires in here and in the front room.'

For a few moments, we sipped our coffee in silence, the only sound that of the flickering fire.

'So,' said Freddie, 'the collector was my piano teacher, Philip Nash. He taught me for four years at Chetham's until I left to go to Cambridge.'

'The name's familiar. Was he also an accompanist?'

'He was, yes. A very fine accompanist. He retired in about 1969.'

'Did you stay in touch, or did his gift of songs come out of the blue?'

'I didn't know about the gift, but we did stay in touch. Largely by letter and telephone, but from time to time he appeared in recitals in Oxford and sometimes, he stayed here.'

'He and Mum got on well,' said Emily.

'They certainly did,' Freddie laughed. 'Marie-Odile and I were married in Paris, where she was born, but my mother hosted a splendid celebration party here to welcome us back. I was touched that Philip made the effort to come and after that, he was a regular visitor for many years.'

He fell silent, gazing into the fire as if lost in memories of days gone by.

'I remember one time he stayed with us was after a song recital for which he'd played at the Sheldonian. It was 1966 and the concert was part of a series of events marking the fiftieth anniversary of the death of George Butterworth. It was such a wonderful concert I can still remember everything about it. Philip and the baritone soloist performed the two groups of Housman settings—*Six Songs from A Shropshire Lad*, and *Bredon Hill and Other Songs*, as well as some arrangements of Sussex folk songs, and one-off settings of Stevenson, Shelley, and Oscar Wilde.'

He paused again.

'After the concert, he and I went out for a meal, and he opened up in a way he rarely did. He told me the most astonishing thing—that his older brother, Vince, had served under Butterworth in the First World War.'

'Good heavens.'

'Vince wrote home regularly, and his letters were full of praise for his Lieutenant, who by all accounts was a brilliant soldier, always looking out for the well-being of his men. Though he was thought of as posh, Vince said he was trusted and respected by men of all ranks. Vince loved him and was devastated when Butterworth was killed by a sniper at the beginning of August 1916.'

'I've often wondered what he would have gone on to achieve if he'd lived. The body of work he left behind is so tantalisingly small.'

'He stopped composing when he enlisted and destroyed many of his manuscripts before he left for the front. And of course, he was never to write again.'

'What's the text by Oscar Wilde?' I asked. 'He seems a strange choice of poet for Butterworth to set. Their outlooks were very different.'

'You're right, but it's not typical Wilde. The poem was *Requiescat* and Wilde wrote it when he was a student in Oxford. It's dedicated to the memory of his sister, Isola, who died unexpectedly when she was just short of her tenth birthday. Wilde was twelve and he continued to grieve deeply for her throughout his life. It's a truly beautiful song.'

'What happened to Philip's brother?' Emily asked.

'He was killed by machine gun fire a few weeks after Butterworth was shot.'

Freddie finished the last of his coffee.

'It was obvious Philip adored his brother.'

'Like Wilde adored his sister,' Emily said quietly.

Freddie nodded.

'I suspect the performance of that song stirred up painful memories for Philip. I've always thought that was why he chose to open up to me that night. Anyway, he was a wise man and a good friend, and I miss him.'

He pursed his lips and I could tell he was struggling to keep his emotions under control.

'On the day of his funeral in June, I was speaking at a conference in Glasgow, and I'll always regret not being there to mark his passing.'

'Did you know he was building a collection of songs?'

'I had an inkling, but I had no idea it was so extensive.'

'When did you know Philip planned to bequeath it to you?'

'His solicitor wrote to me in May and told me that Philip was very ill and was being looked after at home by a palliative care nurse. It was a shock to hear he was so near the end. The letter asked me to visit as soon as possible so I could see the collection before Philip died.'

Freddie stood up and took his empty cup over to the work surface, from where he picked up the manuscript he'd left there earlier.

'I went as soon as I could,' he said as he came back to his seat. 'Sadly, the day I went, the solicitor had been called away on urgent family business and didn't meet me as arranged so I wasn't able to ask him what he knew about the collection and whether it was coming to me in its entirety or whether some of it was excluded from the bequest.'

'Where did Philip live?'

'In Tarporley in Cheshire, about thirty miles from Manchester, in a house memorably called The Red House—like Britten's place in Aldeburgh. I'd never been there before and didn't know what to expect because Philip was always very private about his life away from work. It was a handsome, detached house of pale red brick, on a quiet road, and with a lovely garden at the back, surrounded by trees. I saw very little of the inside of the house—just two large rooms on the ground floor where the collection was kept and Philip's bedroom on the floor above.'

'How was the music stored?' I asked.

'Chaotically! Some of it was in box files—lots of them—some in filing cabinets and some in larger archive boxes and crates. Many of the pieces, however, were loose in piles on desks and all over the floor. Some of the archive boxes were dedicated to a single composer like Britten or Vaughan Williams, but I found works by those composers in the loose piles, too.'

'What did Philip tell you about the collection?'

'Not much, I'm afraid. He was suffering from Pulmonary Fibrosis and by this time, he was very weak. Talking tired him because he was struggling to breathe. I learnt that he ordered much of the music from Forsyth in Manchester and Taphouses in Oxford, but some he found in second-hand book shops stacked in corners in ragtag piles, unsorted. He also went to house clearances and auctions and bought all sorts of stuff, some of it sight unseen—just mixed crates of music scores, not all of which he seemed to have unpacked.' He smiled. 'Perhaps Philip hoped he might one day find a lost song by Schubert. He was well known for giving copies of his songs away, so musicologists live in hope that one or more may yet turn up.'

We all laughed.

'Have you been able to get a sense of the scope and quality of the collection?' I asked.

'It arrived only a few weeks ago, so I've not had time to do more than dip into it, but I think it will be a mix of good, very good and average. In terms of scope, there are some madrigals and Purcell songs, but Philip said most of the songs are from the late Victorian era onwards, when composers drew on the rich heritage of English poetry to inspire their song writing.'

'It will take some organising,' I said.

Emily was laughing. 'You're right, it will.'

'Freddie's lucky to have his very own in-house librarian and archivist,' I teased.

'Very lucky indeed,' Freddie said. 'Fortunately, I've secured a grant from a charitable trust that will enable me to pay Emily for up to a year to begin with. It's also covered the cost of taking specialist advice on how best to organise and catalogue the collection.'

'How much of that had Philip done?'

'A little organising, but no cataloguing. For the last ten years his eyesight was failing and by the end, on top of his respiratory issues, his vision was limited. He had some help from a composition student at the Royal Northern, which is why some of the larger groupings are in archive boxes, but in reality, we'll need to start from scratch.'

Freddie was studying the manuscript on his lap. 'Take a look at this,' he said, handing it to me.

It was a handwritten song for tenor and piano called *Requiescat* by Philip Nash to a poem by Oscar Wilde, in memory of Vincent Nash. I looked at Freddie in surprise.

'So Philip composed as well?'

'I didn't know that. He never spoke to me about it. Look at the dedication written at the top of the first page.'

I read out loud: '*Part of a song cycle of ten songs,* Into the Silent Land, *dedicated to Catherine Haldane.*'

'Who was Catherine Haldane?'

'I've no idea,' Freddie said, shaking his head. 'As I said, Philip was very private and there was never any gossip about him.'

I looked more closely at the song and saw that in the top right-hand corner, written in blue ink, was the number ten.

'Emily found it, paper-clipped—presumably by accident—to a song by Howells, but it's the only one of the ten songs we've found so far,' Freddie said. 'The others may be gathered together in a group somewhere in the collection or scattered randomly through the boxes, as this one was.'

'I wonder if the name of the cycle is from Christina Rossetti's poem *Remember*?' I pondered. '*Remember me when I am gone away, Gone far away into the silent land.*'

'It could be,' Freddie said with interest. 'If so, there may be a setting of that poem, too.'

I flicked through the song, thinking its range and tessitura would suit me.

'Would you mind if I borrowed this as well as the Quilter? I'll have time to look at it over Christmas.'

'Where are you spending Christmas?' Emily asked.

'I'm working up to the 23rd, and again on the 28th, so it's not practical to go to Cairo. I have an open invitation to spend Christmas Day with Johnny and his wife, and that's tempting, but they're expecting their first baby in January, so this is their last Christmas together as a couple.'

'Then why don't you come here on Christmas Day?' Emily suggested.

The invitation took me by surprise, but before I could answer, Freddie said, 'Do come—and bring Philip's song. We can work on it together round the piano. I'd love to hear it.'

Christmas Day

'Did I warn you,' Emily asked as she ushered me into the hallway, 'that whenever we have guests at Christmas, Dad always devises a game or activity for everyone to be involved in?'

She saw my alarmed expression and laughed.

'Don't worry. It's normally painless and can be good fun.'

'I'll take your word for it,' I said, handing her a bottle of red wine. 'I might need a few glasses of this before the fun and games start.'

'Never fear, we'll make sure you're in the festive spirit.'

And they did. Lunch was traditional and delicious, turkey with all the trimmings followed by a Christmas pudding drenched in brandy before it was set alight. The preparation of the meal had been a joint enterprise between father and daughter and the atmosphere was cheery but unforced. While we ate, Freddie revealed nothing about what he was planning and as my inhibitions were allayed by red wine, my curiosity grew, and I began to look forward to whatever he had in store.

After we'd cleared away, Freddie led us to the large room off the hall at the front of the house. It was a handsome drawing room, the walls covered with a complex, swirling William Morris wallpaper in green and slate which, though faded and peeling in places, still retained some of its original opulence. A grand piano vied for dominance with the wallpaper, but the room nevertheless had a comfortable lived-in feel, with a large welcoming sofa, and matching armchairs. Three smaller comfy chairs had been arranged around the fire, to the right of which stood a Christmas tree that almost touched the ceiling.

'The wallpaper is stunning,' I said. 'What is it?'

'It's called Pimpernel,' said Freddie. 'Morris chose it for himself when he was decorating his dining room at Kelmscott House.'

He went to the piano and picked up a small book and some stapled sheets of paper, which he handed to me and Emily.

'This is my old copy of *Under Milk Wood*,' she cried. 'We read it aloud in school at the end of a summer term when I was in the sixth form.' She was flicking through the pages. 'Where did you find it?'

'In a box in the attic when I was looking for the tree decorations. The book is mine and I took your script into college and made a few more copies, thinking it would be fun to read it today, even though it's not Christmassy in any way.'

'Do you know it?' Emily asked me.

'I do. We did a production in school, and I was the First Voice.'

'Then you must be First Voice again,' Freddie said. 'And many other parts as well.'

We divided the male characters between us, while Emily took all the female voices. Before we began, Freddie opened his copy of the book.

'It has an excellent introduction,' he said. 'I'll read you some of it. "This 'play for voices' conjures up the intimate dreams and waking lives of the inhabitants of a Welsh seaside village. It's bawdy and beautiful, and its colourful characters lust and love, gossip and fantasise. The play opens at night, and each character is dreaming. What they dream of tells us much about their personality." Here are some of my favourites,' Freddie said.

'"Organ Morgan: the church organist, dreams of music and orchestras. Cries out 'Help' in his sleep.

Mrs. Organ Morgan: dreams of silence.

Mrs. Willy Nilly: dreams of being spanked by teacher, every night of her married life.

Mr. Pugh: School Master, dreams of murdering his wife."'

We all laughed and settled down to begin.

'This should take about an hour and forty-five minutes,' Freddie said.

'And afterwards we'll reward ourselves with tea and mince pies,' said Emily.

'Sounds good to me,' I replied, readying myself to speak the opening words.

Freddie was a characterful reader, especially in the comic moments, while Emily brought both sensitivity and unexpected wit to the characters she voiced, able to convey Polly Garter's sadness for her lost love, Little Willie Wee, as well as Mrs Ogmore-Pritchard's preference for dead husbands. The time sped by and when I turned to the last page, I realised how alive I had felt spending time with the "chosen people" of Llareggub.

'What a wonderful way to spend a Christmas afternoon.'

'I told you it would be painless,' Emily teased, as she left to go to the kitchen.

'You know Alex, you should definitely do opera,' said Freddie. 'You brought real dramatic intent to all your characters. Those interpretive instincts will undoubtedly bring you success on the concert platform, but it would be a waste if you didn't take those instincts onto the opera stage as well.' He chuckled. 'I could actually visualise your Mr Pugh concocting "a fricassee of deadly nightshade" to poison his wife.'

I laughed, too.

'It's a joy to read. The characters are so distinctive.'

I went out into the hall to collect the bag in which I'd brought Philip Nash's song. Emily soon returned with the promised tea and mince pies, and as she placed them on a low table in front of us, she looked slightly flushed, her eyes sparkling in the firelight.

'Still thinking of Little Willie Wee?' I teased, 'or Mog Edwards or even Sinbad Sailor?'

'That would be telling,' she laughed, as she handed me a cup of tea.

I helped myself to a mince pie, and sat back, enjoying the moment, and feeling a long way from anything else in my life.

'So,' said Freddie at last, standing up to lift the lid of the piano. 'I see you have Philip's song there. Shall we look at it together?'

'I'd love to,' I said, standing up to place the copy on the music ledge above the keyboard.

Freddie switched on a floor lamp that stood to the right of the piano and sat down, and I stood close enough to him and to the light that I could see the music.

'So, first of all, did you know the poem?' he asked me.

'I didn't, but I thought the pathos of Wilde's lyrics were perfectly matched by the music.'

Freddie nodded. 'Let's give it a go.'

Tread lightly, she is near
 Under the snow,
Speak gently, she can hear
The daisies grow.

All her bright golden hair
 Tarnished with rust,
She that was young and fair
 Fallen to dust.

Lily-like, white as snow,
She hardly knew
She was a woman, so
 Sweetly she grew.

Coffin-board, heavy stone,

Lie on her breast,
I vex my heart alone
She is at rest.

Peace, Peace, she cannot hear
Lyre or sonnet,
All my life's buried here,
Heap earth upon it.

'What do you make of it?' Freddie asked, as the last notes of the long play-out faded away.

'I like it. It's full of tenderness and conveys a powerful sense of loss.'

Freddie was turning the pages as I spoke.

It's skilfully written,' he said. 'I'm impressed.'

'And hopefully,' I said, 'there are nine other songs for you to discover.'

There was no date of composition on the manuscript and I wondered what was going on in Philip's life when he composed it.

And who was Catherine Haldane?

Spring Awakening

'That summer in Ireland marked the end of my childhood. I longed to go home, but going home was a step into a frightening new world—very different to the one I left behind. One of the doctors who operated on me said that adversity teaches endurance and resilience and if it's true, I have polio to thank because it forced me to dig deep, to somehow find reserves of grit and perseverance.'

We had walked to the far end of Hinksey Park and were standing on the bridge that stretches across the lake, enjoying the stillness, and alone apart from the coots and moorhens who circled below us.

'Walking was held up as the Holy Grail of recovery,' I explained, 'so it's become second nature to me to walk everywhere.'

The silence was broken by loud squeals of delight. The coots took off at speed towards the bank and we turned to see a small child, throwing lumps of bread into the water and trying to wriggle free from a man who was holding him tightly round the waist. The boy was bouncing up and down with excitement.

'Look, Dad,' he cried. 'That duck took the bread right out of my hand!'

The scene brought back thoughts of my own father. He'd been concerned and attentive while I was in hospital in Cork, but when we went back to London, he withdrew more and more into himself. Unable to cope with what he saw as my altered range of possibilities, he began to retreat from family life. It meant our relationship was forever changed by my illness.

I became well-acquainted with loneliness during those five years of rehabilitation. I was in and out of hospital and when I recovered, I was sent away to boarding school, with my parents starting new lives on a different continent. It was a bewildering, disorientating time.

Now, I was used to solitude, and I'd learnt to be self-reliant, but I valued friendship, and I enjoyed good company. Romantic relationships seemed to elude me and for some reason I'm unsure about, I believed I was destined to be alone. During my teenage and student years I was painfully shy and self-conscious, an awkwardness magnified by the embarrassment I felt about my wasted leg. I was more self-possessed now and women seemed to like me, but I mistrusted their interest and assumed they pitied my misfortune or admired my determination. After the success of that momentous *Messiah*, there were often women at stage doors or in theatre bars who were fulsome with their praise and appreciation, but I pursued none of them. I disliked the casual encounters other singers engaged in when they were away from home, and Johnny said my reserve only enhanced my appeal, but that was not deliberate or calculated on my part.

By the beginning of January, Emily's ankle was fully recovered and we started walking together at weekends. The outing to Hinksey Park was the first of many.

'What does your father do in Cairo?' she asked as we recrossed the bridge and headed back into the park.

'He works at the British Embassy.'

'And your mother?'

'She works part-time in one of the Thomas Cook offices in Cairo, arranging excursions for European tourists.'

'How did she get into that?'

'She fell into it, I think, for something to do.'

Emily looked at me quizzically.

'Going to Cairo took my father to a job he enjoyed and enabled him to escape from everyday parenting, but for my mother, it provoked mixed feelings. She knew Cairo well and loved it, but she hated the thought of leaving me behind at boarding school. Her sense of abandoning me compounded the terrible guilt she felt about my illness and all its repercussions.'

Emily nodded, listening intently.

'She was unwell and depressed that summer and it was for her benefit that we were in Ireland. She's never forgiven herself for exposing me to harm.'

'That's a heavy load to bear.'

'It is. For a time, at least, it shattered my parents' happiness. My father did mute penance and devoted himself to his work, while my mother was transformed from a carefree young wife into a woman resigned to be in pain.' I paused. 'There were no more miscarriages—I think they stopped trying…'

We'd passed the tennis courts and the duck pond and were heading towards the football pitch and the adventure playground beyond it.

'They met a director from Thomas Cook at an embassy party, who said they could use someone like my mum. She speaks fluent French and can get by in German, so she can deal with a variety of visitors, even if they don't speak English.'

'Does she enjoy it?'

'Yes, I think so, in a way, but she's a clever woman and she seems unfulfilled.'

'Are your parents proud of what you've achieved? They must be, surely?'

'They are. They love music and one of the drawbacks for them of living in Egypt is that they rarely see me perform. I send postcards and ring them regularly to tell them what I'm doing, so I guess they get vicarious pleasure from hearing about it.'

'Whatever they had hoped you might achieve if you hadn't contracted polio, I'm sure it must give them great joy to know that you found your own way. It's as if it was meant—that you are here to make music.'

I gasped.

'That's a wonderful thought to hold onto,' I said, taking her arm as we manoeuvred around some children who were cycling unsteadily towards us.

We left the park and headed up Abingdon Road towards the city centre.

'What was your mother like?' I asked. 'Was she musical?'

'She could appreciate music, but I wouldn't say she was musical. She was more into outdoor life and physical wellbeing.'

Emily shook her head.

'She was so full of fun, so full of life. I still struggle sometimes to accept that she's not here—not anywhere—anymore.'

She looked momentarily downcast but tried to disguise it with a wan smile.

'And what about you?' I asked. 'Do you play an instrument or sing?'

'I take after my father to an extent,' she laughed, 'but Grade VI piano was my limit. I'm lucky, though, to be someone who can be affected and moved by music. It's always been a big part of my life.'

We stopped on Folly Bridge and looked down at the river, quiet and undisturbed by watercrafts of any type. I shivered as a dank wind gusted off the water.

'The punts look rather sad, don't they?' Emily said, pointing at the untidy clutter of boats below us.

'They're waiting for spring. And aren't we all?'

She smiled up at me. 'They'll be out on the water again at Easter. That's not too far off.'

The mulled wine we drank that day in the Head of the River was the first of many drinks we enjoyed together in Oxford's galaxy of pubs. And we began to walk regularly. We wandered through Christ Church Meadows and Magdalen Deer Park, and in the vast oasis of the University

Parks we could lose ourselves until the light failed. Ambling along, side by side, it felt easy to talk freely, and during these wintry walks we began to get to know each other.

As spring approached, my feelings for Emily grew so naturally, so gently, that I barely realised what was happening. Love blossomed quietly, over breakfasts in the covered market on Saturday mornings, during simple suppers eaten at my kitchen table, and in late night phone calls whenever I was away. All my limiting beliefs about relationships were challenged by a caring soul I knew I could trust. By the time daffodils were brightening the parks and gardens, my insecure heart knew it had found a safe home.

Father and Daughter

Marie-Odile Fairfax was a force of nature; a woman whose energy changed the atmosphere of any room she walked into. She was so full of life, it was as if she couldn't get enough of the world and Freddie sometimes thought that like a bird migrating from some far-off tropical clime, she had landed in Oxford by mistake and would one day take off in search of somewhere more exotic. After death carried her to the undiscovered country from which no traveller returns, her absence in his life remained so profound it was as if the absence itself was a solid entity.

In their grief, father and daughter cleaved together for succour and solace. Cast adrift in a fearsome tempest, Freddie came to think of his daughter as Prospero thought of Miranda, a cherubin that preserved him, with a smile infused with a fortitude from heaven. For himself, Freddie resolved that his loving and uncomplicated relationship with his daughter, and his passion for his work were enough. Life with Marie-Odile had been an unimagined joy and, when she died, he knew he had been inestimably lucky to have met and married her. He believed he had used up more than his fair share of good fortune.

Strong as their bond was, however, unlike Prospero, Freddie never wanted to control or contain his child. As her mother's daughter, he respected her right to follow her dreams and make her own choices. He hid his dread of the empty house that would be his when she left to go to Aberystwyth, and waved gaily each time he drove away, having deposited her there at the start of a new term. They spoke regularly on the phone, and he was always full of good advice until one day she protested, 'Dad, please stop giving me advice and just listen.' He learnt and listened, and when her first serious love affair ended badly during her final year, he offered comfort, not critique.

When she moved back home, he was relieved to discover they still had the same interests and sense of humour in common. Their relationship wasn't ended by her four years away but was renewed and continued to evolve.

Physically, Emily was a constant reminder of her mother—the same bright eyes and ready smile, the same neat build. She was similarly open and positive too, but in many ways, she was more like her father—studious, bookish and comfortable in the academic environment which Marie-Odile had found stuffy and snobbish. Even in her early teens, reading was more than a distraction from the pain of bereavement. She was interested in the subtleties of human psychology and books were a window to a world beyond her own and offered intimate encounters with other human beings—albeit fictional ones—which enlarged her knowledge and sympathies of lives lived beyond her own limited experience.

She did well at school, though at first, she had to be coaxed to engage with more sociable activities than reading. It was with her English teacher's encouragement she discovered a love of the spoken word and a delight in drama, but she had no aspirations to be an actor. It was with books she wanted to work.

She relished her time at university and though she missed her father, she made good friends—something that was a feature all her life—and it was there she had her first experiences with the opposite sex. After several short-lived dalliances, her most serious boyfriend was a history student who she at first found dazzling. He was intelligent and articulate, and she was flattered that he had noticed her, but their relationship was never easy. Minor disagreements could spiral into massive arguments during which he would lash out unpredictably and then, equally inexplicably, go silent for days. It ended when she discovered that weekends in Edgbaston to visit his parents, were in fact trysts with a long-term girlfriend he'd omitted to mention. When it was over, she realised that anxiety had bubbled constantly beneath the surface. It was this man who taught her how easy it was to be seduced and infatuated by a veneer of charm and charisma.

It was Alex who showed her what love looked and felt like. The readiness and kindness with which he took on the role of gallant rescuer when he found her in St Giles on that frosty, foggy night suggested he would be someone she could trust and rely on. It confirmed the impression he'd made during the recital that evening. She'd been drawn to him, physically and emotionally, from the start. His intelligent face with its large expressive eyes and wide mouth had a sweet, sad beauty, and when he sang it was with warmth and intensity and a joy that seemed to glow from within. He was a thoughtful and accomplished performer, and with his gentle mannerisms and generous heart, she saw a man who allowed his emotions to reflect the deep passion he felt for his craft.

Having shunned romantic attachments since her final months in Aberystwyth, Emily had been single for over a year by the time she met Alex. They fell in love slowly, their relationship underpinned by solid friendship, so that it was never a source of uncertainty or doubt, even when Alex was away and communication was constrained.

It was not surprising that the song collection played its part in bringing them together, but it did more than that; it also cemented a deep friendship between Alex and Freddie. Emily gave silent thanks when her father welcomed Alex into their lives and grew to love him as much as she did. Though Freddie might dread the prospect of losing a daughter, he clearly cherished the experience of gaining a son.

Bright is the ring of words

In January 1984, Emily started work on the song collection, a slow, painstaking process that demanded all her qualities of diligence and patience. Her work plan was devised with the help of an archive specialist who'd been recommended by an acquaintance at the Bodleian. Robin Gould had spent his whole career in archives and now in semi-retirement, was offering consultancy advice. Behind black-framed glasses that were too big for his surprisingly boyish face, his eyes looked shrewd but kind and he had a bright, good-humoured expression. Emily warmed to him immediately and he quickly impressed her as someone who knew his trade.

'My goodness, what an abundance of music,' he said, on first surveying the boxes piled across the floor of the basement. 'Between eight and ten thousand pieces you think?'

'That's right.'

'Have you done any sorting yet?'

'No, we haven't. We've looked in some of the boxes to get a sense of what type of music is there, but that's all.'

'That's good, because I would recommend that the first phase of the work should be spent simply looking at what you have, without doing any sorting or listing at all.'

'Really?'

'Absolutely. This will show you what is actually here. You think the collection contains exclusively songs, but there may also be correspondence, programmes and other memorabilia. At this stage, by all means, reunite obvious strays, but try to avoid assigning material to preconceived categories.'

They were sitting at a desk sharing a pot of coffee and a plate of biscuits and Emily was taking detailed notes.

'Did the collection arrive in one consignment?' he asked.

She nodded.

'Who prepared it for transportation—do you know?'

'Not specifically. Dad said there were some boxes ascribed to specific composers, but the rest of the music was in filing cabinets or unmarked boxes or loose in piles on floors and desks, so I guess the solicitor arranged for it all to be packed into these containers.'

Robin rolled his eyes.

'So, there's not even a rough inventory?'

Emily shook her head.

'It seems to have come to us in a rather haphazard way. Dad had no idea Philip Nash planned to make him this bequest and by the time Dad went to view the collection, Philip was too ill to talk much, and the solicitor didn't volunteer any information.'

'Oh dear,' Robin sighed. 'It can be frustrating to have to work with what you inherit without knowing what may have been accidentally left behind or deliberately omitted.'

'Have you ever been involved in sorting out a music collection?'

'Yes, I have. As part of my degree, I won a scholarship which offered me an overseas placement and I worked for a year in a private classical music archive in America.'

'What a fascinating experience. What was the collection?'

'Nineteenth and twentieth century American music. The collector was a wealthy philanthropist, who also commissioned pieces from some of the composers. He was prepared to spend time and money putting the collection in good order and growing and maintaining it. Currently it's housed in a stunning round library in a wing of his mansion in Virginia. He's in his eighties now and when he dies, the collection will be donated to the Juilliard School of Music.'

'Philip Nash hoped that his collection would eventually end up somewhere like that.'

'Did any endowment come with the collection?'

Emily shook her head.

'Dad's been able to secure a small grant that will cover my part-time salary for a year and leave a modest amount for materials and secretarial support.'

'That's something. Anyway, going back to the beginning of the process: as you survey what's here, record the contents of each box and give each box an interim number, but don't give reference numbers to individual items yet.'

Emily nodded.

'And then, I assume, I would start sorting the items by composer.'

'That's right. And at the same time, check every item for signs of damage or mould and set aside any that require attention. Use acid free boxes to file the songs by composer and go back to them later to arrange each composer's work in some sort of order—chronologically or by Opus number, if there is one.'

'How would you deal with any single songs or materials such as press cuttings or programmes?"

'To begin with, I would simply put them into boxes marked miscellaneous and deal with them at the end.'

He took off his glasses to rub his eyes and laughed.

'Some archivists get very worked up about the use of the word "miscellaneous" in a file title, arguing that saying something like this is ducking your responsibility to describe the contents accurately, but I've always felt it's a reflection of reality. In life we do create accumulations of odds and ends that don't fit anywhere else, and my guess is, you'll come across an array of motley items. If I was sorting these papers, I would create files of miscellaneous material, perhaps in roughly chronological order, in which any cuttings and programmes and so on might be kept separate from the composer or song to which they relate. You'll have to use your judgement and in cases when you're uncertain, your father is likely to be a useful sounding board. I tend to think of assorted loose papers, of different sizes and odd shapes, as fitting best into those box-files with a spring-loaded metal clip clamping onto the documents to keep them in place.'

He had finished his mug of coffee and readily accepted the top-up Emily offered.

'So, now you have your songs sorted into composers and chronology, you will have to list all the items in detail. I advise you to write out onto slips of paper—in pencil only, not pen, in case you accidentally mark the music—the composer, the title of the song, the poet, date of composition or publication and any other relevant information. Eventually, all the slips of paper will be gathered together and glued or pinned in chronological order onto sheets of A4 paper. At this point, each item should be given a distinct reference number written in pencil onto the pieces of music and onto the corresponding description of the item on the list.'

He helped himself to another biscuit.

'Does that make sense?'

Emily nodded and poured herself some more coffee.

'It does,' she said, thinking what a long time all that would take.

'When the list is complete and you know exactly what the collection consists of, I assume your father will write an introduction, explaining where the materials came from, who collected them, as well as information on the music manuscripts themselves.'

'Oh yes, he'll enjoy doing that.'

'The next stage is when you'll need secretarial support—someone to type up the list, using carbon paper so there's at least one other copy. This will produce lots of sheets of A4 paper and these can be put into ring binders or bound into volumes to form a catalogue.'

Emily could see Robin eyeing up the last remaining biscuit and pushed the plate towards him with a smile. Brandishing a chocolate bourbon, he said, 'And now the end is in sight. The final task will be to index the collection, using index cards to form several subject indexes. I'm guessing you might index by the name of the composer, name of the song, by poet, by first line of the song, and by reference number, so that anyone wanting to access the collection can easily find what they want.'

'I feel tired just thinking about it,' Emily laughed. 'How long do you think this will take? I'll be working on it two days a week.'

Robin was silent for a moment. 'You might get it done in the year for which you have funding, but a lot will depend on the complexity of the sorting job and other unpredictable factors, but I suspect at two days a week, the job will spread over quite a long period. It will be a test of endurance, that's for sure!'

For the remaining time he was there, Robin donned white gloves and looked into some of the boxes, exclaiming over songs he knew and commenting on the condition of some of the scores. When it was time for him to leave, they stood at the front door to say goodbye.

'I hope this has been helpful and hasn't served to confuse or daunt you.'

'Not at all,' said Emily. 'I can't wait to get started.'

He reached out to shake her hand and held it tight. 'It's an enormous privilege to work on something like this, so above all, enjoy it.'

And with a slight bow, and the doff of an invisible hat, he was gone, out into the chilly January day.

Some time, shortly after this, Alex came to visit while Emily was working on a box that Philip Nash, or one of his helpers, had sorted into songs by Vaughan Williams.

'Sometimes, I find handwritten notes or press cuttings clipped to a song or a set of songs. Like this.'

She passed him a yellowing cutting from *The Daily Telegraph* headed *Poem of the Week* which was pinned to one of the *Songs of Travel—Bright is the Ring of Words*.

'I'm used to hearing those words sung,' she said, 'but reading them as a poem, I was struck by how vibrant and defiant they are, yet somehow tender, too.'

Bright is the ring of words

When the right man rings them,
Fair the fall of songs
When the singer sings them.
Still they are carolled and said –
On wings they are carried –
After the singer is dead
And the maker is buried.

Low as the singer lies
In the field of heather,
Songs of his fashion bring
The swains together.
And when the west is red
With the sunset embers,
The lover lingers and sings
And the maid remembers.

Unnoticed by either of them, Freddie had come downstairs and was standing in the doorway to the basement listening as Alex recited the poem out loud.

'I love that poem,' he said as they turned to greet him. 'What gutsy confidence Stevenson had that his words would survive down the ages. The poem reminds us that while all artists must eventually die, the beauty of their work will remain as a testimony of their lives.'

Kindred Spirits

I knew hardly any of Gerald Finzi's music apart from choral works I'd sung at Christ Church and St Paul's Cathedral, where I was briefly a Vicar Choral. I had no idea that Finzi's delicate, lyrical songs would form such an important part of my recital career, and I had Freddie to thank for this.

One Sunday morning in February, he found me examining a box of songs labelled Gerald Finzi 14 July 1901 to 27 September 1956, in which I found a catalogue of his complete works called *Absalom's Place*, to which Finzi had added a postscript in 1951. I showed it to him.

"A serious and possibly fatal illness has now been confirmed by the doctors. At forty-nine I feel I have hardly begun my work. 'My thread is cut, and yet it is not spun; And now I live, and now my life is done.'

As usually happens, it is likely that new ideas, new fashions & the pressing forward of new generations, will soon obliterate my small contribution. Yet I like to think that in each generation may be found a few responsive minds, and for them I should still like the work to be available. To shake hands with a good friend over the centuries is a pleasant thing, and the affection which an individual may retain after his departure is perhaps the only thing which guarantees an ultimate life to his work."

'For the last five years of his life,' Freddie said, 'Finzi knew he was suffering from a terminal illness, that his time was likely to be short. He died in Oxford, at the Radcliffe Infirmary, when he was only fifty-five—the same age I am now. He was concerned that his music would be quickly forgotten, but anyone who takes the time to really listen to it, will find that it still speaks with a directness and simplicity that touches the heart.'

'One of the Finzi boxes was damaged,' Emily said, 'so I emptied the contents into one of our new boxes and I couldn't help noticing how many of the settings are to poems by Thomas Hardy.'

'Really?' I said, with interest.

'That's right,' Freddie said. 'Thomas Hardy's Collected Poems would have been one of Finzi's desert island choices, I'm sure. He must have set about fifty of Hardy's poems and there are unfinished fragments of many others.'

The basement was kept at a consistently cool temperature and Emily shivered, so Freddie suggested we continue the conversation upstairs.

'Finzi loved words as much, if not more, than he loved music and Hardy's poetry seemed to resonate with him like no other,' he said as he made a cafetière of coffee.

'What do you think particularly appealed to Finzi?' I asked when we'd settled ourselves around the fire in the kitchen.

'I think Finzi felt a strong sense of kinship with Hardy the man. Hardy had lived through a period of considerable change and right to the end of his life, he remained a radical. He'd supported women's suffrage, opposed empire and racism, and stood behind the poor and disenfranchised. And he wrote about subjects that Finzi cared about: the world's natural beauty, the futility of war, and the pressure of passing time.'

He paused as if he was recalling some of the poems.

'Time and destiny, the accident of chance in man's life, and the power of memory to crystallise the past. All these themes appear in the poems as well as in the novels. It's very rare that a composer and poet seem to be so perfectly in sympathy with one another, but Hardy's friends speak of him as a gentle and humane soul, and that description certainly applies to Finzi.'

Emily was listening intently to her father's description of the connection between the writer and the composer, but when she spoke, she was frowning.

'I have very mixed feelings about Hardy,' she said at last.

Freddie and I looked at her with surprise.

'Go on,' I said.

'I love the novels. I devoured them all when I was a teenager. I remember a teacher at school catching me reading *Jude the Obscure* and being appalled. "Aren't you rather young to be reading that?" she asked.'

We laughed.

'I started feeling ambivalent when I studied Hardy for A Level. We explored his obsession with the women in his novels and his relationships with his two wives. What I saw was a sensitive novelist who twice turned out to be a neglectful husband. Neither Emma nor Florence Hardy could compete with their husband's passion for Bathsheba and Tess. He seems to have been a man who found writing easier than loving or living with a partner.'

'Ah,' said Freddie. 'The big question: can you separate the artist from the art?'

Emily shook her head. 'I'm not sure.'

'How true is the following statement,' Freddie asked. 'An artist's work should have value in its own right, no matter what sort of life the artist led, even if they have hurt or harmed others?'

'I struggle with that,' said Emily. 'During my final year in Aber, I did a placement at the Dorset County Archives. They hold a huge amount of material relating to Hardy and the Archivist arranged for me to visit Max Gate, Hardy's home near Dorchester. It's owned by the National Trust, and though it's not currently open to the public, the tenant is expected to open the house on request to academics or writers. The tenant at that time had done a doctorate on some aspect of Hardy's work and he was a fascinating guide. I was shown all over the house and gardens but what made the most impact on me were the two attic rooms in which Emma Hardy lived for almost twenty years. They're so mean and bleak. I couldn't imagine living like that, utterly rejected, and avoided by a man working away in his study below, completely preoccupied with people he invented.'

'And what about you, Alex? You studied him. Do you think an artist's work should be judged only on its merits?'

I'd listened to the conversation with growing interest because I, too, had come up against this conundrum in my own studies of writers and composers.

'Perhaps we accept that premise when it comes to some artists, but not others?' I said noncommittally. 'Maybe we're not always consistent or even-handed?'

Freddie and Emily looked at each other and nodded.

'I see the irony—and the difficulty—with Emma,' I went on. 'Ignored and shut out in her lifetime, as soon as she died, she inspired in Hardy a passion that overrode everything else, a passion that must have been hard for his second wife to stomach. The outpouring of poems he wrote in 1912-13 are nothing less than love songs to his dead wife.'

'Finzi had a long and happy marriage but like Hardy, his was a sorrowful and brooding spirit,' said Freddie. 'They both chose melancholy themes about the transience of love and life, but for all that, they both had a miraculous ability to blend joy along with regret. That's a remarkable talent and one reason why I believe their work has lasting resonance.'

Come to my arms, Myfanwy

One Saturday in early spring, I was singing *Elijah* at Chester Cathedral and Emily suggested we made a weekend of it together, travelling up on the Friday and returning to Oxford on the Sunday morning. She offered to drive and to make all the arrangements.

I knew she had booked us into a hotel about fifteen minutes from the centre of Chester, but when we made our way north on the Friday afternoon, she didn't drive straight there. I hadn't been concentrating on the route we were taking but suddenly noticed that we seemed to be making a detour into Wales.

'Are you kidnapping me?' I laughed. 'If there's a ransom for my release, I'll pay it out of my concert fee.'

'Don't make me laugh. I'm trying to follow these brown tourist signs.'

I looked up and in surprise I realised we were heading for Theatr Clwyd in Mold.

'A night at the theatre?'

She nodded and after a few miles further, she turned up the steep approach road that led into the theatre car park. Still saying nothing, she led the way up the steps into the theatre. Once inside, she picked up our tickets and a programme at the box office and chose a table in the café and handed me the programme. The front cover showed Dylan Thomas in his shirtsleeves and bow tie, poised over some writing, a cigarette hanging from the corner of his mouth, and his podgy face puckered with an expression of defiance.

'*Under Milk Wood,*' I cried. 'How fantastic.'

'Whew. So far, so good,' she laughed.

The foyer was filling up with people arriving for something to eat and drink before the performance, so leaving our coats on the backs of the chairs, we joined a queue and ordered quiche and salad. While we ate, I flicked through the programme, stopping at the centre page spread on which the cast list appeared, and which had a picture of Thomas with a pint of beer in his hand and a devilish look in his eye.

When it was time to go in, we made our way upstairs and into the auditorium. There was no stage curtain and the designer had given the play the simplest of settings: a black box with a steeply raked floor in the centre. To the side at the front was a writing desk on which paper and pens and a bottle of beer had been placed. The house lights slowly dimmed, while the stage was thrown into complete darkness. The audience fell silent, holding their breath, waiting for those famous first lines. Through the gloom, I could just make out a figure walking down the raked floor towards the audience, and as a spotlight found his face, the actor spoke the words "To begin at the beginning" and a collective murmur of recognition went round the auditorium.

From that first moment, we were drawn into the magical world of Dylan Thomas's earthy, full-blooded characters, brought vividly to life by a company of actors whose versatility was astounding. Though they spoke with heavy and sometimes hilarious Welsh accents and played up the human frailties of the townspeople, these were likeable flesh and blood characters sharing their lives and loves and losses.

The evening sped by until finally once more, with the stage in darkness and with a spotlight again illuminating his ghostly face, the First Voice declared "the suddenly wind-shaken wood springs awake for the second dark time this one spring day." The stage lights lifted slowly to reveal that the whole cast had gathered silently around him. The audience roared their approval and demanded half a dozen curtain calls, before filing off into the night—or the bar—in high spirits.

'Shall we stay for a drink?' I asked.

'Why not?' said Emily.

We stood at the bar, waiting to be served.

'That was terrific,' she enthused.

'It was,' I agreed, 'but I thought it was only opera producers who get singers rolling and writhing around the stage while expecting them to sing at the same time!'

'It's beyond, isn't it?' said a woman's voice behind us.

We turned round and I recognised the red-haired actress who'd played Polly Garter, looking less blowsy in the flesh than she'd done on stage.

'You were wonderful,' Emily said. 'All of you.'

'Thanks,' said the woman. 'Glad you enjoyed it. I always think people in the front row can hear me wheezing when I'm lying flat on my back and trying to sing.'

She laughed and took a swig of beer, before raising her glass to us and moving off to join friends she'd spotted in the crowd.

We took our drinks to a table in front of floor to ceiling windows which in daylight must have offered spectacular views. We watched as more members of the cast gathered at the bar.

'There's Mr Mog Edwards,' I said, pointing out a slightly built man wearing stylish titanium glasses and with thinning grey hair, cut short.

'He was perfect as Mr Edwards,' Emily said. 'He looked and sounded just the part.'

'"I am a draper mad with love",' I mimicked, taking her hands in mine and gazing into her eyes. '"Throw away your little bed socks and your Welsh wool knitted jacket, I will warm the sheets like an electric toaster, I will lie by your side like the Sunday roast".'

She laughed and blushed and I blushed, too.

'"Myfanwy, Myfanwy, before the mice gnaw at your bottom drawer will you say…"'

'"Yes, Mog, yes Mog" she whispered, "yes, yes, yes".'

In her beautiful brown eyes, I saw unmistakable desire, and later that night, before she fell asleep in my arms, I told her that I loved her more than all the flannelette and candlewick in the world.

Let us Garlands Bring

Throughout those early weeks of the year, I immersed myself in the songs of Gerald Finzi and learnt as much as I could about the man and his life. It was clear that the brevity of human existence was a significant preoccupation for him. His father died when he was only eight; all his uncles had predeceased his father and, by the age of seventeen, he had lost all three of his brothers and his teacher, Ernest Farrar. All this made for a world of uncertainty and an unnaturally heightened sense of time passing.

My initial focus of study was on two song cycles, one of which was set to poems by Hardy—*A Young Man's Exhortation*—and another, *Let us Garlands Bring*—to five well-known poems by Shakespeare. I was a fast sight-reader, so the notes usually came easily to me, but I enjoyed learning new repertoire with Johnny and whenever we could be in the same place at the same time, we worked together on these songs. Freddie, too contributed to my understanding of them and seemed to relish the chance to reconnect with his piano-playing past. Finzi wrote truly independent piano parts and the pianist is a key protagonist in his songs. Between them, they brought piercingly perceptive insights and sensibilities to these settings, in part because they valued the words as much as I did.

I was impatient for a chance to perform the songs in public and an opportunity arose sooner than expected with an invitation to sing at Gregynog Hall in July. Ever since the Davies sisters, Margaret and Gwendoline, bought the house in 1920, it had been full of music and poetry. Even after both sisters had died, events continued to be held throughout the year, and that summer, the organisers were planning a series of concerts to mark the birthdays of composers who were born in July. They wanted to celebrate Finzi's birthday on the fourteenth and they approached Dominic, my agent, about the availability of one of the other singers on his books. Fortuitously, that singer was already booked up for the whole month, and they accepted Dominic's suggestion that I would make an ideal alternative.

Luckily, Johnny was also free that day and we began at once to plan the programme. We decided to include the two song cycles and, for contrast, would offer songs by contemporaries of Finzi's whom he loved and admired—Vaughan Williams, Hubert Parry, and Ivor Gurney.

As the concert was on a Saturday, it was a chance for Emily and I to spend a few days away together and we booked two nights at a small guesthouse not far from Gregynog. We left Oxford early on Friday morning and broke the journey with a stop in Shrewsbury to wander round the medieval town. We spent over an hour exploring the stalls in the covered market and had lunch at a café selling produce from the owner's farm.

The guesthouse was a former sheep farm and stood alone at the end of a steep track which led into the mountains and had breath-taking views over the surrounding countryside. When we were making our slow approach up the unmade track, a group of friendly bird watchers were tramping down to a pub in the village we'd just driven through. They stood aside to let us pass and when I wound down the window to say hello, they urged us to walk to the top of the hill beyond the house where they had spotted a pair of red kites.

A short while later, refreshed by tea and scones provided by the charming owners, we set off up the hill. Despite my limp, I loved walking and wherever work took me, I tried to explore as much as possible on foot. I knew my limitations and I tended to walk alone so as not to slow down other walkers, but when walking with Emily I was free of such anxieties because we talked as we walked and seemed effortlessly to fall into step together. We sat on a tuft of grass and surveyed the scene around us, and I imagined it as it had once been during the summer months, with sheep grazing upon the highest hilltops. Now, with the sheep long gone, but with red kites criss-crossing the cloudless blue sky, there was a spartan beauty about the landscape, peaceful and benign in the bright July sunshine.

We had booked for dinner and as soon as we entered the dining room and saw one large table set for four, we realised it would be a communal affair. There were two other people staying that night, an Englishman called Max and his Polish wife, Jowita. They were on their honeymoon and at first, we felt awkward, afraid we would be in the way of what they might have anticipated would be an intimate supper for two, but we need not have worried because they were extremely sociable and proved excellent company. Conversation flowed easily, ranging from football to politics to travel and books and music. Jowita told us that when she was eighteen, she'd unexpectedly won a piano competition that required contestants to play Chopin's formidably difficult *Minute Waltz*. Her father was so impressed that he rescinded an earlier edict that she must follow his example and go to university in Warsaw, and allowed her to come to Britain instead, to study engineering at Imperial College, which was where she met Max. Their happiness was plain to see and they seemed to delight in each other's company. Max was a burly, well-built man but I was struck by the tenderness in his eyes whenever he looked at his wife. They enjoyed the evening as much as we did, and we stayed up long after our hosts had gone to bed. By the time we came down for a late breakfast the next morning, Max and Jowita had left, heading for the mountains of Snowdonia, but it was one of those fleeting encounters that are never forgotten.

We spent the rest of the morning relaxing in the garden and when Johnny arrived, we walked down the track to the pub for lunch. After that, we drove the short distance to Gregynog to rehearse. Emily knew the place from her student days because the house was now owned by the University of Wales and run as a training and conference centre, but neither Johnny nor I had ever been there before.

It was a spectacular black-and-white mansion buried in the Welsh countryside near Newtown. The Music Room was timber-framed with three large mullioned and transomed windows and had been converted by the Davies sisters out of the Billiards Room. We were looked after by Oriel, a solidly built woman with an easy-going authority and a breezy willingness to make sure we had everything we needed.

'It should be a good audience,' she said. 'There's been a lot of interest locally, and regional critics from *The Guardian* and *The Observer* have asked for tickets.'

That surprised and unnerved me, and while Emily and Johnny were pleased we would get some exposure from the concert, I had hoped that my first public performance of the Finzi songs would be away from the scrutiny of hard-nosed critics.

Emily sat in for the rehearsal and gave us helpful feedback on balance and audibility, especially on my spoken introductions. Between the rehearsal and the concert, the organisers provided a tea of sandwiches and cakes, but I ate little as nerves began to dampen my appetite. Immediately before a concert, I tended to retreat into myself, and Johnny and Emily knew I was best left to my own devices. While Johnny munched his way through a plate of carbohydrates and showed Emily photographs of his six-month-old daughter, I slipped away to have some time on my own.

I was keen to get out into the grounds, but Oriel had invited us to explore the house if we had time. The Davies sisters had been avid and discerning collectors, notably of French Impressionists and post-Impressionists, creating one of the most important private art collections in Britain. Though over two hundred works had been donated to the

National Museum of Wales, some pictures remained at Gregynog, hanging in public rooms, and bedrooms and corridors all over the house, as they did when Gwendoline and Margaret made Gregynog their home. As I wandered around the downstairs of the house, I thought how remarkable it must have been to listen to exquisite music surrounded by paintings by Monet, Renoir, and Cézanne, and as I opened a door that led into the garden, I found that thought quietly uplifting.

At the front of the house, sweeping lawns were set off by ceramic fountains, marble statues and roses in every conceivable colour. I wandered away from the house until I found myself in the water gardens, where the only sounds were those of birdsong and humming bees. It was an enchanted place and as I breathed in the soft, rose-scented air, I contemplated the musicians who had been there before us—Elgar, Vaughan Williams, and Holst, not to mention Benjamin Britten and Peter Pears—and the thought served to galvanise me.

I went back inside with renewed energy, the slightly sick feeling with which I had eyed the generous refreshments now replaced by a desire to get on with the concert. Emily had taken her place in the auditorium and Johnny was alone in the dressing room, running his hands gently over the keys of an upright piano, flexing his fingers and crooning quietly to himself. Someone had left us a handful of the concert programmes, on the back of which was a reproduction of the engraved glass window in the church of St James in Ashmansworth, the village where Finzi lived for the last seventeen years of his life. Laurence Whistler designed the window to commemorate his good friend and it celebrates a 'family' of English composers and the inspiration they drew from the English countryside. It shows a tree amongst whose roots appear the initials and birthdates of fifty English composers, including Finzi. Around the edges of the tree are quotations from four English poets, reflecting Finzi's love of poetry and lyrical writing.

Music, when soft voices die (from the poem by Percy Bysshe Shelley)

Music, when music sounds gone is the earth I know (from *Music* by Walter de la Mare)

The music in my heart I bore (from *The Solitary Reaper* by William Wordsworth)

Music to hear, why hear'st thou music sadly? (from *Sonnet VIII* by William Shakespeare)

Emily and I had visited the church a few months earlier. The village is less than an hour from Oxford, an easy drive onto the North Wessex

Downs. I knew that Emily would study the reproduced image, and I hoped she would recall the afternoon we spent there and that the memory would gladden her heart, as it did mine, as I took my place alongside Johnny on the platform.

As soon as the two men made their way onto the stage, Emily saw with relief that Alex had regained his equanimity and was beaming at the packed rows of people. She had found a seat halfway back, on the central aisle, and as Alex moved to the front of the platform and began his introduction, she was pleased to discover she had an uninterrupted view.

'Gerald Finzi was born in London eighty-three years ago today. He died young, just two months after his fifty-fifth birthday, but he left behind a fine body of work, key to which are his wonderful songs. In many ways they define him because his greatest inspiration—and greatest works—came from his love of English poetry.'

Alex smiled and Emily relaxed.

'Good evening, ladies and gentlemen. I first encountered Finzi's music when I was a choral scholar at Oxford and later when I sang in the choir at St Paul's Cathedral, but I have recently discovered his songs and I confess I am now a devotee, so I'm delighted and honoured to have this opportunity to celebrate his life here in this beautiful music room.'

There was a ripple of applause.

'Finzi's instinctive feeling for words is exceptional, and his music is immediately recognisable by its yearning melodic lines and wistful harmonies.'

He spoke with sincerity and assurance and though Emily had heard these introductions during the rehearsal, her attention was held throughout.

'We think of Thomas Hardy as one of the great Victorian novelists,' Alex went on, 'but he was also one of the great twentieth century poets and in many ways, his poems are a distillation of the novels. We generally don't think of Hardy as a source for song texts but in fact, in the history of English song to date, only Shakespeare, Walter de la Mare and A E Housman have been set more often than Hardy.'

People seemed surprised by this and there was a rustle of whispered asides.

'Finzi started setting Hardy's poetry very early in his career, and the cycle with which we're going to open tonight's concert was begun in 1926, while Hardy was still alive. The songs come from seven different Hardy collections and from one of his dramas, and they form a cycle created by Finzi himself, not Hardy. This cycle neatly encapsulates both men's obsession with passing time. It's divided into two parts, each prefaced with a quotation from *Psalm 90*. The first is headed *Mane floreat, et transeat* ('In the morning it flourisheth, and groweth up') and the second *Vespere decidat, induret et arescat* ('in the evening it is cut down, and withereth'). But this is not to say that the whole cycle is full of introspective longing for things to be other than the way they are: *Budmouth Dears* is a romp as we watch the girls "fresh as peaches, With their tall and tossing figures and their eyes of blue and brown." These Budmouth dears return again, now elderly, in *Former Beauties* and a snatch of the "gay tunes" of the past echoes in the piano part.'

Alex looked across to Johnny and smiled and after a brief pause, they began. It seemed to Emily that his singing miraculously blended melancholy with nonchalance, allowing the poignancy of the texts to speak. She thought how perfectly nuanced the balance between singer and pianist was, and with what conviction and confidence they delivered the whole cycle.

In the interval, she stayed in her seat and studied the programme. It contained brief biographies of Finzi and the two performers as well as the texts of all the songs and a reproduction of the Finzi window on the back. She loved Whistler's concept of music as a symbolic tree, with its branches budding into notes, and as she studied the initials of the composers chosen because their music was said to have nourished Finzi's imagination, she was propelled back to the warm Spring day, shortly before their weekend in Chester, when she and Alex had stood in the church porch, gazing at the window, just feet away from where Finzi was buried. When they later stood in silence by his gravestone, she had suddenly cried out in a mixture of shock and pain. Something had bitten her on the back of her neck and she had rubbed the place that was stinging to see if she could feel a lump. She could find no sign of anything and was about to shrug it off when Alex lifted her hair to one side to look for himself. To her surprise, he leaned down and kissed her where the neckline of her dress ended—a light, lingering kiss, the gentleness of which sent tremors fluttering through her body. When she turned to face him, she saw that he was looking at her as if she were something rare and precious.

She was roused from this reverie by two women easing their way past her to their seats further down the row. One of them sighed loudly as she sat down and said to the other, 'It's hard not to fall in love with the sound of that voice.'

She saw Emily smiling at her and blushed.

'Well, you can dream, can't you?' said her friend and they both laughed, just as Johnny and Alex made their way back onto the platform to enthusiastic applause.

'We'll start the second half,' Alex said, 'with songs by three composers who were of particular significance to Finzi. He was a close friend of Vaughan Williams, and the older composer was influential and supportive. He was also a visitor to Gregynog in the 1930s, so it seems doubly appropriate that we should begin with two of his songs. The first, *Orpheus with his lute*, the text taken from Shakespeare's *Henry VIII*, is one of his most popular settings, while *Silent Noon* paints a picture of lovers experiencing the drowsy heat of a summer's day in the English countryside and is a setting of the pre-Raphaelite artist and writer, Dante Gabriel Rossetti.'

These songs made a delightful and accessible start to the second half and were followed by two unashamedly romantic settings by Parry—*Bright Star* to words by Keats—and *My Love is Like a singing bird*, an impassioned love song to words by Christina Rossetti. Not for the first time, Emily marvelled at the way Alex's face lit up when he sang and in some of these settings, a smile seemed never far away.

The final song in this group was *Sleep* by Ivor Gurney to a setting by John Fletcher.

'Ivor Gurney was equally gifted as a poet as well as a composer,' said Alex, 'but his life was a tragic one. He was wounded, gassed and shell-shocked during the First World War and spent much of his later life in mental institutions. He was only forty-seven when he died and Finzi became a great champion of his work, determined to ensure that he was remembered as one of the most gifted artists of his generation.'

When the song was over, there was a hushed silence as if the audience didn't want to break the mood it had established. The vocal line soaring over the gentle rocking of the accompaniment was an unforgettable cry of distress from the depths of the soul, and the applause when it came was sustained. Alex waited for it to die away and began his introduction to the final set of songs.

'We're going to end with Finzi's best known song cycle, *Let Us Garlands Bring*, a group of Shakespeare settings which Finzi dedicated to Vaughan Williams on his seventieth birthday. I'm sure the poems will be familiar to many of you—perhaps you studied them at school, or you've heard them in stage productions or even in settings by other composers. All these poems have been set multiple times, but these settings by Finzi are among the finest. Feste's second song in *Twelfth Night*, *Come away, come away death*, is a powerful lament, whereas *Who is Silvia?* from *Two Gentlemen of Verona*, is a charming ditty, an admiring portrait of a beloved woman. *Fear no more the heat o' the sun*, from *Cymbeline*, is a gentle meditation on the passing of time, on growing old and the dissipation of life's fears in death, the great leveller. These words inspired Finzi to one of his most profound creations and Vaughan Williams said it was one of the loveliest songs he had ever heard.

'The remaining two songs of the collection, *O Mistress Mine* from *Twelfth Night* and *It was a lover and his lass* from *As you like it* provide light relief. *O Mistress Mine* is a call for a kiss, now, rather than waiting and risking losing the opportunity to life's uncertainties. *It was a lover and his lass* is one of Shakespeare's best-known verses, exultant in the very idea of love. Listen out for the syncopated accompaniment which lends the song an invigorating sense of well-being and happiness. Only briefly does a grey cloud appear in the third verse, when, for a moment, there's a sense of regret, "How that life was but a flower in springtime". But this is soon dispelled by the jubilation of the last verse.'

In the first song of the set, Alex sounded so fragile and innocent Emily thought her heart would burst with love for him, but in the final songs his voice glowed with ease and optimism. At the end, the audience erupted, having been carried on a musical journey encompassing love and life in all its plentiful variety. Some of the audience were on their feet, calling for more. Alex and Johnny held hands and bowed, lifting their heads to reveal wide smiles of pleasure and relief. At last, Johnny went back to the piano and the clamour subsided.

'Thank you,' Alex said. 'Thank you very much. We'll leave you with one final birthday gift, a song written by Vaughan Williams in 1901, the year of Gerald's birth. I'm sure many of you will know *Linden Lea*. The words are by the Dorset folk poet William Barnes and tell of the happiness and satisfaction known by those who lead a rural existence. In this splendid manor house in the heart of the glorious Welsh countryside, what could be a more fitting finale.'

When it was over, Alex and Johnny held hands and bowed again and again, and with the applause still ringing out behind them, they left the stage, waving goodbye until the auditorium door closed behind them and they were out of sight.

Looking Forward

By the end of July, Emily had completed her initial survey of the collection and had almost finished sorting the music into individual composer categories. The process had taken longer than she anticipated, and she was disappointed that it failed to uncover any other songs by Philip Nash. She was irked that the collection had been bequeathed with so little information about what it contained, and with Freddie's agreement, she wrote to Philip's solicitor seeking some answers.

Dear Mr Medlicott

My father, Frederick Fairfax, was bequeathed a collection of music from your client, the late Philip Nash, and I am the archivist responsible for sorting and cataloguing it. I have some queries which I hope you can help me with.

Are you aware if any works were excluded from the gift or if any manuscripts might have been stored separately from the main body of the collection and been overlooked? (In particular, I believe there may be songs composed by Mr Nash as part of a song cycle). I also wonder if you have come across any papers or diaries which might throw light on how and why the collection was built and what ambitions Mr Nash may have had for it. Finally, are there any surviving family members who might be able to answer any of these questions?

Yours sincerely

Emily Fairfax

The solicitor's reply was polite but only partially helpful.

Dear Miss Fairfax

Thank you for your letter regarding the estate of the late Philip Nash.

I am not aware of anything having been specifically excluded from the bequest to your father, though as you suggest, it is possible that some items were stored separately and were therefore not obviously apparent to us when we packed up the collection to transport it to Oxford. As to family members, only one cousin is still alive. Due to complications with the lease, Mr Nash's house remains unsold and his possessions, including his extensive library, remain in situ. When the issues with the lease are resolved and we are able to prepare the house for market, I will let you know should we uncover any further music manuscripts which could legitimately be thought to be part of the song collection.

You may be interested to know that proceeds from the sale of Mr Nash's assets

are to be donated to his chosen charity, Mind.
  Yours sincerely
  Arthur Medlicott

'Arthur Medlicott?' said Freddie when Emily showed him the letter. 'I'm sure that's not the person I was due to meet at Philip's house.'

They were in the basement and Freddie opened a drawer in one of the desks and took out a slim cardboard file, from which he extracted a typed letter headed Medlicott Solicitors.

'Yes, look,' he said. 'This is from Alan Medlicott.'

'Perhaps Arthur took over when Alan was diverted by the family emergency you mentioned?'

'Yes, that's a possible explanation.'

With a shrug, he added the letter from Arthur Medlicott to the file and put it back in the drawer.

Meanwhile, following favourable critical response to his recital at Gregynog, Alex's diary began to fill up for the next couple of years. Between his oratorio commitments, he continued to build his recital repertoire. The songs of Finzi, Britten and Vaughan Williams remained key to his programme building, but the song collection provided access to the works of other composers—like Quilter, Ireland, Warlock, and Howells—with whom he also developed an affinity. Summer slipped into autumn and soon he was busy with concerts of Christmas music and *Messiah*s. With no commitment on his birthday that year, he and Emily were able to go out for a celebratory meal. They went to a new restaurant on the Banbury Road, created out of a Victorian Glasshouse that had stood on the spot since 1897 selling indoor and outdoor plants, flowers, fruit and vegetables. At lunchtime, the restaurant was light and airy but by night the ambience was transformed by candles on the tables and hundreds of tiny fairy lights draped around the windows and on the large indoor trees.

As they enjoyed glasses of pre-supper champagne, Alex took Emily's hands in his. He stroked the fingers of her right hand, watching the cluster of diamonds on her mother's engagement ring sparkle in the candlelight.

'Your left hand is bare,' he said, looking directly into her eyes. 'Shall we change that?'

She looked down at her hand and at first, she frowned, his comment having taken her by surprise. When she looked up again, she could not mistake the look of intent in his eyes. He said nothing and at last she laughed.

'Yes,' she said, lifting each of his hands in turn to kiss them. 'Let's change that.'

They were married the following summer, a small wedding for close friends and family.

Alex's parents flew over from Cairo for the engagement party in January and were delighted with their future daughter-in-law. Their wedding gift was a week's stay at the Grand Hotel Imperial in Dubrovnik, where they had honeymooned in 1950. Built at the end of the nineteenth century, the hotel stood in a prime position just outside the walls of the old town and had stunning views from its extensive terraces. On their last night, Alex and Emily went to hear Beethoven's *Ninth Symphony* performed outdoors in front of the Cathedral. Under a clear sky and with sea birds circling overhead as if they too were listening, they sat enraptured as four soloists from four different European countries joined together to sing the *Ode to Joy*. It was a joyous ending to an idyllic start to their married life.

They were now living together for the first time and before their wedding, they gave Alex's flat a much-needed makeover. It was up two flights of stairs on the top floor of a substantial semi-detached Victorian house and it was characterful but shabby, with little having changed since Ruth died. The rooms were well proportioned and there was a spare bedroom which had been Alex's room when he stayed with his aunt as a boy. The flat's best feature was a surprisingly spacious living room, big enough to house a baby grand piano, and with handsome floor to ceiling windows overlooking the treelined street. Freshly painted, with new curtains throughout, and three Turkish rugs brought from the house in Park Town for the living room and main bedroom, the original features came back into focus. Over time, the sagging sofa and chairs were replaced and soon they'd created a home that felt truly their own.

Alex's career was building steadily, and he spent as much time learning new repertoire as he did in performance. He had mastered two more song cycles by Finzi and was working on two substantial pieces Finzi wrote for tenor and orchestra. He was also having language coaching to support his study of the German repertoire. Inevitably, his work frequently took him away from Oxford, and though Emily came to concerts whenever she could, time spent at home together was especially precious. They tried then to live as fully and normally as possible, going to the theatre and cinema, to concerts and opera, but equally enjoying walks in the countryside and quiet times at home or with Freddie.

Emily was pleased she was only a short distance away from her father and glad the continuing work on the collection gave her reason to see him regularly. She had hoped the project might be done in a year, but the sorting alone had proved complex and time-consuming and with only two days a week available and the resulting need to pick up momentum again each time she started, by the end of 1984, the job was nowhere near completion. At that point, the funding ran out and the trust was unable to offer any further support.

Meanwhile, Lincoln raised the idea of Emily becoming full time, but she was reluctant to abandon the song collection and leave her father in the lurch, even without funding to pay her. It was Alex who came up with a possible solution. He suggested that Emily ask Lincoln if they would allow her to transition to full-time working in a year's time, before which she would work four days a week. This would leave the more achievable challenge of securing funding to pay for one day a week of her time on the collection. The College was pleased with this proposal and helped Emily find support from an archive funder whose original settlor had been a Lincoln alumnus.

This meant that work on the collection was able to continue throughout 1985, and by the end of that year, three of the indexes were complete.

Emily heard nothing more from Medlicott solicitors, but she occasionally thought about The Red House and wondered who had bought it.

Before Life and After

As time went on, I seemed to be away from home more than ever. A nomadic existence is part and parcel of life as a professional singer and I grew accustomed to living out of a suitcase, coping with wearying long-distance travel and constantly fretting about the condition of my voice. But wherever I was, and whatever the trials of life on the road, I was sustained by my happiness with Emily. She was an essential part of my life, supporting and encouraging me at every turn with her unwavering love and loyalty.

At the beginning of 1986, she started working full time at Lincoln. She had not yet finished the remaining two indexes but was happy to do what she could on those at weekends or on evenings during the week when I was away. When he was free, Freddie helped her, and they enjoyed the chance to share these times together. I worried that Emily might sometimes be lonely but she, like me, had learnt to be self-reliant. She maintained the friendships of her childhood and was not short of company when I was away. One of her school friends had set up a weekly film club at an independent cinema in Jericho. They were a sociable group and after viewing the films they retired to the Old Bookbinders, a nearby pub whose relaxed atmosphere allowed them to push tables together to enable discussions and friendships to flourish.

Emily was also a volunteer at the University's Recording Centre for Blind Students. Once a week, during her lunch break, she would walk the short distance from Lincoln to the New Bodleian and record texts that ranged from ancient history to contemporary poetry. At an event to thank the volunteers, she met Christina, who became one of her closest friends.

'We were invited for Christmas drinks in the Divinity Schools,' she told me, 'and in that rarefied setting, amongst a group whose average age was probably sixty-five, Christina stood out: purple hair, short skirt, thick tights, big earrings, clumpy shoes.' She laughed. 'We made a beeline for each other and ended up leaving early to go out for a meal that went on for hours.'

Despite their very different life-styles—Christina lived on a houseboat on the canal and sold vintage clothes and accessories in the covered market—they relished each other's company and of all Emily's friends, she was the one I came to know best, and I liked her enormously.

If at weekends, Emily and I had no other plans, we would often spend time in the basement of Freddie's house, Emily working on the indexes and me dipping into the catalogues, which were now typed and bound. It turned out that the collection included not only works representing the flourishing of English song in the nineteenth and early twentieth century, but also works by Schubert, Schumann, Brahms, and Wolf. Though Emily bemoaned the paucity of songs by women composers, it was the treasure trove Freddie had hoped for and I enjoyed discovering songs that were new to me and composers whose works I had not previously known.

I was very taken by some songs which were at the lighter end of the repertoire, mostly written during Victoria's long reign and probably performed in middle class drawing rooms by talented amateur singers and pianists. These songs encompassed many moods and styles—comic, elegiac, heroic and sentimental—and I loved them and felt they were worthy of serious attention. I picked out a few of my favourites to study in spare moments. They were a delightful distraction from the more serious repertoire with which I was normally pre-occupied.

I was busy over Christmas that year, but at home for all of January before I left for ten days, five of them in the Netherlands and five in Edinburgh. The night before I left, we had dinner in Park Town and ended the evening with what Freddie dubbed a parlour performance of Victorian ballads. It reminded me of my first Christmas there, Freddie and I at the piano and Emily, our audience, curled up in a chair by the fire.

'Alex, I think you should introduce the songs,' said Freddie. 'Let's do this properly.'

He pretended to adjust an invisible bow tie and looked at me expectantly.

'Then we'll begin with *Tom Bowling* by Charles Dibdin,' I said, in the clipped tones of a BBC presenter from the 1950s, 'a touching song about the death of a sailor. It's one of hundreds of patriotic sea-shanties Dibdin composed and is his most famous song today because of its inclusion in *Fantasia on British Sea Songs*, arranged by Sir Henry Wood in 1905 to mark the centenary of the Battle of Trafalgar and now a regular item at the Last Night of the Proms.'

I loved this song—it was rousing and yet poignant, especially when the melody soared to the upper parts of the tenor voice. When it was over Emily applauded enthusiastically.

'Prepare to be moved to tears by our next rendering,' I warned. '*Annabelle Lee* by Henry Leslie to words by Edgar Allan Poe. It's a lament for the beloved Annabelle, who dies and is buried on the shore where her lover will mourn her for ever.'

'Ah, I know this one,' said Emily. 'It's beautiful.'

'It is,' I agreed. 'Four verses of pure yearning.'

The final verse always gave me goosebumps and none of us spoke until long after the final chords had died away.

For the moon never beams, without bringing me dreams
Of the beautiful Annabel Lee;
And the stars never rise, but I feel the bright eyes
Of the beautiful Annabel Lee;
And so, all the night-tide, I lie down by the side
Of my darling—my darling—my life and my bride,
In her sepulchre there by the sea—
In her tomb by the sounding sea.

'Beautiful,' whispered Emily.

'And to end our short recital, *I'll sing thee songs of Araby* by Frederic Clay. He's become best known for introducing Gilbert and Sullivan to each other, but this little song of his is a gem.'

When we got to the last four lines, I reached down and took Emily's hands in mine.

And all my soul shall strive to wake
Sweet wonder in thine eyes,
To cheat thee of a sigh
or charm thee to a tear!

She did her best to suppress a giggle, but her eyes told me she was charmed, and I thought how lovely she looked. As the three of us enjoyed a nightcap in front of the fire, I pictured families of old, gathered round their pianos, singing songs of love and regret, wistfulness and celebration, absence and expectancy, and thought how all three songs captured a gentle age gone by when such heartfelt outpourings brought consolation and joy.

The following day, I travelled to the Netherlands to give two performances of *The Creation*, one in Eindhoven, the other in Amsterdam. From there I was flying to Edinburgh for another performance of the Haydn four days later, two days before which I was giving a recital with Johnny at the Usher Hall. Though it was a long stretch away from home, the management of the Dutch orchestra had booked us into comfortable hotels near the concert venues, which enabled me to rest and relax between rehearsals and performances. I made sure Emily knew my schedule because we tried to speak every day, wherever I was. Before the second performance, I was getting ready to leave my room to head over to the concert hall, when the phone rang and the receptionist told me there was a call from my wife.

It was a bad line and her voice came and went through a fuzz of hissing sounds and I struggled to hear her, until suddenly the interference disappeared.

'Did you hear what I said?' she asked.

'Try again,' I said. 'The line's good now.'

'I'm pregnant,' she cried. 'Two months pregnant.'

I gasped and almost choked with a mixture of surprise and delight and in our excitement and happiness, we spent the rest of the call talking across each other.

Shortly afterwards, as I waited to make my entrance onto the stage of the concert hall, I knew that Haydn's life-affirming music and his optimism about "the new-created world" would be the perfect outlet for the joy I felt at the prospect of fatherhood which lay ahead.

Winter Words

It had rained for weeks. While I was away, some of the roads into Oxford lay under water for several days, and when I arrived in Edinburgh, grey skies cast a dark and moody pall over the city's imposing architecture.

Nothing, though, could quash my high spirits and as we prepared for our recital, Johnny, too, was visibly buoyed by my good news. The promoter had asked for *The Songs of Travel* so as to have a Scottish element in the programme via the poetry of Robert Louis Stevenson, and was happy to accept Britten's *Winter Words* as the other substantial component of the evening—the two song cycles we'd performed at the Holywell Music Room on my birthday over three years earlier.

First up was the Vaughan Williams, which I introduced with some context about the poet and the songs.

'Robert Louis Stevenson was born in Edinburgh, but as a very young man he began his extraordinary life of travel. Travel that took him well beyond the borders of Scotland. To Europe—famously by canoe and donkey—then westward to New York, and on to San Francisco. Ultimately, he ventured to Samoa, where he spent the rest of his life, revered by the islanders. His *Songs of Travel* evoke sentimental memories of Scotland, but also ponder some of the bigger issues in life. The fourth song, *Youth and love*, is the kernel of the cycle and takes us to its central dilemma: what should we choose, 'love' and by implication a settled life, or 'solitude' and the freedom to wander. The sixth song, *Whither must I wander?* recalls the poet's childhood and the security of home and family which are now long gone. The song reminds us that while the world is renewed each spring, our traveller cannot bring back his past.'

It was the first time I'd performed the cycle in Scotland, and I realised these songs were likely to have special meaning for this audience.

'All these songs still sound fresh and vital, sometimes melancholy, at other times ecstatic, and it's no surprise that they remain so popular.'

At the end, I was aware of a particularly fervent response, as if the audience were proud that a son of Edinburgh could have inspired such stirring music.

We devoted the second half of the concert to Britten, beginning with six settings of folk tunes and finishing with *Winter Words*.

'Our second song cycle tonight is named after Thomas Hardy's last published collection, but the eight poems are from different parts of

Hardy's poetic output. Some think *Winter Words* is Britten's most perfect song cycle. I love it because it marries some of my favourite poems with Britten's masterly settings. The first and last songs address the theme of passing time, the second and seventh take place on the Great Western Railway, while the third and sixth both deal with ornithological matters. Especially wonderful to sing are the story-telling songs, *The Choirmaster's Burial*—also known as *The Tenor Man's Story*—and the tale of the *Boy with the Violin*. The cycle showcases Britten's uncanny ability to conjure musical images from the piano—listen out for the train whistle introduction and bone shaking accompaniment to *The Journeying Boy*, the fluttering wings of the wagtail, the regretful creak of the little table, and the open strings of the schoolboy's fiddle in *The Convict and Boy with a violin*. As for *The Choirmaster's Burial*, it's a compendium of miniature theatrical effects and a gift for any tenor worth his salt.'

The audience laughed.

'These eight poems,' I went on, 'contrast brief moments—a boy's boredom on a long train ride, a certain light in the trees in November—against the vastness of time. The first song, *At Day's Close in November*, is not simply about a windy day in Wessex, but is also a meditation on time and change, the world of yesterday and the unknown vistas of tomorrow. The closing song, *Before Life and After*, remembers a time there was… "when all went well, None suffered sickness, love, or loss, None knew regret, starved hope, or heart-burnings"—and it yearns for such a time to come again.'

The concert was enthusiastically received, but as we prepared to leave, I felt strangely subdued. Johnny was taking the sleeper train back to London, and not wanting to be alone, I walked with him to the station so we could have a quick drink there before his train left. It had temporarily stopped raining and the station bar was not quite as gloomy as others I'd sometimes found myself in and anyway, I was glad of the chance to relax and reflect before I went back to the hotel. I looked round at the other customers—mainly men drinking on their own—and thought we might all be subjects in an Edward Hopper painting.

'Penny for them,' Johnny said, looking up from his whiskey.

'Something about the Britten discomforted me tonight,' I said, shaking my head. 'I think it's the sense of loss that haunts Hardy's writing and which Britten doesn't shy away from.'

I took a slug of whiskey.

'Never mind. Haydn's delight in the wonder of the world will cheer me up, no doubt.'

'Well, his world view was certainly rather different to Hardy's, that's for sure,' Johnny said, downing the last of his drink and getting to his feet. 'You can bask in a benign, rationally ordered universe, with minimal gloom and suffering.'

We laughed as we hugged goodbye.

'So, no sleeper train for you on Thursday night?'

'No, thank goodness. The Dutch management are paying for me to fly to Heathrow on Friday morning. I'll have an early start, but the hotel they've booked for all the musicians is close to a bus stop for the airport. The flight's at nine o'clock, and if it's on time and I don't have to wait long for a coach to Oxford, I should be home by lunchtime.'

'Give my love to Emily—and cheer up. It went well tonight.'

We hugged again and I watched him hurry towards the platform and waited until he was through the barrier and out of view.

On Friday morning, it was raining again. The flight was late arriving in Edinburgh due to poor visibility at Heathrow, from where the plane was coming, but the delay was brief and we were soon airborne, enjoying coffee and croissants.

Two days spent in the sunny uplands of *The Creation* had gone someway to restoring my equanimity, but though my melancholy mood had lifted, I still felt a sense of disquieting unease, which I couldn't explain. I'd spoken to Emily before the concert the previous day and she assured me she was feeling well and was carrying on with life as normal.

'I'm off to see *Chicago* tonight at the Apollo. I know it's not your sort of thing, you old fogey, so I'm going with Christina.'

I teased her that she was a lowbrow at heart, and we laughed.

It took an age for my suitcase to come off the plane and meant I missed the coach I had hoped to catch. I now faced a long wait for the next one, so I took my time walking from the baggage collection area to the arrivals hall. As I was looking around, wondering where to go to kill the time, I scanned the gaggle of people who were standing at the barrier, looking at the arriving passengers in search of whoever they were waiting for. And among the crowd, I saw Christina and Johnny. The sight of them there together was bewildering. Was it a coincidence or did they know each other? And why were they there?

As my mind raced and my heart rate quickened, it became clear that this was no innocuous chance meeting. Christina looked shattered, her face shiny and pinched, and when Johnny saw me, he closed his eyes and bowed his head. I realised that for some dread reason they were waiting for me. I hurried through the exit, and they moved slowly along the barrier to join me. I heard myself repeat the word 'no' over and over again, as if it was some mystic chant that would ward off whatever heartbreak was to come, and all would be as it had been. I stopped and waited, looking from one to the other until Johnny, his face gaunt with misery, stepped towards me, and as he took me in his arms, I felt my legs give way.

Leaden skies

There was an eyewitness who saw it all: a twenty-year old undergraduate from Keble, heading back to his rooms in college. The student, who was called Oliver, was walking up St Giles, intending to cross the road at the zebra crossing near the church. He told the police it wasn't raining but the roads were very wet following downpours during the evening. As he approached the church, Emily was cycling slowly alongside him, but then a fast-moving car passed too close to her and soaked them both as it hurtled through deep standing water on the road's surface. Oliver said the shock of the drenching seemed to knock Emily off balance and for a moment he thought she might part company with her bike, but she steadied herself, though in doing so, she drifted towards the middle of the road and was hit by a bus that simply couldn't avoid her.

Oliver ran across the road to the lodge at St John's College and asked the porter to call the emergency services. The stricken bus driver placed his jacket under Emily's head, but while they waited for the police and ambulance to arrive, they could see that nothing could be done for her. The police took away Emily's crumpled bicycle, her saddle bag and her shoulder bag, in which they found her diary and address book. She was very organised, and it was no surprise that on the inside cover of the diary she had listed her next of kin. It was almost midnight by the time the police arrived to break the news to Freddie, having first gone to our flat in Bardwell Road and got no answer. Freddie phoned Johnny, hoping he would know where I was staying in Edinburgh, but though Johnny knew I was moving from the cheap hotel where he and I had stayed, he didn't know the name of the hotel to which I'd gone. The police drove Freddie to the canal and helped him identify Christina's boat, but she didn't know how to contact me either. Eventually, it was decided that she and Johnny would go to Heathrow to break the news to me there. Christina would get an early coach and Johnny would meet her at the airport and then drive us all back to Oxford.

It was surreal to think that while all this was going on in Oxford, I was sleeping soundly in Edinburgh, blithely unaware of what was about to come crashing down upon me.

Now, as I sat with Christina in the back of Johnny's car, heading back to Oxford, I felt the future slipping away. The next week, the next month, the next year were suddenly unimaginable. So many hopes and dreams would now never be fulfilled. Our story would be for ever unfinished.

I feared for Freddie as much as for myself and I stayed with him all that day and overnight, not wanting to go home to an empty flat or to leave him alone. We talked and cried and drank whiskey late into the night. As we at last made our way upstairs to bed, I couldn't help saying, 'No matter how I may try to fill the gap left by Emily's death, I know that part of me will be for ever inconsolable.'

'Which is how it should be,' he sighed. 'That's how we keep alive the love we don't want to let go of.'

An Old Belief

That night I dreamt I was being bundled into the back of a cream-coloured ambulance, just as I was during the terrifying summer of 1956. In the dream, however, I was an adult, not a child, but bizarrely, I was wearing Andy Pandy pyjamas. Some people were huddled near the back of the ambulance—Johnny and Emily were there, with my parents and others I didn't recognise—but no-one got in with me.

'I don't want to go. Please don't take me away.'

No-one moved and the ambulance took me on a long journey across rough country roads, and every little bump it encountered was excruciating so that my whole body hurt. I was sobbing and calling for my mother, but there was no-one to hear me.

I awoke with a lurch, not knowing where I was, until I remembered I was in the room which had once been Emily's at the top of the house in Park Town. As feelings of despair and desolation overwhelmed me, I buried my face in the pillow and wept.

Fragments of the dream remained, confused and upsetting, but I was not surprised that my subconscious had taken me back to a childhood trauma, a psychological crisis that rivalled the physical assault of the polio virus. I'd faced the acute phase of that illness alone, bereft of the emotional support of my parents, apparently abandoned by them, whereas before, if I was hurt or unwell, my mother was always there to hold my hand or offer a soothing drink. Now, more than thirty years later and beset by a new calamity, I needed her again.

When I told her the awful news, she spared me platitudes, knowing that words of consolation are notoriously easy to say, and can sound trite or banal. Instead, she shared something from her own experience.

'You may feel overwhelmed by all the terrible tasks a death brings with it, but when Ruth died, I found it extremely comforting to know there were things I could still do for her, that there were ways in which she still needed me. Someone had to choose the coffin and the flowers, the hymns, and the readings, to select a headstone and devise the wording of the inscription. Doing all this for her did help me.'

I had no idea what Emily would have wanted. We had only just begun our journey through life together and had never talked about endings. I realised that even in death, I wanted to keep her close, to have a grave at which to leave flowers, a place where I could sit in quiet communion with her, and as Marie-Odile was buried not far away in Wolvercote Cemetery, it seemed right that this should also be her daughter's resting-place.

I couldn't face going home, so for the time being, I stayed with Freddie, and it was Christina who prepared the flat for my parents, changing the sheets and stocking the fridge. They got a flight from Cairo as soon as they could and insisted they would make their own way from the airport to Oxford so all I had to do was meet them at Bardwell Road. They looked tired and drawn, but were unconcerned for themselves, their attention entirely on me. After they'd unpacked and recovered from the journey, we sat at the kitchen table eating a fish pie that Christina had left for us.

'I'm sorry we didn't make it to see you in Cairo.'

My parents looked at each other and carried on eating.

'We sensed that Emily was reluctant to come,' my father said at last.

I couldn't deny it, she was, and it was one of the few areas of friction between us.

'She was put off by so much she'd heard about Cairo. The noise, the traffic congestion, the pollution, the general pandemonium.'

'All true of course,' my father replied, 'but most visitors, once they've got the measure of all that, are seduced by the history of the city and the warmth and good heartedness of the Cairenes.'

'I used all those arguments, but Cairo's particular brand of exoticism seemed alien to her—I think she would have been more comfortable among the ruins of Pompeii or Knossos.'

'I always hoped she'd come round to it at last,' my mother said tearfully, before changing the subject to that of the funeral.

It was to be held at St Margaret's Church, where we were married less than two years earlier by the same vicar who would now conduct the funeral formalities. He offered to come to Freddie's house to discuss the service, and his visit was the prompt we needed to begin making decisions about music and readings.

Seventeen years earlier, Freddie had been making these same decisions for his wife's funeral.

'How did you choose the music for Marie-Odile's service?'

He sighed.

'I chose one of the hymns—*The Day Thou Gavest Lord is Ended*—and I let Emily choose the other. She was only ten at the time so the hymns she knew and liked were the ones they sang at school. She chose *All Things Bright and Beautiful* because she liked the words.'

I was so dazed by shock and grief that at first, I found it hard to even register if I knew these hymns, though of course, I did.

'I'm sure they'd be fine,' I said, and being as shattered as I was, he agreed.

I suggested we should have a choral motet or anthem, as I knew that a choir based at Pembroke had offered to sing if we wanted them to.

'Did you have anything like that at Marie-Odile's funeral?'

'Yes, we did. I wanted some classical music, and I wanted something I thought would move and console, but I struggled to choose a piece of sacred music because what can console us if we have lost our belief in God and the afterlife?'

I nodded in bleak agreement.

'At first, I thought of a secular piece like Pearsall's *Lay a Garland*, but then something rather extraordinary happened to change my mind. I'd gone into Oxford because the only black suit I possessed was looking past its best and I decided to buy a new one. While I was there, I called in at Magdalen to leave a book for a student whose tutorial I'd had to postpone. As I came out of the porter's lodge, I heard the faint sounds of the choir and the organ from the chapel nearby. I decided to take a few quiet moments to listen, and though I slipped into the building as unobtrusively as I could, Bernard, the Director of Music turned round and saw me. We knew each other of course and he had heard about Marie-Odile, but to my surprise, he left the choir and came to offer his condolences. He was very kind. I asked him what they would be singing at Evensong that night and he invited me to stay and listen while they rehearsed it.'

'What was it?'

'It was one of Parry's *Songs of Farewell*, the fourth one—*There is an Old Belief*. He asked me if I knew it and I said I knew of it but could not recall it. I remember he smiled, possibly having recognised that I was not fully with it.

'"It's the most serene of the six settings in this collection," he said, "and it was sung at Parry's funeral at St Paul's Cathedral in October 1918."

'I remember becoming interested when he told me that.

'"Parry's choice of the texts for these songs is thought to reflect his longing to escape the violence of a world at war, and to find peace in a heavenly realm, guided there by the redeeming power of faith."'

'He looked at me, perhaps hoping for a response, but though I had no desire to appear churlish, I had none.

'"Wait a moment," he said. "Let me bring you a copy of the score so you can follow the words."

'He scurried up the aisle towards his music-stand near the choir stalls and spoke briefly to the singers, the boys among them having started to fidget. He came back and handed me a copy and told me something about the text.

"The Scottish poet, John Gibson Lockhart, was best known as the biographer of his father-in-law, Sir Walter Scott, but he was also greatly affected by bereavement through the later part of his life. He lost his wife and several of his children in just a few years, and it was after this string of losses that he wrote *There is an Old Belief*."

'And with that, he hurried back up the aisle, leaving me to ponder the concept of the redeeming power of faith and the prospect of finding peace in some heavenly realm. I wanted to cry out, "You can't fob me off by saying I'll see her again in some mythical afterlife. I want her to come back now." I had never felt as much of a pagan as I did at that moment, longing to be like Orpheus, descending into the underworld, to lead my lost Eurydice back into the light.'

At that, Freddie paused, and I could see he was fighting back a mixture of emotions.

'And then,' he said, 'the choir started singing. I looked down at the music and quickly scanned the words and I confess, they brought shivers down my spine. As I listened, it seemed to me that the music was exerting an uncanny control over my whole nervous system as if it possessed narcotic powers. The piece is richly scored in six parts, vibrant, *a capella* choral writing, in which Parry conjures up an incredible sound world. The music conveys a desperate sense of longing, but strangely, it isn't morbid. It seemed to have an optimistic radiance that affirmed the power of words and music to comfort and console. In those four or five minutes I felt transported to another world, and it made me realise that even for non-believers, sacred texts, sacred music, can offer moments of emotional connection.

'I sat there for a while longer and when I got up to leave, I managed to get Bernard's attention. I walked up the aisle towards him, intending to return the music. He met me halfway and I thanked him. "That was wonderful. The rapture in that final cadence truly did seem to bring a glimpse of paradise tantalisingly close." He took both my hands in his and squeezed them. "At times of grief and despair," he said, "there is something unsayable about the experience that only music seems able to express. Keep the copy—you may find a use for it." We embraced and I left, but I've always been grateful to him for the lesson he taught me that day.'

We were in the basement and Freddie got up and went over to the door.

'Let's go upstairs,' he said.

I followed him up and into the front sitting room, where he went over to the piano.

'I keep the music here at all times,' he said, handing it to me. 'Schola Cantorum performed it at Marie-Odile's funeral. Perhaps you would like it sung at Emily's?'

Parry may not have conceived *The Songs of Farewell* as ecclesiastical repertoire, but their vision of heaven's joys have found a natural home in religious settings and I had sung them several times at Christ Church and St Paul's. I pictured Freddie, newly widowed and disconsolate, sitting alone in Magdalen Chapel, finding himself unexpectedly moved and uplifted by a sacred motet. Not quite a damascene conversion, but a profound moment, nevertheless.

The Songs were written at the end of Parry's life, at a time for him of great personal despair, and yet as I re-read the wistful words, I felt they exuded a sense of peace and hopefulness.

There is an old belief,
That on some solemn shore,
Beyond the sphere of grief
Dear friends shall meet once more.
Beyond the sphere of Time and Sin
And Fate's control,
Serene in changeless prime
Of body and of soul.
That creed I fain would keep
That hope I'll ne'er forgo,
Eternal be the sleep,
If not to waken so.

So, we agreed on the music, and with help, we chose the readings. Johnny offered to read from *Ecclesiastes*, and I asked my mother to choose something and to read it herself, if she felt able. We were in Summertown, shopping for supplies, and I asked her if she had made a choice because the funeral director needed the details for the order of service.

'If you agree, I'd like to read *Remember* by Christina Rossetti.'

'That would be lovely. What made you choose that?'

'When we came to meet Emily for the first time, when you celebrated your engagement, Emily talked about her work at Lincoln and when she described the library there as one of the most beautiful in Oxford, I said I'd love to see it. She offered to show me round and I was thrilled to have some time with her alone. Do you remember?'

'I do.'

'When we were there, a student stood up, packed his bags, and walked away, leaving a couple of books behind him on the desk. One was a collection of Christina Rossetti's poetry. Emily picked up the books and replaced them on the shelves and, over lunch, she told me the story of the missing song cycle, the title of which seemed to come from the opening lines of Rossetti's poem *Remember*.

'No other songs ever came to light,' I said, 'and Emily wondered if they had been deliberately excluded from the collection or simply mislaid.'

'Yes, she told me that, too. She also told me the cycle had an intriguing dedication.'

'It did. It was a mystery Emily hoped would one day be solved.'

On the day of the funeral, the greatest shock was seeing the hearse and realising that the flower-bedecked coffin, which I had chosen, now contained the lifeless body of my beloved wife. Though I had sat with her in the undertaker's chapel of rest, and kissed and caressed her, this was the first time her death felt real and final.

The service went by in a blur as if I was watching it happen to someone else. Afterwards, everyone said how moving it had been. The Isis Singers sang the Parry with touching youthful purity and genuine emotional conviction, while Johnny, having navigated Bach, Brahms and Vaughan Williams on the organ, scrambled down to the nave to read *A Time for Everything*. The final lines caught my attention and though I recognised all too keenly that this was a time to weep and to mourn, I wondered if there would ever again be a time for laughing and dancing. My mother delivered her reading quite beautifully and, whereas much of what was said that day passed me by, I heard every word of Rossetti's poem.

Remember me when I am gone away,
Gone far away into the silent land;
When you can no more hold me by the hand,
Nor I half turn to go yet turning stay.
Remember me when no more day by day
You tell me of our future that you plann'd:
Only remember me; you understand

It will be late to counsel then or pray.
Yet if you should forget me for a while
And afterwards remember, do not grieve:
For if the darkness and corruption leave
A vestige of the thoughts that once I had,
Better by far you should forget and smile
Than that you should remember and be sad.

The poem was difficult enough to hear, but the Eulogy was almost unbearably poignant. I was grateful that Lesley, the Director of the Recording Centre for Blind Students, volunteered to give this, because neither Freddie nor I felt up to the task. In a former life, Lesley had been a deputy head teacher at Emily's secondary school so had known Emily when she was a withdrawn twelve-year-old. Though I heard only snatches of what she said, Lesley's final words—a message from a student—moved me to tears.

'Hassad is from Istanbul,' she said, 'and English is his third language after Turkish and French, so for him I had to find readers who could adjust the speed at which they naturally read to a tempo that was slightly more measured, without being laboured. After the first tape Emily made for him, he said, if possible, he would like her to do all the recordings he needed. He never met Emily, never knew the beautiful, vibrant person I'd seen her become, but he said he liked not only the warmth and clarity of her voice, but the sense that she read everything with a smile on her face and kindness in her heart.'

At this point, Lesley paused, and I thought she'd finished, but in fact, she was simply gathering herself.

'That was how he pictured her in his mind's eye.'

Afterwards, as the churchyard cleared and we prepared to leave for the cemetery, a young man approached me and held out his hand.

'I'm Oliver,' he said. 'I'm very sorry for your loss.'

In my state of numbness, it took me a moment to realise who he was. He was slightly built and looked younger than I expected, no more than a boy, and I thought how horrible it must have been for him to witness what happened.

'Thank you for coming and thank you for everything you did to help.'

He shook his head.

'I wish I could have done more.'

'I know.'

'I wanted to give you this,' he said, handing me a small package wrapped in brown paper.

'What is it?'

'While we were waiting for the ambulance, I found it in a puddle on the side of the road. I could tell it was a book and I guessed it must have fallen out of your wife's saddle bag because the bag had come away from the bike and split open. It was in a Blackwell's plastic bag so it wasn't totally saturated, but it was wet so I took it back to my rooms, hoping I could dry it out there slowly enough that it would be salvageable. It's not perfect, but it's still in one piece and I was able to ease most of the pages apart. In any case, I thought you would want to have it.'

I gasped, quite overwhelmed by his thoughtfulness.

'Thank you so much. I can't tell you how much this means to me.'

He smiled and bowed his head, and before he walked away, he reached out and held me in a shy embrace.

Much later when my parents had gone back to the flat and after Freddie and I had shared a night cap and he had gone up to bed, I at last felt able to open the package. I tore open the wrapping paper and eased out the book from inside the Blackwell's bag.

To my surprise, it was a tourist guide to Egypt.

I opened it carefully and something fell out onto the floor. It was a greetings card, shrink-wrapped in cellophane, its brightly coloured image showing an illustration of the owl and the pussycat sailing away in their pea green boat. I peeled away the wrapper and opened the card. On the left-hand side were the words of Edward Lear's poem.

The right-hand side simply bore the greeting *Happy Valentine's Day*.

PART 2
Spring 1987 to Spring 1988

To Cairo

That year, winter seemed to have taken such a stranglehold over the natural world, it felt like spring would never come. Freddie was more accepting of the normal cycles of the seasons than I was. We talked about the metaphors that winter carries and he was receptive to its call to go to ground and hunker down, to stay with his loss, in the hope that the renewal he would eventually see in nature would encourage him to go on living. He was granted compassionate leave of absence and took himself away to a silent retreat in the Black Mountains near Abergavenny.

In Oxford, everywhere looked dull and drab and decayed and provoked in me a despairing sensation that nature had closed down, not to renew but to die. I recalled the first winter Emily and I were together when we had looked forward to spring with so much anticipation. Now, though the bare trees and bleached out skies drained my depleted spirits, I perversely also dreaded the arrival of spring flowers—the daffodils and tulips which had once heralded the blossoming of our love. So much must now be faced without Emily. Birthdays, anniversaries, Christmas…

My instincts urged me to escape this bleak new world and flee towards warmth and light. I knew that wherever I went I would carry my grief deep inside me; that I couldn't simply leave it behind and forget it for a while. But if I had to face it, let it be somewhere that vibrated with colour and energy and life. I cancelled all my engagements for the next two months and went to Cairo, a city that swarms with life—chaotic, unpredictable, and captivating.

I also felt a strong need to be with my parents. What I would do once I got to Cairo, I had no idea. On the flight there, I found myself recalling my early visits, when I was still at school. I remembered how unfamiliar everything had felt at first—the heat, the sounds, the smells; how different everything and everybody looked—men in white robes and sandals, women in full-face veils, cars sharing the roads with donkeys and carts, and buses, so overloaded that bodies hung onto doors and limbs stuck out of windows.

As a schoolboy I was not allowed to navigate the city alone. One or both of my parents were always with me, and in the safety of their company I could enjoy these bizarre exoticisms. Sometimes, for a treat, I was taken to what was then the Omar Khayaam Hotel, and is now a Marriott, a few blocks away from where my parents live in Zamalek. The hotel was formerly the Gezira Palace and much of it was furnished with original pieces. On one memorable occasion, my father allowed me to peek into some of the reception rooms at garden level and the ballrooms on the first floor. I had never before seen such splendour and it felt extraordinary to sit in one of its ornate cafés eating ice cream out of a silver dish.

As I grew older and became more independent, and had seen more of the world, I recognised that Cairo is unlike any other place on earth. It doesn't have graceful boulevards and cobbled squares. Its oldest parts have not been tamed and made tourist friendly, and I will never forget how shocked I was when I realised that less than a mile away from some of the smartest Nile-side hotels there are mud-brick houses where water comes from spigots in the street and women wash clothes in the river. It's a vast city of diverse worlds and gross iniquities, but on each visit, I became ever more entranced by its exhilarating anarchy and its good-natured people. Cairenes believe that God in his mercy has endowed them with the strength of character to endure their hardships. The muezzins bellowing out the call to prayer five times a day through speakers on top of the profusion of minarets that dot the skyline are a reminder that it is faith and hope that keep them going. They persevere and somehow, they cope, and I hoped I would absorb some of their fortitude.

My flight landed at five o'clock in the afternoon, when I knew the roads would still be clogged with heavy traffic and the fifteen-mile journey to Zamalek might take as long as an hour. Outside the arrivals hall, the heat and the hubbub hit me, but to my relief there was a line of black and white Ladas and Fiats, mostly old and battered and no doubt badly maintained, all waiting for customers. I leant through the window of the nearest car and told the driver my destination. He leapt out and heaved my suitcase into the boot and I got in up front alongside him, knowing it's considered odd or unmannerly for a lone male passenger to sit in an empty back seat by himself. The driver showed no inclination to talk, and apart from occasionally singing along to the atonal Arab music blaring on his radio, he remained silent.

Daylight was fading fast, and it was dark by the time we approached Zamalek. When we crossed the October Bridge onto Gezira Island, the lights were coming up all over the city and the cruising restaurants moored alongside the Corniche looked like floating fairy palaces.

In Zamalek, Cairo's most fashionable residential district, there are more embassies than in any other part of the city. My parents lived in a nineteen thirties apartment on Ismail Mohamed, a few doors away from the Cyprus

Embassy. Once there, the driver hoisted my suitcase onto the pavement and I handed him thirty Egyptian pounds which he took without comment, giving me a friendly nod before he jumped back in the car and roared off into the night.

Yousri, the *boab* who looked after the building, seemed to be expecting me. He greeted me with a friendly handshake before lifting my case onto his shoulder and leading the way to the lift. 'Welcome, Mr Ingram, sir, welcome to Cairo.'

'*Shukran*,' I said. 'How are you?'

'*Allah karim*,' he replied.

"God is generous" was his habitual reply, but I knew from my parents what long hours he worked and how little he lived on, and I felt humbled by his stoic acceptance of his lot.

We went up in the lift to the second floor and he carried my suitcase to my parents' door, where he pressed the buzzer. My father answered and exclaimed with pleasure to see me. He handed Yousri a folded Egyptian note and spoke to him in Arabic before ushering me inside.

'Do you have any plans for while you're here?' my mother asked me later while we were having dinner.

'Not really. I think I'll want to dip in and out of the city, enough to lose myself in its mayhem and revisit a few special places, but I realise how exhausted I am and right now it feels tempting to simply sit in the garden at the Marriott and doze in the sunshine.'

'That sounds a good balance,' my father said. 'We thought you might like to go out for dinner a few times. There are some excellent new restaurants in Zamalek and the Moghul Room at the Mena House is still as reliable as ever. Some people think it's the best restaurant in Egypt.'

'I'd like that, but I hope you won't find me miserable company.'

'Oh darling, of course we won't,' my mother protested. 'It's wonderful to have you here.'

'We could have early evening drinks by the pool at the Mena House— the best place in Cairo to see the Pyramids flood-lit and rising beyond the palm trees.'

I laughed. 'Dad, you sound quite poetic, but seriously, that sounds lovely.'

'You will, of course, have to brave the dreaded Mugamaa,' my mother said, 'and it would be a good idea to get it out of the way. I can come with you tomorrow if you like.'

'Yes please,' I said with feeling. 'If I went there alone, I'm not sure I'd ever make it out again.'

We spoke little that first night. I had virtually no conversation and went early to bed in the room that had always been mine, apart from the couple of occasions when Ruth and I had come together, and I'd been relegated to the single room. Next morning, I was woken by the sun streaming through the lightweight curtains. The room overlooked the street and shared a balcony with the large sitting room next door and before I showered and dressed, I stepped outside to feel the warmth and take in my new surroundings.

My father had already left for work and my mother was in the kitchen squeezing oranges. She poured some juice into a glass and handed it to me.

'What can I get you?' she asked.

'I'm not really hungry.'

'You'll need something to fortify you for the Mugamaa. Let me at least make you some tea and toast.'

'Okay, thanks. I can manage that.'

When we went down in the lift an hour later, Yousri was outside sitting on a battered wicker chair, and I wondered if he'd been there all night.

'Taxi, madame?' he asked my mother.

'*Min fadlak, Yousri. Midan Tahrir—Mugamaa,*' she said, and Yousri rolled his eyes in sympathy.

By western standards taxis in Cairo are cheap and there's never one faraway. Yousri seemed to be able to magic them out of thin air and often knew the driver—many of them were his cousins. While he stepped into the road, to flag down the first available car, I looked up and down the street and saw that many of the buildings had their own *boab*, sitting on bits of cardboard or rickety old chairs, generally being helpful to residents and keeping an eye on things in return for tips—*baksheesh*. Many of them, like Yousri, were Nubians and with their long robes, coloured turbans and dignified demeanour, they lent a genteel air to the tree-lined street.

'*Shukran,*' I said, handing him some notes as my mother climbed into the taxi that had pulled up.

The relatively unhurried air of Zamalek was soon left behind as we made our way into the hectic metropolis. We were heading to the heart of the city and Midan Tahrir (Liberation Square), Cairo's equivalent of Time or Trafalgar Square. The focal points of the broad, bustling square are the Nile Hilton and the domed Museum of Ancient Antiquities, but everything is dwarfed by the monstrous Mugamaa, a grey Stalinist hulk which my father described as one of the world's most depressingly ugly buildings and where I needed to register the address at which I was staying. I had done this on previous visits and now as then it felt like stepping into a scene from Kafka's *The Trial*. It involved trudging up several flights of stairs circling a huge stairwell, standing in long queues, and being prepared to be told by a dead-eyed clerk that you were on the wrong floor or in the wrong queue, and being directed somewhere else to stand in line and wait your turn for another bored bureaucrat to check your papers. My mother was used to it, because whenever they had visitors, she would accompany them here, and I was grateful for her reassuringly competent presence. After remarkably few missteps, our mission was accomplished, and we rewarded ourselves with coffee on the terrace of the Nile Hilton.

I was aware that my mother was studying me closely while pretending to be interested in the comings and goings around us.

'How are you, Mum?'

She looked surprised to be asked.

'I'm fine,' she said at last. 'Sad for you; worried about you.'

I nodded, knowing there was no point in telling her not to worry.

'How long do you think you'll stay?' she asked.

'I'm not sure. I booked an open return flight so I can be flexible, but I think somewhere between two and three weeks.'

She looked pleased at that.

'Do you have any thoughts about what you'd like to do this afternoon?'

I shook my head.

'Do you have to be anywhere?' I asked.

'No, I'm not working today. If you wanted to do something gentle to ease yourself into life in Cairo, we could head back to Zamalek and go to the Mahmoud Khalil Museum. It's in a beautiful neo-Islamic villa near the Marriott and has an impressive collection of nineteenth and twentieth century French paintings and sculpture.'

I was happy to go there, and it was indeed a fine collection—all the great Impressionists were represented—and it was an exquisite little house. There were few other visitors and we could stroll around at our own pace. I stood for some time in front of a painting by Toulouse-Lautrec called *The Singing Lesson*, with the teacher accompanying the student at a piano on which stood two lamps with bright red shades. My mother joined me, and we stood together in silence, until I sighed and turned away.

'I keep wondering what Emily would have made of Cairo, keep wanting to tell her about what I'm doing and seeing, and then the reality hits me. I feel almost guilty standing here, admiring these magnificent paintings in this lovely house, when she will never do that, here or anywhere.'

My mother nodded and squeezed my arm.

'I'm sorry I'm so glum, such poor company, but I am glad to be here and grateful that you're here with me.'

We walked on, arm in arm, and I knew I could talk as much or as little as I wanted. We went home via the Marriott so that Mum could call at the bakery in the hotel's shopping mall. We'd had no lunch and decided to stop for tea and cake in the café where, as a boy, I'd enjoyed ice cream in silver dishes.

'Emily would have loved that museum,' I said after a while. 'She often spent her lunch breaks in the Ashmolean. Visiting art collections was something she never tired of.'

'And she'd bought a guidebook to Egypt,' my mother said.

'Yes, perhaps she'd come round to the idea of a visit. I'm sure she would have wanted your grandchild to know you.'

I sighed.

'We'll never know now.'

Encounters

The next day I was even more exhausted. Being in Cairo means submitting to an almost perpetual assault on the senses and I knew I would have to recover at least a modicum of strength and energy before I could subject myself to it, so I decided to spend the day quietly, somewhere I could feel the warmth of the sun on my face, just being, and perhaps reading.

The Marriott has an unusually tranquil garden, with trees and lawns and hidden corners where you can discover statuary dating from when the Palace was built in the 1860s. I bought a day ticket and found a sun-bed in a peaceful spot, well away from the poolside area. I was not a swimmer. It had not been part of my rehabilitation—the focus being on physiotherapy and walking—but at any rate, I was too self-conscious about my leg to expose it in swimming trunks or shorts. Lying in the shade of a palm tree in light-weight linen trousers and a T-shirt, I felt inconspicuous.

But anyway, a disability like mine carries no stigma in Egypt. There's a famous Pharaonic stone carving showing a priest with a walking stick, a withered leg and foot deformities characteristic of polio, evidence that the disease has been endemic in the country for centuries. Other disabilities are common, too, since conditions that would be treatable in the west go untreated here because people can't afford the treatment. A disabled traveller, whatever their disability or disfigurement, does not attract the same embarrassed reaction from Egyptians that they can do elsewhere. For Egyptians, it's God's will, to be accepted and made light of. *Allah karim.*

I settled down, hoping to doze in the sunshine, but for a while I took in the sights and sounds around me—the gardeners tending the flower beds, the waiters delivering snacks and drinks, visitors applying suntan lotion and studying tourist guides. A woman walked towards me on her way back into the hotel and I saw that she was heavily pregnant.

Thoughts of the child that would never be were never far away, but neither was the uncomfortable truth that part of me was angry with Emily for not taking greater care of herself and our unborn child. I had never cycled in Oxford and always thought it a perilous activity, with buses in particular seeming to resent sharing the road with pesky cyclists. Much as I hated feeling this way and knew it was unreasonable, I wished it could all have been different, that Emily had abandoned her bicycle for the duration of her pregnancy and taken instead to walking. I tried to brush the thought away, but it had taken hold.

I adjusted the bed and sat upright, before turning to my book in the hope it would distract me. Usually, I read voraciously whenever I travelled, books being trusty companions in situations when I might have been bored or felt lonely. Normally my taste was eclectic but, on this trip, I was anxious to avoid anything romantic or sentimental, so I opted for the short stories about Rumpole of the Bailey, hoping their caustic wit and worldly wisdom would be an innocuous diversion.

But it was hard to settle and to focus. I would read a page or two before my head was once again full of thoughts of Emily. Grief, I discovered, was a constant companion. I was contemplating leaving when an elderly waiter approached and asked if he could get me something from the bar. I hesitated, not sure I wanted to stay.

'A beer, sir?' he ventured. 'A sandwich? Pastrami is good.'

I knew I had nothing better to do.

'Thank you,' I said. '*Shukran.*'

This brief connection with another human being, his quiet courtesy, had shifted something within me. I felt calmer, more willing to sit with the pain and at the same time, absorb and enjoy the serenity of the old palace garden. The same waiter returned again during the afternoon, first to take away my empty plate and glass, and later, to suggest a cup of tea, which I accepted. There was something soothing about his unobtrusive efficiency and in his eyes, I saw decency and kindness. His name was Sayed and before I left, I sought him out to thank him and give him a final tip. He had helped me get through the day.

I walked back, knowing my parents were going to an embassy event and would not be home until late. On a street corner a short distance from their apartment, I saw a woman standing alone with a bucket at her feet containing bunches of tight-budded roses. I stopped to look, and she gave me a tired smile, but said nothing. I looked down to read the sign on which she'd written the price and noticed that her bare left arm was withered, and her left hand was small and misshapen. The roses seemed incredibly cheap, and I handed her twenty Egyptian pounds in a single note. She began to look for change but I waved it away and smiled, hoping to convey to her that I didn't want any. She reached down to select four bunches of the apricot-coloured flowers and I saw that there was now just one bunch left. As she handed me the flowers, I offered her another five pounds and pointed to the remaining bunch, hoping that by taking them all, she would be able to go home. She handed me the extra bunch and her large, brown eyes shone with gratitude. As I thanked her, she placed her right hand on her heart and bowed her head.

Once back in the flat, I appraised the available vases I found in the kitchen cupboards. I could put one bunch in each of two small glass vases for the bedrooms and the other three bunches into a large turquoise vase for the sitting room. This was my favourite room and everyone who visited agreed it was a superb living space. It ran the whole depth of the flat, from the side on the street to the back, overlooking a paved courtyard garden. The courtyard end was the dining area and could be closed off from the sitting room by double doors, but my parents tended to keep these doors open so that the full impact of the room could be appreciated. The walls were painted white, and the floors were wood block, and locally sourced wall coverings and rugs gave it an authentic, middle eastern appearance, offset by western sofas and chairs. I set the roses onto a low, Moroccan coffee table and left one of the small vases in my bedroom.

I hesitated before going into my parents' room but decided it was no intrusion to simply leave flowers on a dressing table. Their room overlooked the garden and was large and cool, the distinctive smell of my mother's favourite perfume still lingering in the air. On one wall there were framed reproductions of lithographs produced in the 1840s by the Scottish artist, David Roberts. They were beautiful: intricately detailed and apparently painstakingly accurate, they showed a Cairo little changed since the rule of the Mamluks many centuries earlier. Elsewhere, there were family photographs, some on the dressing table and others on a chest of drawers. I found a space on the dressing table for the flowers and began to look at the photos.

Most of them were black and white. Both sets of grandparents on their wedding days, sharing a double frame, hinged in the centre. I smiled. Even on this day of days, my maternal grandmother looked as if it was all a terrible disappointment to her while her new husband wore his habitual expression of genial bemusement. My paternal grandparents stood stern and erect, as if smiling was poor show on such an important day. A happier portrait caught my parents on their big day, with Ruth looking uncomfortable but good-humoured in her ill-fitting bridesmaid's dress.

And now in full colour, here were Emily and I at our wedding. Emily wore her mother's wedding dress and looked radiant in the porch of St Margaret's Church, Freddie alongside her, handsome and proud in his pale grey suit. I picked up another, of Emily and I gazing into each other's eyes as we walked down the aisle of the church as man and wife. I put it back in its place next to an almost empty bottle of perfume and turned away with a heavy sigh.

I moved over to the chest of drawers to a cluster of black and white photos of me as a young child. In one, I was standing on my head, in another, I was grinning at the camera while building a sandcastle, my arms and legs looking surprisingly sturdy. By shocking contrast, in another picture, I was captured looking earnest and pensive, my eyes appearing almost too big for my face. I was in a wheelchair, with a rug over my legs, and a teddy bear on my lap. One of the pictures was larger than the others and was positioned so that it was the centrepiece. Here, I was older and when I looked more closely, I remembered exactly when and where it was taken. It was the spring following my tenth birthday and my calliper had broken and been sent away to be repaired. While it was gone, I was keen to show everyone that I could function just as well without it. I wanted to look and behave like other boys, and though I couldn't play sport, walking without a calliper signalled a return to something approaching normal life. I was in our back garden in London, and it must have been a warm day, because I was bare-chested and wearing only shorts. I looked scrawny and under-developed for my age, but I'd assumed the pose of a body builder, legs apart and arms folded across my chest, and on my face, I wore an expression that was a mix of effort and resolve.

I swallowed hard. It was poignant seeing my younger self so physically frail and yet so brave and resolute.

I was about to leave the room, when my eye was caught by another photograph on my mother's bedside table. Her reading glasses were laid on top of a paperback book next to a jar of Pond's cold cream and a box of paper handkerchiefs. Behind all this was a small black and white photo. I sat on the edge of the bed and picked it up. Here I was in that same back garden, in a tin bathtub, being sponged down by my mother, who was wearing an elegant sleeveless dress with a wide belt at her waist. I was chubby and dimpled, with curly blonde hair, and could only have been about two or three years old. My head was thrown back and I was laughing as if I was being tickled, and my mother was laughing like I have rarely seen her laugh since.

Mother and Son

My parents used the single bedroom as an office, somewhere to deal with household bills and personal paperwork and it was here, in a built-in cupboard, I found dozens of photograph albums, arranged in order on the cupboard shelves, with the years they covered written on a label on the spine. I sat on the floor with my back against the bed and worked my way through them from the year of my birth onwards. I pored over them until my back and legs ached and I was forced to stand up and move around. At last, I put everything back in its place, closed the cupboard doors and went into the kitchen in search of something to eat.

In case I wasn't tempted by anything in the fridge, my mother had left the phone number of a reliable local delivery company. The pizza I chose from them was delicious and after I'd washed it down with a couple of beers, I took myself off to bed, opened my book and tried to pick up from where I'd left it earlier in the day.

I didn't hear my parents come home and that night, I slept better than I'd done in weeks. When I awoke quite late the next morning, the roses on the dressing table were giving off a sweet perfume, and as I turned over to look at them, there was a light tap on the door and my mother peeped in to see if I was awake. I sat up and rubbed my eyes and she came to sit on the bed, looking dressed for going out.

'Thank you for the roses,' she said. 'Very thoughtful of you.'

I smiled, glad not to have missed her.

'Did you buy them from a young woman in the street?'

'I did.'

'That's good. Whenever I see her on that corner, I always buy from her. How was your day?'

'I got through it and it was good in parts. I feel more rested. Are you off to work?'

'No, I'm going out for a couple of hours, but I wondered if you might feel like having lunch together. I thought we could go to the Cairo Tower.'

'I'd like that.'

'Good,' she smiled. 'I'll book a table for one o'clock and meet you at the main entrance.'

She leant forward to kiss my forehead and I smelt her familiar perfume, the one she'd worn since she was pregnant with me, and discovered it was the only scent she could tolerate.

The Cairo Tower is one of the tallest buildings in Africa, its partially open lattice-work design intended to evoke a pharaonic lotus plant, an iconic symbol of Ancient Egypt. I was early and when my mother arrived, I was standing a short distance away from the bottom of the tower, looking up at it.

'It looks like a wickerwork tube.'

She laughed. 'The food may be rather average, but no other restaurant can offer the same views.'

'Does it still rotate?' I asked, as we made our way towards the lift.

'Apparently it does one complete rotation every hour.'

The lift took us to the fourteenth floor, and a waiter standing near the restaurant entrance led us to a table by a window, from where the views were truly spectacular.

'I never get tired of this,' my mother said. 'Zamalek is the perfect location for a tower like this, because from here you can see far off to the east and the west of the city.'

'It's staggering,' I said. 'How tall is it?'

'One hundred and eighty-seven meters—taller than the Great Pyramid of Cheops. It's very popular with tourists so we include it on many of our day tours. You can see so many landmarks of the city from the observation deck on the floor above. The Egyptian Television Building, the Saladin Citadel and of course, marvellous views of the Nile. And though they're a long way away, you can even see the Pyramids.'

'Even at a distance, there's something magical about actually seeing them there, almost part of the city.'

'Will you go out to Giza while you're here?'

'I thought I'd get up early one morning to be there before the tourist buses arrive.'

'Good idea.'

I was trying to study the menu while also taking in the view.

'Is there anything you recommend?' I asked.

'I've found it's safest to stick to *mezzes*. They'll do a platter for us to share and it's really quite good.'

'I'd be happy with that. And a beer perhaps?'

A waiter appeared and wrote down our order. When he left, I looked around. All the tables were set with crisp white linen and bright red paper napkins and every table had a tall, narrow vase containing a single red rose.

'Tell me about the rose-seller,' I said.

My mother looked surprised. 'Not much to tell, or at least, not much that I know. She's there on that corner, without fail, once a week. Sometimes she has a little girl with her. She only sells roses. They come from somewhere along the Nile valley. Flowers always seem to be plentiful here.'

'I noticed that her left arm and hand were withered, and I guess she had polio?'

'Yes, I've always assumed that, too. Polio is still endemic in Egypt, despite repeated immunisation campaigns.'

'Seeing her, reminded me of all those children I was in hospital with in Ireland and I wondered what her experience of the disease might have been here, in an even poorer country.'

My mother looked discomforted but then the waiter reappeared with our beers. 'What are your memories of that time?' I asked her.

'It was awful. The hospital was packed to capacity, understaffed, overwhelmed. Not being allowed to be with you in those first few weeks, phoning the hospital for news, never sure what to believe. The closest we could get was the other side of the door to the ward, peering in through a small porthole window.'

She had picked up her napkin and was plucking at it as she spoke. After a few moments, tiny shreds of red tissue paper littered the table in front of her, like tiny rose petals, and I laid my hands on hers to make her stop.

'I feel so guilty that we exposed you to such danger,' she said, pulling her hands away. 'I feel responsible for everything you went through.'

'Mum, please don't upset yourself.'

'We were selfish, your father and me. We needed that holiday—a complete change of scene by the sea and a break from the endless round of appointments with specialists. And we were ignorant, too. We didn't realise the danger we were heading into.'

'How could you know? Polio isn't like other diseases. Even the doctors didn't fully grasp at first that it was the better-off and most isolated who would be the most vulnerable.'

I used the side of my hand to push all the shredded pieces of her napkin together and then scooped them up and put them in my pocket.

'Cedar Lodge might have looked safe, but in fact, it was more dangerous to live there than in the worst slum housing in Cork. Who would have thought that?'

'I know,' she said, shaking her head. 'It was a very middle-class disease, at its worst in the relatively well-off southern suburbs of Cork. But this was so contrary to popular perception. We all associated epidemic disease with poverty and dirt, but in fact, polio was most at home in places where clean water and sanitation were robbing communities of natural immunity.'

I took her hands in mine and squeezed them, just as a waiter appeared with a large platter laden with food. We withdrew our hands and he placed the platter on the table between us. Noticing that my mother had no napkin, he took one from an empty table nearby and put it alongside her cutlery.

'This looks good,' I said to him. 'Come on, Mum. Dig in.'

She unfolded her napkin and placed it on her lap, and I could see she was struggling to regain her composure. She looked out of the window, and I followed her gaze, feeling there was something calming about being so high up in the sky above the city, knowing that below and beyond us it teemed with its usual clamour and intensity. I cursed myself for thinking we could talk about the past without one or both of us becoming upset. The awkward start threatened to derail our lunch and I did what I could to make conversation, but it was as if a light within her had gone out. Sharing the *mezzes* was comfortingly companionable and somehow, though our appetites had been blunted, we managed to make modest inroads into the array of appetisers before us.

Afterwards, the taxi dropped us at the Marriott for Mum to make her regular visit to the bakery, and it was as we were walking back to the apartment that she opened up again.

'I know you loved Jeanie and I hope you know how grateful I was to her.'

The mention of Jeanie was unexpected.

'She came along at just the right time. You were so quiet and withdrawn, so listless, we honestly thought you were dying. It was Jeanie who brought you back to us.' She paused. 'More than that, she seemed to make you want to live again.'

'She did,' I said quietly. 'She found a way through to me.'

'I saw that, and though I was happy and relieved, I felt inadequate and a little jealous. I could accept that it took medical professionals to make you physically well again, but I found it harder to accept that it was a nurse who was able to revive your spirit.' She hesitated. 'And I saw how much you loved her.'

I had no answer to that because I wasn't going to minimise, let alone, deny, my feelings for Jeanie or the vital part she'd played in my recovery. By now, we were nearing the apartment. Yousri was sitting on his wonky old chair, chatting to an armed guard who was going on duty at the embassy a few doors away. As soon as he saw us, Yousri clambered to his feet and scurried towards the lift. Before we stepped in, my mother stopped and turned to him.

'How's your son, Yousri? Is he better?'

'*Na'am*, madame,' he replied and raised his hands in prayer. *'Il-hamdu lilla. Shukran.'*

My mother smiled and clasped his hands in hers, in which I'm sure there was a generous tip.

'Il-hamdu lilla,' she said. 'Thanks be to God.'

Once inside the apartment, I told Mum to sit down while I went into the kitchen to make tea. We drank it in the sitting room where there were two sofas facing each other on either side of the coffee table, but rather than sitting opposite, I sat next to her.

'What's the matter with Yousri's son?' I asked.

'He's had a nasty infection—at one point the doctors thought it might be meningitis, but tests ruled that out, thank goodness.'

I wanted to ask her about the photos but didn't know how to casually introduce the subject. Fortunately, she helped me out.

'Penny for them,' she said, with a smile.

I laughed. 'Sorry, but I was thinking about sick children again.'

She sipped her tea and looked at me over the rim of her mug.

'When I put the flowers in your bedroom yesterday, I couldn't help noticing all the photos you have on display. Quite a collection.'

She nodded.

'It got me thinking I'd like to see more, so I looked around for any albums you might have.'

'Did you find them?' she asked. 'In the study?'

'I did.' I paused. 'I was struck by how many photos there were of all of us—me in particular—before I was ill. Apart from some taken the summer I threw away my calliper, there seemed to be relatively few of me after 1956.'

She said nothing and I waited. At last, she adjusted her position on the sofa so that she was turned towards me.

'There are two I keep on the chest of drawers as a reminder of how far you've come: one of you in a wheelchair looking rather woe begone and the other when you're showing us how well you can cope without your calliper. But apart from these, I didn't want to be reminded of what the illness had done to you…'

Her voice trailed off, and she turned her head away so I couldn't see her expression. After a long silence, she turned back to look at me.

'You were such a bonny little boy—always smiling, always on the go, always jumping about. We'd promised to take you to Buff Bill's Circus in Cork so you could see the acrobats and the trapeze artists—you were so excited, but it was cancelled and it was only later we discovered it was due to the polio outbreak. In the garden at Cedar Lodge, I loved watching you practice your somersaults. You said you wanted to fly, so you'd throw yourself through the air over and over again, trying to soar as high as possible.' Her voice broke. 'That's how I wanted to remember you. After we came to Cairo, we weren't with you for much of the year, so we relied on school photos and any that Ruth took and sent us.'

'I guessed that might be it,' I said, crushed to think my mother couldn't bear to be reminded of how much I'd changed. It was as if she thought I was damaged goods. I bit back the bitter riposte I might have made and then, to my horror, I saw she was crying.

'You've no idea how guilty I felt at abandoning you at boarding school when you'd been through so much and when I knew there was a danger you'd be teased or, worse, bullied, for being different.'

'Dad went away to school, so I assumed it was the norm in our family.'

'It was the norm,' she agreed, 'but I've always felt it was wrong—cruel even—to desert you when you were vulnerable and needed us. Your father persuaded me that if you went to a school in Oxford, Ruth would step in and look out for you.'

'And she did,' I assured her.

'Yes, I know she did, and that added to the guilt I felt. Yet again I was relying on another woman to be there for you when I wasn't. I knew your father badly wanted the job at the embassy, but I was torn. I loved Cairo, having lived here as a child, and I've enjoyed the life we've made here, but it doesn't take away from the fact that we put our needs before yours.'

I knew all this, but hearing her pour out such self-reproach, all these years later, was a shock.

'Mum, I never wanted you to feel like this.'

Her face was streaked with tears, and I saw how much the guilt and regret had gnawed away at her. The photographs of my early years seemed to represent a fixation on a charmed life before polio struck and changed everything.

'Were you bullied?' she asked at last.

'I was certainly mocked. Some of the boys, especially the sporty types, liked to mimic my limp, and that was one reason I spent so much time on my own studying. But I also needed to work hard to catch up. Books and music not only took the place of football and gymnastics, they gave me a purpose. I wanted to show you that I could make the best of my life.'

I took her hands in mine. They were wet with tears she had tried to wipe away.

'Emily thought that perhaps it was meant to be—that I'm here to make music—and that belief has given me strength.'

That set her off crying again and I stood up.

'I'll fetch some tissues.'

I went into her bedroom to get the box from her bedside table. I also picked up the photo she kept there.

'I love this photo,' I said. 'I never knew I was such a cherubic little chap! And you look quite the elegant young mum.'

She blew her nose and took the photo from me.

'That was my favourite dress,' she laughed. 'It was white and covered with dramatic dark green leaves. I smile whenever I look at this photo and see you chuckling away in the bathtub.'

She put the photo on the coffee table in front of us and sighed. 'That was a happy time.'

Looking at the boy I once was, I was suddenly overwhelmed by feelings of anguish and dread. I had survived one major setback in my life, but I had no idea how I would navigate the long, heart-breaking journey I now faced, and I laid my head on my mother's shoulder and wept.

Chaos and Curiosities

In the days that followed, I threw myself into the city's pulsating street life. One advantage of Cairo's density is that many places are within walking distance of Midan Tahrir and though Cairo can be tough on travellers with mobility problems, walking is arguably the only way to experience the full gamut of surprises the city holds in store. The pavements may be uneven and rubbish-strewn, congested with vendors and pedestrians, but people weave gracefully around each other, and the prevailing mood on Cairo streets is one of genial bustle. Faces show energy, curiosity and good humour and rarely do you encounter the resignation and irritation characteristic of a city like London.

Bereft and hollowed out, I needed to be distracted. Sometimes I wandered without purpose, simply to experience the city in all its chaos and contradictions, to disappear into its seething mass of humanity. Finding my way around Cairo's vast sprawl was frequently bewildering and several times I got lost, but Cairenes are remarkably helpful to visitors, and invariably I found someone who would go out of their way to steer me in the right direction. These friendly strangers had no idea what brought me to Cairo, so their kindnesses felt like gifts.

Sometimes I caught myself seeing the city through a strange, shimmering blur and at those times, I knew I was not fully engaged or absorbed in what was around me. Though it was an effort to shake off such torpor, I forced myself to focus on something out of the ordinary, whatever it might be. Gaudy, hand-painted hoardings; little Suzuki vans competing with traders with impossibly laden barrows; barefoot urchins humping garbage onto donkey carts; the pungent aromas of herbs and spices mixed with the odours of livestock and petrol; time-warped coffee shops that looked like something out of a David Roberts lithograph.

Sometimes I lingered amongst the old men in the coffee shops, watching the hustle and bustle around me. Other times, when I was weary of seemingly thousands of vehicles, jamming the roads, belching out clouds of noxious fumes, I sat on the Corniche or the terrace of one of the riverside hotels, gazing at the feluccas drifting sedately up and down the Nile. But mainly, I roamed the city, content to go wherever fancy or fortune took me. I carried a map and a guidebook, but rarely consulted them and if I chanced upon a mosque or a temple, I visited if the mood took me, or simply passed on by if it did not.

On one of my rambles, I ventured into the Khan al-Khalili, an immense conglomeration of markets and shops selling everything from glassware, leather goods and brass work to books of magic spells and prayer beads. As I wandered through the narrow, twisting alleyways, I was assailed by shouts of "Hey mister, look for free" or "just to look, not to buy." One trader with milky eyes and a sly, gap-toothed grin offered me some crystal beads, saying "very cheap, very real."

I was making my way out of this maze-like area on my way back to Midan Tahrir and found myself walking behind a young woman who was clearly a visitor. She was small and blonde, and her bare arms looked sunburnt and sore. She kept referring to a street map as if she was looking for somewhere, when a salesman stepped out of a doorway, intent on enticing her into his shop. I stopped and watched, concerned she might be at risk, and to my alarm, she allowed him to take her inside. I approached the shop and looked into the open doorway. It was so dark, I couldn't at first make out what sort of shop it was, but coloured lights high up on the walls gave a faint glow and when I looked closer, I realised it was a perfume shop, not the sort you found in the marbled malls within international hotels, but a private emporium selling pure essence as well as cheaper substances diluted with alcohol or oil. I hesitated, unsure whether I should go in and look out for her, when the salesman saw me and welcomed me inside, where the young woman was smiling and looked unperturbed.

'One minute, sir, if you please. You can look for free,' he said, before turning back to the woman. I hovered at a distance, making a pretence of looking at the shelves of different perfumes.

'What perfume do you wear, Madame?' he asked. 'We have it here, very cheap.'

She laughed and looked unconvinced.

'Why do you laugh?' he asked, feigning offence.

'My perfume isn't a well-known one,' she said.

'I will know it. You tell me, Madame.'

'No,' she said, holding out her wrist to him. 'You tell me!'

She seemed to be enjoying the interaction and he leant forward but took care not to touch her. He screwed up his eyes before straightening up and pronouncing, 'Azurée by Estée Lauder.'

The young woman's eyes opened wide, and she laughed again, this time with surprise.

'Am I right, Madame?'

'You are,' she said, clearly impressed.

He walked over to a shelf and picked up a small bottle, half full of golden coloured liquid. He took off the stopper and invited her to try it. She dabbed a small amount on to her inner arm and waited a moment before she lifted her arm to sniff at it. The look on her face said it all and now it was his turn to laugh.

'It's good, yes?'

She nodded. He put the tester bottle back on the shelf and picked up a full bottle.

'Sixty-two Egyptian pounds in London. Thirty Egyptian pounds here, for you, Madame.'

The woman thought about it for a moment and after taking another sniff at her arm, she reached into her bag for her purse and handed him three ten-pound notes. He took them with a bow, placed the bottle of perfume in her bag and escorted her to the door, where he kissed her hand before bidding her goodbye. She thanked him and nodded at me before continuing on her way down the street.

It had been a totally straightforward encounter and even if I had not been there, I don't believe the man had an ulterior motive in tempting her inside. He was a good salesman and he'd identified a likely customer. Now he turned to me.

'Sorry for the wait, sir. You see something you like?'

I had picked up a bottle labelled Chanel N°5 but as he approached me, I put it down on the counter.

'For your wife, sir, perhaps?' he said, picking up the bottle.

It was an innocent question, and I should have expected it, but I was off guard, and it stung me. I saw him glance discreetly at my wedding ring, and when I shook my head, he held my gaze and nodded as if my eyes had revealed my story.

'For my mother,' I said. 'May I smell it, please?'

He went to a shelf and took down a tester bottle and a small strip of absorbent fabric, onto which he sprayed a dash of perfume. He held it in front of me and it was instantly recognisable as the scent my mother had worn all my life.

'You like it, sir?'

I smiled. 'My mother likes it. I'll buy it for her. How much is it, please?'

'Thirty-five Egyptian pounds, sir.'

He picked up the bottle from the counter and slipped it into a cotton bag with a tie neck.

'Your mother will be happy, sir.'

I nodded and handed him the money. He hesitated for a moment.

'Wait, please.'

He disappeared into the back of the shop and reappeared with something in his hand. He took the cotton bag from me and said, 'A small gift for you, sir. No charge.'

It was a bar of Floris soap.

'It's very good, sir, very popular.'

He slipped it into the bag.

'Thank you,' I said, taking the bag from him. 'I'll enjoy it.'

I went on my way towards Tahrir, but after going a short distance, I stopped and looked back. He was standing in the shop doorway and when he saw me looking at him, he waved.

A Pharaoh's Journey

I had seen Tutankhamun's treasures many times before, but I couldn't resist another visit to the Egyptian Museum, a place as eccentric as Cairo itself. On previous visits, I'd made the mistake of trying to see everything the museum contained, and dizzied by the chaos and clutter, the poor lighting and unhelpful captioning, I'd ended up frustrated and exhausted. This time, I decided to limit myself to a dozen of the rooms that housed the riches of the boy king's tomb.

I went early to avoid the crowds who would pile in as soon as the tourist buses arrived, and without the racket of competing tour guides, it was relatively quiet. This was a relief, because in rooms jam-packed with visitors jostling each other between cabinets containing everything the pharaoh would need in the afterlife, it was easy to forget that we were there to contemplate the short life of a young man; to forget that these wondrous funerary relics represented a craving for something beyond death.

The ancient Egyptians believed that at death the soul began a journey full of challenges. Hence, the model boats that would miraculously enlarge in order to carry Tutankhamun across the rivers of the underworld, the cases that contained food for the journey, the doll-like entourage of workers to accompany the pharaoh into the hereafter. There were cabinets containing the young king's bows and arrows and his boomerangs, his chariots and the wilting bouquets of flowers that were laid with him in his tomb. And there was Anubis, ancient Egypt's jackal-headed guard dog of the dead—reclining, paws outstretched, watchful and alert, protecting the king's tomb.

Meeting the guardians of the underworld clearly required serious preparation.

More than five thousand artefacts were brought to Cairo from the Valley of the Kings in Luxor, three thousand miles south. And every single item was a miracle of craftsmanship. A gilded wooden figure showed the boy king on a skiff, poised ready to strike his prey with a harpoon, or surmounting a wonderfully life-like panther, or striding forward on sandals much larger than his feet. There was a small, gilded bed and the little armchair made for him when he was a child and buried with him when he died at the age of nineteen. His staffs and walking sticks—all one-hundred and thirty of them—were not only covered with gold but inlaid with precious stones and decorated with tiny falcons or cobras. This Golden

Boy—who was he? I asked myself. Boy warrior, boy hunter, boy king, fearlessly navigating the netherworld? Or a gentle soul, with a club foot, who walked with a stick? The contradictory depictions of Tutankhamun intrigued and moved me.

I lingered longest over the legendary death mask, exquisite with its beaten gold inlaid with lapis lazuli and other gorgeous gems. There was something ineffably poignant about that face, gazing serenely into some hoped for afterlife. Though I found it hard to leave, the room had become busy and noisy, and I was tiring. In the bookshop downstairs I bought postcards, one of which showed the beautiful alabaster chalice which was found in the entrance to the antechamber of Tutankhamun's tomb. Around its rim was inscribed a wish for the spirit's long life—a desire that saw the chalice become known as the "wishing cup".

May your spirit live, may you spend millions of years, you who love Thebes, sitting with your face to the north wind, your eyes beholding happiness.

At seven o'clock the next morning, a taxi dropped me on the road by the Mena House Hotel. I paid the admission fee to enter the Giza Plateau, though I didn't intend to go inside the pyramids. I had done this on a previous visit and my weaker leg had struggled with the steep, uneven steps and low ceilings. I had over three hours before the site would be overrun by tourists and I simply wanted to soak up its magical aura. The three pyramids are visible from the upper storeys of buildings all over Cairo, though postcards artfully obscure this proximity to the city, showing the monuments against a backdrop of boundless desert. The contrasts and contradictions here are startling and somewhat surreal. While the pyramids stand solidly inscrutable, for most of the day every visitor has to run the gauntlet of camel and horse hustlers, souvenir hawkers, and would-be guides. Even at this early hour, I watched a group of women being assailed by purveyors of postcards and pyramid-shaped paperweights.

I struck out across the desert plain until I was almost completely alone, save for a few other solo visitors like me looking for solitude and the space in which to savour the magnificence of the scene and to reflect on what had led the ancient Egyptians to build such incredible mausoleums. Apparently, not a fear of death, but a desire for eternal life. I thought of Freddie's struggle to choose music for Marie-Odile's funeral when he had neither belief in God nor the afterlife and how by chance, he had encountered the quiet hopefulness of Parry's *An Old Belief.*

"That on some solemn shore, Beyond the sphere of grief Dear friends shall

meet once more."

I thought of Emily, alone in her silent tomb in north Oxford, and I wondered how much more bearable our separation would be if I believed unequivocally that we would meet again in another life.

I turned back and headed towards the Sphinx. With his body of a lion and face of a god, he had been staring out of the desert sands for centuries. Carved almost entirely from one huge piece of limestone and wearing the royal headdress of Egypt, he seemed both unknowable and all-knowing. I stood before him, hoping to absorb some of his wisdom and endurance and in that moment, I knew I needed to go home and sit at Emily's graveside and then begin the journey into the rest of my life.

The Moghul Room

My parents were to join me at five thirty for drinks, followed by dinner in the Moghul Room, so I spent the rest of the day in the garden of the Mena House Hotel. I positioned myself under the shade of a jacaranda tree, from where I could see the tops of the pyramids just beyond the hotel perimeter. The Mena House had always been a favourite place to spend a lazy day, largely because of its proximity to the pyramids and its surprising tranquillity and I was glad my father suggested it.

I'd slept badly the night before and spent the afternoon in a state somewhere between brooding and dozing. For the last couple of weeks, I'd pushed myself to the limit in the hope that exhaustion would distract me and keep sadness at bay, and to an extent it did, but for much of the time I ached with silent misery. Sometimes I feared I was teetering above a sheer drop, below which lay a chasm of loneliness. Death had stolen the future I'd hoped for and as I began to contemplate going home, I wondered what life there would be like. Somehow, I would need to find a way of carrying on. I had no idea what part my work would play in this. Would it ever again be spiritually rewarding or life-affirming, or would I find it soul-crushingly sad to sing of love and loss?

My parents arrived in good time, just as the sun was sinking behind the palm trees. It was still pleasantly warm, and we sat at a table near the pool drinking gin and tonic and watching the light fade. As it grew dark, the pyramids remained in full view, now magically illuminated by skilfully positioned lighting.

When we'd finished our drinks, we moved inside to the restaurant. The décor was opulent—a representation of India aimed at tourists—and we were seated in a cosy booth which offered privacy but allowed us to see out into the restaurant. When a waiter brought the menu, my father rubbed his hands with glee and my mother laughed.

'George, I know you're itching to do this. Why don't you choose for all of us and whatever comes can be a wonderful surprise for me and Alex.'

'Suits me,' I said.

My father knew his Indian food and would choose well.

'Okay,' he said, summoning a waiter and proceeding to rattle off an order of side dishes and mains.

'What are you drinking, Alex?' he asked. 'Will you have one of the Indian beers?'

I nodded and leant back on the plush banquette.

'Have you enjoyed these last two days—museum and pyramids?' my father asked.

'Yes, I have. It was a good idea to do them early in the day and I'm glad I restricted myself to the Tutankhamun rooms yesterday.'

'Very wise. The place is unmanageable if you try to see it all. They say there are almost one hundred and forty thousand items on display. It's crazy.'

I nodded. 'I think I enjoyed Tut's treasures all the more by focussing on just a dozen or so rooms. I bought postcards of some of the loveliest items, though photos don't do them justice.'

I reached into my rucksack for my book and retrieved the card of the wishing cup that I was using as a bookmark. I handed it to my mother.

'It's beautiful. Look, George, the inscription is the one on Howard Carter's gravestone.'

'Ah, yes,' he said, taking the card from her.

'You've seen his grave?'

'We have,' my mother replied. 'It's in Putney Green Cemetery. It's rather moving. It has his name and the description "Egyptologist, Discoverer of the Tomb of Tutankhamun 1922," and then the inscription that's on the chalice.'

My father was still studying the card. 'Apparently, at the end, Carter was a lonely figure. Reports say there were only a handful of mourners at his funeral. He was an outsider, fiercely independent, an awkward man to deal with by all accounts and he'd stepped on a great many toes.'

'He searched the Valley of the Kings for six years before he discovered the tomb,' my mother said, 'and then he catalogued every one of the five thousand three hundred treasures with detailed descriptions. It took him years.'

'And the scandal is he received no recognition of any kind from the British government,' said my father. 'But he'll never be forgotten for the gift he gave the world. Every single treasure he found brought ancient Egypt back to life.'

He gave me back the postcard, just as a waiter brought our beers.

'Have you managed to settle to much reading?' my mother asked, watching me put my book away.

'Sort of. I finished *Rumpole of the Bailey* and I've started *Rumpole's Return*. The stories are a good length for the amount of concentration I can muster at the moment.'

Both my parents nodded in understanding.

'I wondered if you might find poetry something you could dip into,' my mother said.

I shook my head. 'I'm sure I would find poetry too emotional.'

I thought of the torrent of poems Thomas Hardy wrote to his dead wife and wondered how long it would be before I could face reading them again.

"Woman much missed, how you call to me, call to me..."

My father looked uncomfortable but was saved by the arrival of the meal.

'How have you found Cairo on this trip?' he asked, passing me a side dish of okra.

'A bit like the museum,' I laughed. 'Crazy. The traffic seems even worse than ever, more cars and more fumes.'

'And the driving,' my mother exclaimed. 'Rather than slow down or brake, drivers beep their horns furiously to signal to the car ahead to get out of the way, or to alert pedestrians that they intend to run a red light.'

'Yes, what is it with traffic lights?' I asked.

'Ah,' my father laughed. 'Egyptian drivers obey police signals rather than traffic lights.'

'Typical,' I laughed.

'And when you cross the road, you're dicing with death,' my mother said.

'The trick is to be bold,' my father counselled. 'Dithering or freezing midway confuses them. You have to keep going.'

'Fortunately, I've realised that,' I said, helping myself to some chicken. 'But I really like the Cairenes. I've encountered enormous kindness and very little hassling.'

'Did you go to Groppi's?' my mother asked.

'I did. It was very disappointing. The cake was stale and the coffee insipid. It wasn't at all like Olivia Manning described it.'

'Well, she was writing about it as it was during the war—its heyday. I'm afraid it's gone downhill since then.'

'Will you have any engagements when you go back?' my father asked.

'Not immediately. I cleared my diary for two months, so I'll have time to see what state my voice is in before I have to sing in public again.'

My mother looked at me anxiously.

'Right now, I can't imagine standing in front of an audience and making a decent sound.'

'We've got tickets for the opera next month,' said my father. '*The Barber of Seville.'*

'When's the new opera house due to open?' I asked.

'Some time next year. From what I've heard, it will be an impressive complex.'

'I'll miss the Gomhouria, though,' my mother said. 'It's such an exquisite theatre and so welcoming.'

My father nodded in agreement. 'How's the meal?' he asked me.

'Delicious, thank you.'

I paused. 'And thank you for putting up with me and looking after me. I've been thinking I should make plans to go home. I thought I would look for a flight in the next couple of days.'

I saw a look of concern pass between them.

'Only if you're sure,' my father said.

'I have to face it sometime.'

'When will Freddie be back in Oxford?' my mother asked.

'I'm not sure, but he's due to go back to work for the new term.'

'What will happen to the archive now?' my father asked.

I shook my head. I couldn't imagine anyone but Emily working on it, but I knew that Freddie would feel he owed it to her and to Philip Nash to finish the job.

'I think most of the work is done, apart from the indexing, and I'm not sure how close Emily was to completing that.'

'Perhaps that's something you and Freddie might work on together?' my mother said.

I thought about the suggestion and nodded. Perhaps we might.

We arrived back at the flat just as the telephone in the hallway started to ring. My mother answered it while my father and I went into the sitting room, my father heading for a sideboard in the dining area on which they kept bottles of whiskey, brandy, and sherry.

'Whiskey?' he asked, unscrewing the bottle, and lining up three of the cut glass tumblers they kept on a tray.

'Alex,' said my mother, coming in from the hall. 'It's for you. Dominic.'

I frowned in surprise because Dominic had said he would contact me only if something arose for which he needed an immediate answer. I took the glass my father handed me and went out to take the call. When I returned to the sitting room fifteen minutes later, my glass was empty and my father stood up to go to the drinks tray, from which he picked up the whiskey bottle.

'You look as if you need another one,' he said.

'What is it?' my mother asked.

I sat down next to her, and my father topped up my glass.

'The Cairo Symphony Orchestra is performing *Elijah* at the Gomhouria the day after tomorrow and a few hours ago the tenor soloist was rushed into hospital with appendicitis. The conductor is Kaspar Edberg who I sang with recently in Holland and Edinburgh. He's asked if I'm available and able to do it, not knowing I'm already here in Cairo.'

'Will you do it?' my mother asked, wide-eyed?

'I must be mad, but yes, I will. They're bending over backwards to make it as easy as possible for me to agree. Someone will deliver a score here in the morning, a complete set of concert dress will be ready for me to try on at the theatre tomorrow evening and Dominic's negotiated an eye-watering fee.'

'Danger money, I suppose,' my father said with a grin that turned into a grimace.

My mother was still looking at me anxiously.

'I know what you're thinking,' I said. 'Less than two hours ago I was saying I couldn't imagine singing in public and not making a fool of myself, and here I am accepting an engagement at two days' notice.'

I took a slug of whiskey.

'But maybe I just need to get back out there again, without too much time to think about it. I love *Elijah* and the tenor only has two arias and a few other bits and pieces. It's not as if it's *The Dream of Gerontius*.'

'Good for you,' my father said, raising his glass to me.

'Maybe,' I said, squeezing my mother's hand, 'it's a gift I didn't know I needed.'

Elijah

Next day, I made my way to the Gomhouria theatre in Downtown. The area was once stylish and fashionable but though still lively, even vibrant in places, much of it now looked tired and down at heel. The theatre, though, was beautiful, with an ornate façade and an inviting auditorium. I had been there in the past to see performances of opera and ballet, but I had never been backstage. I was to meet the Orchestra Manager at the front entrance so he could walk me round the building to the stage door and take me to my dressing room where I would meet Mr Al Sakka, the tailor.

'He's the best tailor in Cairo,' Mostafa assured me as he led me down a long, shabby corridor to my dressing room, the door of which already bore my name. 'If the measurements he was given were correct, the suit will fit you perfectly,' he whispered, before he tapped lightly on the door and led me inside. 'Here is Mr Ingram.'

The room was small and brightly lit by lightbulbs surrounding a wall of mirrors above a counter on which I saw the tools of a tailor—scissors, thread, needles, and measuring tape. Mr Al Sakka was waiting for me alongside a clothes rail on which hung my concert dress: a black tuxedo, a white dress shirt, and black trousers. Shiny black dress shoes and black socks were placed neatly below the trousers, while on the counter lay a black cummerbund and a white bow tie.

Mr Al Sakka smiled and bowed before stepping forward to shake my hand. He looked like I imagined a tailor in Savile Row might look, his own black suit well cut and of good quality, his grooming immaculate. His face was lively and expressive, but his manner conveyed calm competence and I felt instantly at ease with him.

'I will leave you together now,' Mostafa said, 'and in the break, if you are happy to wait, I will bring Mr Edberg along to talk to you.'

I thanked him and turned my attention to Mr Al Sakka and the clothes. Suddenly the fact that I was doing this concert felt alarmingly real and I think he sensed my anxiety.

'Do not worry, sir,' he said kindly. 'We will have everything perfect for you. If anything needs alteration, it is no problem. Are you ready to try on?'

I smiled and despite my dislike of baring my left leg, I undressed and waited for him to pass me the clothes. He handed me the trousers first, and to my relief, they fitted perfectly—neat at the waist and over the hips, but not too tight. The shirt was the finest Egyptian cotton, crisp and well-ironed, the tuxedo lined with soft black silk and more elegant than any I had ever owned. I sat down to put on the socks and shoes and the outfit was almost complete, apart from the cummerbund and the bow tie, which Mr Al Sakka secured. He adjusted the shoulders of the jacket and flicked some imaginary fluff off a lapel and looked at me admiringly, before turning me round to face a full-length mirror.

'You look magnificent,' he said.

I laughed. 'I really do! You're a magician. I have never had a concert suit that looked so exquisite or fitted me so perfectly. Even the trousers are exactly the right length.'

He bowed and I could see he was beaming with pride. 'Is it comfortable, sir?' he asked, stepping nearer to feel the waistband. 'Enough room here?'

'It's perfect. I'm very grateful to you.'

'It's my pleasure, sir.'

'You must have been working many hours to have everything ready in such a short time.'

He smiled. 'Tonight, I will go to bed early.'

'Do you work in Downtown?'

'Very close, sir, on Sharia Abdel Khalek Sarwat, not far from Midan Opera, and we live above the shop.'

'What should I do with the clothes tomorrow night after the concert?'

'Take them,' he laughed. 'They are yours now.'

I shook my head in disbelief.

'It's correct, sir. The management have paid me for the clothes and the Maestro, he told me when I brought them here, that you are to have them, as a gift from the orchestra.'

'I will treasure them, and whenever I wear them, I will think of you.'

He bowed again and began to gather up his sewing kit, preparing to leave. 'I wish you all the best for the concert tomorrow and safe journey home.'

'*Shukran*.'

When he'd gone, I changed back into my own clothes and got out the score which I'd brought with me in case the conductor wanted to give me markings. I'd liked him when we worked together on *The Creation*. He was courteous and considerate to everyone, from the leader of the orchestra to the stagehands. In private he spoke quietly, his Swedish accent manifest in sing-song inflections which were rather endearing; on the podium he communicated without histrionics of any kind, and it was always clear what he wanted.

I reached up to turn on the relay system, so I would know when the rehearsal paused for a break. The chorus were singing *Be Not Afraid*, which seemed apposite. On the countertop was a call sheet. Today's rehearsals were for the orchestra and chorus only, with none of the soloists required, though my fitting was shown on the schedule: Six p.m. in dressing room three, Mr Ingram and Mr Al Sakka. The following day, we were all rehearsing in the afternoon, with the concert starting at seven thirty.

I looked at the list of soloists. I didn't know the soprano and alto and guessed by their names they might be Scandinavian. I swallowed hard at the sight of the bass-baritone's name next to mine. Dominic had told me the line-up but seeing it in black and white brought home to me the company I was keeping. I had seen Joshua Norman give a towering performance as Wotan in *The Ring Cycle*, and I hoped he was as forbearing as he was said to be friendly. I was anxious about my voice, unsure if it could do what I needed it to. I'd done some vocal warm-up exercises before I left the apartment and to my ears, it sounded as fragile and uncertain as I felt, but at least I would look good, and maybe that knowledge would embolden me.

An outbreak of chatter from the relay speaker signalled that the rehearsal had broken. I turned down the volume and opened the score at the recitative and aria which were the tenor's first entry, but then I heard voices outside in the corridor and the door opened.

'May I come in?' asked Kaspar.

'Of course,' I said, getting to my feet to greet him.

He looked at the rail of clothes and went over to touch the jacket. 'Nice, I think?' he said, looking at me.

'Beautiful,' I said, with feeling.

'That's good. And how are you, dear Alex?'

Before I could answer, he held me in a brief embrace and then sat down in the chair next to mine.

'Thank you for doing this for us. When I asked for you, I had no idea what had happened to your Emily. I am very sorry.'

'Thank you,' I said, touched that he'd spoken Emily's name. 'I haven't sung since we did *The Creation* in Edinburgh, so I hope I won't disappoint you.'

He shook his head. 'Don't think like that,' he urged. After a pause, during which he looked at me long and hard, he asked, 'Do you like this music?'

'I love it.'

'I thought so. I heard from a colleague that you sang it beautifully at a performance in Chester Cathedral a few years ago.'

'That was a special one. Emily was with me that night. It was the first time she'd heard a live performance of *Elijah*.'

'And there will be people in the audience tomorrow night who will be hearing *Elijah* for the first time and together we can make it special for them, too.'

He was still looking at me intently. 'I was thirty-eight years old when I first conducted *Elijah*—the same age Mendelssohn was when he died. *Elijah* was the final triumph of his career, and I felt I had a responsibility to do justice to him and to the piece. It's a work of such spirit, such heart, and when you sing it tomorrow, I will be with you every step of the way.'

I felt my mouth twitch with emotions I was trying to hold back, and he saw that, and took both my hands in his and squeezed them. He was only a few years older than me, and I admired his willingness to talk so directly and to not ignore the fact that I could not be the same man he had conducted a few weeks earlier.

'It may help if I say a little about how I approach *Elijah*,' he said at last, letting my hands drop. 'Do you know Mr Norman?'

'No, but I saw him as Wotan a few years ago.'

'Ah, good! You will see that he is not only perfect as Wotan, but as Elijah, too. The role of the prophet requires an operatic range of emotional expression, sometimes imploring, sometimes weary, other times defiant. He will set the tone of our performance. As will the chorus and you will see that this chorus is magnificent. I am very pleased with them. The whole oratorio is in reality an opera manqué and should be performed as a piece of riveting Old Testament drama.' He paused. 'Do you understand?'

'I do. We need to maintain a strong dramatic momentum, even through the reflective moments.'

Kaspar nodded. 'That is the challenge.' He turned his head away slightly and seemed to be pondering something. 'As you are here, would you like to try one of your arias to get a feel for the acoustics? If you like, we can give the chorus a longer break and you can sing just for me and the players.'

I hadn't expected this suggestion and at first, I was unsure whether it was a good idea or not, but then I remembered what I'd said to my parents the night before. In effect: "Feel the fear and do it anyway".

'Yes, let's have a go at number four.'

'Good,' he said, getting to his feet. 'I'll ask the Chorus Master to arrange a delay for the choristers and, in a few minutes, I will come back to collect you and we can go to the stage together.'

I nodded and when he'd left the room, I began to warm up my voice with exercises I had built into my practice ever since I was a student. Gradually, the arpeggios became more fluent and free-flowing and my upper range opened up. Shortly afterwards, Kaspar knocked on the door and we walked the short distance to the stage. The choir seats were empty, but the players had come back from their break and were tuning noisily. Kaspar made his way to the podium and suggested I stand near him and in front of the cellos. The cacophony of sound ebbed away until there was attentive silence.

'Thank you, ladies and gentlemen. Please give a warm welcome to our tenor soloist, Alex Ingram, who has stepped in for Mr Romano who is indisposed.'

The players clapped and smiled, and I remembered how good it felt to be part of a team, all focussed on making music together.

Kaspar waited until the noise died away and lifted his arms. 'Before the choir comes back, we will play through number three, the recitative, and number four, the aria, *If with all your hearts ye truly seek me.*'

Turning to me, he said, 'Not too slow, something like this,' and he beat out three four time with his right arm, while crooning the melody of the aria to demonstrate his suggested tempo. 'But I will follow you if you slow down anywhere, at figure A for instance.'

I nodded in agreement and stood half facing him and half turned towards the empty auditorium, and after one chord from the orchestra, we began. Kaspar watched me closely throughout and I felt that he and the players were breathing with me. At figure A, any rubato from the soloist was prone to come apart if the conductor and players pushed on, without regard for what the singer was doing, but not here. We were in perfect synchronicity. After the long final chord had died away, there was a hushed silence until Kaspar lowered his arms. I waited for him to say something, to suggest we try it again perhaps, but to my surprise, the string players began to tap their bows against their music stands and I heard some quiet *bravos.*

Kaspar put down his stick. 'Thank you, ladies and gentlemen. That was a wonderful, sweet sound.'

He turned to me. 'Alex, that was lovely. Tomorrow, if you come to my dressing room half an hour before the rehearsal, we can look at your other music. I very much look forward to it. Now go home and relax. You will see, all will be well.'

The next day my mother fussed over me from the moment I got up, when she made me a delicious breakfast of eggs Benedict and smoked bacon, followed by an extravagant fruit salad. Dominic rang to wish me luck and I was able to thank him for his efficiency in keeping an up-to-date record of my measurements. My mother sent me off with a Tupperware box containing a vegetable rice dish she had made in case I didn't have time to go out for something to eat before the performance. I enjoyed her attentiveness but was glad to be on my way to the theatre.

After I met with Kaspar, I found Mostafa and asked him to arrange tickets for my parents. I then went to settle into my dressing room, and as I was finishing my vocal warm-up, the Company Manager brought me a cup of peppermint tea. The impromptu sing-through the night before had given me an indication of how my voice was behaving and had helped to settle some of my nerves, but I was still on edge and the calming drink was welcome. I was thinking about Johnny and wishing he was there with me to offer his customary words of reassurance, when there was a knock on the door and a man I recognised as Joshua Norman came in holding a gaudy Tutankhamun mug while still managing to look the image of an Old Testament prophet.

'I thought I'd come and say hello,' he said, offering me his free hand. 'If you've no objection, we can drink our tea together.'

'Sit down,' I said, smiling.

His speaking voice was as deep and majestically rich as his singing voice, and his eyes sparkled with warmth and good humour. He was even more physically striking than I remembered, his hair and beard perhaps whiter now and his colouring more florid.

'I heard you were already in Cairo when the call came?' he said.

'I was. I've been visiting my parents who live here.'

'So, you didn't have any concert kit with you?' he said, looking at the clothes rail.

'None at all. It's been conjured up by a wizard tailor organised by the orchestra.'

Joshua laughed. 'Cairo never fails to amaze me. It has the most notorious bureaucracy in the middle east, designed to solve problems which it itself has created, and yet it can rustle up a set of concert clothes in less than twenty-four hours.'

I laughed. He was friendly and down-to-earth, and seemed good fun, but as we talked more, I couldn't help wondering what he was like beneath the easy chatter, and without stopping to think and without censoring my words, I heard myself asking him a very personal question.

'Have you ever had to find a way to keep singing through personal pain or difficulty?'

I watched his expression change and saw that momentarily the muscles in his face seemed to shift and settle somewhere unaccustomed, but his focus on me didn't falter. As he put down his mug and pulled the chair closer to mine, I felt the piercing scrutiny of his brilliant blue eyes.

'I guess you're asking because you're currently in that position?'

I nodded and waited for him to go on.

'The simple answer is yes. I had a daughter who died of leukaemia when she was eighteen. She was our only child and she and I were very close. When she died, I was completely broken. The first time I sang after her death was like an out of body experience, as if I wasn't really there, because Elena was no longer there. Gradually, I realised that all I could do was go on working and hope it would get easier.'

'Did music console you?'

He replied without hesitation. 'It did, of course. There were many pieces that gave me particular comfort, but the work that confirmed I was doing exactly what I needed to do was the Mozart *Requiem*. I was performing it in Paris with a conductor who was deeply religious. Before the performance, he reminded us that this Christian funeral rite, the Requiem, asks an all-powerful God to accept a human soul into heaven. And of course, Mozart had buried four of his six children, so he knew what it was to suffer loss. Those two thoughts were at the forefront of my mind as I sat on the stage, waiting for it to begin. You know how it starts?'

I nodded.

'The first bars are stately and solemn,' he said, 'with the basses sounding dejected and despairing in a dark, minor key that suggests eternal rest may not easily be attained, but almost immediately, a fleeting moment of musical hope arrives. The setting of the phrase *et lux perpetua luceat eis* is utterly sublime, a signal from Mozart that he will take us on a journey from uncertainty into hope. That moment made me realise that what fed my soul was music. Working didn't block out the pain, but it gave me a break from it, and it connected me to my strengths. All these years later, I know it has sustained me.'

The muscles in his face seemed to have reset and he looked more like himself again.

'Who have you lost?' he asked at last.

'My wife, Emily. Six weeks ago, she was knocked off her bike in Oxford.

She was two months pregnant.'

'Ah, so, you came to Cairo to get away, and singing *Elijah* was not part of the plan?'

I nodded.

'I've sung *Elijah* with Kaspar before,' he said, 'and he knows what he's doing. Orchestras like him and he's very supportive of singers. We're in safe hands.'

'Last night, we sang through my first aria, and I was struck by how responsive the orchestra were. Kaspar followed me and they followed him. I'm just hoping my voice won't betray me tonight.'

He nodded. 'The voice can certainly be affected by emotional distress. I learnt to find a way of enduring the pain, but not blocking it or denying it. Work has been a lifesaver, but I still think about Elena every day. Sometimes, especially if I'm feeling apprehensive before a performance, or under the weather, I imagine she is standing in the wings, watching over me.'

I found that image profoundly touching and felt my eyes prickle with tears.

'You won't believe this right now,' he said, 'but grief eventually becomes a visitor, it comes and goes.'

'Thank you for sharing that,' I said. 'I hope you didn't mind me asking.'

'I'm always glad to have a chance to talk about Elena, to say her name out loud.' He leant over and squeezed my shoulder and got up to go. 'Last year, I sang *Elijah* in Boston and in the programme book it said that Mendelssohn once described death as a place "where it is to be hoped there is still music, but no more sorrow or partings". Tonight, my friend, focus on the music, not the sorrow.'

At seven twenty-five, we stood in the wings, waiting to go on. At last, when the audience had taken their seats, the sign came, and Joshua led the way onto the stage. He and I were to stand next to each other in front of the cellos, while the two sopranos, Liv and Nina, were positioned on the other side of Kaspar, in front of the violins. We stayed standing in anticipation of Kaspar's entrance, at which point the chorus and orchestra also got to their feet. After the usual preliminary smiles and bows, everyone sat down, save for Joshua and the chorus, and we began.

I sensed that if I could be caught up in the drama of the piece, I might keep my composure, so my strategy was to bring all my concentration to bear on the score, on the words; to follow the story of Elijah's battle with the Israelites.

I didn't have long to wait for my first aria and when it came, I enjoyed it. What remained for me to do in the first half was a short recitative, so I felt I could relax and enjoy the efforts of the others. The chorus were magnificent throughout, especially in their cries to Baal and in the final chorus before the interval, *Thanks be to God*, when Elijah has summoned rain to end the drought. The music exploded like a storm, the choristers singing in tumult. Uninhibited yet unanimous, they carried all before them.

However, for me, the highlight of part one was Elijah's first big statement, *Lord God of Abraham*. There was something uniquely personal and open-hearted about Joshua's rendering, and I thought back to his performance in *Die Valkyrie* when Wotan casts out his favourite daughter, Brünnhilde, for her disobedience. He embraced her for one last time, and kissed her eyes to sleep, and his deeply affecting aria of farewell was nothing less than a crescendo of grief. I marvelled at how much emotional resilience and courage that must have demanded of him.

The applause at the interval was warm and prolonged and we were in good heart as we made our way down the dressing room corridor. As Nina turned to go into her room, she caught my elbow and whispered, 'Your aria was beautiful, Alex. So tender, so consoling.'

Before I could thank her, she'd smiled and disappeared. A validation lightly given, and gratefully received.

I had slightly more to do in the second half—two recitatives, an aria, and a quartet with the other soloists. It was easy to be swept away by some of the more lyrical choruses, especially *He that shall endure to the end* and my favourite, *He, watching over Israel, slumbers not, nor sleeps* where the words "slumbers not nor sleeps" repeat in lovely, graceful patterns, and were sung with astonishing delicacy by the huge chorus. Joshua's *It is enough, O Lord* and *O Lord, I have laboured in vain* could not have been more heart-rending, showing Elijah as human and vulnerable. Kaspar's tempi were perfectly judged, and he controlled the massive forces with effortless authority, never losing sight of the dramatic thread. My second aria, *Then shall the righteous shine forth as the sun* is often taken too slowly for my liking, but Kaspar allowed me to sing it with a thrilling forward propulsion. The very final chorus, *Then shall your light shine forth*, was a glorious apotheosis, the massed voices creating a wonderful opulent sheen. Elijah had ascended to Heaven in a fiery chariot, his work was done.

The applause was unrestrained and many in the audience rose to their feet, their enthusiasm testament to the work's irresistible power. I was quietly pleased with my own performance and happy to join the others for celebratory drinks in one of the front-of-house bars. My parents came along, too, looking proud and relieved, and comfortable mingling with members of the orchestra, many of whom they had met at other concerts when my father and some of his embassy colleagues had been invited as guests.

I saw Joshua steering an attractive woman towards a table of drinks and went over to join them.

'Alex,' he said. 'Meet my wife, Hilary.'

'Hello,' she said. 'Wonderful performance. I'm on a complete high so I can only imagine how you boys are feeling.'

'I'm glad you liked it. It did seem to go well.'

'One of the best, I thought,' said Joshua. 'I hope you enjoyed it, Alex?'

'I did and thank you for your support. It really helped.'

He put up a hand as if to say don't mention it.

'How long are you in Cairo for?' I asked.

'We arrived two days ago, staying at the Nile Hilton. And,' he said, smiling at his wife and pulling her close to him, 'tomorrow, we're flying to Luxor for a little holiday.'

'How wonderful. I've not been there on this trip, but I love Luxor and Karnak.'

I saw my parents standing nearby and called them over. While they chatted to Joshua, I continued talking to Hilary.

'Do you work in the business?' I asked.

'I do. I used to work at ENO in the costume department, but I'm freelance now, specialising in historical corsetry. I tend to pick and choose my projects so I can travel with Josh if he's going to be away for any length of time.'

'That sounds a good balance, and lovely for Josh to have you with him.'

Josh heard that and said, 'It is indeed. I'm very lucky. *We're* lucky.'

They appeared to have found contentment despite their loss and I envied them.

'We should be going,' Josh said. 'We have an early start.'

I looked at my parents and could tell that they, too, were ready to leave, so Josh and I said our goodbyes to Kaspar, Liv and Nina, and the five of us left together. As we went down the stairs to the foyer, Josh asked, 'When do you go home?'

'The day after tomorrow.'

'Will there be people around to offer you whatever you need when you get back?'

'My accompanist and best friend, Johnny Randall, is coming to stay for a couple of days and I hope my father-in-law will be back in Oxford soon.'

'You get on with him?'

'Oh, I do. I love him. I'm very lucky. Perhaps you know him, Freddie Fairfax?'

'Freddie,' he exclaimed. 'I knew him slightly at Cambridge—fantastic pianist, I recall.'

I nodded.

'We live near each other in Oxford, and we have a lot in common. He inherited a huge collection of art songs and lieder which Emily was archiving. There's still some work needed to finish it, so I thought I might offer to help him with that.'

'Good idea to have a project, to find purpose again, and to be with people who care about you. And look, keep in touch. If you ever want a chat or need a bed in London, here's my card.'

'Thank you,' I said, moved by his kindness. 'I'd like to keep in touch.'

We had reached the foyer now and a member of staff was holding the doors open for us.

'Scribble your address and phone number on here,' he said, passing me the programme that Hilary had been holding.

My parents had gone outside and been able to flag down a taxi. Josh and I embraced and as we moved away from each other, he whispered, 'Onwards, step by step.'

My parents were waiting in the back of the car, and as I opened the front passenger door, I watched Josh and Hilary link arms and set off on foot for their hotel.

I hoped that in time, music would sustain me as it had him. But more than anything, I was glad he had helped me see that it is people, and their unlooked-for acts of kindness, who show us what it means to go on, to keep going, despite everything.

Going Home

On a grey day in mid-March, the air moist with the threat of rain, little in Oxford seemed to have changed since I left three weeks earlier. It was not yet three o'clock when I stepped off the coach, but under a darkening sky, the city looked as jaded as Cairo had been vibrant. As the taxi drove me home, I looked for signs of spring, but it seemed the daffodils had already had their day and hastened away before my return. In Bardwell Road, I expected the pavements to be littered with the confetti of fallen cherry and apple blossom, but to my surprise the trees were yet to bloom. Those weeks lay ahead when their boughs would be laden with clusters of pink and white flowers, and I was glad I would be there to see their display.

The empty flat was a sobering reminder that Emily would not be there to enjoy it with me.

Christina had collected the post from the hallway and laid it on the kitchen table, along with a note propped against a vase in which she had put stems of yellow wildflowers.

"Hi Alex, welcome home. I hope you're not too knackered after your long journey. I've put milk, butter, and cheese in the fridge and a granary loaf in the bread bin. I found these Marsh Marigolds lurking in the bank near the canal and thought you might appreciate the splash of colour. While I was in the flat, the phone rang and rather than let it go to answer machine I picked it up. It was Johnny saying he would arrive this evening, rather than tomorrow lunch time. I've made up the spare bed, so the room is ready for him. Give me a ring at the shop when you fancy a chat and a drink. Love, C xx."

Dear Christina. I knew how hard she, too, would be grieving. She had loved Emily and through much of the funeral service she had sobbed silently and inconsolably into a handkerchief. I visualised her now in her shop in the covered market, utterly at home among the beaded jackets and exotic scarves, herself as quirky and individual as the distinctive clothes she sold. But she was a kind soul. She'd told me she would continue to read for the Recording Centre for Blind Students, and every Christmas she volunteered at a centre for homeless people, doing whatever was required to make the festive season less bleak than it might otherwise be for those with no home to go to.

I started to unpack, cheered by the news of Johnny's imminent arrival. My mother had washed almost everything I'd taken with me and as I stored clothes away in drawers and hanging space, I was aware that other drawers and cupboards were still full of Emily's clothes and I knew that one day, I would have to deal with them. I would keep her books and records, and assimilate them with mine, but her clothes were a different matter.

The post was a mixture of bills, fliers, and belated cards of condolence. An envelope bearing an Irish stamp brought a letter from Eamon. He wrote about his work at the hospital, but the final section of the letter was about the ways in which he was navigating life without Jeanie.

'You may remember how much Jeanie and I enjoyed walking to the coast and into the countryside. Even when she was ill, she continued to be energised by the natural world. One Sunday, not long before the end, we walked through a patchwork of green and yellow fields stretching towards the cliff above a bright blue sea. We stood watching the gulls circling over our heads, calling to each other before swooping down into the waves, and Jeanie turned to me and said, "This is what you will need when I'm gone." At first, I didn't know what she meant, but she went on, "You'll be strong and resourceful, I know, and your doggedness will help you, but always keep your eyes open for flashes of beauty like this, because this is what will keep you going and get you through."

'I still walk by the sea or in the countryside and these rambles are always exhilarating, even on days when I'm weary of life. However low I'm feeling, I try to hold onto moments when I encounter something rare and beautiful.

'To my surprise I also found myself turning to poetry. As you know, I've never been a big reader—not like you and Jeanie—but I've found unexpected comfort in a book of elegies I was given. The bereaved poets describe the bewildering process of grief, but I've also glimpsed signs of healing and hope. These poems are dedicated to the dead, but they're written to be a source of wisdom and consolation for the living who are left behind.'

I was touched he'd taken the trouble to share this and his letter was one of many I kept and occasionally, re-read.

A few hours later, Johnny and I were sitting in the corner of an Italian restaurant in Summertown. It was an old-fashioned, authentic trattoria run by a family from Naples, most of whom spoke only broken English despite having lived in Oxford for years. Perhaps to remind them of their homeland, their sound system played nothing but choruses and arias from Italian operas.

'So how was Cairo?' Johnny asked.

'It was just what I needed. A city that though it's frenetic most of the time, also has this pervasive sense of timelessness. There are swanky international hotels and shiny new shopping malls, but there are whole districts that have been there since medieval times, jam packed with people whose lives seem not to have changed much for centuries.'

'It sounds astonishing. How were your parents?'

A waiter delivered our pasta and salads and we were all set, both of us hungry after hours of travelling.

'My parents were fine, and it was good to be with them. I needed a certain amount of looking after, even if it was just suggestions of where to go or outings with one or both of them to places I might not have visited on my own. One evening, I met my father for a drink after he finished work. He took me to a famous old hotel, the Windsor—eminently dignified but not somewhere you'd necessarily expect to find running water in your bathroom. The bar is extraordinary. Wealthy Egyptians drinking cocktails in décor designed to evoke the Swiss alps.'

We both laughed, but then I thought of Emily.

'Time and again, whenever I saw something to marvel at or laugh at, I thought how extraordinary the world is and then I'd remember that it's now a world without Emily.'

Johnny grimaced and nodded.

'Have you heard from Freddie?' he asked. 'You'll be glad when he's back.'

'I will. I sent him a couple of postcards from Cairo and there was a message from his housekeeper on my answer machine, saying he'll be home on Sunday. She's put the heating on to get the house aired and she'll leave him a meal to reheat.'

I was quiet for a moment as I recalled how withdrawn Freddie was before he went away. 'He's been on a silent retreat, living in very basic accommodation, miles away from anywhere.'

'I guess even when a loss is shared, people look for different ways to get through it.'

'Yes, that's right. I was glad to have quiet time alone, but I needed company as well. I'm so glad you're here now. I was dreading these first nights alone in the flat and I wonder if Freddie is feeling anxious about returning to normal routines.'

'It's odd to think that in all these weeks he hasn't talked to anyone about his feelings or his memories of Emily.'

'I was glad of any opportunity to reminisce about her with Mum and Dad, but interestingly, Mum and I also talked about my childhood—about the polio, all the years of treatment, and then life in boarding school after they took off to Cairo.'

"Was that awkward?'

'In some ways, it was. My mother feels enormous guilt about taking me to Cork and exposing me to the virus and then abandoning me to St Edward's.'

'How do you feel about that?'

'It was good to have it acknowledged, but I feel sad for her.'

'What about your dad?'

'He's harder to read. Not so forthcoming. How's your dad doing?'

Johnny sighed. 'He seems so much older. The age gap between him and my mum is more apparent than ever. They made it to my concert last night, though—the first time in ages they've heard me play—and they both insisted I should leave this afternoon, rather than in the morning. My father—bless him—said that your need was greater than his.'

'Yes, bless him. What were you performing?'

'Some of Dad's favourites: *Frauenliebe und Leben* and a selection of French and Russian songs.'

'Sounds lovely.'

Johnny nodded. 'First-rate mezzo, too. She did well.' He reached for the bottle of wine and topped up our glasses. 'Tell me about *Elijah*. How was your voice?'

'I was worried it would sound tight and slightly strangled, especially on the top A flats, but it was remarkably free and open.'

'That must be reassuring. And how was Joshua Norman?'

'He was exceptional—and extremely nice. Everyone was very supportive. It was an altogether good experience and I'm very glad I did it.'

'It would have been understandable if you'd said no. It took courage to do it.'

'Maybe. The tenor has very little to do, but his two arias are beautiful, and I was afraid I wouldn't be able to do them justice, that grief would all but throttle me, but when I came to sing them, I felt absolutely in the right place, vocally and emotionally.'

I was absentmindedly fiddling with my dessert spoon when Johnny reached over and put his hand on mine.

'You may not believe this right now, but I'm sure making music will help you live through this grief and survive the sorrow.'

The archive

The next morning, we walked down Banbury Road towards Park Town, stopping on the way in North Parade to buy milk and biscuits. It felt strange going into the empty house, but Johnny had asked to see the archive, and I knew Freddie wouldn't mind. I left the provisions in the kitchen and led the way downstairs to the basement.

'It will be cooler down here,' I warned, as I opened the lower door.

When Johnny gasped with admiration at the sight that met us, I realised how hard Emily must have worked to turn the mountains of unsorted boxes into the immaculately organised collection that now lined the shelves. Every box had a label on the front indicating the range of composers whose works were inside.

'Arne, Thomas,' said Johnny, reading from the first name on the first box before scanning the shelves until he found the second name on the last box, 'to Wood, Charles. What an array of names—every major figure in British music seems to be here.'

'And plenty of Europeans and Americans, too.'

I went over to one of the shelves and took off a large bound volume, one of several, all inscribed with a letter of the alphabet. 'This is what the catalogue looks like—every single item is listed and has a reference number.' I handed it to Johnny and moved over to another set of shelves. 'And here are the indexes,' I said, picking up a box of index cards. 'The intention was to have five separate indexes: composer, poet, song name, first line, and reference number. They're very time consuming to compile, especially for someone working alone, as Emily was.'

'How far did she get?' Johnny asked, flicking through the box I handed him.

'As far as I know, she'd completed four of them and made a start on the fifth.'

'What a wonderful resource—all these songs gathered together in one place. Do you think Freddie will hold on to it or will he look for a permanent depository—somewhere like the English Folk Dance and Song Society at Cecil Sharp House?'

'I suspect he won't want to part with it for a while because there's so much of Emily in it. He may use the excuse of the unfinished index to hold on to it for now and find someone to complete it—a postgraduate student, perhaps. I might even offer some help.'

'Good idea.'

'Have a look at these,' I said, handing him two hard-backed books. 'Emily found them invaluable. The writer, Stephen Banfield, is a Lecturer at Keele University, and in 1985 he published an expanded version of his 1979 DPhil thesis on English song. It's a catalogue of over five thousand songs by fifty-four composers written between roughly 1900 and 1945.'

'Wow, this is a hefty piece of research,' Johnny said, studying the contents list before flicking through the pages.

'You stay and look around, and I'll bring some coffee and biscuits.'

While I was waiting for the kettle to boil, I wrote a note to Freddie to welcome him home and tell him that Johnny and I had spent time in the archive.

A few minutes later, we settled at an empty desk and shared a pot of coffee, and I could see that while I'd been upstairs, Johnny had been making jottings in a notebook he always carried with him.

'What's all that?' I asked, pointing at his notes.

'I've been wondering what your plans are and thinking about how the archive might feed into them.'

'My next concert is Britten's *Spring Symphony,* and there are bookings for various Bach and Handel oratorios, but I need a catch-up with Dominic to update my schedule. Of course, I'll be learning Quint for next year, and at some point, I'll pick up the German coaching I've been having on *Winterreise* and start learning that.'

'If you don't go mad and take on too much, I think work will be your friend.'

'I hope so,' I said, topping up his coffee.

'The archive might provide inspiration for recital programming. You have a fantastic feel for poetry, and you can use your choice of songs to reflect on any aspect of life. The archive gives you enormous scope, so I scribbled down some ideas for thematic programming. Have a look.'

He pushed the notebook towards me, and I studied his list of suggested groupings.

Shakespeare in Song
Songs of Travel
Love and Loss
Songs of the Seasons
Housman and his Composers
Songs of Grief and Healing
The Pity of War

Songs of Innocence and Experience
Benjamin Britten Remembered
Time and Destiny—Songs of Thomas Hardy
Words and Music—The Composer as Poet
Once upon a time—Songs that tell a story
Where's Home—Kennst du das land?

What he was proposing made sense and I was interested, but in my present state, I blanched at the prospect of exploring the more overtly emotive categories.

'It would be fun to devise a programme that's a Song Palindrome,' he said. 'It's a clever way of showing how different composers have reacted to the same words. You don't programme them side by side, but in different halves of the concert. The words have more agency when they're heard twice in an evening, and listeners are better able to appreciate them as poems. What do you think?'

'I like the idea, but it would be a lot of work.'

'It would, but we know how creative and absorbing it can be.'

I nodded, but said nothing, still feeling the task was beyond me.

'Perhaps,' said Johnny, 'we could work up some ideas together.'

'I'd love that,' I said, touched by his efforts to motivate and support me. 'Right now, I'm not up to tackling this alone. At times, everything seems utterly pointless, and doing anything much seems daunting. But I need to rediscover a sense of purpose, and I have to earn a living, so that's imperative as well as motivation.'

I considered the list again, and as if he'd read my mind, Johnny said, 'Some of these ideas might interest Freddie for his broadcasts. He likes a theme, doesn't he?'

'He does, and developing themed programmes would give Dominic some solid ideas to put to festival and concert promoters.'

Johnny looked pleased I was at least showing interest and had not dismissed the ideas out of hand. 'The majority of recitalists focus on the German and French repertoire so English song tends to be neglected. By shifting the focus, you'd be offering something different and distinctive.'

'And actually, because of my love of poetry, I'm particularly drawn to the English repertoire anyway.'

'And so that you're not singing without a break, you could introduce the songs and tell the audience anything about their provenance that might be curious or unexpected, and if I'm accompanying, I'd be happy to do some of that as well.'

'Really?' I said, surprised.

'Absolutely. I did that the other night. The mezzo was a lovely singer and a delightful personality, but she was terrified at the thought of speaking directly to the audience.' He paused and seemed to hesitate. 'While you were upstairs, I flicked through some of the index boxes and a couple of cards caught my eye because they had writing on both sides.'

He leant over to retrieve his notebook and pulled out two cards from the back which he pushed towards me. The first was from the composer index and was for a setting by Benjamin Britten of a French folk song, *La Belle Est Au Jardin D'amour*. I turned it over and there in Emily's typically even handwriting was the note: *There's a recording of this song by Peter Pears and Benjamin Britten. It's a sad and haunting story of a beautiful young girl who confides the secrets of her heart to a dove, while her father and her lover search for her in the garden.* The second was from the poet index and was for the John Masefield poem, *Sea Fever*, set by John Ireland. Emily's note for this read: *Masefield disapproved of the setting because of its slow tempo, but Ireland considered it his finest song. Despite the royalties it earned him, Masefield loathed it, largely because of the dirge-like performances it often received. Nevertheless, according to a poll carried out by the BBC in the 1930s, it was the most popular song of any description heard on the wireless.*

I bit my lip, hoping to stave off a threatened wave of tears.

'There may be more of her annotations elsewhere in the indexes, so I wanted to forewarn you.'

I gulped and nodded. 'Oh, Emily,' I said at last.

'I have that recording of the French folk song,' Johnny said, wanting to defuse the moment but not changing the subject completely. 'Britten's playing of the accompaniment is sublime—so perfectly judged. If I could emulate any accompanist, it would be him.'

'Perhaps we could do it sometime?' I ventured at last.

'We certainly could. I had another thought, too—though not something you would pursue straightaway. You told me about the song Emily found by Philip Nash and how it appeared to be part of a cycle. Did any of the other songs turn up?'

I shook my head.

'You also told me about the intriguing dedication and said the whole thing was a mystery Emily hoped would one day be solved. Well, perhaps in time, you might try to do that. Some research in the Tarporley or Nantwich area might throw up information about a Haldane family, for instance, and who knows where that might lead?'

The empty chair

I had missed Freddie and was looking forward to seeing him and hearing about his time in Wales, but grief is so personal, so differently experienced, I didn't know what to expect from him. I hoped we would provide fellowship for each other in our loss, but I feared that one or both of us might reveal a grief that was too ragged and raw to make us the easy companions we had once been.

The day after he got back, I called round for a nightcap, having had a pub meal in Jericho with Christina. At first, I was alarmed to see how much thinner he looked, but his face wore the ruddy complexion of someone who had been outside in all weathers and was in good health. He had lit a fire in the front sitting room and there we sat, as we so often had, cradling our whiskeys, but both painfully aware of the empty chair between us.

'How was Christina?' he asked.

'Sad, but she's doing her best to keep going. I took her out to thank her for all her kindness—not just when my parents were here for the funeral, but when I got back from Cairo. She'd been into the flat and stocked up with the basics and made up the spare bed for Johnny. I also wanted to ask her if there's anything of Emily's she'd like to have as a memento.'

'Are you beginning to think about what to do with her things?'

'I'm not ready to face it yet, but Christina said that when I feel the time has come, she'll help deal with the clothes and shoes and bags and so on. I guess charity shops would be glad of some of it. How about you,' I asked, 'is there anything you would like to have?'

'I don't think so, thanks. I have quite a lot left from her school days—pictures she drew for me, a scarf she knitted, Father's Day cards…'

His voice trailed away and when he spoke again, he didn't lift his eyes out of his whiskey.

'Have you thought what you might do with the wedding dress?'

'I wanted to ask if you had any thoughts about it, given that it was Marie-Odile's.'

He looked up at the mention of her name.

'I'm happy to leave that to you, Alex. Frankly, I couldn't bear to have it in the house. The dress would be a forlorn reminder that they're both gone.'

My heart ached for him. I had no idea how he could bear the loss of the two people he had loved more than anything else in the world.

'I don't want it either. I could offer it to Christina for her shop. It's exactly the sort of thing she specialises in.'

'I think that would be totally appropriate. They were such good friends. One thing—I would like to look at any recent photos you have. I'd like to have one or two enlarged and framed.'

'I'll look some out for you to choose from. Christina would like to see if there's a piece of jewellery that might suit her. Their style and tastes were very different, but you never know.'

Freddie smiled. 'Indeed.'

'How are you adjusting to being home?'

'I'm glad to be back. I was away for long enough.'

'How was it?'

'Bracing,' he said with a wry smile, 'but it was what I needed. The countryside was beautiful, so the walking was good. We worked on the land, too—tending the fruit and vegetable gardens, sowing and planting for future growth. The food was tasty and wholesome—I don't think I encountered a single preservative for the whole time I was there! And the silence suited me. When I arrived, I was almost mute anyway—still stunned by shock and misery—and it seemed that most people were escaping something or other, so there was a kind of unspoken solidarity between us.'

'Now I've got used to you being leaner than before, you look well,' I said.

'That's something I suppose. And how was Cairo? And your parents?'

'Cairo was just what I needed, and I was glad to be with Mum and Dad. To my surprise—and relief—they seemed to know how to be with me. After the first couple of days, there was no stiltedness between us and we settled into a comfortable *modus vivendi*. It made me realise how much time we've spent apart, and I was sad about that, as I think they are, especially my mum. They came to the airport to see me off and even my father was visibly upset when I headed away from them towards passport control.'

I sighed.

'I love Cairo. It's one of my favourite places and because Emily had never been there with me, I didn't have those sorts of memories or associations to contend with—just all the other ones.'

'I kept waiting for her to visit me in dreams,' Freddie said, 'but she never did.'

'Take it from me, dreams are a mixed blessing. They provide only temporary balm. You wake up and that first bleak moment of recollection simply reinforces the reality of the loss.'

He nodded.

'I went into College today, and as I walked down Cornmarket, I found it hard to understand why people were going about their normal lives, oblivious to my pain.'

He got up to refill our glasses and for a while we were both silent.

'By the way,' I said at last, 'I met Joshua Norman in Cairo and he remembered you.'

I told him about *Elijah,* and he was impressed that I'd done it.

'Was it exhausting?' Mustering the courage to take to the stage and sing in public?'

'Quite the opposite actually. I felt unexpectedly rejuvenated during and after it.'

'And now?'

I laughed.

'Ah, there's the rub. I have to pick up my career, get back to work.'

'What did Johnny make of the archive?'

I told him how impressed and inspired Johnny had been by it and outlined his idea of programming recitals around themed songs, and Freddie was pleased and interested.

'I'm meeting Dominic next week to talk about how we want to develop my work over the next few years, so I'll be telling him about these ideas then.'

'That's good. You need a sense of purpose. We both do. Dostoyevsky said, *the mystery of human existence lies not in just staying alive, but in finding something to live for.'*

Staying alive

And so, we went on. Freddie returned to work and was soon immersed in the familiar rhythms of a Trinity term at Oxford. I met the challenge of Britten's fearsome *Spring Symphony*, somehow managing to navigate the score's many mantraps. The mixed choruses of adult singers and boy trebles gave rumbustious renderings of the choral sections, joyously conveying the work's exuberant depiction of the progress of winter into spring and the reawakening of the earth and of life. It seemed an appropriate way in which to resume my career.

And spring did come at last. The trees on my street burst into bloom and the days got longer. Though I had lived alone in the flat contentedly before my marriage to Emily, it was there more than anywhere else that I missed her, and I sometimes felt very lonely. Life seemed to be happening somewhere else in a world I was no longer fully part of.

On my first visit to her grave, I made my way through what seemed like a sea of gravestones, until to my horror, I realised I was lost. The cemetery was vast and maze-like and at her internment, I had not taken note of markers that would help me find my way back to her. I was almost in tears, when one of the gardeners took pity on me and steered me to an office where I confessed to a kindly man called Ted that I couldn't remember where my wife was buried. Ted looked after me with a gentleness I guessed was the hallmark of his daily dealings with people who were sometimes distraught. He consulted his records before taking out a map on which he painstakingly highlighted in yellow marker pen the route from the office to Emily's grave. I was very grateful when he offered to take me there, and as we made our way, he pointed out memorable features which might help me remember the route next time I came. Though I was abject with misery and mortification, his deep, gravelly voice was strangely calming, and I listened and looked closely as we made our way to Emily's grave. In time, of course, I could have found my way there in the dark, but I always looked out for one particular headstone that had struck me on that first distressing visit.

It was tall and four-sided and beneath it lay a husband, his wife, and two sons who had died within two years of each other, aged twelve and thirteen. The wife had died fifteen years before her husband, and he had chosen the inscription: *She is watching and waiting for me.*

Fifteen years without her earthly presence by his side. I wondered if such certainty helped sustain him.

A year passed and I somehow survived the milestones I had dreaded—Emily's birthday, our wedding anniversary, and of course, the date of her death. At least once a month, I took flowers to her grave, now marked with a black marble headstone, the inscription of which gave her name, the span of her life, and the words *Beloved wife, daughter, and friend. A woman much missed.*

I hoped that work would be my saviour, the reason to keep going. In the spring of 1988, I sang Quint in Britten's opera *The Turn of the Screw.* Though the role suited my voice, and I had prepared for it well, I came to believe it was the right role at the wrong time—or more likely, the wrong role in the wrong opera.

Throughout the seven weeks of rehearsals and performances, I felt I was being sucked into a world of sheer malevolence. Tumbledown set designs and unsettling lighting created an air of desolation around the forsaken country house at Bly, providing the perfect backdrop for a production which evoked an atmosphere that was as much menacing as haunting.

Most productions of the opera tended to take an enigmatic approach to the true nature of the children, attempting to combine superficial childish innocence with sinister undercurrents, but this one was much more overtly sexual. The ghosts, Quint and Miss Jessel, got much closer to the children than most productions would dare. These children were lost souls, living in a world of the depraved. The young singers playing Miles and Flora were exceptional, the boy perfectly suggesting Miles's dangerously damaged innocence, the girl, even more knowing and calculating. Miles's highly sexualised behaviour with his sister was unnerving, the director coaxing extremely creepy performances from both of them. There could be no redemption for any of the wretched inhabitants of Bly.

It was a joyless experience and I was glad when it was over and I could return to the 'normal' world.

Freddie and I tried to have dinner together once a week and we quickly fostered the comradeship I had hoped for. He was working hard and though he didn't immediately resume his broadcasts, he began planning future programmes and this gave us much to talk about as I expanded my knowledge of the song repertoire.

Johnny and I met regularly to explore the archive and try out new songs. An invitation to give a themed programme came sooner than we expected, and interestingly, came not from a music promoter but from the organiser of an academic symposium. A university in the Midlands was holding a weekend of discussions on *Walter de la Mare—poet and storyteller*, and the organiser wanted to include in the schedule a recital of songs set to texts by de la Mare.

The idea was a gift because—Shakespeare apart—de la Mare ranks with A E Housman and Thomas Hardy as the poet most beloved by song makers. We were spoilt for choice. Our job was to choose the best songs—and find settings for the tenor voice—and link them together with a narrative that would make sense of our selection. *Arabia* by Denis Browne chose itself as the opening song because it was the first poem by de la Mare to be set to music and sadly, it was Browne's last song before his death on the Gallipoli peninsula in 1915 at the age of only twenty-seven. It was a precious fragment from a foreshortened life. We found three other single songs to include by Arthur Bliss, Gerald Finzi and Ivor Gurney, but the bulk of the material came from three composers who were particularly associated with de la Mare—Cecil Armstrong Gibbs, Benjamin Britten and Herbert Howells.

I had grown to love the songs of Howells and wished he had devoted more of his talents to this repertoire. He concentrated his song-writing attention on one poet and by sheer weight of numbers, his settings of Walter de la Mare form nearly half his output and the two men were life-long friends. If I were to choose just one of his songs, it would be his setting of *King David*, a song which Howells said he was prouder to have written than almost anything else he composed. The poem tells of the Biblical King David who is so full of melancholy that nothing can lift his spirits. Even the finest musicians of the day cannot take away the sorrow that haunts his heart. Only when he walks in his garden and hears a nightingale singing in a nearby tree does he feel lifted, and yet this little bird is oblivious to the King's dark feelings, and presumably is simply singing to catch a mate, or for the joy of singing. The setting is subtle and understated, the melody, rich and warm, and it was another song that had prompted Emily to write an entry on the back of the relevant card in the composer index.

Composed in 1919 when Howells was twenty-seven years old, King David is regarded as one of the greatest songs written in English in the early twentieth century. Howells's career as a composer was severely affected by the sudden death from polio in September 1935 of his nine-year old son, Michael. It was something from which Howells never recovered, and though he gradually returned to composing, the effect on his song-writing was profound. Of his forty or so published songs, the majority were written before 1935. Many commentators feel that Howells was potentially one of the finest writers of English song in the twentieth century, but after Michael's death, he turned his energy towards larger scale, religious works.

I'd not known about the death of his son and I wondered how Emily had come across this information. Sometime later, when I was rummaging through a file of miscellaneous materials in the collection, I found a programme for a concert of Howells's music. A lengthy biographical note of the composer revealed that on Tuesday, September 3rd, 1935, Michael was busy mowing lawns. Three days later he was dead from a severe case of bulbar polio.

These hidden notes triggered conflicting feelings in me. On the one hand, I dreaded stumbling across them, because I found it almost unbearably poignant to think of Emily responding to a poem or a song and being moved to convey something she thought interesting or significant.

On the other hand, I longed to find more of them because through these personal commentaries she seemed vividly present to me, and I felt a strange comfort in this unexpected communion with her. So, whenever I consulted the indexes, as well as having feelings of trepidation, I couldn't always resist the temptation to go looking for notes rather than staying focussed on whatever had been my real reason for consulting the records.

Johnny and I enjoyed planning the de la Mare programme, but to his frustration, I still shied away from repertoire that dealt with loss and grief, so our choices were constrained. My heart was too bruised and burdened to confront subjects and songs in which Johnny felt I would excel, but which I feared would overwhelm me. I remained resolute about this for many months until something happened to change it.

Catharsis

It was a Sunday morning in late April and Freddie and I were drinking coffee on the patio outside his kitchen. Birds were singing away in the trees at the end of the garden—proud songsters as Hardy called them—piping away without a care in the world, but I was feeling stuck and out of sorts. Freddie had been studying me intently but said little.

'It seems to me,' he said at last, 'that since Emily died, you've had a problematic relationship with music, and the work you've done this last year has not brought you much joy.'

I nodded.

'I'm not talking about your experience on *The Turn of the Screw*, though clearly that was difficult. It's more that I sense you're afraid of music that is sad or sorrowful. Am I right?'

He had found me out and I shrugged. He put his empty mug on the small table between us and leaned back in his chair.

'I once heard a musician say that singing sad songs can be healing because it gets the hurt out into the open. And people enjoy listening to sad music, don't they?'

'Why is that I wonder?'

'It's an intriguing paradox. Psychologists believe that rather than prolonging sorrow, engaging with art that is sad may actually be therapeutic.'

I frowned. 'I'm fearful of music that mirrors how I'm feeling. I'm afraid that even something that's vaguely wistful will propel me into despondency, so my enjoyment is precarious and inconsistent.'

Freddie knitted his fingers together and placed his hands beneath his chin. 'What about the sacred texts you encounter in your oratorio work?'

My relationship to this music had also become full of challenges and contradictions and I struggled to find an answer.

'After Marie-Odile's funeral, I found the way I listened to sacred music changed. Until my encounter with *An old belief* in Magdalen Chapel I'd never let that sort of music *in*, if you know what I mean. I knew plenty of sacred music, of course, but even when I could acknowledge the beauty of the music or the skill of the writing, as a non-believer, I heard it without letting it touch or move me. This, I thought, was music for other people, not for me. But then I realised that these settings—of psalms, Requiems, Stabat Maters, and the like—tell us that other generations have felt exactly as we feel and we are not alone in our fear and despair and our need for comfort.'

'That's true. Musicians in every generation have set those words to music. One day last week, I'd been to London for a session with Johnny, and when I got back to Oxford, I couldn't face the empty flat. I thought of spending an hour in the Old Tom, so I headed down St Aldates, but instead of going into the pub, I slipped over the road and went to Evensong at Christ Church. The choir sang a wonderful setting by Howells of Psalm 56—*Be Merciful to me, O God*. It's about keeping faith in the midst of fear, and it was somehow indomitable.'

'Ah, courage inspired by faith, I presume.' Freddie paused. 'I have another question for you. If you avoid songs that deal with love and loss and grief and so on, how long can you go on doing that before you run out of repertoire?'

I shifted awkwardly in my seat because Johnny had made the same point at our recent session which had ended in stalemate and left us both feeling discouraged.

'I know,' I muttered. 'It's something I have to face up to.'

'Most of us have music that reminds us of people or places or particular times in our life. One of music's superpowers is the way it can transport us from the present to the past, and listening to some music will trigger memories that can be powerfully emotional.'

'Memories I fear would waylay me.'

'But nostalgia is a complex emotional experience. There's a tendency to put "positive" and "negative" labels onto our feelings. Happiness is good, sadness is bad. But our relationship to music defies these simplistic categorisations. The music we've loved and connected with during our lifetime helps form the core of our identity.'

He leaned forward. 'I'd like you to try something. Let's go inside.'

I followed him to the front sitting room and he handed me a song that had been left on the music rack.

'Remember this?' he asked.

It was the setting of *Annabelle Lee* I had sung to Emily on the last night we ever spent together. I swallowed hard.

'Of course,' I said, handing it back to him.

'I remember you warned Emily she might be moved to tears.'

'I did—and she was.'

Freddie sat down at the piano. 'It was the last time the three of us were together. Could you sing it now? It would mean a lot to me.'

I felt a fluttering of anxiety in my stomach, but before I could object, he started playing, and when I heard the lovely lilting rhythm of the introduction, I closed my eyes and sang. Sang "of a love that was more than love", sang of "my darling—my darling—my life and my bride in her sepulchre by the sea".

As the final chords died away, I could see that Freddie's hands were shaking. He smiled up at me briefly, before folding his hands in his lap and bowing his head, but not before I saw that his eyes were full of tears. The intense sadness of Poe's poem of everlasting love beyond the grave, perfectly matched by Henry Leslie's beautiful melody, combined to create something that was both exquisite and heroic.

I leant down to wrap my arms around Freddie's drooping shoulders and something seemed to shift. I'm not sure what it was—the light coming through the window perhaps—but I remember it as a moment when our shared grief was briefly assuaged. It taught me that in searching for pathways out of despair, back to life and light, I would have to face my heartache and trust that strength and solace would be found in music and kinship.

PART 3
Spring 1988 to Spring 1993

When I set out for Lyonnesse

The mahogany bureau in my sitting room had belonged to Freddie's grandmother and was where Emily did her homework throughout her teenage years. She was attached to this family heirloom and brought it with her when we married. After she died, it became part of the furniture, until one day I decided to start using it. Inside, I found an unused notebook Emily had bought from the V&A and this became the journal in which I recorded my ideas about poetry and song.

On the first page, I listed the suggestions Johnny had put to me twelve months earlier. I then wrote each proposition at the top of a new page, leaving several pages in between each to allow space for notes. Finally, I turned to my many books of poetry. There were a few collections by individual poets, but mostly, they were anthologies—compilations of poems by century or by type—English poetry, war poetry, love poems, and so on—some arranged alphabetically, some chronologically and others, thematically. I was faced with a vast array of poetry, but for the first time in a long while, I began to read. At first, I read without being systematic and allowed myself to go where fancy took me, and these diversions frequently led me to unexpected discoveries, which I noted in the journal.

When I was ready to start thinking about thematic groupings, I faced up to the most challenging and began with the poetry and songs of Thomas Hardy. At first it was hard to know where to start because Hardy wrote almost a thousand poems and covered most aspects of human experience—time, memory, love, loss, fear, grief, anger, uncertainty, death—but I forced myself to persevere and gradually a long list of possibilities took shape.

This study of Hardy's poetry reminded me how often in his writings he explored the dream of love's joys, yet he lived more of its disappointments and frustrations. He and his first wife, Emma, were married for almost forty years, but their happiness was short-lived, their love soured by Hardy's neglect, due in part to his tireless preoccupation with his writing and his susceptibility to infatuations with other women. It was Emma's death in 1912 that was the catalyst for an outpouring of poetry in which he tried to rediscover a love he had forgotten but now longed for. He was filled with sorrow and remorse at their long and bitter estrangement and after her death, he attempted to recreate a great romance.

He went on writing poems about Emma to the end of his life fifteen years later, and there are at least eighty love poems about her. But only one—*Ditty*—was published in her lifetime. Set by Finzi in his song cycle *A Young Man's Exhortation*, the poem basks in contentment, disturbed only by the unbearable thought that chance might never have brought the poet and his true love together. Another love poem—also set by Finzi—*When I set out for Lyonnesse*, is about the magic of falling in love, coming out of cold, lonely darkness into a life of shining possibilities. This poem provoked another of Emily's notes in which she made plain her misgivings about Hardy and her sympathy for his rejected wife. On the back of the card in the poem index, she wrote:

Hardy put the date 1870 beside this poem—the year he met Emma in Cornwall (Lyonnesse)—but he did not publish it until after her death. On its publication, he told a friend it was exactly what had happened forty-four years earlier. He could have included it in any of his earlier collections after 1898, when he first began to publish poetry, but he chose not to, perhaps because by then it was too painfully incongruous. Did Emma ever read this poem and realise it was about her husband's first dazzling meeting with her?

I hoped she had.

Freddie was delighted I was actively using the collection, and though he asked me not to take any music away with me, he was happy for me to study it at the house until I'd decided whether it was worth buying my own copy. If I was still in the basement at the end of a day, we would often spend the evening together and much fruitful conversation was had over dinners or nightcaps. When I'd come up with a list of Hardy songs, we discussed it over his famous Spag Bol.

'Among my degree notes on Hardy, I found a quote attributed to Emma: "He understands only the women he invents—the others not at all".'

'Bleak, but probably true,' said Freddie, eating while glancing down at the list I'd passed him. 'Did you enjoy doing this?'

'Mostly, I did. Being immersed in Hardy could be gloomy work, but alongside the wistfulness and the sense of loss and tragedy, there's also a capacity to enjoy, to be grateful, and that surprised me. There's a rousing setting by John Ireland of a poem called *Great Things* that's full of excited, delighted pleasure. It's a list that starts with cider and ends with impassioned flings.'

Freddie frowned.

'It's not on your list.'

'It's not. I have a sense that it's better suited for a baritone. I can imagine Josh giving a rollicking good rendering of it.'

'Fair enough,' Freddie conceded. 'So which ones are you drawn to?'

'Inevitably, many of them are by Finzi, but I did look for others—so there are songs by Bax, Bliss, Britten, Gurney, Holst, Ireland and Vaughan Williams.'

'*Her Song* by Ireland is lovely,' Freddie said. 'The poem is said to represent the ghost of Emma and the setting is very poignant.'

'There's a setting in the same vein by Finzi of *The Phantom Horsewoman*. It was written in the immediate aftermath of Emma's death and is Hardy encountering the ghost girl rider he once knew and still loves.'

'I like your idea of including alternative settings of the same verse, and there are some interesting options here.'

'Yes. Take *Weathers* by Finzi and Ireland. It's highly untypical of his poetry and yet it's been set more times than any other single Hardy poem. It begins "This is the weather the cuckoo likes" and continues in the style of an Elizabethan verse. *The Oxen* has three very different settings by Britten, Finzi and Vaughan Williams and is Hardy musing at Christmas on his lack of faith and his regret for it.'

'Hardy once said he'd been looking for God for fifty years, and that if God existed, he thinks he would have discovered him.'

'Typical Hardy,' I laughed. '*Proud Songsters* is about the very short life cycle of the birds in our gardens who sing as if all time were theirs. Britten's setting in *Winter Words* is short and joyful, but there's a very different interpretation by Finzi, which is longer and elegiac in tone—and both work equally well.'

A clock somewhere in the house was chiming the hour, and heard from a distance, it was a doleful sound, and quite out of the blue, I felt a melancholy mood descend on me. I got up to get a glass of water and when I sat down again, Freddie was looking at me with concern.

'Are you okay?'

I shook my head.

'So many of these poems, these songs, have struck a chord.'

Freddie said nothing but nodded to show he understood.

'Take *Proud Songsters*, for instance. Have we not thought we had all the time in the world to enjoy love and life only to have it snuffed out in an instance?'

'Indeed.'

'And Finzi's setting of *The Clock of the Years* is a horribly misguided Faustian pact, yet I found myself sympathising with the poor, trusting poet.'

'What's it about?'

'It's a fantasy in which a spirit can make time go backwards, but only at his own whim. So, the poet's beloved is brought back from the dead, then taken back to her youth and childhood and babyhood until "it was as if she had never been".'

Freddie pushed his plate away and shuddered.

'I'm grateful to have only happy memories of my time with Marie-Odile and glad that those memories are not blighted by guilt or remorse like Hardy's.'

I nodded.

'The love between Hardy and Emma seemed to quickly descend into irreparable bitterness and resentment. To quote the man himself: *If I have seen one thing, it is the passing preciousness of dreams.*'

'You know, Alex, this is mournful material to spend time with,' Freddie said. 'And I'm not simply talking about the songs of Hardy. As you get deeper into the song repertoire, you'll discover that its predilection is for the sorrowful, it dwells on pain as much as it extols pleasure. It forces us to confront how chance and choice and circumstance converge to give us the lives we have, to make us who we are. But one day, you may be glad you didn't let sadness squeeze the creative impulse out of you, that you explored what happens when words meet music, that you discovered moments of revelation, of surprise, of catharsis.'

We grow accustomed to the dark

'For goodness' sake, Alex—you need to start enjoying yourself again. When did you last have some fun? For instance, when did you last see West Ham play?'

I laughed. 'Not necessarily guaranteed to be a source of either fun or enjoyment.'

'Fair point, but you know what I mean.'

The questioner was Luke, the baritone I'd shared a flat with in Earl's Court and who for years had been my regular companion at home matches. Luke loved football, but having grown up in the Netherlands, he was a devoted Ajax supporter and could be a happy neutral at matches in the English league.

'So?' he insisted.

'Not for a while,' I conceded. 'But I follow their progress, which is hard enough. Sixteenth last season, this year could be worse.'

Luke shook his head and tutted. 'Shame on you! I never had you down as a fair-weather fan. Come on, let's give it a go.'

He would not be deterred and go we did. Even when the play was dismal and the results disappointing, going achieved Luke's purpose of getting me back into the habit of engaging with what he called normal life. Though he was not comfortable talking about Emily's death, he proved a staunch and faithful friend, undaunted by my grief and my reclusive tendencies. I had other people in my life like him who cared about me, but grief is isolating, and I'd become something of a loner. I rarely joined other musicians for post-performance drinks, fearing I would be poor company and a drain on the enjoyment of others.

But the music world is a small one and itinerants, like me, are often lonely, and glad when our paths cross with old acquaintances. Luke had secured a salaried position in a leading chamber choir and not long after he took up his place, I was the tenor soloist in Bach's *B Minor Mass*, in which his choir were also performing. After the concert at St John's Smith Square, the condition for me staying the night at his new flat in Putney, was to accompany him—and most of the other musicians—to a nearby pub. I'd forgotten how good it felt to unwind with fellow performers and reflect together on the highs—and sometimes, the lows—of the performance just given. I knew a couple of the other choristers from St Paul's and I enjoyed reminiscing with them about past times without needing to dwell on my recent troubles.

Time passed, and life was busy. Luke and I met up for football excursions as often as our schedules would allow, persevering through the snakes and ladders of relegation and promotion which characterised these years. Freddie resumed his broadcasts and he and I maintained our custom of having dinner together every week, if possible. My parents visited a few times, and when a couple of concerts were cancelled at short notice, giving me an unexpected gap in my schedule, I spent a week with them in Cairo.

Johnny and I developed and performed many of the thematic ideas he'd mapped out that day I first took him to the archive, and my singing career remained a mix of recital work and oratorio. I found particular success as the Evangelist in Bach's *Passions* and his music became a mainstay of my work, but at the same time, I became known as what one commentator described, an ideal exponent of Benjamin Britten. His many songs continued to feature in my recital programmes, but his *Serenade for Tenor, Horn and Strings* and *The War Requiem* also became part of my repertoire.

Around this time, Josh rang to invite me to a performance in Oxford of *Falstaff*, in which he was singing the title role. This was a surprise because he was not listed on any of the advance publicity I'd seen.

'I've been sharing the tour with another chap,' he explained, 'and he was due to do the Oxford show, but he's struggling with vocal difficulties, so I've taken over the whole run.'

He gave a typically virtuoso performance in a production that was a hoot. It made the most of the many comic moments in the piece and earned the kind of enthusiastic laughter you rarely hear in an opera house. As a self-aggrandising but eloquent Falstaff, Josh put his voice to hilariously undignified use, but at the start of Act Three, when he huddled alone on the stage, drying off after having been unceremoniously dumped in the Thames, he made Falstaff's humbling feel ineffably poignant.

Josh and some other company members were staying at the Randolph and a group of us ended up in the hotel bar sharing a platter of sandwiches and drinking beer and whiskey. A young man sitting next to me and Josh introduced himself as Adam Lucas, a conductor who I knew was building a reputation as a Britten specialist. He had recognised me immediately.

'I heard you at Snape,' he said. 'Your recital *Remembering Britten*. It was fantastic—I was sorry not to have seen you afterwards to congratulate you, but I was rushing to catch the train back to London.'

'Thank you. It was very scary singing that programme in a place where Pears and Britten would have performed the same music.'

'Well, you needn't have worried. You and your accompanist are a formidable team.'

I laughed. 'Britten was Johnny's favourite accompanist, so for once, I think he was more nervous than I was.'

'What do you have coming up next?' he asked.

'More song recitals and a lot of Bach oratorios.' I was curious. 'What brought you here tonight?'

'I wanted to see Josh sing Falstaff.'

'How do you know each other?' I asked, looking from one man to the other.

'I was conducting my first ever *War Requiem* and the baritone soloist pulled out a week before the performance. Josh stepped in to save the day.'

Josh raised his glass and said, 'Glad to be of service.'

Adam raised his glass in return, and they exchanged warm smiles.

'Do you have any opera lined up?' Adam asked, turning back to me.

I shook my head. 'Not at the moment.'

'One of my next projects is *Curlew River*. We've been auditioning, without success, for the Madwoman. Would you be interested? I think the role would suit you.'

The suggestion took me off guard and while I searched for a response, I saw Josh looking at me expectantly, as if willing me to say yes.

'Who's your agent?' Adam asked. 'May we have a conversation about dates and so on?'

I gave him Dominic's details and he promised he'd be in touch. Shortly afterwards he left to drive to his parents in Cheltenham.

'You should consider it,' Josh said. 'I didn't want to say this when he was here, but he's very good and very nice. The *War Requiem* is a test for everyone involved and he was completely on top of it.'

'Other people have suggested I do the Madwoman, but I've steered clear of opera ever since *The Turn of the Screw*.'

'I know that was a bad experience for you, but you shouldn't let it put you off *Curlew River*. Quint and the Madwoman are worlds apart.'

'Have you ever done *Curlew River*?'

'I've sung the Ferryman a couple of times, but I've always envied the tenor playing the Madwoman—it's such a sympathetic role, fragile yet strong. Cruelly named, though. She's a widowed noblewoman wandering the earth, unhinged by grief, seeking her lost son, and initially mocked in the attempt.'

He struck me as a discerning judge and his words persuaded me.

'Okay. I'll tell Dominic I'm interested. Can I get you another drink?'

He pointed at his glass to indicate the same again, and by the time I got back from the bar, the remaining group was dispersing, leaving Josh and I alone.

'How are you otherwise?' he asked when I sat down with our drinks.

'Better—but the world still seems empty without Emily. It makes me realise what comfort I got, whenever I was away, to know that she was there, somewhere. I missed her during our times apart, but I could look forward to being home with her again and that gave me a powerful sense of well-being.' I sighed. 'Missing her now feels very different, but she's still stitched into my life in all sorts of ways. Little things, like I still use her method to keep my T-shirts tidy, taking out the whole pile to choose one so they get less messy.'

Josh stroked his beard and nodded. 'Those little things. I know.'

'I've only recently dealt with her clothes. Fortunately, her friend Christina helped with the grim process of going through the wardrobe and drawers. I knew I had to part with the stuff, but it somehow felt disloyal, and I confess, I've kept a red jumper she was wearing on the night we first met.'

'I remember that process. Like you, we put if off for ages, but afterwards I realised we'd been in danger of preserving Elena's room as some sort of shrine. Even at the time, it didn't feel healthy.'

I nodded and for a while we were both silent.

'I loved your performance tonight,' I said at last. 'The way you can combine knockabout comedy with pathos and humanity—it's a wonderful talent.'

Josh shrugged. 'The role's a gift. It allows me to show both sides of myself.'

That gave me pause for thought.

'My mother remembers me as a high-spirited, playful child, and sometimes I long to be able to tap into that boy, the child I used to be, the man I might have become. But I think life may have made me a melancholy soul.'

'That may be what makes you such an effective singer of lieder.'

'You could be right. Do you know Emily Dickinson's poem, *We grow accustomed to the dark?*'

Josh shook his head.

'She says that darkness is part of our lives, something we grow accustomed to and become comfortable with.'

'Or at least, we accept it,' Josh said, looking deep into his pint. 'Do *Curlew River*,' he said at last, looking up. 'It may help you work through your grief. Be that noblewoman searching for her son. It's a remarkable portrait of intense love and inner crisis—but at the end, there's a glimpse of healing and resolution.'

I did agree to be considered for *Curlew River* and was invited to a working session with Adam Lucas and the director, Simon McCabe. The music of *Curlew River* presents particular challenges, largely because it has no time signatures, and the bar lengths change freely, so they asked me to come prepared to work with them on parts of the score. They also invited me to sing two pieces of my own choosing, ideally both of them to be in English.

Freddie knew *Curlew River* well and advised me to sing contrasting pieces that would convince them I would be able to convey a distraught soul whose only purpose left in life was to find her missing child. It seemed obvious that one of these pieces should be by Britten, and I chose *Since she whom I loved*, the sixth song from *The Holy Sonnets of John Donne*, which was an elegy for Donne's beloved wife. He had risked his life for the love of Anne More (grandniece of Sir Thomas More), and this sonnet was an outpouring of grief at her death. Britten's setting is tender and compassionate; by turns, anguished and calm, and I chose the song not only for its themes of yearning and consolation, but because of its unusual surges and hesitations and because Britten put rests in the vocal line in unexpected corners, avoiding the obvious breathing places.

When I was pondering what else to sing, Freddie was preparing a broadcast about Handel's final oratorio, *Jephtha*.

'He'd worked too hard, drunk too much and he was very tired,' Freddie said as we were sharing dinner one night. 'He was sixty-six years old, and he was going blind. Not surprisingly, but unusually for him, he was behind schedule. He must have felt desperate, yet despite all this, *Jephtha* contains some of his most ravishing music.'

I knew the piece and like many stage-works of the period, *Jephtha* hinges upon a vow to make a sacrifice if victory in battle is assured, a vow that cannot be broken, that demands a submission to destiny. In the hour of Jephtha's triumph, he is horrified by the realisation that it is his daughter, Iphis, who must die because of the vow he made. I immediately thought of *Waft her angels*, the aria in which Jephtha prays for angels to guide his daughter's spirit to heaven.

'Good idea,' said Freddie. 'The way it expresses the devoted love of a broken-hearted father is very touching.' He laughed. 'And you'll be able to show off some impressive no-breath acrobatics. But seriously, it will suit you well.'

He must have been right because after I'd sung it at the start of the working session, Adam sighed and declared, 'That was sublime. No wonder such an eloquent prayer was answered by the timely intervention of an angel.'

After that, I relaxed. Auditions can be terrifying and gruesome, but the more informal format of a working session allowed me to show what I could do and how I might approach a role, and it seemed a meaningful way for a director to judge whether or not he could work with someone. I was excited when I was offered the role, and time spent learning it and studying its provenance dominated much of the next year.

It's one of three Church Parables Britten wrote and it was based on the Japanese Noh play, *Sumidigawa*, which Britten and Pears saw performed in Tokyo, and which Britten said was seared into his memory. Scored for seven instruments and an all-male cast, the main role is that of a mother who has lost her son. Britten intended the piece to be performed without a conductor, so Adam would lead the performance from a chamber organ within the ensemble.

Freddie had seen two different productions of *Curlew River*, including the first, and his vivid recollections were fascinating.

'The audience in Orford Church on that first night were transfixed,' he said. 'We all knew we'd witnessed something new and special—an extraordinary attempt to fuse two disparate traditions: the classic Japanese Noh drama and the medieval mystery play. There we were, in an ancient church in Suffolk, watching a collision of east and west: the transplanting of a Japanese tale to the fenlands of East Anglia. Dramatically and musically, it was worlds away from anything Britten had composed before.'

He fell silent as if lost in memories of that night in Suffolk. We were eating at the Italian trattoria in Summertown and it seemed incongruous that we were being regaled by a series of Verdi's most rousing drinking choruses, but Freddie seemed not to notice. When he next spoke, he was obviously still hearing monks chanting plainsong in a medieval church in Orford.

'At the end, the voice of the boy soprano who plays the spirit of the Madwoman's son emerged so suddenly from out of the sound of the chamber orchestra that you could hardly believe it was there.' He shook his head, as if in wonder. 'Mystery and miracle. I remember leaving the Church feeling transformed by the experience.'

'It sounds astonishing. How similar—or different—was the other production you saw?'

'The premiere production had the singers masked, as they would have been for the Japanese Noh play, and that didn't worry me at the time, but it created a sense of otherness that was not a feature of the production I saw in France.'

A waiter arrived to clear away our plates and, after he'd gone, I refilled our wine glasses.

'Before that performance began, the director explained that in her concept of the work, a group of performers who've experienced a transition from trauma to hope, are travelling around telling this tale as an act of love.'

'Did it work?'

'I wasn't sure about the determinedly workaday costumes, but overall, it did work, partly due to the church setting, which helped convey the idea that the production was a gift of hope. Its message seemed to be "take comfort, things will get better".'

Crossing the Curlew River

We began rehearsals in February 1991, shortly after the fourth anniversary of Emily's death. By then, Marie-Odile had been dead for over twenty years and Freddie had been single ever since. He told me this after he'd been a witness at the registry office wedding of a colleague who was marrying for the second time after many years of being a widower.

'Have you ever hoped to remarry?' I asked.

He shook his head.

'I never expected it to happen, and it never has. A woman in the music faculty showed interest in me for a while, but there was no spark, not for me at any rate. No rush of attraction, no desire to become closer.'

I found it impossible to look into my own future and know how I would feel if I was still alone after twenty years. Sometimes that awful journey from Heathrow to Oxford in the back of Johnny's car, seemed to have happened only yesterday; at other times, it seemed part of another lifetime. For now, a new love felt unlikely. It was not that I never met women I found attractive, but more that I felt somehow shrunken inside and only fully confident when I was immersed in work.

I was glad to have something as different as *Curlew River* to get to grips with. We rehearsed for three weeks in an unused church in London—four principal singers and a chorus of eight pilgrims—initially with piano accompaniment. The ensemble was scheduled to arrive towards the end of the rehearsal period, along with two boys who were to share the role of the child and cover for each other. It was a strong cast, several of whom I already knew, including Leo who was playing the Ferryman, Julian who was the Abbott, and Guy who was the Traveller. Because I had done virtually no opera, I was afraid I might feel like an outsider among people who were used to being part of a company, but I soon felt at home. On day one, we met the designers of the set, costumes, and lighting as well as the Production Manager, Electrician, and Wardrobe Supervisor. There was a three-strong stage management team of Assistant Stage Manager, Deputy Stage Manager and the Company Stage Manager, Christos, whose job was to make sure we were well looked after.

As we gathered over coffee, Bruce, one of the chorus men nudged me when the costume designer arrived, armed with sketches.

'Good luck with the costume, Alex,' he whispered. 'Let's hope they don't get you dressed up to look like Edna the Inebriate Woman.'

My look of alarm provoked loud guffaws from the other men, one of whom reminded us that Peter Pears had famously objected to his costume in the original production, telling the composer: "Really, Ben, I just can't work in this frock."

I need not have worried. My costume was designed to signify that the woman was of noble birth, a simple robe that would be broken down to show she had travelled a long way and was dusty and bedraggled. Everything about the staging was to be minimal. A pathway of stones, a cross, a simple skiff and a white canvas sail. All the costumes were sober and plain, in varying hues of brown and beige, and we were to be unmasked, with the lighting used to illuminate our faces so that our expressions could communicate to the audience as much as our voices did.

Having heard the production design described, Simon talked about the piece itself.

'"What are those birds?" asks the Madwoman. They are, of course, curlews—conjured up by a skittering, flutter-tongued flute—high above the land where she is looking for her lost son.' He paused. '*Curlew River* is about the search for peace; the universal, all-consuming need to know what and why. In learning what happened to her son, the Madwoman can come to terms with his loss and so leave her madness behind and move on.'

Simon had once been an actor and his telling of the story was at times theatrical yet always felt sincere.

'I want us to create an atmosphere of timeless magic. At the beginning, accompanied by flickering candles and the sound effect of trickling water, the Monks will process into the church, with their feet crunching along a path of stones, chanting the plainsong *Te lucis ante terminum—To thee before the close of day*. The Abbot summons the audience to watch his monks enact a mystery and a wonder. The Ferryman steps forward to say that a memorial service is to take place that day at a shrine on the far bank of the Curlew River. A Traveller enters and tells of his intention to cross the river, but the Ferryman delays departure to listen to the demented singing of a Madwoman who is approaching the boat, crying out to her lost child. After some resistance, the Ferryman agrees to take the woman across the river and during the crossing, he relates the story of a stranger who arrived, a year before, accompanied by a young boy of noble parentage who subsequently died from illness and exhaustion. The Madwoman questions the Ferryman and it becomes clear that the child was her abducted son.

'Her grief is overwhelming. She has come so far only to find him dead by the side of a foreign river. Her madness intensifies and the Ferryman tries to console her by leading her to the grave of her son, but she finds nothing to comfort her. Finally, she is persuaded to say a prayer at his grave. They all join her in singing, and as the song culminates, they hear the voice of the boy's spirit joining in with them. The Madwoman rejoices to hear his voice again, and the whole company falls silent in awe. The boy's spirit then appears in full view above the tomb and the Mother, now cured of her madness, sings an Amen. The Monks then process out of the church, chanting the plainsong with which the work opened.'

The room was silent and still.

'It's a quiet piece,' Simon concluded, 'but ultimately cathartic.'

We were due to give two performances at Brecon Cathedral as part of a music festival. Shortly after rehearsals began, Dominic heard that if the production was a success in Brecon and if enough venues and funds could be secured, the show would tour the following spring. This possibility appealed to me. It would be a new experience and give me the opportunity to develop the role in different settings and in front of different audiences.

Halfway through the third week, the instrumentalists arrived, and Adam took his place among them at the chamber organ. The sound world was transformed by the arrival of the Viola, Double Bass, Harp and Percussion, with the Flute the alter-ego of the Madwoman and the Horn the alter-ego of the Ferryman. The two boys joined as well. Henry was twelve years old and his experience in other stage shows gave him a remarkably grown-up poise. Ryan was a year younger and was small for his age, but he was a lively little lad, eagerly revelling in this new experience. Together they brought a different energy into the room and just as we were all beginning to flag after long days of intensive rehearsal, they lifted everyone's spirits.

On the final day in London, there was no Christos and Simon told us that his father had been taken seriously ill in Greece and was not likely to survive.

'We told him he must go at once to be with his family in Athens. Hopefully, by the time we get to Brecon next week, we'll have found a replacement.'

Christos was friendly and funny and we'd grown fond of him so the news cast something of a pall over the group, but we had to press on as planned. In the afternoon there was a floor run to be done and before that, final costume fittings—and for me, a chance to try out my wig: a long plait that would be as dishevelled as my costume.

When the day was over, I was glad to head home for a few days break.

I'd spent the first week with Josh and Hilary and the second and third weeks at Luke's and I needed some quiet time alone before the rigours of the coming week.

On the following Monday morning, I arrived at the Cathedral in good time for the eleven o'clock call. Six of us, including Adam and Simon, were staying in a guesthouse on the other side of town, not far from the Regimental Museum. It was old-fashioned and spartan, but it was warm and clean and the landlady gave us a good breakfast, so we had few complaints. Some of the others were not so fortunate and we arrived at the Cathedral to find four of the chorus men gathered near the entrance, surrounded by their luggage and deep in conversation with a woman I didn't recognise. She was dressed in casual blacks, and I guessed she was the new Company Stage Manager.

The crew had been busy since early morning rigging up lights, setting up the ensemble positions and laying out the props. The central aisle had been transformed by a carpet tightly packed with pieces of gravel to create the path down which the monks would progress at the beginning and end of the opera. Some of the players were already seated and tuning, the two boys perched near the front, watching all the comings and goings, with Gemma, their chaperone sitting alongside them.

Signs handwritten in bold black marker pen directed us to our makeshift dressing rooms. The players were to use the Clergy Vestry on the ground floor which was also set up as a Green Room with tea and coffee making materials. The twelve male singers were upstairs sharing adjoining space in the large Choir Room and the small Library, while the boys were to use a windowless Robing Room across from the Choir Room. The morning session was to be out of costume, so as everyone arrived, we gathered in the nave waiting to begin.

'Don't you just love a freezing cold cathedral on a Monday morning,' said Guy, who showed no intention of taking off his duffle coat, scarf and gloves.

I laughed but nodded in agreement. It was indeed very cold. The four chorus men left their luggage among the pews and when they came to join us, we learnt that the bed and breakfast they'd been booked into bore close resemblance to a doss house and they'd checked out early and had breakfast at a café in town.

'The dead rat we had to step over on the front path was an ominous sign,' said Bruce.

'The final straw for me,' said Miles, 'were the long, black hairs I found on my pillow. And you don't want to know about the bathroom.'

'The whole place was disgusting,' said Hugo.

'Can you move somewhere else?' Simon asked them.

'The new Company Manager's on the case,' Miles replied.

'She seems very competent,' said Hugo. 'Very calm and collected.'

'We told her we'd double up to share rooms, if necessary,' said Miles.

'Desperate times demand desperate measures,' said Bruce, shaking his head in mock horror.

We all laughed, glad of their forbearance and good humour.

The morning's rehearsal was a *sitzprobe*, when we would sing seated alongside the players, with the intention of integrating our performances in the new setting and acoustic. It was a stop-start affair, mainly to address issues of balance and ensemble, but we finished a few minutes short of one o'clock when we were due to break for lunch.

Just before that, I noticed the Company Manager come into the cathedral and make her way quietly towards us down the South Aisle, thus avoiding the noisy gravel path. She stood discreetly to one side and when she saw that Adam was about to announce the break, she stepped forward.

'Adam, could I have a moment with the company before lunch please?'

'Of course. Go ahead.'

'Hello,' she said, addressing us all. 'I'm sorry I wasn't able to greet you individually before the rehearsal started, but you may have gathered we had a slight accommodation problem.'

She said this with a smile which must have reassured the men that their problem had been resolved.

'I'm Lillian Baranski, your Company Stage Manager for the next few days, and before the afternoon session, I'll try to get round you all to say hello. If you have any problems, let me know and I'll do my best to sort them.'

She was softly spoken but had a quiet authority, and though she looked slightly flushed and a few flyaway strands of hair were coming away from her ponytail, she inspired confidence.

'Bruce, Miles, Hugo, Sam—can I have a word please?' she said, picking out the men who were currently homeless.

She took them to one side and though I couldn't hear what was said, from the way Bruce winked knowingly at the others, I guessed all was well. She handed Miles a piece of paper and the four of them collected their luggage and walked towards the main door.

While I looked around to see what others were doing for lunch, I saw that Lillian was now with Leo, Julian and Guy and I went to join them.

'Hello. I'm Alex Ingram.'

'Madwoman of this parish,' whispered Leo.

'Much maligned,' I said, feigning offence. 'But welcome, Lillian. I hope you settle in quickly and we don't cause you too much trouble.'

'It's the pilgrims on my ferryboat you've got to watch out for,' said Leo. 'Troublemakers.'

She laughed and moved away to chat to the players, saying over her shoulder, 'I'll make a note!'

It was a long day, with an afternoon rehearsal in costume and a dress rehearsal in the evening. During both sessions, the lighting designer and the electrician were still plotting the lighting design, so while we performed, they experimented around and above us. The evening session was run without stopping, with a notes session at the end. Afterwards, many of us went to a nearby pub for a reviving drink. Bruce and the other men were more than happy with their new accommodation, and when Lillian arrived with the rest of the crew, they clamoured to buy her drinks in thanks.

'How did you find somewhere so good at no notice?' asked Adam.

'Basically, I got lucky,' she said with a smile. 'I went into a property agent, explained the problem, and asked if they had any suggestions or could point me in the direction of anyone who might be able to help. Miraculously, some months back they'd sold a guest house to a couple who'd been renovating it and were due to open in a couple of weeks. I waited while the agent rang the owners to ask if they were in a position to put up four men for two nights. To my amazement they agreed, seeing it as a sort of dry run. It's just down the hill from the cathedral so I went to see it. The bedrooms look comfortable and though the kitchen isn't quite finished, they were confident they could provide breakfast. I thought we were unlikely to find anywhere better.'

'Fantastic,' said Adam. 'Well done.'

She shook her head, keen to play it down, but though luck had played a part, I thought how resourceful she'd been and as she blushed under Adam's praise, I caught her eye and smiled.

We were all tired and most people left the pub at the same time, with small groups walking together through the town to their accommodation. The day had gone reasonably well, given the technical difficulties posed by the cathedral, and the musical challenges presented by the piece, but I was glad to be working with people who were used to making opera and who were not phased in the final days of rehearsals when lighting and costume added new layers to an already complex process.

The next morning, we had a final dress rehearsal with a photographer present. I had lunch with Leo and Guy but was glad to have the afternoon free to spend time alone, preparing myself for the performance. I went down to the canal which was not far from my digs, and I was walking along the towpath away from the town, when I heard boys' voices calling me and saw that Henry, Ryan and Gemma were kneeling down on the opposite towpath, throwing chunks of bread to a cluster of excited ducks. I waved and watched them for a few moments before I walked on. Henry was singing that night and Ryan the next and both sets of parents were making the trip from London to see their sons perform.

I carried on walking for a while and stopped when I came to a bench near the water's edge where I sat for a while. It was bright and cold, but I was wrapped up well and it was good to feel the sun on my face. Watching the stately progress of brightly painted narrow boats, some with potted plants and flowers on their decks, and gazing at the ducks, swimming around in endless circles, was wonderfully soothing. As I focussed on the mesmeric rhythms of canal life, I felt some of my anxiety about the coming performance dissolve.

It was early when I arrived back at the cathedral, but I wanted to take my time and not feel rushed. I was the only performer wearing a wig and makeup and I knew that Scott, the Wardrobe Supervisor and Dresser, would want to get me sorted before he dealt with all the others. I went to tell Lillian I was in the building so she could sign me in and I found her placing programmes and envelopes on each of the music stands. She was still dressed in black, but the casual sweatshirt and jeans had been replaced by smart trousers and a neat jacket over a subtly sparkly top.

'You look very elegant.'

'I'm sure you'll outdo me once you're in full Madwoman mode,' she said with a laugh. 'Are you okay?'

'I'll be fine when I've submitted to Scott's ministrations.'

'I'll tell him you're here.'

I was sharing the Library with the other three principals and when I arrived there, our clothes and shoes were laid out waiting for us. A trestle table and four chairs had been set up in the middle of the room, and I saw that at each place, there was a white envelope with a name on it. I opened mine to find a postcard showing the beautiful stone reredos in the cathedral's Sanctuary. On the back, Lillian had written *Dear Alex, I know you will be a truly noble and moving Madwoman. All the best for the two performances in Brecon, love and best wishes, Lillian.*

I realised she had written cards for everyone and I was touched by her thoughtfulness. I propped up the card just as Scott came into the room.

'You're early,' he said. 'Have you eaten?'

'I had a good lunch, and some fruit and yoghurt before I left the digs.'

He looked at me askance, as I knew he would, and produced a Tupperware dish of dried fruit and nuts which he put on the table in front of me.

'I've got some cheese sandwiches, too, if you get hungry,' he said, placing his hands on my shoulders. 'But let's get started. Costume first, then makeup, then wig.'

His capable, kindly manner was reassuring and relaxing and he was ideally suited to a job which involved seeing performers when they were feeling exposed and anxious. Once dressed, I sat back and let Scott work on my face. Simon did not want me to look like either a woman or a ghoul; he simply wanted my eyes to be emphasised against a slightly ashen complexion. Scott worked slowly and carefully, knowing that Simon would check the finished look. Finally, he secured the wig, making sure it was as comfortable as possible. Once it was in place, he held up a mirror and even I had to admit that in its deliberate state of decrepitude, the wig was rather affecting.

'You look gorgeous,' said Leo, blowing me a kiss as he took his seat opposite me. 'Those eyes!'

The other two arrived soon afterwards and the four of us settled into our separate routines. Lillian's cards were opened and admired.

'She's been good, hasn't she?' Guy said. 'Gets on with it, no fuss and always helpful.'

'I think Bruce fancies his chances,' said Leo.

'Well, he'd better watch himself,' said Julian drily. 'She's not a woman to be messed with.'

He was a quiet, mild-mannered man and this tart comment seemed out of character and therefore all the more notable. Guy and Leo gave each other knowing looks and when Lillian came in to wish us well, I watched to see how she and Julian interacted, but saw nothing out of the ordinary. As soon as she'd gone, Simon arrived to give his verdict on my make-up, and before long, it was time for all the men to gather in the corridor outside the door on the east side of the cathedral. Though I didn't process in with them and didn't sing until almost fifteen minutes into the opera, I waited with them so I could feel part of the performance from the outset.

When clearance was given, the ASM opened the door and the eleven men paced slowly into the cathedral and down the path of stones, the haunting sound of their plainsong causing me to shiver with anticipation, even through the now closed door. I waited for the door to be opened again on cue, in time for me to hear the Ferryman ask the Traveller "what is that strange noise up the highway there?" I started singing from beyond the open door, gradually moving into the Cathedral and eventually, making my way down the path towards the Ferryman's boat, on which the Pilgrims and the Traveller were about to set off across the river. As I got closer, members of the audience turned and craned their necks to look at the poor, crazed woman who was being taunted and ridiculed, with Leo and Guy as Ferryman and Traveller particularly convincing as men of a certain bravado who would yet be swayed by human suffering.

Even with its relatively sparse orchestral textures, Britten's music sounded rich and strange in the high-vaulted cathedral, and the minimal set lent itself to eye-catching effects, particularly when the ferryboat's billowing white sail was raised. The piece is only seventy minutes long and it seemed to pass by in a flash. When I knelt at the boy's grave, I felt my heart pounding as Henry's clear, piping treble voice called out to me and could be heard above the singing of the monks. When the spirit of the boy appeared in a slash of white light and he told his mother to be at peace, it was almost overwhelming.

As we processed away down the gravel path towards the back of the cathedral, singing the same plainsong that had opened the piece, the audience sat in silence, but when we exited out of the east door and it closed behind us, we heard an eruption of applause. We processed back in to take our bows and I stepped among the players to collect Henry, who had retreated into the darkness out of sight behind the percussion. When I brought him to the front and we bowed together, it was as if I, too, was experiencing the Madwoman's redemption.

The schedule for the next day was different. We were free in the morning but were called late afternoon so that Ryan could have a final rehearsal of his scene, especially the moment when he had to stand on a high platform behind the players to appear out of almost black-out into a dazzling flash of light. He had done one of the dress rehearsals, but due to his lack of experience, Simon and Adam felt he needed the reassurance of another rehearsal.

After a long lunch with Julian and Guy, I decided to go straight to the cathedral. By now it was almost four o'clock and my plan was to make a cup of tea and take it up to the dressing room, but before that I decided to have a quiet moment in the cathedral. I thought some of the crew might be around but in fact the place was deserted, save for a couple of people in a pew towards the front. When I moved closer, I saw that it was Lillian and Ryan and Lillian had her arm around the boy's shoulder. I walked to the end of the pew to find out what was wrong, and Lillian looked up and smiled.

Look,' she said to Ryan. 'Here's Alex.'

The boy looked up, his eyes full of tears. I edged into the pew to sit next to him.

'What's up little fella?'

'My parents were meant to take me out for lunch, but they haven't arrived and I'm afraid they're not coming.'

I looked at Lillian in alarm, hoping she knew more.

'Gemma's gone to see if anyone in the cathedral office has taken a message and not known what to do with it. Henry's with her, and I said I'd sit with Ryan until she comes back.'

I wanted to reassure the poor boy but didn't want to offer platitudes that might turn out to be misplaced. Did his parents have busy city lives that might have got in the way, I wondered? Might they think that missing this was little different to missing a sports day or an end of term nativity play? For Ryan's sake, I hoped not.

'London's a long way from Brecon,' I said. 'Perhaps they're stuck in traffic and have no way of getting a message to you.'

He sniffed and nodded but didn't look convinced. I saw Lillian glance at her watch.

'Do you need to be somewhere else?' I mouthed, over Ryan's bent head. She nodded.

'The flautist was sick all night, so we spent the morning looking for a replacement.'

'Oh dear, the curlews.'

'Indeed, but hopefully the principal flute from the CBSO is on her way. I said I'd meet her in the carpark at four o'clock and bring her in here to go through the score with Adam.'

'You go,' I said. 'I'll look after Ryan.'

'Is it okay, Ryan, if Alex looks after you for a while? I won't be far away.'

He shrugged and nodded.

'Did Ryan have any lunch?' I asked.

'Yes, Gemma made sure of that.'

'Shall we go and look for rabbits in the churchyard?' I suggested. 'I saw a couple of babies yesterday.'

'Okay,' he said, shuffling to his feet.

If his parents arrived when we were outside, we would see them.

'The rabbit holes are over there in the far corner,' I said, leading the way across the churchyard towards the boundary wall. 'If we're quiet, we might see them.'

We walked side by side in silence, and I prayed we would see something distracting. Though we waited patiently for about ten minutes, no rabbits appeared, but we did see three grey squirrels scampering across the grass ahead of us as if they were in a race. One of them scooted at high speed up a tree trunk while the other two, after a moment's indecision, disappeared into a bush.

Ryan chuckled with delight and wanted to wait to see if they would reappear.

'There,' he cried, pointing. 'Look!'

He jumped with glee having spotted them again, when behind us, I heard a woman's voice calling him and we both turned round, squirrels and rabbits forgotten.

'Mummy!' Ryan cried, hurtling towards a woman who crouched down, waiting for him to run into her outstretched arms.

I followed at a short distance and saw a man hurrying through the lychgate to join his wife and son. I introduced myself.

'I said I'd look after Ryan while his chaperone went to check if you'd been in touch with anyone at the cathedral.'

'Thank you,' they said together.

'I'm so glad we got here before the rehearsal so Ryan could stop worrying,' his mother said.

Ryan was still snuggling up against her.

'We've had a very difficult journey,' said his father. 'We set off in plenty of time but were stuck behind a lorry spillage which closed the motorway miles from the next exit where we might have been able to make a detour.'

'But you're here now,' I said. 'So, all's well—and here's Gemma. She'll look after you.'

I left them and went inside to the Vestry, where Lillian was making a cup of something.

'They're here,' I said. 'That panic's over and Gemma's looking after them now.'

'Thank goodness. I'm so relieved for Ryan. And the flautist is here, too. I'm taking her a cup of tea—she's in the cathedral with Adam. She seems very together.'

I laughed. 'Just as well—the flute has a starring role.'

'Thanks for helping me out,' she said, as she made her way to the door.

The rehearsal went well, and I sensed that the change of flautist and boy treble would add something new and different to the dynamic of the performance. As it had the night before, the seventy minutes seemed to fly by. The flute's symbolic curlew cries were poignantly lyrical, and when I sang the mother's desolate soliloquy at her son's tomb, my voice and the flute seemed to come together as one.

And as the Spirit of the Boy, Ryan was the personification of innocence. For one so young, he brought not only a radiant tone, but impressively precise diction and intonation. And in the final moments, as he sang a promise to his mother that they would meet in Heaven, he did something that neither he nor Henry had ever done in rehearsal: he opened his arms wide so that in his white, shroud-like robe, he looked like an angel. As he disappeared into the darkness, his final, ethereal *God be with you, Mother* was spine-tingling.

When it was over and the audience had gone home, the crew still had work to do. The cathedral and the dressing rooms were to be cleared and restored to their normal state and the props, clothes and lighting rig had to be packed and loaded into a waiting truck. Meanwhile almost all the singers and players made their way to the cathedral's tithe barn, where the festival promoter had laid on drinks and snacks.

I enjoyed chatting to the flautist who stayed for a quick drink before driving home to Stourbridge. Ryan's parents were there briefly, clearly proud of their son but exhausted by their taxing journey. As soon as they left to go back to their hotel, Henry and Ryan asked me to sit with them on a shabby sofa they'd requisitioned. While they tucked into a late-night feast of sandwiches and lemonade, Gemma was enjoying some social time without her two young charges in tow. She'd impressed everyone with how expertly she managed the boys. They were mainly well-behaved, but she combined the role of good-humoured big sister—she was twenty-six—with an unerring ability to judge the few times when she needed to haul them back in line.

'Whew,' Ryan said, like a seasoned old pro. 'I needed this.'

'You did very well,' I said. 'Both of you.'

'Henry set the bar very high last night,' said Ryan, shaking his head. 'I was afraid I'd mess it up.'

I laughed. 'Well, you didn't. I couldn't have done what you two did when I was your age.'

They grinned and shoved each other playfully and I thought how lucky they were to have had such a thrilling experience and I hoped it had kindled a love of performing. They chatted comfortably to me and to each other, until I could see they were beginning to flag, and Gemma decided to get them off to bed before they became over-tired. She pulled them to their feet and having wished me good night, they set off round the room saying slightly bleary goodbyes to everyone else.

Simon and Adam had been standing to one side, deep in conversation, but when they saw me stand up, they beckoned me over to join them.

'It looks as if a tour will happen next spring,' said Simon. 'I hope you'll be up for it?'

'I certainly will. I can honestly say this has been one of the highlights of my career.'

'It was obvious how invested you were in the piece and in the role,' said Adam. 'You sang it with such beauty and such aching intensity, it was very special.'

'Thank you, Adam. That means a lot.'

'You were a hit with the festival promoter, too.' He pointed to a man standing with his back to us. 'He's keen to invite you back sometime.'

'I'd be pleased to come back.'

I was tired now and tempted to leave, but the arrival of the crew gave the gathering a new lease of life, and I helped myself to another beer. Most people were hovering around a table still bearing plates of sandwiches and sausage rolls, but we stood back to allow the latecomers easy passage to the food. People moved around, joining different groups, drinking, and chatting and not for the first time, I thought what an unshakable feeling of goodwill there was amongst everyone.

After a while, Scott started moving chairs that had been stacked against a wall.

'Let's sit down, for goodness' sake,' he said, arranging the chairs into a circle. 'I'm dead on my feet.'

Some people moved away to get more drinks, but most people sat down. I found myself between Guy on one side and Lillian on the other.

'How was the get-out?' I asked.

'Pretty straightforward, thanks. Everyone mucked in so we got it done quite quickly.'

'Do you have another project to go on to?'

'Five days at home and then London for a few weeks at the South Bank as an Events Manager—they're short-staffed until someone new starts so they need an extra person short-term.'

'You seem to do a bit of everything.'

'I do. I like to have variety—it stops me getting bored. For small groups like this, I'm often Company Manager or equivalent. In larger companies—opera or theatre—I'm usually DSM on the book.'

'So, you read music, then?'

'Oh yes. I studied score reading as part of my stage management training, but I play the piano anyway, which helps.' She laughed. 'But I can't sing for toffee.'

'I've been wondering about your name. Is it Polish?'

'It is. I was married, very briefly, and my husband's grandfather was Polish. I'd changed my name before I started working professionally and I decided to keep it, even after we split up.'

She was so matter of fact about it, I didn't think any expression of sympathy was expected. She didn't ask me about my marital status, but her next question surprised me.

'What happened to your leg?'

I told her and she nodded.

'I thought you might have had polio. My mother caught it in the 1940s when she was a teenager and it affected her legs, too.'

She was drinking out of a bottle of pale ale and paused to take a swig.

'She's wearing callipers again now and sometimes has to use a stick, but she's never let anything hold her back.'

'Did she go out to work?'

'Oh yes. Before the polio, she wanted to be a pastry chef and for a long time that's what she was. She made fancy cakes for a smart hotel that served sumptuous afternoon teas, and after that, she worked in a baker's shop that made all its bread and cakes on the premises. Her speciality is lemon drizzle cake—it's delicious.'

'Do you think you and your father were affected by the disease?'

She tilted her head on one side and narrowed her eyes as she thought about her answer.

'I was aware from an early age that my mother was different to other mothers, but watching my gran and my dad deal with it, seeing how supportive they were of her, and how stoic and uncomplaining she was, I suppose I just accepted it.'

She took another slug of beer.

'What about you? Do you ever think "without all that, could I have done all this?"'

'You mean adversity builds character and resourcefulness?'

'Perhaps.'

'Having polio certainly forced me to rethink what I could do, what I might become. Without polio, I might not have discovered music.'

'And like my mother, you didn't let what happened break you.'

'No, I didn't. It worries me, though, that one day—who knows when—I may develop post-polio syndrome. It seems that past heroics count for nothing, because you don't conquer or overcome polio in any meaningful sense.'

It was the first time I'd confided to anyone, apart from Eamon, my fears I might be struck down by debilitating new pain and weakness, and Lillian's face registered concern and recognition before she rightly guessed I hoped we could change the subject.

'What's coming up next for you?'

'A mixture of Britten, Finzi and Schubert, including a few works I've never performed so far—enough work to keep the wolf at bay.'

'Have you heard about the tour next Spring?'

'I have. And you?'

'Yes, Simon says he'd like me to be involved, and the festival promoter has asked if I'd be interested in coming back here next year to look after the artists.'

We were interrupted when a member of the cathedral staff came in and said, 'We need to close up now, please, if you wouldn't mind drinking up as quickly as possible.'

'Where's home?' Lillian asked me as we crossed the bridge over the river and turned right into the town.

'Oxford. How about you?'

'I have a flat in Macclesfield. I wanted to stay close to my parents— they're not getting any younger. I'll be glad to have a few days at home checking in on them.'

She was staying in the same guesthouse as Gemma and the boys.

'Good night, everyone,' she said, as she arrived at her front door.

'Thanks for looking after us so well,' said Simon, and everyone joined in with thanks and hugs and good wishes for a safe journey home.

'It's been a pleasure,' she said. 'Hope to see you all next year.'

Onwards

A few weeks later I gave my first performance of Schubert's *Winterreise*. I'd been working on it for years, but it had taken a back seat while I concentrated on my repertoire in English song. Though *Winterreise* is generally regarded as the greatest of all song cycles, it can seem intimidating for both singer and listener: twenty-four songs to be performed without a break; seventy-minutes of singing; longer than the time taken to perform many an entire operatic role. The learning alone took months, much of it spent delving into the unravelling psyche of Schubert's protagonist. At the beginning of the cycle, we find him betrayed by the girl he loves and setting off on a journey he hopes will somehow yield personal revelations. He describes everything he's walking through—the snow and the ice, the freezing wind, the barking dogs. His despair is profound, and as the weeks drag on, he becomes ever lonelier. By the end he's in a state bordering on madness. But there are moments of beauty and tenderness, too, and in contrast to the underlying bleakness, the music has energy and passion. What I tried to convey was the stoicism of the man, his determination to face the tribulations of life with courage and defiance.

Through all the long period of learning, thoughts of Schubert were never far away. In his final year, when he knew he was dying, he wrote quickly and urgently, and from that tenacity and spirit emerged what for many people is his crowning achievement. I'd resolved not to tackle it until I was sure I could do it justice, because it's more than a collection of gloomy songs. It's a drama, too, almost a piece of theatre, and though the wanderer is a young man, it requires maturity to fully understand this introverted protagonist, and I was almost forty when I sang it for the first time.

The venue was St George's Brandon Hill, a concert hall in the heart of Bristol, converted from a two-hundred-year-old Georgian church, with crystal clear acoustics. Johnny had performed the work several times before, so I could depend on him to see me through any passages of uncertainty or weariness, when perhaps the summit of the mountain seemed a step too far. At the end, and after a silence from the audience that seemed to go on for several minutes, stunned applause gradually swelled into noisy approbation. The mountain had been safely negotiated.

I no longer avoided songs of love and loss, and over the next few months, we gave several recitals. The last one before I left for two months in America was at the London home of a well-known patron of the arts.

His large flat in Kensington was on the ground floor of a converted hotel, and in a room that had once been a ballroom, he and his wife hosted regular chamber recitals. They made the room available to companies wanting to hold fundraising soirées, and to artists keen to try out a programme they would later record or perform in a more public setting. Sometimes, they mounted their own events to raise funds for the charitable trust they'd established in memory of their son, Alistair, who had died when he was twenty-one. Alistair and Johnny had been school friends and Johnny regularly took part in such events, often pro bono. When he suggested we offer them one of our themed programmes, I was happy to agree.

They wanted something light and accessible, and we were pleased when they chose a programme that emerged as we got to know more repertoire but which we'd not yet performed. We called it *The Lark in the Clear Air* after a traditional Irish folk song I had first sung as an encore, and which once elicited a piece of feedback I have never forgotten. At the end of a concert, two elderly women waited for me at the artists' entrance and asked if I would sign their programmes. They'd both enjoyed the concert but admitted they'd approached it with contrasting expectations. One of them was a regular concertgoer; the other described herself as a classical music virgin. The connoisseur said her measure to judge if a concert had been a success was if she felt in a better place at the end than she'd been before the concert started. As she thanked me, her face was flushed with pleasure, but her friend was reluctant to speak, saying she did not have the right words to say what she felt.

'There are no "right words",' I assured her, as she handed me her programme. 'Please, just speak from your heart. I'd like to know what you thought.'

Though she still looked slightly flustered, this seemed to encourage her.

'If you were to ask me which singers I usually like to listen to, I'd say people like Frank Sinatra and Nat King Cole and Tony Bennett and ....'

'And Harry Belafonte and Perry Como and Johnny Mathis...?' I asked.

'Yes, that's right! They have this way of bending the melodies around the words. And you did that, too—especially in the last song. I loved that.'

She laughed. 'To be honest, I hadn't expected to enjoy the evening at all, but I really did.'

'Thank you. I admire those singers, too—and like you, I love the way they marry words with music so naturally and expressively.'

I handed her back her programme.

'I've written down the name of the last song so you can listen out for it.'

Johnny had heard these exchanges and we reflected on what the woman had said as we shared a pint in a nearby pub.

'You made a convert there,' he laughed. 'It makes you realise that classical song and popular song shouldn't be seen as different animals. After all, they tend to choose the same subject matter, and both aim to create a sense of intimacy and connection.'

For the concert in Kensington, I sang of skylarks and nightingales, curlews and cuckoos, blackbirds and wagtails. We saved *The Lark in the Clear Air* for the encore, relishing its enchanting melody and its serene optimism, as the sweet sound of the lark matches the poet's confidence that his love will be requited.

Afterwards, fortified by champagne and canapés, we circulated among the audience who had stayed behind for refreshments. I was introduced to a couple who owned a large country estate in Shropshire where they were planning to establish a summer opera festival. "We have exciting plans," they told me. They'd heard me perform in *The Turn of the Screw* and the Britten recital at Snape—and expressed the hope that I would one day perform in their newly converted theatre.

A few days later, I flew to the States for a tour with an American orchestra whose Music Director had a passion for English music. It was his mission to introduce lesser-known works to audiences in his homeland, and over a period of two months, from Baltimore to Philadelphia and New York to Boston, we gave performances of Britten's *Spring Symphony*, *War Requiem* and *Serenade for Tenor, Horn and Strings* as well as two works with orchestra by Finzi I had never before performed: *Dies Natalis* and *Intimations of Immortality*.

Dies Natalis is the work for which Finzi is probably remembered more than any other and I'd wanted to perform it ever since I first learnt it several years earlier. In this cantata, Finzi turned away from the world-weariness of Thomas Hardy to the wonder and rapture of a little-known seventeenth-century poet and preacher, Thomas Traherne, who died in 1674 aged thirty-seven. His work had fallen into oblivion until it was rediscovered and published in the early twentieth century. The texts Finzi chose from Traherne expressed the amazed vision of a new-born child experiencing the world for the first time and his settings brim with hopefulness and a guileless and wide-eyed enthusiasm for the world. In similar vein, his setting of Wordsworth's *Intimations of Immortality* from *Recollections of Early Childhood*, is a touching lament for the passing of childhood innocence.

Spending so much time with these two works in rehearsal and performance, made me contemplate how much we are defined by our childhood experiences. I had once been a spirited and carefree child, until an ill-timed family holiday led me to become someone different. In these works, Finzi urges the listener to hold fast at all costs to an optimistic vision of the world, whatever hardships life throws one's way.

Those months in America gave me space in which to breathe and reset. The change of scene, the chance to explore new places and experience a different culture refreshed and renewed me as much as the music did. I felt ready for life again.

And awaiting me when I arrived home was an invitation to sing Aschenbach in *Death in Venice* at the new opera festival in Shropshire.

Lillian

Nicole placed her hands on my shoulders and smiled at me in the mirror.

'So, who normally cuts your hair?' she asked.

'An elderly barber in Oxford, who doesn't always wear his glasses.'

She laughed. 'You're a long way from home then,' she said, running her fingers through my hair and smiling at me with interest. 'Are you on holiday down here?'

'No, I'm singing at the cathedral tonight.'

'So you need to look decent,' she said with a nod of understanding.

'Well actually,' I admitted, 'I wear a wig for the show, but my hair needs cutting so I thought I'd have it done while I have a few hours to spare before the rehearsal.'

Nicole was the manager of a unisex salon in the centre of Truro where I'd turned up shortly after nine o'clock, following a suggestion over breakfast from Lillian, who was going there herself later that morning.

'Let's get you shampooed then,' said Nicole, leading me into the back of the salon, where she eased my head gently over a washbasin. I closed my eyes and waited while she ran the water until it was a comfortable temperature. After she'd applied and lathered the shampoo, she began to massage my scalp, her fingers firm but not rough. It was remarkably relaxing, and by the time she was rinsing my hair, and patting it dry with a towel, I was feeling quite drowsy. Back at her cutting station, she worked confidently but carefully, checking in the mirror at regular intervals.

She chatted easily, telling me her father had helped her establish the business and asking me about myself. To my surprise I chatted back, telling her about *Curlew River* which was what had brought me to Truro. In response to one of her questions, I even told her about Emily. At that, she stopped cutting and put her hands on my shoulders, and I could tell from the look on her face that she, too, knew about loss. When she resumed her work, she told me she was newly married for the second time, her first husband having been killed in Northern Ireland. Occasionally, her hands brushed my neck or my cheek and I realised she was the first woman to touch my bare skin since Emily died. In my working life, hugs were given freely and the dressers I'd worked with, like Scott, were always extremely tactile, but they were all men. It felt different being touched by a woman, even in the innocent context of a hair salon, and it made me aware how starved I'd been of physical or sensual closeness.

When it was done and I'd paid and put on my coat ready to leave, Nicole leaned forward and gave me a light peck on the cheek. 'It was nice to meet you,' she said. 'Good luck tonight.'

I closed the door behind me but looked back at her through the glass. I held her gaze and she waved and I knew I would remember this brief encounter as a gift of kindness and connection.

I was enjoying the novelty of being part of a travelling company who would be on the road together for several weeks. The producer had been able to reassemble most of the original cast, and we'd picked up where we left off a year ago in Brecon, quickly assimilating a couple of newcomers who replaced two of the monks. There was a new Assistant Stage Manager as well, and she, Lillian and Gemma, plus three members of the ensemble, were the only women in a company of almost thirty, an unusual imbalance—but then *Curlew River* is itself unusual.

As is Truro Cathedral, the second venue on the tour. Only just over eighty years old, it was designed and built during the reign of Queen Victoria in an ambitious attempt to emulate the great builders of the medieval era. The Victorians managed to create an extravaganza of Gothic Revival architecture, with rose windows, flying buttresses and soaring arches. From a distance, its three tall spires are a prominent feature of the skyline and inside, the immense height of the building creates a sense of awe made all the more wondrous by the light streaming through the stained-glass windows.

When I arrived, the far end of the cathedral was a hive of activity as the crew worked at speed to get everything ready for the run-through at two o'clock.

'What happened to your hair, Alex?' quipped Bill, the electrician, as he and the Production Manager moved a tallescope from one side of the nave to the other.

'Don't take any notice of him, Alex,' said Lillian, who was walking behind them carrying a pile of ensemble parts. 'It looks very smart.'

'Thank you,' I said to her, while pulling a face at Bill.

'How was it?' she asked.

'Absolutely fine. Thanks for the suggestion.'

She nodded. 'I'd better get on—nothing is straightforward in these cathedrals, so everything takes longer than it should. I'm glad I booked my hair appointment for the lunch break!'

I sat for a while in the choir stalls, marvelling at the ornate high altar and the brightly coloured mosaic floor. I was struck by how challenging these buildings must be for lighting and technical crews, often having to work at great heights—hence the tallescope—and striving to achieve theatrical effects in a place of worship. Lillian had her own specific tasks to undertake, but she kept a watchful eye on how others were getting on and was always ready to help if needed. She had a practical intelligence that made her ideally suited for a job demanding an ability to problem solve under pressure.

I'd driven down the night before, not wanting to risk the long journey on the day of the performance. We were responsible for our own travel arrangements, but unless we told her we were making other plans, Lillian booked accommodation for everyone, the costs of which were borne by the producer as a way of boosting our modest fees. After the first performance at Southwark, when most people went home or to friends, we all stayed in the same hotels, and because Lillian could negotiate favourable party rates, we would normally end up staying in better accommodation than we could have afforded if we were booking for ourselves. The aim was to treat us all as equals and to engender a camaraderie and *esprit de corps*. And for those of us staying at least one night in most towns, it was obvious we would become close, sharing tables at breakfast, and relaxing together in any down time, especially after performances.

In Truro we stayed at the Alverton, a grand building—now slightly faded in places—which until a few years earlier had housed an order of nuns. The hotel barman agreed to stay open for as long as we wanted him to, which meant the crew could look forward to a drink after they'd finished the get-out. When they arrived an hour or so after the rest of us, we pushed tables together so we could sit in one large extended group and we made a good-humoured, if slightly rowdy, gathering.

Lillian stood at the bar chatting to Bill, and as I watched her, I thought how changed she was by her new hair style, which had provoked many approving comments. Her hair was still long, but to Lillian's dismay, Nicole had given her a fringe. As a result, her blue eyes seemed to have much more definition and were now an arresting feature in her small, pale face. She was clearly self-conscious about all the attention and was dismissive of the compliments, vowing she would get rid of the fringe as soon as she could.

'Cheers,' we said to each other, clinking glasses, after she sat down next to me.

'Interesting hotel,' I said.

'It is. It's the only one reasonably close to the cathedral that was able to accommodate us all.'

She was tucking into a packet of crisps and offered me one.

'Did Nicole tell you that she met her new husband here?'

'Really?'

'It was at a Christmas dinner organised by the Chamber of Commerce—he's a solicitor.'

"I liked her very much. She was easy to talk to. My usual barber in Oxford doesn't do much more than grunt, but Nicole was the sort of hairdresser I'm sure her clients confide in.'

Lillian laughed. 'Hairdressers are dangerous. They'd make good private detectives—I spent an hour with her and she could probably tell you the story of my life!'

'And what would she tell me?' I asked, emboldened by several beers.

'Well, we seemed to spend most of the time talking about husbands and marriage.'

'Ah,' I said, wondering what to say next. In the end I asked her how long she'd been married.

'Only three years.'

'What happened?'

'Stefan was more complicated than I realised.'

'In what way, more complicated?'

She sighed. 'He had a special childhood girlfriend, but they split up before he and I met, and I assumed they'd lost touch. After we'd been married for a couple of years, she wrote to tell him she'd married a man she met on holiday. After that, his whole world seemed to fall apart. Like he was broken.' She frowned and shook her head. 'From then on, he just opted out of our marriage.'

'That must have been awful for you.'

'It was brutal. I had no idea she still meant so much to him. I've asked myself if there were clues I missed—or chose to disregard.' She sighed before taking a long slug of beer. 'It seems so long ago now. I was married at twenty and divorced at twenty-three. Since then, I've had to make another sort of life.'

'Where is he now, do you know?'

'I've no idea. For a time, about twelve years ago, he was living on a croft in Shetland. Perhaps he's still there. He'd been a budding lighting designer, but he gave it all up. It was as if hearing about her new life made him rethink all the decisions he'd made about his own.'

I shook my head, thinking how confusing and crushing that must have been for her.

'It made me feel I was not enough, that I could never be enough,' she said, tapping the side of her glass. She laughed, but it sounded hollow and hard-edged. 'It changed my attitude to love, that's for sure.'

'What do you mean?'

She shrugged. 'I don't trust it. How could I?'

The silence between us was long and awkward.

'I know you lost your wife,' she said at last. 'I'm sorry.'

'It's five years since she died, but sometimes, it still feels like yesterday.'

Gales of laughter from people sitting near us suggested someone was telling a long, rambling story. I looked around bemused, but because we'd missed the beginning of the saga, I took the opportunity to change the subject and asked Lillian what she'd be doing between performances, when typically, there was a break of three or four days.

'I'll go home when I can, or head to London. I can stay with a friend I was at the Guildhall with. How about you?'

'I'll go back to Oxford.'

'Do you have any other gigs to fit in during the tour?'

'No, I told my agent I wanted to focus on this for the duration. And on the days off, I need to get on with learning Aschenbach for next spring.'

'Is that for the new festival at Stonehurst?'

'That's right. How do you know about it?'

'They've advertised for crew, and I've applied to be DSM on the book.'

'If you got the job, you wouldn't be that far from home, would you?'

'A couple of hours or so, I think. Close enough to get to see my parents on days off.'

She offered me the last of the crisps.

'Are your parents still alive?'

'Alive and well, I'm pleased to say. They live in Cairo—they have a good life there. My father works at the British embassy and my mum for Thomas Cook.'

'Do you get to see them?'

'I do, not as often as I'd like, but they're coming over later this year to hear me sing *Winterreise* at the Wigmore.'

'I'd love to hear that. You must give me the date.'

I'd wondered what audiences we'd attract for a niche work like *Curlew River*, especially somewhere like Truro with a relatively small population outside high season, but I need not have worried. The advance publicity made generous use of the excellent reviews we'd received in Brecon and at

Southwark at the start of the tour, and even in Truro, people came to see us.

The performance in Southwark was particularly thrilling, partly because the cathedral was packed with an audience avid to hear the work, but also because most of us had friends or family there. Josh and Hilary, with whom I'd stayed for the three days of re-rehearsal, came along, as did Johnny and Luke, and Freddie and Christina came down from Oxford together, the first time she had ever seen me perform.

'You're playing a mad woman?' she'd said with disbelief when I first told her about the project. 'Now that I have to see!'

All of them came for a drink afterwards and Christina was unashamedly overcome by the experience, it being completely new to her.

'When it ended,' she said to everyone at the table, 'I wanted to see it all over again. It was so powerful.'

I was thrilled by her reaction, as I was to see Freddie and Josh reconnecting after so many years. While they caught up with each other, Hilary and Christina talked about vintage clothes; Johnny and Adam had animated conversation about Britten's instrumental writing; and Luke and I talked about West Ham.

'You're going down,' he said gloomily. 'You haven't won in the league since the beginning of February.'

'I know,' I said, equally gloomily. 'Let's hope they bounce straight back up.'

It was late when we left and when Josh and I said our goodnights, he hugged me and whispered, 'It's nights like these that help you keep going.'

I was grateful for the days off between performances because I found life on the road tiring. The producer had been able to raise funds from the Arts Council on the basis that the tour would cover as wide a geographic spread as possible. So, having opened in Southwark and gone next to Truro, we performed at the cathedrals in Wells, Worcester, Lincoln and York, with the tour ending in the church in Suffolk where *Curlew River* was first seen in 1964. Every venue was different and presented its own unique challenges, technically and acoustically, but we were well rehearsed, and the crew were highly skilled and endlessly resourceful.

As the final performances approached, I realised how much I would miss everyone when it was over, and we went our separate ways. We were giving two performances at Orford Church and staying a short distance away in Aldeburgh. It proved the perfect ending and the three nights and two days we spent there were idyllic. I felt as if we were simply on holiday at the seaside—joining long but good-humoured queues for fish and chips; watching Bruce and Leo race along the beach with Henry and Ryan on their backs; late night drinks in the Cross Keys pub mitigated by huge breakfasts at the White Lion Hotel the morning after; and a private visit to the Red House. After the final performance, there was a gathering at the hotel. Gemma had allowed the boys to stay up later than usual, and they were still enjoying themselves when the crew turned up almost two hours after the rest of us arrived.

'There were times tonight,' said Adam, 'when I caught myself thinking that almost three decades ago, Britten had sat in those very pews watching his work for the first time.'

'Perhaps he was up there watching us tonight,' said Leo.

'Well, at one point I thought I heard the ghost of Peter Pears wailing in the choir stalls,' said Guy.

'No, no,' said Bruce. 'That would have been Alex!'

'Very funny,' I said, but I laughed, nevertheless.

'What's funny?' asked Ryan, coming to stand next to me.

'As usual, Bruce is taking the mickey.'

'You know I love you really,' Bruce said, putting his arm round me and pulling me into a hearty bear hug.

'Is he giving you trouble?' Scott called from the other end of the bar. I laughed and moved round to join him.

'Let me get you that,' I said, 'to say thank you for looking after me.'

We chatted for a while before he suggested we go and sit with the rest of the crew. They were tired and slightly bedraggled, but relieved that all had gone well for the final get-out. Lillian swapped seats with Bill and came to sit next to me. During the afternoon she'd asked for my address and phone number and given me hers.

'Let's keep in touch and do let me know the date of your Wigmore. If I'm in London with a night off, I'll come.'

I looked at her as she reached across the table to grab a couple of sandwiches and I thought how pretty she looked with colour in her cheeks and with the tension of the day all gone.

'Are you doing the Brecon Festival again next year?' I asked.

'I am. Why? Will you be there?'

'It looks like it. My agent is having discussions about two possible concerts—a solo recital and a performance of *Serenade to Music*.'

Henry and Ryan came to say goodnight and as more and more

goodbyes were said, I wondered if any of our paths would cross again. I decided it was time to go to bed and went over to bid *au revoir* to the other singers and then came back to the crew table to do the same. Scott stood up and gave me a hug.

'It's been a pleasure,' he said.

Lillian had been bought another beer but she, too, stood up and we embraced. As we eased away from each other, I looked into her eyes. Was it my imagination or was that hope I saw there? To hide my consternation and uncertainty, I pulled her close so that her face was buried below my shoulder. I kissed her cheek and when we moved apart, she was smiling.

Hephzibah

A few months later, when we were meeting in his office to go through my schedule, Dominic told me there'd been some upheaval in the creative team for *Death in Venice*.

'Adam is still down to conduct, but the festival founders sacked Simon McCabe and his designer because they disliked their concept. Too minimalist or something. Not enough trappings. They've brought in a director, designer and choreographer whose production of *Eugene Onegin* they admired in Aix-en-Provence.'

He was frowning and I could tell he feared this would not be a straightforward engagement.

'I heard about that *Onegin*,' he said. 'By all accounts, it was extremely lavish, but I gather it was not a happy show.'

'In what way?'

'I don't know. I've not been able to get to the bottom of it.'

He was still frowning.

'What is it?' I asked.

'I just sense these people at Stonehurst are amateurs. As they say, "a little learning" …'

If he was right, I wondered how that would play out in practice.

'The other thing I've heard is that they've cast a woman in the role of Tadzio.'

'Is she a dancer?'

'Yes, her name's Romy Tyler.'

'I suppose it might work…'

By the look he gave me, it was obvious that Dominic was sceptical.

'Don't forget, Tadzio is a teenage boy who Aschenbach becomes utterly infatuated with, so unless Romy Tyler can look suitably youthful and androgynous, it could put a rather different slant on the story.'

'Fair point. It's intriguing, though.'

'You think?' said Dominic, not sounding at all convinced. 'She's on tour at the moment playing Eppie in a production of *Silas Marner*. I might try to catch it.'

'I've seen posters for that somewhere,' I said, and later, as I made my way via the underground to Paddington, I spotted them. The London season was some weeks off, but the poster listed the venues at which the show was playing before then, and one of them was the Apollo in Oxford. I could see it there.

I'd read the book at university and loved it. I remember my tutor explaining why Silas gave the child the Biblical name Hephzibah, or Eppie for short, meaning "my delight is in her". He said her purpose in the story was to be a catalyst to transform Silas's life in a way that his precious gold coins could not. I was touched by the idea of a child bringing a lonely man out of isolation and spiritual desolation, giving him hope of future happiness.

In the ballet, two different dancers played Eppie. The first was tiny and brilliantly conveyed the young child, capturing her toddling gait as she wandered into Silas's cottage, instantly and unmistakably curious and good-natured, and soon completely devoted to her new father. Romy Tyler played the older Eppie and from the moment she appeared, I was transfixed—by her abundant, curly auburn hair glowing in the stage lighting, by the tenderness with which she showed her love and devotion to Silas and by the strength of character she displayed as a young girl growing into womanhood.

Afterwards, I walked round to the stage door, unsure whether to go backstage to say hello to her. My old shyness kicked in, and at the very moment I decided against it, a group of dancers emerged and made their way towards George Street. Romy was in the midst of them, laughing at something one of the others had said. She looked so cool and self-assured, I felt strangely overawed, and I turned away in the direction of Gloucester Green and headed home.

Lillian and I kept in touch sporadically—we sent each other occasional postcards and she rang me from time to time. She couldn't come to *Winterreise* at the Wigmore Hall in November, but she came to hear us perform it a few months earlier in the concert hall at the RNCM in Manchester. Afterwards, we had a drink in the bar. She'd grown out her fringe and was wearing her hair with a centre parting and a ponytail, but otherwise, she was unchanged. I was pleased to see her but uncomfortably aware that Johnny was observing us closely, no doubt wondering if there was anything going on between us.

'By the way,' she said, 'I got the job at Stonehurst. They rang me today to make the offer.'

Later, we walked with her to her car before continuing on foot to our hotel.

'She likes you,' said Johnny with a chuckle. 'She likes you a lot. The question is—do you like her as much?'

I didn't know. I still found it hard to believe I would ever be able to commit to more than friendship with anyone; to allow myself to fall in love again and risk all that that entails. Might I simply need longer before I was ready to love again? Might Lillian be the 'right' person at the wrong time? I didn't know that, either.

In Search of Aschenbach

When in later years I looked back on the events of 1993, that line in Shakespeare's *All's Well That Ends Well* seemed particularly apt: "The web of our life is of a mingled yarn, good and ill together."

A few days into the new year, I was lying on the sofa, re-reading *Death in Venice* when the phone rang.

'Happy New Year,' said Adam, sounding far from his usual upbeat self.

'How are you?' I asked, sensing all was not well. 'Is everything alright?'

He sighed and there was a long pause. 'I felt I should call you myself to tell you what's happened.'

I swung my legs onto the ground and sat upright, wondering what was coming.

'I've been agonising about this decision all over Christmas, and it's not been easy, but I've decided to withdraw from *Death in Venice.*'

'Are you ill?' I asked with concern.

'No. Not ill.'

'So, what's happened?' I asked, wondering what on earth it could be, but remembering Dominic's disquiet about the project.

'Do you know Douglas Drake, the designer?'

'No, I don't.'

'He and I got off to a bad start at the model showing in the autumn and when we worked together on another show in December, it was clear to me that I couldn't contemplate working with him again.'

I was a novice at opera, but I knew that in the operatic hierarchy, conductors were often treated as semi-gods so it surprised me that a designer could have such a negative impact on a conductor that he would resign from a project. I knew Adam to be a man of honour and I guessed that his decision must be a matter of principle and more profound than simply a clash of personalities.

'I'm very disappointed,' he said. 'It's an opera I've longed to conduct and I know you will make the perfect Aschenbach.'

'I'm disappointed, too,' I said, 'but I've no doubt you must have had very serious misgivings to have come to this decision.'

We talked a little more and after making myself a coffee, I rang Dominic.

'So, what do you know?' I asked.

'Some time back, Adam told his agent he had reservations about the creative team. Apparently, at the model showing, Adam questioned some aspects of the design—something to do with sight-lines—and Douglas Drake bit his head off and belittled him in front of everyone. Then in December, Adam was asked to step in at short notice on a new production of *Billy Budd*. The original conductor had been taken ill and Adam arrived just as rehearsals moved into the theatre. He said it was obvious that everyone was fraught—not just because of the change of conductor—though that can't have helped—but because the designer, Douglas, had been a pain from the word go. The crew were exhausted and disaffected—the original props supervisor had walked out—and the singers were stressed and demoralised. They were working on a steep rake, which was very tiring, and one or two of them complained about persistent back ache. When Drake started interfering during Adam's rehearsals, Adam spoke to him privately with no success, so complained to the management about what he judged to be unreasonable behaviour, but no-one would stand up to Drake.'

'He sounds like a bully. Oh dear...'

For several months before this, I'd been immersed in studying the score and the text, the role of Aschenbach being by far the most substantial I had ever undertaken. I learnt that Thomas Mann took his family to Venice in 1911, and like Aschenbach, he too, was feeling creatively blocked. I was intrigued to discover that almost all the events he described in the novella actually happened to Mann himself: the encounter with a mysterious traveller in a Munich graveyard that inspired his journey to Venice; the sighting of an elderly fop on board the ship that took him there; the truculent gondolier who took him over the water from Venice to the Grand Hotel des Bains on the Lido; the appearance of a fascinating Polish boy with whom he became obsessed; and the advent of the last European outbreak of cholera.

Dirk Bogarde's performance in the Visconti film sent me to the volumes of his autobiography in which he recalled the gruelling process by which he assumed the character of Aschenbach. For the five months of filming, he lived an isolated and solitary existence, seldom socialising with his colleagues, and eating little so that his crumpled suit hung off his shrunken frame. One image stayed with me: "Daily, I sat alone on the Lido beach in my little cabana, aloof and distant, as silent and yearning as von Aschenbach himself... My main objective was to remain in total, exhausting concentration at all times and under all circumstances in order to contain this spirit which was so alien to myself. It was a fragile thing; I was constantly terrified that he would at one moment or another slip away from me."

In Britten's treatment of the book, Aschenbach is rarely offstage, and the opera is essentially a monologue, punctuated by conversations with a variety of characters in and around the hotel. The roles of Tadzio, his family and his friends are played by a mix of dancers and actors and though they never speak, they represent life and vitality and the conflict of age surrounded by youth and beauty.

Freddie had seen the original production and proved an excellent sounding board. We would sit on opposite sides of the desk in his teaching room in Park Town, each of us with a copy of the full score open in front of us, and a piano on hand if we wanted to work on a section.

'I must say, I think *Death in Venice* is a daring venture for a new opera festival,' he said. 'Even now, twenty years on from its premiere, I wouldn't expect to find it on the country house opera circuit.'

I nodded in agreement.

'I admire the piece,' he went on, 'but it has considerable longueurs. Seventeen continuous scenes divided into two lengthy acts—it's not an easy prospect and they may struggle to get an audience.'

'I think the founders want to launch the festival with something that's bound to attract interest and attention, exactly because it isn't the normal fare of country house opera companies.'

'I'm sure it will do that, but it won't be cheap. All those small roles—it needs a large cast.'

'I don't think money's a problem. Word is, they've already spent millions creating rehearsal rooms and a theatre out of buildings on the estate.'

'So, where are you in your thinking about the piece and the role?' he asked.

I felt like a student again, being asked to analyse a novel I had only skim-read, but on this, I had done my homework.

'Aschenbach is a tricky character,' I said at last. 'The key theme I think Britten took from Mann's novella is the helplessness of intellect in the face of exceptional, untouchable beauty. The piece simmers with all Aschenbach's struggles—emotional conflict, artistic torment, philosophical despair, the lot. Some people say that Aschenbach was the anti-hero Britten most identified with, but he may be the hardest with whom to connect.'

'I agree,' said Freddie. 'It's hard to worry overly much about someone suffering from just writer's block. You somehow have to take the audience right into his troubled heart and make us care about the fate of a man who's flawed and self-obsessed. Thomas Mann's Aschenbach was a harrowed, spent figure with a dead wife and a grown-up daughter who'd already left home to get married. Perhaps in some way the production will explicitly link the loss of Aschenbach's creative spark with the death of his wife.'

'Maybe.'

'In fact, using the death of his wife could be a way of arousing the audience's sympathies right from the start—something for you to discuss with the director.'

I made a note and hoped the director and I would develop the sort of relationship where I could volunteer ideas like that, confident he would at least listen to them.

'Many of the scenes,' Freddie said, 'are just Aschenbach and the audience. The opera begins without an overture and we're hurtled immediately into the mind of the writer as he meditates on his artistic fatigue. He questions his beliefs and moral certainties in bare recitative, with just piano and a few percussion instruments underneath. There needs to be an intimacy about these monologues, and rather than them seeming tedious, they need to convey the confusion and anguish of the man so that his ultimate disintegration is believable.'

We worked hard on these monologues, trying to achieve a variety of sounds and colours in order to capture the man's fluctuating moods and emotions. When we stopped for coffee or lunch, we chatted generally about the piece.

'The opera has a magical transcendental ending,' I said, 'whereas the novella comes to a very matter of fact close: *And before nightfall, a shocked and respectful world received the news of his decease.*'

'An example of what music can conjure that words alone cannot.'

'Did I tell you that they've cast Tadzio with a young woman?'

Freddie looked astounded.

'Why would they do that?' he gasped. 'That seems utterly perverse. To my mind, this is an opera that stands or falls on the casting of the beauteous vision who is Tadzio. Whether the production plays down the sexuality or embraces the homoeroticism full on, you preclude either of these approaches by casting the object of Aschenbach's infatuation as a woman.'

'I've tried to fathom the reason, too. I saw the dancer play Eppie in *Silas Marner* and I can see why the choreographer of *Death in Venice* might specifically want to work with her. She has a captivating stage presence, but

I wonder how such dazzling charisma will translate into the enigmatic persona of Tadzio—a pre-pubescent boy, inaccessible and unattainable.'

'Unless she can convince as a boy,' said Freddie, 'I think it will take away something important from a work that should feel ambiguous and unsettling.'

Those Eyes

In late March 1993, a few weeks before we began rehearsals for *Death in Venice,* I was performing on two consecutive nights at the Brecon Festival. I was due to meet Johnny at the cathedral at two o'clock, but I was early and had plenty of time to enjoy the bright spring sunshine. I bought a sandwich and on my way to the cathedral I lingered on the bridge over the river and stood gazing down at the fast-flowing water. When I walked up the hill and turned into the cathedral grounds I was struck by the tranquillity of the place.

Once inside the building, I headed for the Clergy Vestry and found Lillian there replenishing the tea and coffee supplies. Her face lit up when she saw me, and her smile gave my spirits a lift. We hugged and as she pulled away, she asked, 'How are you? In good voice?'

'I'm fine, thanks. How's it going here?'

'Very well. We had a lovely concert last night—the Brahms *Requiem* in the version with two pianos—and the first night concert was a huge success—an early music consort with countertenor and soprano soloists.'

'How's tonight looking?' I asked, flicking a switch on the kettle and preparing to make a cup of tea.

'Very healthy. Tomorrow's already sold out so it's possible that some people who can't get tickets for that will book for tonight instead.'

'Tea? Coffee?' I offered, but she shook her head.

'No thanks.'

'It's so unseasonably warm I thought I'd take this outside. Do you have time to join me?'

'Of course,' she said, grabbing her jacket from a peg on the wall.

We made our way down the corridor and back into the cathedral, before exiting through the main door that led into the churchyard.

'Do you think the Dean would mind if we perched on a tombstone over there in the sunshine?' I asked.

'Let's go for it,' she said, leading the way.

'This weather is amazing,' I said as we settled ourselves on the widest and flattest tombstone on which I could safely rest my mug of tea. 'I remember how bitterly cold it was when we were here for *Curlew River.* This is a very pleasant surprise.'

I closed my eyes and lifted my face to the sun.

'So,' I said. 'Tell me your news, while I drink my tea and eat this sandwich.'

She sighed.

'I've not much news about myself, but my dad's not well.'

I could see she was concerned.

'I'm sorry to hear that.'

'He had a stroke a few weeks ago and the doctors assured us there would be no lasting damage, but he seems slow to recover his energy and strength.'

'How's your mum coping?'

'She's remarkable. Dad's always seen himself as her rock, her protector, but now he's having to depend on her.'

'That can't be easy for him, or you.'

'It's upsetting to see him look so unlike his usual self—so wobbly and frail.'

I heard a catch in her voice and she bit her lower lip. I'd never before seen her lose her composure and I reached over to put my arm around her shoulder.

'When will you get home again?' I asked.

'In a couple of days when I leave here, so I'll see them then, but if Dad doesn't pick up soon, I'm worried about how they'll cope when I'm away for *Death in Venice*.'

'Hopefully, he'll be on the mend by then,' I said, squeezing her shoulder before I took my arm away.

'Thanks, Alex. How about you—how's life?'

'Okay, though the shine has been taken off the prospect of *Death in Venice* by Adam's withdrawal.'

'Why's he pulled out?'

'He had a bad experience with the designer and decided he couldn't face working with him again.'

She looked surprised.

'Who's taken over?'

'Someone called Rhodri Pearce.'

'I don't know him. Do you?'

I shook my head.

'I'm intrigued by your programme for tonight,' she said, changing the subject. 'How did you put it together?'

'It was a joint effort between us—with some input from my father-in-law, Freddie.'

'It must take a huge amount of research to curate a programme like that.'

'It does,' I laughed. 'And a fair bit of discussion and debate, too! Hopefully, we've achieved a range of moods, so not all the songs are gloom and doom.'

'It's a lovely title—*The Passing Preciousness of Dreams*. Where does that come from?'

'It's a line from a song by Gerald Finzi to a poem by Thomas Hardy called *A Young Man's Exhortation*.'

I sang the line.

If I have seen one thing, It is the passing preciousness of dreams

'That's very poignant,' she said, looking into my eyes.

'You'll hear the complete song tonight,' I said, holding her gaze.

A voice calling us made us both jump.

'*Talley-ho!*' sang Johnny, making his way through the grass towards us.

I stood up and we hugged, before Johnny turned to Lillian to say hello.

'So you've got an easy day today, Lillian. Just me and Alex to look after and we're very well-behaved.'

She laughed.

'Will you be able to sit in tonight?' I asked her.

'That's the plan. Once we've settled all the late-comers, I'll squeeze in somewhere.'

Lillian's knowledge of the song repertoire was limited, so she was glad that the lyrics were reproduced in full in the festival programme, accompanied by notes that Johnny had written. She hoped her ignorance would not spoil her enjoyment, though her real interest was in hearing Alex perform the music for which he was becoming increasingly acclaimed. *Winterreise* had been her first experience of this repertoire, but not even reading the English translation of the German words beforehand had fully prepared her for so intense an encounter with existential misery. Seeing and hearing Alex convey a man's mental disintegration in merciless detail had unnerved her. As his lonely wanderer made his way through the harsh winter landscape, she felt that what was being revealed was the inherent loneliness of the human condition. In the final song—*The Hurdy Gurdy Man*—when the wanderer meets a beggar man standing barefoot on the ice, grinding away with numbed fingers, the dogs snarling at him, his little plate always empty—the despair and desolation seemed doubly magnified.

In stark contrast to that bleak finale, this recital began with a cheerful song by Thomas Campion—*There is a garden in her face*—in which the poet compliments the woman he loves in extravagant terms. The cathedral was almost full, but Lillian had spotted an empty seat near the front into which she was able to slip just as Alex and Johnny were about to begin.

'Good evening, ladies and gentlemen,' said Alex. 'It's good to have so many of you with us tonight to share this programme of some of our favourite songs. Songs that consider themes of love, loss, and longing—and others that suggest joy and delight and contentment. Many of these songs are gay and light-hearted like the one by Thomas Campion you've just heard. Others are deeply introspective, and some are painfully sad, but though such music can make us feel sorrow more intensely, at the same time this music has the power to bring solace and healing.'

Lillian noticed people nodding as if already in agreement with him.

'Campion was a contemporary of our next wordsmith, William Shakespeare,' Alex went on. 'The next group of songs, *Let Us Garlands Bring*, are five settings by Gerald Finzi of song lyrics from four different Shakespeare plays, all dealing with love and the passage of time.'

The music was unfamiliar, but Lillian enjoyed the way the songs moved from grief to acceptance to end in high spirits, and she marvelled at how naturally Alex captured fluctuating moods and feelings. His voice was key to this, of course, but it was as much through his soft, expressive eyes that he conveyed the rapture of love and the bleakness of despair.

He was a long way from the barnstorming operatic tenor voices she was more accustomed to and though those voices could be viscerally thrilling, she was captivated by his ability to inhabit character and emotion so sincerely and intimately. His diction was beautifully clear and unaffected, and he had a particular way of tilting his head and adjusting how he held his body that she found very touching.

Johnny introduced the next song saying it was a setting by George Butterworth of a poem by Oscar Wilde. He said it was one of the very few songs that Butterworth did not destroy when he signed up in 1914 for the war in which he would lose his life.

'Thankfully,' Johnny said, 'he preserved his unsurpassed settings of Housman's *A Shropshire Lad*, but he kept only three other songs and this setting, *Requiescat*, was written by Oscar Wilde in memory of his sister who died just before her tenth birthday.'

It was a melancholy little song and Alex's performance was hushed and tender—perfect for an epitaph to a beloved sister. The final song of the first half—*Silent Noon* by Vaughan Williams—was serene and romantic whereas the second half began in an altogether different vein with a mournful song by Elgar called *Pleading*, which the programme note explained he had written when he was feeling particularly depressed. He chose the poem by Arthur Salmon because it fitted his dejected mood at that time.

Will you come homeward from the hills of Dreamland,
Home in the dusk, and speak to me again?
Tell me the stories that I am forgetting,
Quicken my hopes, and recompense my pain?
Will you come homeward from the hills of Dreamland?
I have grown weary, though I wait for you yet;
Watching the fallen leaf, the faith grown fainter,
The memory smoulder'd to a dull regret.
Shall the remembrance die in dim forgetting–
All the fond light that glorified my way?
Will you come homeward from the hills of Dreamland,
Home in the dusk, and turn my night to day?

Alex's pure and plangent tone conveyed a powerful sense of loneliness and Lillian felt it stir something inside her that she normally kept at bay, and for much of the concert her mind drifted to thoughts about her own life and experience. Despite her busy schedule, she was sometimes lonely. Following the abrupt ending of her marriage, she took up a life of touring and temping. For the most part, she enjoyed it, but she sometimes felt isolated in a world where relationships were often short-lived and superficial. In low moments, she longed for a more settled existence, for more grounded and authentic friendships. Sometimes she wondered about the different paths she might have taken, but then she told herself, "I'm thirty-seven now and I'm good at what I do and this is the life I know".

When she heard Alex talking about Thomas Hardy, one of her favourite writers, she snapped out of her musings.

'These quiet and reflective songs by Finzi continue the theme of transient happiness, the last fleeting moments of youth and innocence.'

In the first song, *A Young Man's Exhortation*, Lillian listened out for the words "the passing preciousness of dreams" and they came in the final stanza in a melodic phrase that Alex sang with telling wistfulness. Before the second song, *The Sigh*, Lillian glanced down at the programme note, just readable in the half light. "The speaker is recalling the life he had with his beloved wife but can't stop wondering why she sighed when he kissed her for the first time. What was troubling her? What sadness was she concealing? They married and loved each other well, yet she never confessed why she sighed. The mood of the song is contemplative, almost at peace, yet a little hesitant, a little regretful. Does Hardy want the reader to wonder whether or not one can ever truly know another's heart completely?"

Alex's performance of the song matched its mood—delicate and pained, yet loving and compassionate—and for the rest of the concert Lillian's thoughts were about him and his experience of love and marriage. He seemed to be in that shifting, changing place of grief—able to get on with life, to laugh and have fun and even find joy along the way, but not ready to loosen the ties that still bound him to a past love. Would he ever love again? Did he believe that he might meet another woman who was the 'right fit' for him?

She sighed, not knowing the answer. Still brooding about lost or unrequited love, the next songs—*When I am dead my dearest* by John Ireland to a poem by Christina Rossetti and *Waly, Waly* by Benjamin Britten—seemed sadder and more sombre than anything that had gone before. When the Britten was over, Alex stepped forward again.

'After that sad lamentation of broken love,' he said with a rueful smile, 'our next song is in more hopeful vein. Though Yeats's poem for *The Cloths of Heaven* is poignant and has a beautifully symbolic ending, the lighter spirit of the composer Thomas Dunhill shines out in his delicate setting.'

Had I the heavens' embroidered cloths
Enwrought with golden and silver light
The blue and the dim and the dark cloths
Of night and light and the half-light,
I would spread the cloths under your feet:
But I, being poor, have only my dreams;
I have spread my dreams under your feet;
Tread softly because you tread on my dreams.

Lillian closed her eyes, thinking how carelessly her ex-husband had trodden on her dreams. She had moved on from *him* and had accepted that they were not right for each other, but she'd never again allowed anyone else to get close enough to hurt her. Perhaps that's why her attraction to Alex felt so disconcerting.

After the final chords of the long playout, there was a hushed silence before the audience broke into enthusiastic applause and this time, Johnny stepped forward.

'Our final song,' he said with a wide smile, 'should send you away with a skip in your step and a light heart. It's *Love's Philosophy*, a very popular setting by Roger Quilter of one of Shelley's most romantic poems. In essence it's a poem of seduction. It's a manifesto for 'free love' and says that no-one should stay single. One critic summed it up beautifully: "As chat-up lines go, it's better than most."'

People around her were smiling and Lillian saw that Alex, too, had enjoyed his friend's introduction to what was a joyous song, which they performed joyfully. At the end, Johnny left the piano and he and Alex joined hands and bowed. The man sitting next to Lillian turned to his companion and said, 'that was simply wonderful.'

Yes, thought Lillian. The applause continued until Johnny raised his hand to indicate he had something to say.

'Thank you so much.'

He waited while cries of "encore" rang out around the cathedral. 'Okay,' he said with a laugh, 'we'll leave you with two more offerings: a folk song in French arranged by Benjamin Britten called *La Belle Est Au Jardin D'amour* in which a young girl confides her secrets to a dove; and a well-known traditional song, *The Lark in the Clear Air*. If any of you are familiar with the actual song of the skylark, you'll know that it consists of rapturous outpourings sometimes lasting unbroken for several minutes. This song is similarly rapturous.'

Lillian didn't understand the French words but the way the song moved between an air of contentment to something more sorrowful gave it a bittersweet quality, whereas the final song was unequivocally optimistic.

Dear thoughts are in my mind and my soul it soars enchanted,
As I hear the sweet lark sing in the clear air of the day,
For a tender beaming smile to my hope has been granted,
And tomorrow she shall hear all my fond heart longs to say.
I will tell her all my love, all my soul's pure adoration,
And I know she will hear my voice and she will not answer me nay,
It is this that gives my soul all its joyous elation,
As I hear the sweet lark sing in the clear air of the day.

It brought the concert to a perfect conclusion and as Alex and Johnny made their way out of the cathedral, a woman sitting in front of Lillian turned to her companion and whispered, 'Those eyes! He lets us see into his soul through those eyes.'

Later, in a nearby pub, the couple who'd been sitting next to Lillian approached them and asked Alex and Johnny to autograph their programme.

'We're coming tomorrow as well,' the man said, 'but I doubt it will surpass the pleasure you've given us tonight.'

'Thank you,' said Alex. 'That's very kind.'

'My wife's a singing teacher,' the man said, 'so she knows a thing or two.' The woman blushed.

'As a matter of interest,' she said, 'do you ever give masterclasses?'

'I haven't so far,' Alex replied, 'but it's something I've thought about.'

'My students could learn so much from you,' she said with a laugh. 'It's a miracle how you're able to contrast genuine vulnerability with moments of radiance.'

'Wow, that's nice,' said Johnny as the couple moved away to a table on the other side of the bar.

'It is,' said Alex, shaking his head as if he didn't believe her.

'She's right,' Lillian said. 'I couldn't have found those words, but she's right.'

'Did you enjoy the programme?' Alex asked.

'More than I can say. I hadn't expected those songs to trigger so many memories, so many different moods.'

'That's what music never fails to do,' Johnny said, raising his glass.

At the end of the evening, they parted company outside the guesthouse where Alex and Johnny were staying. They both kissed her goodnight, but it was Alex who waited and watched while she walked the short distance down the street to the flat she was renting above a photographer's studio. As she put the key in the door, she looked back and to her delight, she saw him watching her.

The next day, she was busy getting ready for the festival's final concert, with the morning spent greeting the instrumentalists and singers as they arrived for the afternoon rehearsal. Including technicians and orchestra porters, she had over forty people to manage and support and the rooms available for them were full to bursting. Most of the performers already knew each other—the singers had had a separate rehearsal in London the week before—and there was a convivial vibe among them which made Lillian's life easier. Everyone arrived safely and on time, though one of the singers had forgotten his black concert shoes and having turned up in grubby trainers he was forced to borrow an enormous pair of black gym shoes Lillian found in the Choir Room.

The theme of the concert was *Serenade to Music* and the conductor rehearsed the programme in order so they could also practise the moving of chairs and stands that would be necessary. The first piece was Hugo Wolf's short and lively *Italian Serenade,* followed by Mozart's *Eine Kleine Nachtmusik,* and after a short break, by Elgar's *Serenade for Strings.* Alex was involved in the final item, the *Serenade to Music* by Vaughan Williams for sixteen solo voices with lyrics adapted from Act V of *The Merchant of Venice* in which the lovers, Lorenzo and Jessica, sit under the stars and become enraptured by the music of the spheres. Alex and a few of the other singers sat in for the entire rehearsal until it was their time to sing, at which point, Lillian had to round up the others.

'It would be easier herding cats,' she joshed as Marcus, one of the baritones, hurried into the lineout just in time to forestall any irritation from the conductor, while his soprano girlfriend, Amanda, simply rolled her eyes.

Once the concert itself was underway, Lillian slipped into a reserved seat at the front, so that if for any reason she was needed, she would be close at hand. In fact, she was able to relax and enjoy the music, particularly the final work. The conductor had handpicked the soloists because the work was composed for sixteen voices who as well as their solo contributions, in some places sing together as a choir, sometimes in as many as twelve parts.

As soon as the piece began and the first notes of the exquisite violin solo were heard, it was as if the air in the cathedral had been sucked out, with several hundred people holding their collective breath. The violin solo was the precursor to a soprano's delicately ascending line, "Of sweet harmony", sung by Amanda with remarkable control and purity. Lillian knew *The Merchant of Venice,* so the text was familiar. And though Vaughan Williams had cut words, phrases, and whole lines, and moved and repeated others, she felt he'd paid tribute to Shakespeare in music that was almost celestial in its loveliness. If she closed her eyes, she could imagine herself in a Mediterranean garden on a sultry summer's night. She tried to pick out all the individual solos, but it was the climactic moments when the singers joined together—"Such harmony is in immortal souls" and "Draw her home with music"—she found the most thrilling. The piece finished with a touching repetition of the violin and soprano solos, the violin's singing tone perfectly matching that of Amanda's "Soft stillness and the night...Become the touches of sweet harmony."

The last night party in the tithe barn was a high-spirited affair, made all the merrier when the reason for Marcus's earlier tardiness was explained. He waited until everyone had joined the gathering before he asked for the floor. He was very well-liked, but a known joker and Amanda looked a mixture of amused and suspicious.

'First of all, folks, apologies for keeping you waiting this afternoon. Unprofessional, I know, as my beloved was quick to point out...'

People cheered and those nearest to her, applauded Amanda and gave her a thumbs up.

'The thing is,' he said, 'I was on a mission. A mission that had to be accomplished before the rehearsal began. Now it's the moment of truth.'

Some people "oohed" and there were a few titters as Marcus reached for Amanda's hand and drew her towards him. When he got down on one knee, she gasped and then laughed.

'Voice of an angel, my heart's desire—will you marry me?'

With a flourish he produced a small box from his pocket and opened it to reveal a gold ring with a single diamond. Everyone's attention was now on Amanda, who was studying the ring closely before gently pulling Marcus to his feet.

'You silly sod!' she cried at last. 'Of course I will.'

At that, he picked her up and swung her in his arms until she told him to stop. He put her down carefully and began easing the ring onto her left hand. It was a lovely moment. Everyone crowded round to congratulate them and within minutes the party was in full swing. Lillian was worried the drinks laid on by the festival organiser would quickly run out, but at his own expense, Marcus had arranged extra supplies so there was no danger of a drought.

'Just doing my bit for the local economy,' he said, when someone thanked him for his generosity.

'Not to mention the purchase of an expensive engagement ring!' quipped someone else.

The concert had been warmly received and the festival organiser told Lillian it had been the most successful festival so far and he hoped she would come back the following year when the main event would be Bach's *St John Passion.* She said she'd be delighted and had to stop herself suggesting that he ask Alex to sing the Evangelist.

For now, she and Alex sat next to each other in a large group that included the conductor and some of the other singers. At one point, Lillian looked up and saw that Marcus and Amanda were standing quietly together, away from the others. Amanda looked radiant and Lillian watched as she covered Marcus's face with kisses. When Lillian turned back to her drink she saw that Alex, too, had been watching them. He looked pensive and Lillian was afraid that such a very public display of love and happiness would trigger memories so painful that he would hurry away to his hotel.

But he recovered his equilibrium and stayed. Conversation flowed and there was much storytelling and laughter and Lillian sensed he was glad to be there, sharing in the general *bonhomie*. As people drifted away from the table to circulate or retire to their digs, they found themselves alone, until Amanda came over to say goodnight.

'Marcus told me you're both working on *Death in Venice* at Stonehurst. I'm playing the Strawberry Seller, so I'll see you there—though blink and you'll miss me!'

'I like her,' Alex said after she'd gone, 'and I have a feeling we'll all need to stick together.'

'You're anxious about it?'

'I am. I'm not sure what to expect.'

'Well,' she said, putting her hand on his, 'you'll have at least two friendly faces around.'

'I'm glad of that,' he said, closing his hand around hers.

He held her gaze and, in that instant, she knew how the evening would end and she looked forward to the moment when they would, at last, be alone together.

A Dangerous Thing

William Clyne inherited Stonehurst from his godfather, Maurice Craig, a wealthy, childless eccentric who was a close friend of William's mother. Rumour had it that they were more than friends and that Maurice was in fact William's biological father. He certainly took a life-long interest in the boy and from his early childhood, William was a regular visitor to the house, allowed to roam freely in the gardens and surrounding woodlands.

Maurice was an enthusiast of all things Italian and when he bought Stonehurst, the nineteenth century farmhouse had been empty and neglected for so long that he had it demolished and in its place, he built an adaptation of the Italianate villa designed by John Nash at nearby Cronkhill. The central part of the house was rectangular, with a circular, three-storey tower to the north and a square, three-storey tower to the west. There was a music room on the ground floor of the circular tower with a staircase leading to a bedroom and bathroom on each floor above. The square tower housed an impressive library, and fine art hung on the walls here and in the reception rooms in the main house.

When William was older, Maurice began taking him to Covent Garden and Glyndebourne and thus was kindled an abiding love of opera. By his late twenties, a well-paid job in the city enabled him to attend as much opera as he wanted. Glyndebourne became a regular summer pilgrimage, and it was on a late train back to London from Lewes that he met his future wife, Marjorie. She, too, loved opera and though not well-paid as an administrator at a music publisher, she was sometimes given tickets that a colleague or client couldn't use.

They married two years later, and Marjorie moved into William's flat in Pimlico. They had no children and after William's parents died, their wealth increased and they were able to venture into philanthropy. But as well as supporting a few favoured arts organisations, they harboured dreams of setting up something of their own, and in the year they celebrated their fortieth birthdays, Maurice's death and his generous benefaction made this dream a possibility. William gave up his salaried position and took on a consultancy role, meaning they could live for some of the year in Shropshire, while retaining a flat in London. As soon as they moved into the villa, they began transforming the estate into somewhere capable of hosting a summer opera festival. When finally, the largest barn had been transformed into a theatre seating five hundred people, they were ready.

Their years of mingling with the great and the good at Covent Garden, Glyndebourne, Aldeburgh and the like meant that they had met many people who worked in opera. The Clynes regarded themselves as opera aficionados and believed that with Marjorie's knowledge of the classical music world and William's financial acumen, between them they knew enough about the business to make a success of it.

William intended to fulfil the role of Artistic Director, making all the decisions about repertoire and principal artists and creatives. In the first year, they planned just one production—*Death in Venice*. They converted one of the outbuildings into offices and made three key appointments: an experienced Head of Music, Glen Reed, who recruited a fine répétiteur, Neil Brown; a Technical Manager, Roger Hubbard, who had recently been let go by one of the opera companies the Clynes supported; and Tara Clayton, a General Manager who had previously worked at the Lion Hotel in Shrewsbury. The bulk of the administrative work would fall to her, working alone until the arrival of a small festival team—many of them volunteers—in the months leading up to the first festival in May 1993. The operational burden was significant, more than the Clynes had envisaged, and Tara had no experience of budgeting for opera or pulling together the infrastructure and staff essential for the efficient and professional management of a festival in a country house setting.

It's possible that neither of the Clynes knew Alexander Pope's *Essay on Criticism* or grasped the acuity of its most well-known quotation, "A little learning is a dangerous thing". If they had, they might have recognised that a small amount of knowledge can mislead people into thinking they are more expert than they actually are; can make them overestimate their knowledge and abilities, which can result in costly mistakes being made.

They certainly underestimated the importance of clean, comfortable, and safe accommodation for people whose work required them to spend weeks away from home.

'The days are long,' explained Deborah, the Company Stage Manager, 'and everyone works incredibly hard, with huge demands made on them. This can lead to exhaustion and stress and if their digs are grim, it can pile extra pressure on top of everything else.'

Her warnings went unheeded—hence the many disgruntled observations that could be heard in the Green Room on the first day of rehearsals.

'It's obvious that no-one took the trouble to inspect the digs or vet the hosts.'

'Booking theatre digs is like playing roulette—you never know what you're going to find when you get there.'

The creative team had no such difficulties on this score. The conductor and the director were put up by the Clynes in the round tower at Stonehurst, with access to their own kitchen and sitting room in the main house, while the designer and choreographer, who were married, stayed in a cottage where William and Marjorie had lived briefly when work on the estate was particularly disruptive.

As for the rest of the company, Tara sent out a digs list less than two weeks before rehearsals began. Stonehurst was an attractive village, well served with shops and cafés, two pubs, an Indian restaurant and a traditional chippy, but its only hotel, a famous coaching inn, was closed for refurbishment, and the immediate area had limited options for bed and breakfast or self-catering. In an attempt to address this, and at the same time, sensing there was some local hostility to the idea of an opera festival, William promoted the positive impact that several dozen people staying locally for almost six weeks would have on the local economy and encouraged people to open their homes and make spare bedrooms available to rent. He was keen to engender goodwill, but his appeal was only partly successful. Many locals disliked the prospect of being overrun by outsiders and didn't relish the inevitable noise and disruption of hundreds of cars streaming up and down narrow country lanes before and after performances.

Lillian, Deborah, and Sian, the ASM, were staying in a large house with a young couple, their two small children and several boisterous dogs; while Romy and the dancers playing the Polish Mother and the Governess were housed with an elderly couple who had three draughty attic rooms available. The rest of the company were scattered among local pubs, guest houses and private homes of varying quality. A common complaint amongst those staying in private houses was the lack of locks on bedroom and bathroom doors and the irritations of sharing a kitchen with strangers. Keen to ensure their privacy and to save money at the same time, several of the chorus brought caravans and were parked on a site nearby.

Alex wanted to live on his own and asked Dominic to find him somewhere self-contained. This task fell to Caroline, Dominic's formidably efficient assistant, who also had to find a place for Richard Gibbs, another of Dom's singers, who was playing the multiple baritone roles. Caroline was quietly in love with Alex and knew Richard would kick up a fuss if he was unhappy with his accommodation, so well before the festival's digs list arrived, she'd booked them into two cottages a few doors apart in a quiet mews off the main street of the village.

Visconti had apparently told Dirk Bogarde: "You must live the book. We make a study of solitude, of loneliness." Though Alex had no desire to live in the sort of social vacuum that Bogarde endured, he sensed that to fully inhabit Aschenbach's problematic personality would demand discipline and a willingness to stay close to his doomed alter-ego and protect himself against too much external stimulus. He was not sure what this would mean for him and Lillian. They'd not seen each other since Brecon, but given their intimacy there, he wanted to say, "allow me some space for now and then let's see", but he worried that if she felt hurt and rejected by this, it would cause awkwardness between them that he was anxious to avoid.

Death in Venice: rehearsals

As the company prepared for a presentation from the creative team, the atmosphere in the rehearsal room was a mix of nervous apprehension and tentative excitement. Chairs were laid out in semi-circular rows for cast and crew, while the director, designer, and choreographer faced them from behind two large tables pushed together. Lillian, Glen, and the assistant director, Frank, sat alongside them, slightly apart, while Neil listened from the piano. Rhodri Pearce was surprisingly absent and during her introductory welcome, Deborah explained that he'd been assisting on a production in Germany and having arrived back in the UK at the weekend, he would not be joining until the next day.

The presentation began with an introduction to the opera by the director, Anthony Carey.

'I'm guessing that for most of us, this will be our first experience of working on *Death in Venice,* so before Douglas describes the design concept, I'll say a little about the opera's provenance and its key themes.'

He had a calm, commanding presence and gained the full attention of everyone in the room.

'It was Britten's final opera, written when he was ill with the heart condition that would kill him three years after the premiere in 1973. It's a deeply personal piece, written for Peter Pears, and throughout its composition, an ailing Britten didn't know how much music he had left in him.

'The libretto adapts Thomas Mann's 1912 novella and tells of an ageing writer who goes south to Venice in search of inspiration and release from the pain of writer's block. There he becomes enthralled and obsessed with a beautiful young Polish boy, Tadzio. Venice meanwhile is in the grip of cholera and the city empties around Aschenbach as tourists flee the infected city. At the end, as decay and disease take hold, and overwhelmed by his desire, Aschenbach slips into fever, and eventually dies.

'The whole piece is very much about Apollonian light versus Dionysian darkness: order, intellect, and harmony versus chaos, passion, and intoxication. We see this in the complex character of Aschenbach. Where we would expect a respected and artistically revered protagonist to behave soberly and honourably, instead we have a character who can provoke disdain for his obsessions, his selfishness and his irresponsibility—for instance when he fails to tell Tadzio's mother about the danger the spreading cholera epidemic poses to her family.'

The atmosphere shifted when Douglas Drake "walked" the company through the set model. He had an unmistakable air of self-importance and arrogance, while by contrast, his wife, Camilla, was quietly spoken and self-effacing. She carried herself with the grace of the dancer she had once been, and it was clear the dancers felt comfortable with her.

After the presentation, everyone was encouraged to study the costume designs which had been pinned onto screens at one end of the room. Douglas said his aim was to recreate a cloistered world of wealth and privilege, of sophisticated gentility, a world in which a leisured class drifted about at a fashionable resort. There were elegant suits and dresses in cream and pure white, enormous hats and pastel parasols, with Aschenbach in a beige three-piece suit.

After this, the whole company was invited to view the theatre and the dressing rooms, and at the end of the morning, while the creative and technical teams held a production meeting, the cast decamped to the Green Room for lunch. Over sandwiches and juices laid on by the Clynes, there was much discussion about the design concept.

'So,' said Ashley, the countertenor singing Apollo, 'the opera opens in a graveyard and shifts scenes continually: a boat to Venice, the bank of the Lido, the travel bureau, the beach, canals, bridges and piazzas, various rooms in the hotel. Question: how do you depict all this in a theatre with modest technical facilities and no fly tower? Answer: chocolate-box realism, overflowing with painstakingly busy goings-on—tourists strolling, chatting and twirling parasols, hawkers and beggars straggling and pestering, children frolicking and fighting.'

'Plus, a never-ending parade of paraphernalia,' groaned someone else. 'Luggage, beach huts, deckchairs, sofas, potted palms…'

'Not to mention an enormous gold statue of Apollo,' said someone else.

Lillian and Sian came in to grab coffee and sandwiches before the start of the afternoon session and someone asked them what the crew thought of it.

'It will be busy,' said Lillian. 'There's a lot going on.'

'A lot to go wrong,' muttered Sian as she closed the door behind them.

For most of the first day, Alex was a silent observer, as if subconsciously he was getting into character, watchful and wary, weighing up the people who would be his companions for the next six weeks. Like Aschenbach, he was instantly fascinated by "Tadzio". With loose auburn curls, long limbs, and high cheekbones, Romy Tyler was undoubtedly striking. He guessed that in due course her hair would be cut and styled to achieve a more androgynous look, but he wished this had been done before rehearsals started so that he could develop an obsession for a "boy" rather than an undeniably beautiful woman. While pondering how he and she would manage this, he observed how she interacted with others. She didn't flirt in an overt way, but she had an indefinable quality that was cool yet seductive, and it was obvious that several of the men were drawn to her.

He watched Lillian making notes in a hardbacked exercise book and thought she looked pale and tired. She'd called him before he left Oxford to say she wouldn't be travelling to Stonehurst on Sunday afternoon as planned but was driving down very early the next morning. Her father had had a significant setback and she wanted to spend a last night with him and her mother.

'How are you?' he asked when they met in the rehearsal room. 'You look peaky. Are things tough at home?'

She laughed half-heartedly. 'I feel like a battery that needs recharging.'

That evening, they drove to a nearby pub for supper. They didn't stay long because Lillian was tired after her early start, but it was a chance to reconnect.

'How are your digs?' Alex asked.

'It seems to be a chaotic household, but I think it will be okay. How about you?'

'It's fine. My agent—or at least, his assistant—managed to find me a cottage in the village. It's small and rather cluttered but it's warm and clean.'

'You're lucky. Some of the crew are in grotty bedsits they say reek of damp.'

'I gathered that from snippets I overheard this morning. There seemed to be a lot of moaning. How was today for you?'

'I like Anthony and Camilla. But Douglas—what a piece of work he is.'

'Oh?'

'High-handed, patronising—even to the men. Thank goodness he won't be here all the time, but the weeks in the theatre when he is here could be difficult. There are delays on the set build and no date confirmed for when it will be delivered. It's unlikely to be here from week three as originally planned. Douglas and Roger went to see the builders and screen painters a couple of weeks ago and Douglas quibbled about the quality of the finishes and demanded that some bits were rebuilt or repainted. It's already over budget and Roger warned him it's in danger of being too big and heavy for a small crew to handle safely.'

'That's a worry.'

'It is. Hopefully, there'll be enough props to work with in the rehearsal room, though apparently Douglas keeps changing his mind about what he wants.'

'Hey ho. But I thought once we got going, the rehearsal went well.'

'It did. Glen and Neil are brilliant, aren't they?'

'They are. Shame Glen's not conducting—he's an excellent musician and he knows the score inside out.'

As they drove back to the village, Alex wondered if he should bring up his intention to limit his socialising. When he pulled up outside Lillian's digs, she gave him a potential opening.

'I'm sorry I've been such poor company tonight,' she said. 'I'm just knackered. Hopefully, a good night's sleep will do the trick. I need to pace myself. I can see this show is going to be a rough ride and on the odd days when we're not working, I'll want to get to my parents.'

'No need to apologise,' he said. 'I feel the same—about pacing myself, I mean. I know Richard has a lot to do, with seven different characters to play, but you can't get away from the fact that this opera is all about Aschenbach. I feel the weight of that even more than I thought I would.'

'I understand,' she said, reaching out to take his hand. 'I enjoyed tonight. You've cheered me up, even if I still look and sound like a wet rag!'

They leaned together and kissed lightly and then she was gone, through the gate and up the steps of the big old house, with his intentions still unspoken.

Rhodri Pearce did not appear the next day. He rang Deborah to say he had a kidney infection and felt too unwell to travel. It was a full week before he arrived and when he did, he seemed distracted, and though he was civil to everyone, he was also frequently distant and morose.

'It's as if he doesn't want to be here,' said Richard to Alex as they walked back to the rehearsal room one day after lunch.

'I agree,' said Alex. 'It's odd—he's always got his head in the score, but he doesn't seem to know it.'

Richard nodded. 'The first time we ran the strolling players scene, which admittedly is a bit crazy, it was all over the place and he didn't seem able to work out who or what was wrong.'

'Glen knew what the problem was straight away,' said Alex. 'As did Anthony.'

'God knows how he'll cope when he's got a full orchestra in front of him.'

The cast, however, was uniformly strong and despite a lack of confidence in Rhodri and the limitations of not working on the set, under Anthony's clear and purposeful direction the production began to take shape. Ashley was crystal-clear and powerful as Apollo, and in a gold costume made to look identical to the appearance of the statue, he would be a dominating presence whenever he was on stage. In another cameo part, Amanda made a provocative and seductive Strawberry Seller, suitably luscious of voice, but by the end, she would be made up to look visibly—and ominously—ill. Richard was astonishing as the seven harbingers of death who propel Aschenbach on his journey towards catastrophe. From his first entrance, as the Stranger-Traveller in the graveyard, he injected something mysterious and threatening into the drama. He switched nimbly between roles, the oily darkness of his voice conveying sinister charm and unsettling menace in all his manifestations: the lewd, lecherous Elderly Fop; the vanishing Gondolier; the smarmy, ingratiating Hotel Manager; the wheedling Hotel Barber; the crude, leering Balladeer; and the devilish Dionysus. It was a masterful gallery of characters who torment and seduce Aschenbach into abandoning his Apollonian principles to give himself up to "chaos and sickness".

Rehearsals were hard-going, and most people did their own thing at the end of the working day, but the White Swan in the village became the watering hole of choice for anyone looking for company or an escape from their digs. Alex and Lillian had one quiet night a week alone together and sometimes Lillian stayed over in the cottage, but they were both preoccupied by concerns that got in the way of any nascent relationship that might develop between them.

Lillian was worried about her parents, wondering how her mother would cope if her father became seriously disabled or worse. She was also exhausted by the rehearsal process, starting early before the creative team arrived, rarely managing to have a proper break at lunchtime, and with rehearsal reports to produce and circulate at the end of each day.

'Be prepared,' she warned Alex, 'that when we move into the theatre and start rehearsing on the set it will seem as if we're going backwards.'

Alex, meanwhile, was finding Aschenbach a draining character to inhabit. He'd gone back to Oxford for the first two weekends, but after that, decided to stay in Stonehurst in his own little 'cabana', forcing himself to maintain the total concentration achieved by Bogarde, a process that Alex, too, found uncomfortable. The man's feelings towards the boy were complicated, and for any singer, the attraction was hard to pitch. One morning, during a coffee break, Alex found himself standing next to Camilla and he asked her what was intended when they cast Tadzio with a woman. She answered, somewhat unconvincingly, that they thought it would add an extra layer of ambiguity to the drama.

A few days later, at the end of the rehearsal, he and Romy sat down with Anthony to explore the conundrum.

'Aschenbach can never know what the boy thinks of him,' said Anthony. 'They don't speak, and if the boy favours him sometimes with a look or a smile, he favours many other people as well, because that's his nature.'

'But what's in his look?' Alex asked. 'What does it signify?'

'Ah,' said Anthony. 'The quality of the gaze. Well, first, let's ask what's in Aschenbach's gaze?'

'Curiosity,' Alex ventured. 'Admiration. Desire. Confusion. Guilt. Fear?'

Anthony nodded. 'And how might such a gaze be returned?' he asked, looking at Romy.

'Guarded or questioning,' she said. 'It might be kind or cold; it might seem to tease or tempt—or it might be nothing more than a look—a look to be interpreted as he will.'

The inscrutable answer seemed typical of her. Gazing for long hours at her and trying to see past her feminine attractions and imagine her as a teenage boy was becoming increasingly difficult. Whether in character as Tadzio or out, Romy was an enigma. She was extremely tactile with the other female dancers, and especially friendly with Sylvie, who was playing the Governess, frequently draping her arms around Sylvie's shoulders in pauses in rehearsals. Once or twice, late at night, Alex thought he heard her arriving at Richard's cottage a few doors away from his. Another time, he saw her arm-in arm with Charlie, the young baritone playing the English Clerk, going into The Greyhound, the less favoured pub in the village. And whenever Alex found himself held in her gaze, whether it was guarded or questioning, teasing or tempting, or none of those things, he knew she was alert to her own power and allure and that he was in danger of succumbing to it.

Lillian was well-aware of Alex's absorption with Romy. It was impossible for her not to notice it because the whole point of the story was Aschenbach's fixation on the beautiful Polish boy, who in this production seemed to be omnipresent. When Anthony asked Alex and Romy to stay back to discuss Aschenbach's obsession, Lillian was sitting quietly at the production desk, updating the prompt copy and writing up rehearsal notes.

Though she couldn't hear much of their conversation, she knew how immersed Alex was in his role and could see how engrossed he appeared to be in Romy. She found herself envying Romy, feeling jealous of her closeness to Alex, and she realised these feelings, if unchecked, would sour her mood for the remainder of the project.

On the Saturday morning at the end of the third week, Douglas arrived with a hairdresser and after the coffee break, Romy was taken away and didn't reappear for the rest of the rehearsal. When the session finished at lunchtime and they were dismissed until Monday morning, Lillian left for her parents as usual. Having waved her off, Alex walked back to his cottage, but felt restless and, on a whim, he got into his car and drove out of the village towards Attingham Park.

When he arrived at the estate, he followed signs to Cronkhill and parked on the grassy paddock in front of the house. It was peaceful there because the villa wasn't open to the public and his car was one of only a handful. The house stood high on a hill and Alex leant against the car bonnet to take in the views over the estate. Being cooped up in a rehearsal room day after day was tiring and he enjoyed the sense of freedom and release he felt as he closed his eyes and breathed in the fresh air. As he was turning round to face the house, his eye was caught by a figure sitting on the grass further down the paddock. As he watched, the person stood up and started making their way up the slope towards him. The gazelle-like walk was familiar, but it took him a few moments to realise it was Romy. When she drew closer and saw him, she stopped and sighed.

'I came here to escape,' she said. 'I didn't want to face other people until I'd had time to get used to it myself.' She gave a wry smile. 'It seems ironic, if appropriate, that the *Signore* should be the first person to see it.'

She had been utterly transformed. Gone was the abundant head of hair, replaced by a crop of short, tight curls that framed her face so that her features appeared almost chiselled. Her femininity had been stripped away and she was now a juvenile boy. Though of course, she wasn't, and this skilfully manufactured look only heightened his confusion and discomfort.

'Sorry,' he said. 'I'm staring.'

'Well, of course you are *Signore*. It's what you do!' She laughed. 'Are you following me? Imagining we're in Venice?'

He blushed, embarrassed by her mocking tone. 'I had time to kill and thought I'd take a look at Cronkhill. Shall we walk around the gardens?'

She nodded, before linking arms and leading him off towards the house. When they'd seen all there was to see, they drove the short distance to the main house where they had tea in the National Trust café.

'You're staring again,' she chided, as she lavished cream and jam onto a large scone. 'Are you always in character?'

'You look very different,' he said. 'Do you like it?'

She shrugged. 'It'll grow back, so what the hell. The stylist did a good job, despite Douglas watching him like a hawk the whole time and making "helpful" suggestions.' She rolled her eyes and shook her head. 'He gets everyone's backs up.'

'Apart from telling me I'm too young to be playing Aschenbach, I've got off lightly so far. He was pleased with the suit they've made for me and delighted that my limp is for real so that I'll look convincing using a walking stick.'

'So tactful.'

He laughed. 'Do you like working with Camilla?'

'I do, though I sometimes feel irritated about the dynamic between her and Dougie, as she calls him.'

'What do you mean?'

'She gives way to him too much. Anything for a quiet life, I suppose.'

'How are you finding rehearsals?'

She pulled a face. 'I enjoy the games on the beach and the rough stuff with Jaschiu and the demonic craziness of the dream scene, but a lot of the time, I'm bored. How about you?'

'I find Aschenbach energy-sapping. Trying to understand him, trying to make him believable and relatable.'

'Yeah. He's a dry old stick.—No offence.'

'None taken.'

'Seriously, though, you're very good at all that world-weariness and detached aloofness.'

He couldn't tell if she was being sardonic, so he said nothing.

'I love the opening scene,' she said.

'You do?'

'Yes, you, sitting alone at your desk in the darkened study, trying to write but frustrated and dissatisfied, it's remarkable how your voice captures the disillusionment, the lack of inspiration, the joylessness. And the funeral wreath in the graveyard is a sweet touch—very poignant.'

'Hopefully the audience will assume that his wife died recently and that will help them understand his melancholic demeanour and feel sympathy for him.'

'So, do you think he's a repressed perv? After all, he daydreams about he and Tadzio being the sole survivors.'

'I've thought long and hard about that, and I've come to see his enthralment with the boy not so much as the sign of an illicit sexual urge as a wish that his own past life might have been different. That it was not a life spent in cerebral solitude but one enjoyed with others on beaches and in playful games.' He paused. 'I think he's so overcome by unfamiliar feelings that he begins to question every choice he's ever made and to doubt the worth of his art.'

'Wow, that's sad.'

'It is. So, how do you see Tadzio?'

'I think he simply represents an ideal of physical beauty.'

'Androgynous perfection like a Botticelli angel.'

'Well, I'll do my best,' she laughed.

As they walked back to their cars, he asked, 'Do you not go home at weekends?'

She frowned and shook her head. 'Nothing to go home for.'

He watched her drive off ahead of him. She'd suggested that later on he might join her and some of the others for a drink at the Greyhound. The majority of people would have gone home for the weekend, so he had no idea who was likely to be there. Uncertain whether to go or not, he decided that if it was uncongenial, he could simply go back to the cottage.

When he got to the pub, he had to stand aside to allow a group of people to leave, and with the door propped open, he could see the crew sitting around a large table in a corner. On a table next to them were Romy and a few of the dancers. The crew seemed to be playing cards and almost all of them were smoking. It did not appeal, so he let the door swing closed and turned away. His leg ached and he was hungry. The tempting smell of frying fish from across the street seemed to offer a solution for the hunger, but Romy had seen him and come after him, and before he could cross the road, she took hold of his arm.

'What's up?' she asked.

'Nothing's up, but the pub looked very smoky.'

'It is, and *nos amis francais*, Sylvie *et* Gerard, are two of the worst offenders, so why don't you and I escape to the White Swan?'

'Okay. Do you fancy something to eat?'

'Suits me.'

The pub was busy, but they were able to find a table in the section of the bar where food was served.

'I wondered,' Alex said, tentatively, 'what you meant when you said earlier that there was nothing to go home for?'

He didn't expect her to answer as fully and frankly as she did, but over fish and chips washed down with pints of beer, she told him her story.

'My mother, Jenny, was from Cardiff. The daughter of someone high up in the education service who was a very strict Catholic. I think family life with a God-fearing father was difficult, and she was desperate to break away. It was the swinging sixties so as soon as she was old enough, she ran off to London and worked as a temp. When her mother fell seriously ill, she went home to be with her, not realising at first that she was pregnant. Her mother died just as her pregnancy began to show and Jenny was left to face her father's anger alone. He couldn't accept that she'd led her own life for three years and was now an independent woman. He was furious that she was pregnant and set about arranging a private adoption. There was no suggestion he would support her so that she could keep her baby.'

She paused, as if this part of the story still caused her grief.

'My adoptive parents moved to Hertfordshire but split up when I was a toddler. Neither wanted custody of me so I was put into the care of the local authority. I had a series of foster parents until I settled with Vera. She'd once been a dancer and it was her who encouraged me to dance.'

'She must be very proud of you. Does she come to see you perform?'

'She did, but not anymore. She came to Britain from the Caribbean, as part of the Windrush generation, but she went back to Trinidad a couple of years ago. She never got over the race riots in the 1980s.'

'What a story,' Alex said, thinking how much misfortune she'd endured. 'How did you find out about your mother and her family in Cardiff?'

'The local authorities in Cardiff and Hertfordshire were able to tell me the bare bones, but in truth, I know very little, so I fill in the gaps. When I think of my grandfather, I see someone ramrod stiff and grim-faced.'

'And your mother?'

'Ah, Jenny. I think she was defiant and brave but helpless in the face of her father's implacable opposition.'

'Poor woman. Thank goodness for Vera, but such a shame she felt she had to leave Britain.'

'It is. I loved her. I would have been happy to live with her for ever.'

How sad, he thought, and what lonely dejection seemed to hide beneath her blazing outer confidence.

'Where do you live now?'

'I share a house with some students in Shoreditch. The landlord's a cowboy—one of his properties was condemned last year.'

For a moment or two, they were both silent, until Romy laughed and caught his arm. 'Listen,' she said, holding a finger to her ear.

Alex focussed his attention on the background music. He'd been vaguely aware it was a compilation of female singers—Madonna, Mariah Carey, Whitney Houston and Sinéad O'Connor—but now Dinah Washington was singing her wonderfully bluesy version of Noel Coward's *Mad about the Boy*.

'What a voice,' Romy said when it was over, 'and so true—after all, who hasn't loved someone unsuitable at some time or other?'

She laughed and leant towards him so that her face was disconcertingly close to his.

'I mean, look at poor old Aschenbach,' she said, her eyes open wide, as if shocked. 'No matter how hard he tries, he simply can't let go of his shameful obsession, his foolish love.'

Alex blushed and tried to smile, but felt awkward and self-conscious, unsure how to react. Was she flirting, giving him the come on—or simply teasing? At times she seemed to promise intimacy and connection, at others she remained determinedly untouchable. Just as he was thinking she enjoyed seeing him squirm with embarrassment, she tapped him on the nose and said, 'Come on. I'm taking you home!'

At rehearsals the following Monday, aware that Lillian would be watching, Alex tried to act normally around Romy but feared he was painfully maladroit. He persuaded himself that his self-consciousness could be attributed to his impersonation of Aschenbach, but he imagined people saying that he was so convincing in his infatuation with 'the boy', it was as if he wasn't acting.

And there was more than a grain of truth in that. He'd been infatuated with Romy from the start. She was so bewitching, and though she was also brittle and elusive, she was the same glowing young woman who'd charmed him with her goodness and kindness as Eppie. More than ever after that weekend, he didn't quite know who she was, and that added to the turmoil that now consumed him. Behaving normally around her had not been easy at the best of times, but now he found it well-nigh impossible.

Meanwhile, the set was installed in the theatre and the scale of the challenge ahead became starkly apparent. The get-in and fit-up took two whole days, at the end of which the crew were exhausted, some of them having slept on the floor of a dressing room at the end of the first day, and all of them complaining of sore backs and aching arms.

Everything was designed to capture the mythic grandeur of Venice. Beyond pillars and arches could be glimpsed flats painted with piazzas, bridges, and basilicas while the imposing gold-painted statue of Apollo loomed over the scenes in which the God appeared.

Rehearsals progressed more slowly as the lighting and technical logistics were worked through. There was much stopping and starting, which was tiring for everyone, but what was more wearing was the change in dynamic now that Douglas was there permanently and behaving as if he, and not Anthony, was in charge. Having worked together before, Anthony was used to this and knew how to handle it, but Rhodri was not as forbearing as experience had taught Anthony to be. Technical holdups and mishaps ate into precious rehearsal time and the atmosphere was tense.

One irritation Rhodri had to endure was that urgent costume fittings frequently took performers out of rehearsals. The cutters and sewers were working under considerable pressure as Douglas demanded alterations or embellishments. Experiments with wigs and make-up took place as and when possible, and though the look of the show was coming together, the mood was increasingly strained. Even Camilla was noticeably less relaxed when her husband was around, and only Anthony maintained his usual steady focus and equanimity. He valued Lillian's unflustered presence alongside him and appreciated the clear but diplomatic way in which she could voice queries or concerns.

Douglas, however, resented her occasional interventions and frequently dismissed them out of hand. She was particularly concerned that in the Games of Apollo, the presence of the chorus as onlookers plus the huge statue and the beach huts constricted the area in which the dancers could play out their boisterous antics.

'So, what's your point?' Douglas demanded.

'With so little room to manoeuvre,' she explained, 'there's a risk of accidental collisions which could lead to injury. Could we perhaps lose one of the beach huts?'

She hoped that Roger and Camilla would reinforce her concerns but to her astonishment and dismay they said nothing, and therefore the answer came as no surprise.

'We keep all the beach huts. Got it?'

Members of the crew who witnessed this exchange looked on blank-eyed and dispirited, worn down, like Lillian, by the hopelessness of even constructive dissent.

"I need a drink after the day I've had" became a regular refrain and the village pubs were busy in those last couple of weeks. Though she was exhausted, Lillian often joined the others and very occasionally, Alex came along, too. She noticed that if Romy was there, he seemed ill at ease. She'd heard rumours that Romy was involved with Gerard, the dancer playing Tadzio's friend Jaschiu, but she couldn't help wondering if something had happened between her and Alex, a possibility that troubled and upset her.

By now, after weeks of rehearsing with only a piano reduction of the score, the singers were keen to hear the full gamut of Britten's sound world. With the arrival of the players, the rehearsals would be Rhodri's to run as he chose, but he was showing signs of being under great duress, and discord between him and Douglas simmered ominously.

The day before the orchestra stage rehearsals began was Romy's birthday and Sylvie and Gerard decided it would be good for morale for everyone to relax and have some fun together, so they undertook to organise a birthday party. They did a whip round to cover the cost of drinks and snacks and the Clynes agreed that the Green Room could be used. Though most people were too tired to be in the mood for partying, there was a respectable turnout. Sylvie produced a large birthday cake which she cut into squares, and when everyone had a drink and a piece of cake, Gerard introduced Ashley as the evening's floorshow. Neil was already at the piano, primed and ready to start, when, to the accompaniment of whoops and cheers, Ashley sashayed across the room to join him, his lipstick as red as his shiny stilettos.

'Romy,' he said. 'This is for you.' And then, with a knowing look, he pointed to Alex. 'And for you too, Alex.'

Before Alex realised what was in store, Ashley had launched into a flamboyant rendering of *Mad about the Boy*. To more whoops and cheers, he gave a flagrantly camp performance, bending the rhythms to give extra weight to certain words—insane, stupid, misery, joy—and drawing out the melody's haunting minor key like a sexy cabaret artist in a sleazy nightclub.

Romy relished being the centre of attention, but Alex was mortified. He tried to look as if he was taking it all in good humour, that it was all part of the pretence of the production, but inwardly he was cringing and wishing it would be over and he could disappear. He couldn't bear to look at Lillian but caught a glimpse of her flushed and pained expression as she slunk quietly away before the song had ended.

Death in Venice: performances

It was a relief when the first night arrived, and despite a few hairy moments when scene changes were barely achieved on time, the performance went surprisingly well. Lillian's show report recorded errors and mishaps that Frank and Roger would discuss with the company and crew before the next performance, and everyone hoped that with Douglas having left by then, some adaptations might be made. As Lillian had feared, an incident occurred during the Games of Apollo which almost sent Alex toppling out of the deckchair in which he was supposed to be dozing. Gerard had misjudged a sequence of crouches and jumps and come hurtling towards Aschenbach, an accident only averted because Gerard's strong arms enabled him to steady the chair before it tipped onto its side.

Exhaustion, euphoria, and relief in equal measure summed up the feelings of the company at the end of the first performance. They'd got through it and the response from the Clynes and from the audience was enthusiastic. At the drinks reception afterwards, Alex was pleased to be able to unwind with Freddie and Johnny.

'The singers saved the day,' said Freddie. 'There was so much going on, it rather swamped the piece, but without exception, everyone on stage held their own.'

'I agree,' said Johnny. 'I found it wearing that the scenery seemed to be constantly moving, but I was glad our seats were right at the front so we could appreciate the detail in the performances. And thank goodness there was no long supper interval because frankly, systems for managing the audience left much to be desired, and anyway, a long interval would have broken the mood.'

'And that would have been a shame,' said Freddie, 'because over the course of the opera, you achieved what we thought would be impossible— you made Aschenbach sympathetic. It was heartbreaking to see him as a lonely man who thinks he's found joy, and then watch him disintegrate mentally, physically, and emotionally.'

When they left soon afterwards, Alex looked around the Green Room to see who was still there. The dancers had disappeared and Amanda had left with Marcus as soon as the show finished. Lillian was talking to a man Alex didn't recognise, and lacking the energy to be sociable, he slipped away hoping his departure would go unnoticed.

But Lillian, trapped in a boring conversation with Marjorie's brother, saw him leave and, disappointed, she, too, left soon afterwards.

There were three more performances with a day off between each. With the final performance in sight, musicians, dancers and crew resembled marathon runners desperate to get over the finishing line in one piece. During the beach games, flashy cartwheels and tumbles twisted into pirouettes and entrechats as Tadzio and his friends postured and pounced with a boisterousness spilling over into aggression. It was no surprise that a physio was kept busy, easing sore shoulders and strapping tweaked ankles.

During the second and third performances, Lillian and Deborah were concerned that a disquieting dynamic had crept into the scenes between Romy and Gerard. Their duets shifted disturbingly between sensuality and antagonism, and at the end of the Games of Apollo, Romy's body was thrown in the air before it was held aloft by the boys to signify Tadzio's victory. Gerard in particular relished his role in this scene, his muscular strength seeming to threaten danger. Camilla had left after the first night and in her absence, Frank urged the two dancers to tone it down, but he was not confident they took his warning seriously or that anything would change.

There were other issues, too. Lillian and Deborah knew that a drinking culture among technical crews was widely tolerated in the industry, but the *Death in Venice* crew was working on a large-scale production with inadequate resources and were exhausted. Many were living in digs which offered little chance of relaxation or good sleep and it was understandable that alcohol offered an escape. One of the most reliable crew members developed respiratory problems which turned into pneumonia. He was replaced, but his substitute was nothing like as experienced or reliable and Lillian and Deborah were worried enough to raise their concerns with Roger.

'I've seen him worse for wear several times,' said Deborah.

'That hitch during the scene change from the barber's shop into the last visit to Venice was down to Darren fumbling with the brake on the barber's chair,' said Lillian. 'It meant the scene change took longer than it should have and forced one of the others to move a flat on his own.'

'Darren's okay,' said Roger, defensively.

Lillian and Deborah shifted uncomfortably.

'But it's not okay,' said Lillian. 'It's dangerous for anyone to have to move that heavy flat alone—Darren should have been on it as well.'

'Okay, I'll speak to him,' said Roger and walked away before they could say more.

The day before the last performance, Alex and Lillian drove to a craft fair in a nearby walled garden. Its outbuildings had been restored and the garden replanted, and they wandered among stalls selling leather goods and hand-knitted jumpers, jewellery and scented candles, designer cushions and garden accessories. Just as they were thinking about stopping for lunch, they spotted Amanda and Marcus.

'I didn't realise you were still here,' said Alex to Marcus.

'I've come back for the day. I have a concert in Birmingham tomorrow, so I'll stay the night and not have far to go in the morning.'

'Want to join us?' Amanda asked. 'We're about to have a snack in the café.'

'What did you make of the production?' Alex asked Marcus after they'd settled down with bowls of soup and chunks of home-made bread. 'I didn't see you to speak to after the first night.'

'That was my fault,' said Amanda. 'I wasn't in the mood for a party—I was too tired to be sociable.'

'I felt the same,' said Alex. 'As soon as my friends left, I headed off to bed.'

'You did well,' said Marcus. 'All the singers were terrific, but blimey—did no-one ever think that less might be more?'

Alex and Lillian grimaced and nodded.

'The production drove me mad,' Marcus said. 'It was far too busy for my taste. Surely, *Death in Venice* lends itself to a much more minimalist approach.'

'I agree,' said Alex.

'And I didn't think it worked casting Tadzio with a woman.'

'Did anyone?' Amanda asked. 'Romy looked good, but she wasn't consistently convincing as a pre-pubescent boy.'

Alex and Lillian said nothing, both—for their different reasons—uncomfortable that the conversation had turned to Romy.

'Rumour has it,' said Marcus, 'she's been having it off with one of the baritones—Charlie, is it?'

'No,' Amanda insisted. 'Not Charlie—they're old friends—but there's something going on between her and Gerard.'

Lillian was taking all this in but couldn't help noticing how ill at ease Alex seemed and she was glad when Amanda looked at her watch.

'We'd better make a move,' she said. 'We're off to have a look round Shrewsbury.'

'We've still got a few stalls to visit here,' said Alex, 'so we'll see you later.'

The two couples went their separate ways and Alex suggested they seek out the second-hand book stall. Lillian agreed but her mood had changed. She was irritated by the speculation about Romy and itched to ask Alex if he, too, had feelings for the woman.

'Is something the matter?' he asked her later, as they made their way back to his car.

'No,' said Lillian unconvincingly before saying, caustically, 'What is this fascination with Romy? Has every man in the company fallen under her spell?'

She interpreted Alex's look of alarm as proof she had found him out; that he had succumbed—and not only as Aschenbach. They travelled back to Stonehurst in silence.

'What are you doing for the rest of the day?' Alex asked. 'Would you like to go round the house at Attingham Park perhaps?'

By now, Lillian was feeling at odds with herself and knew she'd be poor company.

'No thanks,' she said quietly. 'I think I need to rest this afternoon. I'm going to the Indian restaurant tonight for a last meal with the technical team.'

She sighed, vexed that their trip had ended like this and knew it was her fault. 'I'll see you tomorrow,' she said, when he dropped her outside her digs.

He looked upset, but said nothing. She guessed he'd hoped to lift the tension between them, but she had neither the will nor the energy to put things right.

The meal at the Indian restaurant was Roger's treat to the backstage team, to thank them for their hard work and rally them for one big final effort. He asked the chef to choose for them so they could share a mix of fish and meat and vegetable dishes. Pints of Indian lager were consumed at speed and the group was soon in high spirits. The mood became increasingly gung-ho, with everyone demob-happy at the prospect of putting the show to bed. Lillian had gone along because she didn't want to appear standoffish, but she was disappointed that only a couple of the wardrobe and wigs department were there, and Sian and Deborah had cried off at the last minute—Sian complaining she'd had enough of all the testosterone. Lillian ate and drank little, picking at some naan bread and tarka dhal and sipping a lime soda. The men were clearly there for the duration and would, no doubt, retire later to one of the pubs, so as soon as she felt it was polite, she wished them goodnight and slipped away.

All evening, she'd been thinking about Alex and she'd decided to call on him to apologise for her earlier bad temper. As she made her way up the main street, she saw Romy on the other side of the road, stopping to look in the window of a dress shop before ruffling her cropped hair and sauntering into the mews. In dismay, Lillian turned in the opposite direction and hurried back to her digs.

Ah, Tadzio

Throughout the next day, threatening black clouds hung over Stonehurst, and the air felt muggy and oppressive, providing a fitting backdrop for Britten's tale of death and decay.

At breakfast, Sian and Deborah were concerned to see Lillian looking pale and unwell, with dark circles round her eyes.

'What's up?' they asked her.

'I don't know. I feel really below par, a bit shivery and headachy.'

'Why don't you go back to bed,' Deborah suggested. 'Come in for the crew call. We can cope till then.'

'Thanks, I'll do that. I'll come in mid-afternoon.'

But by mid-afternoon, they had a problem. Lillian was feeling no better and one of the wardrobe team had called in sick, saying she was unable to leave her digs. When the crew started arriving to do lighting and technical checks, the situation was serious. Almost all of them, including Roger, complained, in varying degrees of severity, of being unwell—sickness and diarrhoea being the main symptoms, but several said they felt dizzy, too.

'There are several hangovers,' Deborah said to Lillian and Sian, 'but given all of them ate at the Indian restaurant last night, it sounds like it's food poisoning. Perhaps that's your problem, too, Lillian?'

'Maybe, though I ate very little.'

'How are we going to get through the show?' asked Sian.

'I honestly don't know,' said Deborah, shaking her head.

'Should they take something for the sickness and diarrhoea?' asked Lillian.

'I could go to the pharmacy and ask for advice,' suggested Sian.

She came back with remedies the pharmacist said might help with the diarrhoea and sickness, but not the dizziness.

'Well, that's something, I suppose,' said Deborah. 'The girls in wardrobe have asked if I can help with the quick changes, Richard's in particular. I can't say no, but it means I won't be able to be a floating presence keeping a general eye on everything.'

Frank and the performers arrived for their notes session and, because Roger was in no fit state to brief the crew, Lillian offered to talk them through her show report from the third performance. They gathered in the crew room looking tired and sickly and Lillian wondered how much of what she said they were taking in.

'Obviously, the scene changes could be tricky,' she said, 'but whatever happens, we have to keep everyone safe.'

'Don't worry Lil,' said Darren, getting up to leave. 'It'll be fine.'

Deborah was standing by the door listening and he pushed past her on his way out.

'He's been drinking already,' she said to Lillian when they were alone. 'I wish I could send him home, but we need the manpower.'

'We do. Even at its full complement, the crew is not up to the demands of this production.'

Later, Deborah joined Frank for his notes session with the cast and advised them of the health issues affecting the crew and the wardrobe staff. When the session was over, Alex went to look for Lillian. He'd hoped to see her the night before and had gone to the restaurant to seek her out, but she'd left some time earlier. He felt guilty and confused and had no idea if he could put things right, but he felt honour bound to try. He found Lillian in the wings where she and Sian were checking off the list of personal props. She looked tense and haggard and he feared he was to blame, but for now, because she was busy, there was nothing he could do except wish her—and Sian—all the best for the show.

When he got to his dressing room, Ashley was already there, waiting to have his face painted.

'The sooner this is over, the better,' he said. 'That gold makeup has wreaked havoc with my complexion. Look at me! My face used to be as smooth as a baby's bum.'

Alex laughed, grateful for this attempt to lighten the mood.

Deborah looked in on the dancers who were doing stretching exercises and warming up. Gerard, she noticed, looked unusually sullen, whereas Romy was hyped-up and flushed.

Just before the house lights went down, Frank slipped into the stalls seat reserved for the director. The first five scenes were navigated reasonably successfully, but then came scene six—*The Foiled Departure*. In this scene, Aschenbach crosses the lagoon to visit the city, but fearing the possible effect of the sirocco on his health and pestered by beggars and street vendors, he resolves to leave Venice. He sets off for the railway station but his luggage has been misdirected, so he returns to the hotel and decides to stay on there after all.

Frank felt his heart rate quicken. This scene was always challenging. There were multiple settings—the gondola rides between the Lido and Venice, the railway station, the street scenes, and the hotel foyer; many different characters were involved throughout; and not least, a swift transition was required into scene seven in which the *Games of Apollo* would be played out on the beach.

They were coming to the end of scene six and the wings on both sides of the stage were busy. The crew were preparing to wheel on the beach huts stage right and the statue of Apollo stage left. Ashley was waiting to make his entrance, and the chorus were gathering in readiness to play their parts as hotel guests who watch and commentate on the games.

On stage, Aschenbach returned to the hotel and was welcomed back by the Manager. Alex handed his briefcase, hat, beige raincoat, and brown scarf to Jason, a chorister playing a hotel flunky, before taking a few steps up-stage. In a dramatic lighting change, Tadzio and his friends were suddenly silhouetted beyond him against a blinding brightness. As the lighting gradually returned to its previous level, Tadzio and Jaschiu could be seen pushing and shoving each other, ostensibly in play, though their cavorting looked too rough for Frank's liking. He was equally worried about Aschenbach's scarf which he thought might have slipped to the floor, though as the floor was black it was not obviously visible.

Meanwhile, unbeknownst to anyone, one of the crew lay collapsed in a backstage toilet, having fainted after being violently sick. In the crush of people waiting to go on stage, no-one in the wings realised that they were a man down. No-one noticed that Darren was standing alone behind the statue preparing to wheel it on stage. Lillian, in prompt corner, was busy following the score and cueing choristers and crew and lighting changes.

On stage, Tadzio and Jaschiu's game-playing was becoming even more vigorous, and Frank was horrified when after a sequence of mock-wrestling, a clumsy push from Gerard caused Romy to lose her balance and stumble downstage. This was not meant to happen. She was supposed to stay at the back of the stage with Gerard, out of the way of the upcoming scene change. Frank hoped she would steady herself and retreat to safety, but she seemed dazed and befuddled and stayed crouched down on her haunches with her hands on her head. Alex, too, was taken by surprise but as the stage lights began to dim, he did as he'd been directed and hurried to the front of the stage, singing:

Ah, Tadzio, the charming Tadzio,
that's what it was,
that's what made it hard to leave.

So be it. So be it.
Here I will stay,
here dedicate my days to the sun
and Apollo himself.

A short orchestral interlude began, and the foyer furniture of tables, chairs and potted palms was removed by two choristers playing hotel staff. Darren began to push Apollo onto the stage, but the statue was tall and heavy and needed the weight and heft of two men to keep it stable as it moved. All the other available crew were on the opposite side of the stage dealing with the beach huts, one of which had got stuck.

And Frank had not imagined seeing the scarf slip to the floor. It was there in the darkness and when the wheels on the circular plinth of the statue came into contact with it, the scarf snagged, the wheels jammed and the statue toppled forward and crashed to the floor.

Alex leapt round in shock, and Deborah, standing in the wings amidst the jostle of choristers, realised instinctively that the stage must be concealed from the audience. In the absence of a safety curtain, she reached for the quick-release mechanism that unfurled a painted cloth that was due to come down at the end of the act. Now, what the audience saw was a sepia reproduction of Venice, taken from the beach with the famous skyline of the city visible in a haze of sunshine across the water.

But it was too late.

Everyone sitting in the front of the stalls had seen Tadzio lying prone and lifeless under the full weight of the enormous statue.

If Only

Gerard was inconsolable, his anguish almost visceral in its intensity, his sinewy arms hugging his shaking body as if by squeezing it tight, he could prevent it from breaking apart.

'I pushed her too hard,' he sobbed. 'I was jealous and angry, but I didn't mean to harm her.'

Alex, who witnessed his despair at close quarters, feared that he had provoked Gerard's suspicion and resentment. Lillian had no doubt this was the case and Alex's shattered reaction did nothing to challenge her assumption.

Environmental Health paid a visit to the restaurant and over the coming weeks, the police, the Health and Safety Executive, and the Coroner all endeavoured to piece together a narrative that would explain what happened and why. They heard about the depleted technical team on duty that night, small in number to begin with but weakened further by illness and exhaustion. They examined the stage floor and commented on some unevenness in the way it was joined together. They learnt that a scarf had inadvertently been dropped unnoticed onto this floor, and that the wheels of the enormous statue—manoeuvred by only one man and not the two it required—had snagged on it and jammed so that the statue had toppled forward and crashed to the floor. Gerard told them that in the rough and tumble of their play, he and Romy had accidentally banged heads and he had subsequently pushed her harder than intended. He'd expected that her normal poise and balance would enable her to steady herself, but to his horror she had stumbled and was in the path of the statue when it fell.

And thus, mishap and misfortune conspired to create a catastrophe. The coroner's verdict was death by misadventure. The HSE decided not to prosecute or fine but issued the Clynes with a warning—that crew numbers needed to be adequate for the scale of the production and should include spotters in both wings whose job it would be to look out for—and avert—any potential hazards.

That there was to be no prosecution and that no blame was apportioned was a huge relief, especially to the Clynes and to Gerard, Darren and Jason, but it did little to dissipate their sense of being culpable. The singers waiting in the wings, Frank watching from the stalls, the players seated in the pit—even those who had been merely witnesses and could in no way be held responsible, felt the guilt of simply being part of such a tragedy.

The crew were particularly shaken up because they knew it was their responsibility to keep the performers safe. Deborah and Lillian asked themselves if the show should even have gone ahead with such a compromised technical team, but sensed that even if cancellation had been mooted, the old theatrical adage that "the show must go on" would have prevailed. From the beginning, Lillian had felt that the overblown production concept was ill-judged and that an accident was simply waiting to happen, but she was haunted by thoughts of what she might have done differently. If only she had spotted the rogue scarf or noticed sooner that a crew member was missing stage left and that Darren needed help with the statue or realised that Romy was not wantonly in the wrong place but was dizzy and disorientated following a clash of heads with Gerard. She had seen none of this and even if she had, what could she have done to avert the disaster?

She and the rest of the crew had to wait while the police and the HSE examined the stage and took statements. Only then could they dismantle the set and clear the theatre of props and costumes. It was a dismal task and they worked in gloomy silence. Having seen someone die so needlessly in that awful way, Lillian, for one, knew she would never again feel the same about working in theatre.

She and Alex had barely spoken. She could see he was numb with shock, and she feared he would blame her as much as she blamed herself, so she avoided him, but before he left, he sought her out. He found her in the room that served as a stage management office.

'How are you?' he asked. 'Do you know when you'll get away?'

She mumbled something vague in reply and busied herself packing up her paperwork.

'When the Coroner releases Romy's body, the Clynes will organise a funeral. Will you come?' he asked.

She shook her head.

'I doubt it. I don't think I could face coming back here and anyway, I need to be with my parents.'

His eyes widened in surprise, but he simply nodded.

'I expect you'll be coming?' she said.

'I will. It seems the right thing to do.'

She took that as a rebuke and turned back to her packing.

'Perhaps you'll ring me when you get home,' he said, 'and we can talk properly?'

She shrugged, not looking up from what she was doing.

He could see there was no point in persisting, so he leant down to give her a goodbye peck on the cheek and left.

She followed him to the door and watched him walk down the corridor. His limp seemed more pronounced than before and even from behind, he looked tired and vulnerable. Part of her wanted to run after him, to offer comfort and feel his forgiving arms around her, but she couldn't shake off the suspicion and jealousy that had tainted the last few weeks, and she simply stood in the doorway and watched him go.

PART 4
1993-2006

The Red House

When we are lonely or vulnerable, we can mistake many things for love—admiration, attraction, need—but in my heart, I knew my feelings about Lillian and Romy were ambivalent. In truth, I doubted I would ever again experience a love that grew so naturally and trustingly that I never questioned if I could meet its demands or whether it would bring me happiness without cost. Perhaps my experience of love meant I idealised it. The love Emily and I enjoyed was uncomplicated. It was not weighed down by life, not tested by vicissitude, but remained simple and unencumbered, so perhaps it was not surprising I feared any new liaison would be less straightforward and feel second best.

When Romy 'took me home' and spent the night and much of the next day with me, a fling was all it was for her, as I quickly recognised it was for me. Though outwardly she was attractive and assured, she was unfathomable, hard to pin down, someone with whom you never quite knew where you stood, whose heart you could never quite touch. I'd succumbed to her sensual allure—as I later learnt Richard Gibbs had, too—whereas it was Gerard with whom Romy was entangled in a more meaningful, though volatile, relationship. She came to my cottage on that last night, but she was tipsy and antagonistic after a fight with Gerard, and I sent her away. Seeing her snuffed out like a candle the following night was something I would never forget, the awful violence of it an unwanted reminder of the way in which Emily died.

Lillian was different. She had feelings for me and I cheated on her, and I felt bad about that. She never did call me and when I rang her, there was no answer. When I wrote, I got no reply. If something had happened to her, I had no way of finding out. It was as if she wanted to disappear.

It helped that I was busy and had work and music to sustain me. In the spring of 1994, I went back to Brecon to sing in the *St John Passion*. I wondered if Lillian might be there as Company Manager, but she was not, and the festival promoter told me she had not responded to his offer of work, and he'd been forced to engage someone else.

Time passed and I accepted that Lillian had removed herself from my life, but I thought that one day our paths would cross again, so small was the world in which we both moved.

I never again worked in opera, though offers continued to come my way, and years later, I was asked to step in to play Quint in an open-air production of *The Turn of the Screw* at nearby Myddleton. Despite the convenience it would have offered of being at home throughout rehearsals and performances, I declined.

Johnny and I continued to develop our recital repertoire, with the archive remaining a boundless source of inspiration. Aaron Copland's settings of *Twelve Poems of Emily Dickinson* had for several years been on the list of songs I intended to tackle, and it was another of Emily's notes that finally made me start learning them.

Copland loved Emily Dickinson's poetry and he visited her home and saw the room where she worked. His settings of twelve of her poems are among the most popular of all his music. He particularly fell in love with one poem, The Chariot, *but the title is not Dickinson's - it was changed by one of her editors after she died. Its proper title is* Because I could not stop for death. *In the poem, a female speaker, (assumed to be Emily Dickinson), tells the story of how she was visited by Death, personified as a kindly gentleman. She's taken for a ride in his carriage, a ride that appears to take her past symbols of the different stages of life, before coming to a halt at what is possibly her own grave. Much of its power comes from its refusal to offer easy answers to life's greatest mystery: what happens when we die.*

Was this mystery something that preoccupied Emily? I didn't know, but whenever I sang this song, and visualised the poet riding in a carriage with an incarnation of death, I thought of my Emily who died too young.

I had not forgotten Johnny's suggestion that one day I might go in search of Philip Nash's missing song cycle, but I needed a reason to be in the Tarporley area where Philip had lived. In the late 1990s, I was invited to sing *Messiah* with the local choral society at the parish church of St Mary in Nantwich, about ten miles from Tarporley. Further away in the opposite direction was Macclesfield and I thought if I could get hold of a regional phone directory, I might be able to locate an address for Lillian. I harboured no hope of a relationship, but I was sorry that we'd parted on bad terms and sensed there was unfinished business between us.

I stayed at a small hotel outside Nantwich and as I waited at reception to check in, I saw a set of double doors with a sign above them bearing the words *The Haldane Lounge*. I had no time then to ask who the Haldane was, but this gave me hope that enquiries might bear fruit.

After the concert, one of the tenors, Keith, who was the choir manager, seemed keen to look after me and took me off to the choir's regular drinking haunt. I quickly realised he was an abundant source of local knowledge and once we'd settled down with our second pints, I asked him who the Haldanes were.

'They were once one of the wealthiest and most powerful families in the area,' he told me. 'Back in the day, they owned land all over the place. Some of them were active in public life, too, and did good works. Others, not so much…'

'Was there a Catherine Haldane?'

'There was. I never knew her but by all accounts, she was a lovely girl.'

'What else do you know about her?'

'Why do you ask?'

I told him about Philip Nash and the missing song cycle.

'Philip Nash was very well known around here. He was a brilliant man. You should ask Eve about him—she lives at the Red House now.'

'Who's Eve?'

'Eve Harland. Her late mother was Philip's cousin. Eve and her husband Woody bought the Red House when Philip died. In fact, they were at the concert tonight, because Woody's firm of solicitors sponsor the choir.'

'I certainly will ask Eve,' I said, 'but going back to Catherine Haldane—what do you know about her?'

'Not much, but I remember when she died—it was the same day the King died. February 6th, 1952.'

Over thirty years before Philip died.

'I remember where she died, too,' he said grimly. 'Parkside. It's closed now.'

I looked at him questioningly.

'What was Parkside?'

'It used to be known as the Macclesfield Asylum.'

The following morning, armed with directions supplied by Keith, I set off for the Red House. I found it with little difficulty and from the outside it was much as Freddie had described it thirteen years earlier. There were two cars on the drive, so it seemed I was in luck and someone was at home. The house was double fronted and the rooms facing the road had bay windows and as I walked up the path to the front door, I could hear the sound of a piano coming from the room on the left. The music stopped abruptly when I rang the doorbell, and soon I heard footsteps approaching. The door opened to reveal an attractive woman I assumed to be Eve.

'Hello!' she exclaimed. 'What a pleasant surprise. It's Alex, isn't it?'

'I hope you don't mind me turning up unannounced, but I was talking to Keith after the concert last night and he thought you might be able to tell me more than he could about Philip Nash and Catherine Haldane.'

She looked first astonished and then pleased and stood aside to welcome me inside.

'Come in,' she cried. 'Come in.'

I followed her down the tiled hallway and into the room in which she'd been playing the piano. It was a beautiful room, painted white, with striking black and red floor length curtains and walls lined with books. She beckoned me towards a comfy looking sofa and sat near me in an armchair upholstered in a fabric that matched the curtains.

'I loved your performance, by the way,' she said. 'The whole evening was a joy.'

'It was. I love the commitment and enthusiasm that amateur choirs bring to their performances. It was obvious they were all having a whale of a time.'

'You're right. That's one reason Woody and I support the choir. It's such an important part of the local community. But tell me—how can I help you?'

I told her about the archive that Philip had bequeathed to Freddie.

'I knew something about that because Alan Medlicott told me that Philip's song collection was going to an eminent academic. That was how he described Freddie.'

'Before any systematic sorting of the collection was done, we found this.'

I reached into my music case and handed her the manuscript of the song *Requiescat.* I expected her to be surprised, but instead her reaction was one of sheer delight.

'It's clearly part of a song-cycle,' I said as she scanned the pages, 'but it's the only one of the ten songs that were found in the collection and we've always wondered what happened to the others.'

'They're here,' she said, her eyes shining with excitement. 'I have them! I always wondered if there was a tenth song. And here it is.'

She stood up and went to a shelf of books near the piano and picked out a tall, slim volume which she handed to me. It was a bound book of handwritten songs, all in Philip's neat notation, and all dedicated to Catherine Haldane. I gasped.

'Where did you find this?'

'I didn't find it. Philip gave it to me.'

At a quick glance, I could see there were settings of poems by W B

Yeats, Thomas Hardy, Edgar Allan Poe, Christina Rossetti, and Emily Dickinson.

'You and Philip must have been close.'

'We were. I'd known him all my life and he taught me to play the piano.'

'Did you know Catherine Haldane or did Philip talk to you about her?'

She sighed. 'Let's have some coffee and then I'll tell you what I know.'

She gestured to me to stay while she went to make coffee, and I took the opportunity to study the songs. Even on a cursory look, I could tell that the cycle was a contemplation on love in its many guises. When Eve reappeared with the coffee, we settled down to talk.

'To answer your question, no, I didn't know Catherine. By the time I was born, she had already been admitted to the county mental hospital, but later on, I heard about her from my mother and from Philip.'

'What's her story?'

'It's a sad one, I'm afraid. She wasn't born a Haldane. Her name was Catherine Carshaw and she was Vincent Nash's sweetheart.'

'Philip's older brother.'

'That's right. When Vincent was killed in 1916, Catherine was devastated. My mother described her as an intelligent girl, feisty and high-spirited, but prone to be impulsive and capricious. Mum said that Vincent's death seemed to exacerbate all the unstable parts of her personality and she never recovered from it.'

'Where did Philip fit in?'

'She was ten years older than him but when Vincent died, there was a bond between them and they became friends. As Philip became a young man, he fell in love with her. My mother thought he would be good for Catherine and hoped that when he was older, they might one day marry.'

'What went wrong?'

'Philip went away to university and about a year before he graduated, Catherine upped and married Walter Haldane.' She shook her head. 'From my mother's description of him, he sounds like Captain Troy in *Far from the Madding Crowd*. It was a difficult marriage. It didn't make either of them happy. He was a rogue and she became increasingly erratic. Her mental health was significantly affected by multiple miscarriages and the crisis came when after a very difficult pregnancy, she gave birth to a son, who sadly died when he was three weeks old. Soon after that, she became confused and suspicious and started having delusions and hallucinations. There were manic episodes when she'd appear to be on top of the world and depressive lows when she couldn't get out of bed. Walter washed his hands of her and she was admitted to hospital at Parkside.'

'What a shocking story. Was there a diagnosis?'

'I'm not sure, but today I think it would be seen as post-partum psychosis.'

At that point, I heard a door open and footsteps in the passageway.

'That will be Woody. They're painting his office in Nantwich so he's working at home today. I'll tell him you're here.'

She got up and popped her head round the door.

'Darling—we have a visitor. Come and say hello to Alex.'

He followed her into the room and I realised I'd seen him speaking to the conductor after the concert. He, too, recognised me and I stood up to shake hands.

'Alex is interested to know about Philip and Catherine and Keith suggested he talk to us. He has the missing song from the song cycle.'

'How fantastic,' said Woody.

He was a good-looking man with an inquisitive face and a confident energy.

'Don't let me interrupt,' he said, sitting at the other end of the sofa.

'Eve was telling me about Catherine's illness. She died at Parkside. Is that right?'

'It is,' said Woody. 'Walter didn't divorce her, but he did nothing to facilitate her release, either.'

'Philip visited her until the end,' said Eve. 'He thought she'd grown so used to being in an institution, it would have been very hard for her to adjust to a more independent life in the community.'

'After Philip died,' Woody said, 'we went to look at Parkside and we were astounded by its size—vast and complex buildings covering hundreds of acres, some of it farmed to produce the food they ate. The site is surrounded now by urban sprawl but the Asylum—as it was known locally—would once have stood in complete isolation.'

'Did Philip talk about what it was like to visit Catherine in that place?'

'I asked him that,' Eve said. 'I thought it must have broken his heart to see her confined in that way. He said that though there were undoubtedly cruelties and suffering...'

'...and errors,' Woody interjected. 'Philip said there were people there who shouldn't have been; who'd been put away and forgotten about.'

'But they encouraged visitors,' Eve went on, 'and he and Catherine could walk in the grounds and the woodlands, and there was a plentiful supply of books, and regular art and music classes, so they did try to make life there congenial.'

'He must have been devoted to her,' I said.

'Oh, he was,' Eve said, without hesitation, 'and he grieved for her right to the end. And I mean, to the end. He arranged for her to be buried in Nantwich Cemetery and he visited her grave for as long as he could until he became too ill.'

'Are there any photographs of Catherine?' I asked.

'We have one,' Eve said. 'When we were negotiating the purchase of the house, we asked if we could have or buy some of Philip's books. He'd told us that Catherine loved poetry and said if she was depressed or anxious when he visited, he would read poems to her. There were many poetry books here and no doubt, Philip referred to them when he chose the texts he set to music, and in one of those books, we found a photograph.'

She got up and went over to the same bookshelf from which she'd taken the volume of songs. She handed me a framed head and shoulders photograph which I'd noticed earlier and assumed was a relative of hers or her husband.

'What an expressive face,' I said. 'She was lovely. Do you know when this was taken?'

'July 1916,' Eve said, 'a few weeks before Vincent died. There's a pencilled note on the back of the print.'

She returned the photograph to its place on the bookshelf.

'Whenever I think about Catherine and Philip, it reminds me that life is full of if onlys.'

'It is,' I agreed. I was still holding the volume of songs. 'When did Philip give you this?'

'Not long before he died. He kept the songs in a drawer in a bedside table and it was only after he died, and I had them bound that I saw there seemed to be a song missing.'

'I guess that song had become separated from the others and was bundled up by the solicitors with the music they delivered to Freddie.'

'Did Freddie manage to organise and catalogue the collection?' Woody asked.

'He did. It's an impressive archive now.'

I paused.

'His daughter, Emily—my late wife—did most of the work and since she died, it's been completed by a couple of Freddie's graduate students. Freddie was extremely fond of Philip and he and Emily always hoped we'd discover what happened to his other songs.' I paused again. 'Did Catherine know that Philip had written them for her?'

Eve shook her head.

'We don't know that—and we also don't know when they were written because none of them are dated.'

'Did Philip leave any diaries?'

'We didn't find any personal diaries,' Eve said, 'but he kept diaries recording the concerts at which he'd played and the music he performed. We have them here and you're welcome to borrow them.'

'Thank you. I know Freddie would love to see them.'

'We'll pack them in a box for you when you leave,' said Woody.

'Have any of these songs ever been performed?'

'I doubt it,' Eve said. 'I've played them for my own interest—though the pianist is a key protagonist in most of the songs and the accompaniments are rather beyond me.'

I knew this would be of interest to Johnny.

'Did Philip hope the songs would be performed?'

'I don't know,' she replied. 'Would you perform them?'

'I'd like to study them, if I may, and if I feel they suit me, I'd love to sing them.'

'Take them,' Eve said, 'and let us know what you decide.'

'And if you need any financial backing for a performance,' said Woody, 'we'll help.'

I had learnt more than I'd hoped possible and couldn't wait to show Freddie and Johnny the songs and the diaries, but before I headed back to Oxford, I drove to Macclesfield in search of the only address I had for Lillian. I had no idea how to find it, but luckily, as I was wondering who to ask, I spotted the post office sorting office. The woman on the desk was helpful. She showed me on a street map how to find the address and let me look in an up-to-date phone directory. There was not a single Baranski listed in the area, but to satisfy myself that I had tried, I went to the address anyway. It was a neat, redbrick Victorian terraced house divided into two flats, with doorbells and name labels for each.

Neither of the names was Baranski.

Into the Silent Land

Philip Nash curated and performed many programmes at the Wigmore Hall so it was fitting that his song cycle should receive its first performance there. We wanted the focus of the evening to be on Philip's songs, but to complete the programme and provide a connection to Vincent Nash, we selected half a dozen of George Butterworth's Sussex folk songs.

Freddie agreed to write the programme notes and talk about his friendship with Philip. As part of his research, he went to Philip's diaries, and it was during a trawl of these journals that the past gave up another gift. From within the pages of the volume covering the year 1949 he found a black and white photograph of a man and a woman standing on the edge of an expanse of lawn. The man was looking down at the woman and smiling; the woman looking directly at the camera, her expression one of surprised amusement. On the back of the print, Philip had written: *With Catherine in the garden at Parkside, July 1949.*

'Her face looks rather worn here,' I said. 'I guess age and illness—not to mention years of incarceration—had taken their toll.'

'She would have been fifty-one years old,' Freddie said. 'And Philip, ten years younger.'

He was studying the photo closely and seemed lost in thought.

'July 1949,' he said at last. 'Three months before that, Philip attended the funeral of a girl he had taught at Chetham's. Her name was Laura and she was my first love.'

I looked at him in surprise.

'He consoled me that day. Urged me to carry on, to believe there would be better days ahead. I told him he didn't understand, and I've never forgotten the look on his face when he disputed that. "Oh, I do," he said. "Trust me, I do." Now I know he was no stranger to heartache.'

I worked on the songs with both Freddie and Johnny. Between us, we knew all the poems and I had sung some of them in other settings, but Philip's style was unlike anything else I had ever encountered. It could sound quintessentially English in the way we associate with the likes of Howells and Vaughan Williams, but though there were sometimes snatches of these and other composers in his music, it was not derivative. Philip had clearly not set out to imitate anyone—he had his own voice.

Freddie's study of the diaries was comprehensive—he read every entry—and his diligence was rewarded by the discovery of jottings on some of the poems.

The first two were by Yeats, and about the opening song, Philip wrote:
In August 1946 I went on a walking holiday in Cornwall, and along the route I bought postcards from places I'd been or sights of interest I'd seen. It was a solitary expedition, but I found I could feel less alone if I wrote to Catherine recounting my experiences. By the end of the trip, I'd sent her over a dozen cards and when I next went to see her, they were propped on the mantlepiece in her room. From time to time, she would pick up one or other of them and silently study the picture or re-read what I'd written. I imagine these tokens were a tantalising glimpse of a world from which she'd long ago been removed.

The card she seemed to like best was a water colour illustration of a quaint Victorian style bookshop called The Word Weaver. Its showy curved glass frontage was matched by its colourful book displays and I'd described spending a happy couple of hours browsing there, while sheltering from a heavy rainstorm. Still holding the card, Catherine opened a book on her bedside table and showed me a poem by Yeats called Where My Books Go.

All the words that I utter,
And all the words that I write,
Must spread out their wings untiring,
And never rest in their flight,
Till they come where your sad, sad heart is,
And sing to you in the night,
Beyond where the waters are moving,
Storm-darken'd or starry bright.

She told me how much my words had touched and consoled her, and it gave me great joy to know that my musings had been a source of connection and solace. The idea of my words singing to her in the night inspired me to set the poem to music. The song turned out so well I decided it could form part of a song cycle dedicated to Catherine.

In my mind's eye, I visualised Catherine and Philip enjoying quiet time together in a spartan hospital room; kindred spirits, whose love endured despite being forever lived out in the shadows. It was easy to see why this poem became the catalyst for the song cycle. Its language was tender and felt deeply personal, and Philip's lyrical setting echoed the poem's urgent rhythms and lilting repetitions. With its image of words being winged emissaries tirelessly soaring towards a loved one's heart, this was the most overtly romantic song in the collection and quickly became one of my favourites.

The second Yeats setting was *He Wishes for the Cloths of Heaven,* about which Philip wrote: *Like so many of his poems, this one was written for Maud Gonne, the woman Yeats loved for many years and regarded as his muse. She was clearly an extraordinary woman—actress, activist, feminist, mystic—and in all her complexity, she reminds me of Catherine. Maud and Yeats met in London in January 1889, and Yeats was immediately overwhelmed. It was the start of a mutually obsessive relationship that would last half a century. But what Yeats did not discover until very much later was that less than three weeks before their momentous first encounter, Maud had given birth in Paris to a boy called Georges—a child who died when he was still a baby.*

What powerful resonances this woman must have had for Philip.

The third song, *Because I could not stop for Death,* was the first of three by Emily Dickinson. About this, Philip simply wrote: *I am fascinated by Emily Dickinson. What a strange, sad life she had. She was regarded as eccentric, habitually dressed all in white and living in almost total isolation, largely in her bedroom. And yet, her poems! I love them.*

Because I could not stop for Death –
He kindly stopped for me –
The Carriage held but just Ourselves –
And Immortality.

We slowly drove – He knew no haste
And I had put away
My labor and my leisure too,
For His Civility –

We passed the School, where Children strove
At Recess – in the Ring –
We passed the Fields of Gazing Grain –
We passed the Setting Sun –

Or rather – He passed Us –
The Dews drew quivering and Chill –
For only Gossamer, my Gown –
My Tippet – only Tulle –

We paused before a House that seemed
A Swelling of the Ground –
The Roof was scarcely visible –
The Cornice – in the Ground –

Since then –'tis Centuries—and yet
Feels shorter than the Day
I first surmised the Horses' Heads
Were toward Eternity –

The fourth song was another setting of Yeats, *When you are old,* and another that was inspired by Maud Gonne.

When you are old and grey and full of sleep,
And nodding by the fire, take down this book,
And slowly read, and dream of the soft look
Your eyes had once, and of their shadows deep;
How many loved your moments of glad grace,
And loved your beauty with love false or true,
But one man loved the pilgrim soul in you,
And loved the sorrows of your changing face;
And bending down beside the glowing bars,
Murmur, a little sadly, how Love fled
And paced upon the mountains overhead
And hid his face amid a crowd of stars.

Yeats was 28 when this poem was published, wrote Philip, *and Gonne was 27. It's written about two young people imagining what life will be like when they are old, and although it's specifically about Yeats and Gonne, it could be about any young couple looking ahead to what the future may hold. Yeats invites Maud to cast her mind forward to a time when she is old and grey; to a time when she is no longer a glamorous actress but a frail old woman nodding by the fire. He says that while many men loved her beauty and moments of triumph, he loved her for who she is deep inside; and continued to love her even as her looks began to fade.*

'Perhaps Eve would let us reproduce the photo of Philip and Catherine alongside these words?' I suggested, and I was pleased when she readily agreed.

Freddie found no entries about the fifth song, *The Voice* by Thomas Hardy, but it was a poem I knew well and more than any other Hardy poem, it was this one that had made me fear I would struggle to ever sing of love and loss again. Writing about his grief and longing for his late wife, Hardy captures how hard it is to accept that a person who has died is never coming back.

Woman much missed, how you call to me, call to me,
Saying that now you are not as you were
When you had changed from the one who was all to me,
But as at first, when our day was fair.

Can it be you that I hear? Let me view you, then,
*   Standing as when I drew near to the town*
Where you would wait for me: yes, as I knew you then,
Even to the original air-blue gown!

Or is it only the breeze, in its listlessness
Travelling across the wet mead to me here,
You being ever dissolved to wan wistlessness,
Heard no more again far or near?

Thus I; faltering forward,
Leaves around me falling,
Wind oozing thin through the thorn from norward,
And the woman calling.

I had never before sung a setting of this poem and Philip's song forced me to pay close attention to the meaning of the words. The speaker feels as if he can hear—and almost see—his former love, but he also knows deep down that he'll never meet her again. Her death leaves him in a strange limbo, feeling as if this woman is both always with him *and* lost to him forever. I found this the hardest and most painful of all the ten songs to sing.

The sixth song was *A Dream Within a Dream* by Edgar Allan Poe.

Take this kiss upon the brow!
And, in parting from you now,
Thus much let me avow —
You are not wrong, who deem
That my days have been a dream;
Yet if hope has flown away
In a night, or in a day,
In a vision, or in none,
Is it therefore the less gone?
All that we see or seem
Is but a dream within a dream.

I stand amid the roar
Of a surf-tormented shore,
And I hold within my hand
Grains of the golden sand —
How few! yet how they creep
Through my fingers to the deep,
While I weep — while I weep!
O God! Can I not grasp
Them with a tighter clasp?
O God! can I not save
One from the pitiless wave?
Is all that we see or seem
But a dream within a dream?

Philip's notes said: *In one of his last poems,* A Dream Within a Dream, *published in 1849, the year he died at the age of 40, Poe questions the meaning of life. He muses on the fragility and fleetingness of everything and asks whether anything we do has any lasting or real effect. He wonders whether he has, in fact, been living in a fantasy world. I read the poem to Catherine, and she was particularly taken by the vivid analogy in the second stanza when Poe compares the slipping away of important things in life to the slipping away of the grains of sand he holds in his hand. 'There's something rather desolate about it,' she said, 'the thought that love can seem so certain until, one day, it's suddenly gone.'*

The next song was *They say that Time assuages* by Emily Dickinson. Freddie found nothing in Philip's journals about this poem, but its inclusion in the cycle was not in any way surprising, because the poet's argument is one that Philip himself might have debated: that the idea that time can heal all wounds is a myth—that real suffering never truly goes away; that time is not a remedy for suffering, but rather a test of a person's ability to endure it.

They say that "Time assuages"–
Time never did assuage –
An actual suffering strengthens
As Sinews do, with age –

Time is a Test of Trouble -
But not a Remedy -
If such it prove, it prove too
There was no Malady –

The next song, *We grow accustomed to the dark,* was another by Dickinson and another for which Freddie found no notes. I knew the poem and told Freddie about the conversation I had once had about it with Josh when we'd agreed that darkness becomes part of our lives, something we grow accustomed to and learn to accept.

We grow accustomed to the Dark –
When Light is put away –
As when the Neighbor holds the Lamp
To witness her Goodbye –

A Moment – We Uncertain step
For newness of the night –
Then – fit our Vision to the Dark –
And meet the Road – erect –

And so of larger – Darknesses –
Those Evenings of the Brain –
When not a Moon disclose a sign –
Or Star – come out – within –

The Bravest –grope a little –
And sometimes hit a Tree
Directly in the Forehead –
But as they learn to see –

Either the Darkness alters –
Or something in the sight
Adjusts itself to Midnight –
And Life steps almost straight.

The penultimate song was a setting of *Remember* by Christina Rossetti, from which the song cycle took its name, and which my mother read at Emily's funeral. Philip's note in his diary was brief: *Catherine loved this poem and at her request, I read it at her funeral.*

The most poignant note was written on February 6th, 1952. *Catherine died today. Where have you gone, my darling? Have you vanished into nothingness? Wherever you are, may you at last be at peace.*

The final song was, of course, *Requiescat.*

Philip's very personal choice of poems meant that the song cycle was not only a memorial to a much-loved woman, but was part autobiography as well, and for these two reasons, I found it a challenging undertaking. Learning the songs well enough to perform them by heart in public took time and application. Time remembering and reflecting on my own loves, my own losses, my own sorrows. Even after all the many years of being without Emily—almost thirteen—I still sometimes felt myself, at best—as Hardy put it—"faltering forward".

There were other challenges, too. I began to notice that the muscles in my left leg, my hips and my lower back ached more than ever before. I became easily exhausted and couldn't walk as far as I once had. I feared these new physical limitations were an ominous sign; that hidden damage done by the polio virus many years before meant that as I passed middle age, the disease I had survived in childhood, had an unpleasant sequel in store.

An Untold Story

The pavement outside the concert hall was busy as latecomers jostled to get inside out of the rain, many hurrying to deposit wet coats and umbrellas in the cloakroom before taking their seats in the auditorium. In the dressing rooms, the performers readied themselves, waiting for the call to take to the stage, Alex and Johnny in their usual concert dress, Freddie, striking in black trousers and black polo neck jumper.

At Chancery Lane station, Lillian waited impatiently for a westbound service that would take her to Bond Street, from where it was a short walk to the Wigmore Hall. The station announcer apologised several times for delays on the Central Line, but the notice board now indicated that a train was approaching. She was relieved when she saw its lights come into view, but full of trepidation about the step she was taking.

Since *Death in Venice*, seven years earlier, she'd become invisible to the people whose world she once shared. A world, that for her, was never the same after the disaster at Stonehurst. Since then, secrets and obfuscations had become a way of life, but she was on a different path now, and was ready to tell her story and to make reparation—or try to.

The train crawled towards Bond Street, a destination less than two miles away, and not for the first time she told herself it would have been quicker to walk. She cursed the torrential rain that had persuaded her to take the underground and though when she arrived at the hall, the front doors were closed, she had still made it with enough time to spare to buy a programme. She took her seat in the back row of the stalls, adjusted her headscarf, and scanned as much of the programme as she could before the houselights went down.

A credit on the cover thanked Eve and Woody Harland for making the performance possible, while inside, the texts of all the songs were given in full and there were lengthy background notes written by Freddie Fairfax. There were biographies and photographs of the performers and composer, and of Catherine Haldane, the woman described as the inspiration for the song cycle. She recognised two of the poems because Alex had sung them in Brecon, in settings by other composers, the memory of which took her back to a time when she was full of hope and expectation. She continued flicking through the programme until she came to a whole page devoted to the Philip Nash Song Collection, where there was a photograph and a lengthy note about Emily Ingram and her key role in establishing the archive. Seeing Emily's bright, vivacious face was a shock, because Lillian had trained herself to think of Emily as no more than a ghostly presence from Alex's past, a ghost whose enchantment would surely fade over time. This image of a woman once so vibrant made her doubt that she could be easily erased from memory.

About another ghost, she was also uncertain. Was Romy any more than a casual affair embarked upon during a time of heightened passions and bottled-up desires or did she, too, still haunt Alex's psyche and trouble his peace of mind?

The house lights were lowered and the three performers made their entrance. They walked onto the stage and bowed, before Johnny went to the piano and Alex sat on a chair to the side. Lillian was sitting too far away to see closely, but she thought he looked older. But then, so did she. Life had taken its toll. Freddie stepped forward to welcome the audience and explain that they would start with six folk song arrangements by George Butterworth, after which they would take a short break before the Philip Nash song cycle, which he and Alex would introduce together.

But for Lillian, the evening was already spoilt. The six folk songs barely registered because reading the tribute to Emily had left her feeling deflated, her hard-won confidence draining away inexorably. She hated herself for allowing habitual feelings of inadequacy and jealousy to cast a pall on the evening, but she'd arrived in a highly charged state of mind, and it took little to tip her mood into peevishness.

By the time they came to the song cycle, she was thoroughly out of sorts. Freddie did most of the introductions, but Alex offered observations on the songs from a singer's perspective. He ended by talking about the final song, *Requiescat*.

'It's a prayer for the repose of the dead, and we believe Philip composed it after Catherine died in 1952. I'd like to dedicate this first performance of *Requiescat* to my late wife, Emily, because it was she who found this song and who set us all hoping there might be others that we would one day find. She also shared our desire to know who Catherine Haldane was and what part she played in Philip's life.'

He paused and smiled.

'It was a mystery Emily hoped would one day be solved. And solved it now is.'

Clearly moved by these words, Freddie stepped off the stage and took a seat near the front of the stalls. Lillian tried to quieten her racing mind, to listen to the words, and enjoy hearing Alex's voice again. He sang, as always, with total commitment—declamatory and impassioned, gentle and meditative, whatever the words and the settings required, and always openhearted and sincere. He sang of love and loss and suffering, and she felt convinced that in his heart he was singing about a love that time could not extinguish, a love that would endure to the end.

How foolish she had been to think she could ever compare or compete with Emily.

She'd intended to go backstage afterwards, to congratulate Alex, to admit she owed him an explanation for her silence, to give him a letter in which she told him everything and to ask if they could meet. But this now felt pointless. The belief she had nurtured ever since the collapse of her marriage still held: that being second best would be worse than being alone. And at the end, she hurried away before the house lights came up, the letter stuffed into the bottom of her bag.

Life changes

I was used to some daily fluctuations in my energy or strength, but not giving in to my body had always worked before, so I tended to push on in spite of exhaustion or weakness. But now the fatigue was sometimes debilitating and the loss of power in muscles not previously affected was alarming. The symptoms recalled all too painfully the losses I'd incurred decades earlier, but for almost a year I lived in a state of denial, until eventually, I was forced to face up to the reality of what was happening.

Eamon advised me to go back to the hospital in London where I was treated as a child, recommending two consultants who had experience of patients presenting with post-polio syndrome. Both doctors recommended more rest and less stress, and though moderate exercise was advocated, the emphasis was on conserving energy as the best way of managing fatigue and weakness. They stressed that I should minimise the strain on my legs and lower back and so, in defence of my mobility and independence, a walking stick became part of my arsenal.

By this time, I realised I would also need to develop a new psychological response to the disease, not only because it threatened my sense of who I was, but because it cast doubt on my ability to sustain the career I loved. I found the hospital appointments dispiriting and was touched when Johnny insisted on coming with me whenever he could. One day when we had an unusually long wait, we fell into conversation with an older man sitting opposite us at a small table in the waiting room. He was a former newspaper editor, struck down with polio in 1948 when he was nine years old.

'I was football mad,' he said, 'but playing for England was ruled out.' He looked down at his hands. 'Even though neither of my arms are much good, by working hard to improve my handwriting, I found another way through life.'

'Sounds like my story,' I said. 'I never played for England either, but I've made a good life in music as a singer.'

The man smiled.

'A lot of polio survivors ended up being creative and living inside their heads.'

'I certainly did. For a long time, books and music were my closest companions.'

'Even though there were thousands of us in the same boat, it was lonely being a polio kid, didn't you find?'

'I did.'

'I don't know about you, but I wasn't prepared for this post-polio syndrome,' he said, shaking his head in frustration. 'You think you've gone through all the bad times and suddenly you find yourself getting weaker, experiencing pain and fatigue. A writer I know describes us as victims of an ancient scourge, survivors of some forgotten war, the stuff of old headlines. I went into a deep depression at first. And then I told myself to just get on with it, so I still write and I still enjoy watching football. I hate asking for help, but for the most part, people are kind and want to help.'

Johnny was listening intently. He knew I was struggling emotionally, and that I was worried about the impact on my stamina and my voice.

'Even if your voice changes as your body becomes less robust,' he said at last, 'there'll be other ways you can put your creativity and experience to good use.'

The man nodded.

'You could teach, for instance,' he said. 'Even if your voice does change, none of your other gifts need be wasted.'

That thought sustained me and in time, I accepted the frustrations of living with my damaged body. To avoid over-exerting myself, I organised my performance schedule more conservatively and accepted only engagements I really wanted to do. Beyond changes that were normal through the process of ageing, I didn't notice any negative impacts on my voice. It was perhaps not as consistently sweet as it had once been, nor was the top as effortless, but it had the weight that comes with maturity and my technique was mercifully unaffected.

Gradually, masterclasses with students and emerging artists became a key part of my programme. Johnny was now on the staff of the Royal College of Music and he and I worked together as teachers and mentors with both singers and accompanists, and I was pleased to discover how much I enjoyed supporting young musicians at the outset of their careers.

I still occasionally went to watch West Ham with Luke, but now his son came with us, a strapping twelve-year-old, whose young head was chock full of facts and statistics about all the teams in the Premier League.

During this time, the ground floor flat beneath mine went up for sale. I sold my flat and moved into the garden flat I had often coveted, and which was now much more practical for me. I was sad to leave my top-floor eyrie with its memories of Emily and Ruth, but the move signified something inevitable—the need to adapt to changing circumstances.

I stayed in touch with Christina, and we met every month or so for a pub meal. She still ran her shop in the covered market and remained as kind and quirky as ever, but life changed for her, too. She gave up her houseboat, saying that as she got older, she found it too cold and damp in winter, and she moved to a terraced house in Jericho to live with a man she'd met through a Stop the War march in 2003.

I thought my parents would eventually move back to the UK, but my mother pointed out that Egypt had been her home for over half her life and she feared she would struggle to adapt to living in England again. In late November 2006, the three of us went to Alexandria to celebrate their eightieth birthdays and they told me they felt too old to uproot themselves from the country they loved. I was glad they were in good health and content with their lot, but I'd spent most of my life missing them, wishing they they were not so far away, so I was disappointed.

Of course, Freddie remained a surrogate father. When he turned seventy, he retired from full-time teaching and though he retained an honorary position at Pembroke, he devoted more time to writing and broadcasting. His radio programmes became another new venture for me, and I regularly joined the panels of "experts" with whom he discussed his chosen subject matter. He began to think about how best he could secure the future of the song archive, and as if sent by providence, he was approached by the John Rylands Library in Manchester. He and I went to look around and meet the staff and we both felt it would be a worthy depository for the collection. He could have simply bequeathed it in his will, but though it was a wrench to let it go, he wanted to be involved in its installation and digitisation at its new home.

His life changed in another way, too. A nearby house in Park Town was sold for the first time in years and the buyers threw a house-warming party for their new neighbours. Freddie was not a party animal, so I offered to go with him and be his excuse to leave early if he was bored. In fact, it was a jolly affair. The hosts were generous and easy-going, and Freddie met people he had barely spoken to before. One of these was Clara Wenham, an American in her early sixties who'd been widowed some years earlier. She was tall and statuesque, with thick blonde hair, folded into an intricate chignon, and though at first glance the fine lines around her pale blue eyes gave her a somewhat fragile look, she was a spirited woman who knew her own mind. Later, when Freddie observed, casually, 'well, she was interesting. We seemed to get on rather well,' I couldn't help laughing.

'What's funny?' he asked.

'I'm just imagining how Emily might have described your encounter with the American widow. She'd have raised her eyebrows and said in a loud stage whisper, "She was very beautiful and took a great fancy to Dad, even though he's getting old and decrepit".'

'That sounds like her,' he said, laughing, but soon afterwards, he and Clara began to spend time together. Just when his life might have seemed to be narrowing, she had blown it wide open again, and I could tell he was experiencing emotional fulfilment that was all the more wondrous for being so unexpected.

6 December 2006

Behold, I tell you a mystery; we shall not all sleep, but we shall all be chang'd in a moment, in the twinkling of an eye, at the last trumpet.

I waited at the bus stop on Banbury Road and looked up at the thickening sky. I'd heard that snow was falling all over the Cotswolds and though, so far, it had not arrived in Oxford, daylight seemed to be fading fast and it was not yet one o'clock. I adjusted the shoulder strap of my suit bag and pulled my woolly hat tight over my ears. The mediterranean warmth of Alexandria seemed a world away. Fortunately, I didn't have long to wait for a bus to take me the short distance to the Ashmolean, from where I would walk to the Town Hall. Previously, I would have walked the whole way, but with a long day ahead, it seemed wise to conserve my energy and spare my legs.

I was looking forward to the concert—I never tired of *Messiah*—but a few weeks earlier, my left leg had given way without warning, and I knew I would have to husband my physical strength carefully. I was in good time and once backstage, I hung up my suit in the dressing room I was sharing with the bass and countertenor soloists and made myself a cup of camomile tea. From next door, I heard the sound of a soprano going through her warmup exercises. I knew it was Anna Maxwell, with whom I'd never worked before, and when the singing stopped, I went to introduce myself.

'Hello, I'm Alex Ingram. I thought I'd come to make your acquaintance before we meet on the concert platform.'

'I'm so pleased to meet you,' she said, holding out her hand. 'Please, have a seat.'

As I sat down, my eye was caught by a brightly coloured handmade good luck card propped against her mirror. She saw me looking at it and smiled.

'It's from Michael Manning—the boy in the production of *The Turn of the Screw* I did at Myddleton in the summer. He was brilliant as Miles and such a sweet boy. I was very sad to say goodbye to him at the end, but he's coming tonight, which will be lovely.'

'I did *Curlew River* some years ago,' I said, 'and everyone in the company became very attached to the two boys who shared the role of the son. Strange to think those delightful little boys will be young men in their early twenties now.'

'Ah yes, they grow up, and so will Michael, in no time at all. Am I right in thinking there was talk of you stepping in to play Quint when Harri Gwilym broke his leg?'

'There was, but…' I shook my head. 'I'd made a decision not to do any more opera, and to be honest, it would take a more agreeable piece than *The Turn of the Screw* to make me reconsider.'

'It's a tough one,' she conceded, 'but it worked well, particularly in the outdoor setting.'

We talked for a while longer about our work and our travels, and a little about where we each were in our lives, and I sensed I could have enjoyed playing Quint to her Governess.

'Do you have anyone in tonight?' she asked.

'Yes, my father-in-law Freddie Fairfax and his friend Clara will be here. How about you?'

'My friend Mark's coming, and actually, he'll be looking after Michael, because Michael's mother has a work commitment somewhere in Oxford. She'll leave him with Mark at the beginning and collect him afterwards.'

'How old is he?'

'Just thirteen, but he's small for his age.' She paused. 'It's hard to explain but he can seem endearingly child-like but also old beyond his years.'

'An only child?' I guessed.

'Yes, an only child, and a lonely one, I fear.'

She made her way to the Garden Quad where people were gathering outside the Auditorium. She was apprehensive about the evening ahead and glad she'd worn her smartest clothes and had her hair cut short and restyled. She saw several people she knew, and a group of women waved at her across the crowded foyer. She waved back, but decided against joining them and instead chose to go in and find a seat. A colleague from her office was standing near the entrance door.

'Hey, I like the hair,' he said. 'Are you staying for a drink afterwards?'

'Just a quick one.'

The Auditorium was still almost empty, and she was glad to have some time to gather her thoughts before the discussion began. She studied the sheet the usher had given her. It was headed *Miscarriages of Justice: why do they happen?* The panel was to consist of the Director of Public Prosecutions, a senior police officer, a solicitor, a barrister from the Criminal Appeal Reviews Commission, and a woman whose son had been found guilty of murder and imprisoned for a crime he did not commit. The facilitator was a Professor of Psychology from St John's who had written extensively about moral ambiguities and ethical dilemmas.

She was all too familiar with such quandaries. For too long, she'd been carrying a burden of guilt she knew she would only be able to cast off if she tried to make amends for the harm and pain she had caused, whatever the cost to herself, be it anger or even rejection. All the years of self-justifying had given her nothing but unease, not peace of mind. She'd moved south as if she wanted to be found out, like a criminal returning to the scene of a crime. Regret and remorse proved powerful motivators for seeking reconciliation.

Earlier, on the way into town, her son had asked her to explain what was meant by a miscarriage of justice. He listened intently to her answer, his large expressive eyes conveying his curiosity and intelligence, just as on other occasions the same eyes could signal excitement or anxiety or sadness, their eloquence a continual reminder of his father.

I followed my fellow soloists onto the stage, score in one hand and walking stick in the other. I stood alongside the bass soloist, and to his left so there was space next to me for a music stand on which I could place my score if I needed a free hand to hold my stick. For now, I secured the crook of the stick onto the stand and hoped it would remain there unneeded.

I hated how this must look to the audience, but it was a necessary precaution. Like a sportsman fearing career-ending injury, I never knew if a performance might be my last, if one day all this might be too much for my weakened body to manage, so I determined to enjoy every note. To my relief, I made it through to the end without physical mishap, and I loved every moment. As it always did, Handel's music filled me with a well-pool of joy and gratitude.

When the discussion was over, and while the rest of the audience streamed out into the foyer, she stayed in her seat, reflecting on what she'd heard, the mother's testimony having been particularly harrowing. Her son was utterly traumatised and broken by the experience of being locked away for a crime he didn't commit, and though he was now free, he had been offered neither financial nor psychological support. The injustices of his case were striking enough, but what made the most powerful impression was the mother's tireless campaign to achieve justice for her son. 'He has been wronged,' she said. 'Someone needs to make atonement, to make reparation. There needs to be a reckoning.'

The concert organisers laid on drinks and a simple buffet outside the auditorium in a large open area which was already bedecked with Christmas decorations. Though many of the players and singers had headed straight back to London, there were enough people there to create a cheery buzz. Freddie and Clara stayed for a drink and after they left, I sat down near the Christmas tree next to an empty chair on which I put my suit bag and my coat. I looked around to see if there were other guests I knew. Not far away from where I sat, Anna was talking animatedly to a man and a boy I guessed were Mark and Michael. The boy looked full of beans, and I watched as he and Anna chatted easily, visibly delighted to see each other again. Suddenly, in response to something Anna said, Michael turned and broke away and, in his haste, he collided with my chair, dislodging the walking stick which I'd hung over the back, and almost toppling into my lap. I caught him and held him steady.

'No harm done?' I checked.

'I'm sorry,' he stammered, leaning down to pick up the stick and replace it on the back of the chair.

He looked alarmed, as if he thought he might be in trouble, but when he saw me smile, he smiled back, and we both laughed.

'You must be Michael, Anna's friend. She told me how good you were as Miles.'

He blushed but looked pleased.

'Did you hurt your leg?' he asked anxiously.

'It was damaged a long time ago when I caught polio. It hurts now and then—especially if I've been standing for long periods.'

He nodded as if he understood.

'My gran had polio, too. She has to use a walking stick, and sometimes we push her in a wheelchair.'

'I'm not at that stage yet,' I sighed. 'Where were you rushing off to just now?'

'To get something to eat. Would you like anything? I can bring it over.'

I smiled. His large eyes were almost too big for his elfin-like face and his earnest expression was endearing in such a young boy.

'Could you manage a glass of white wine?'

He nodded vigorously and sped off towards the buffet table. I watched him look along the trays of ready poured drinks until he came to the white wine. Having presented me with a large glass, he raced back to the table to pile a plate full of food.

'Why don't we share it?' he suggested. 'I'll hold the plate.'

As he tucked into a sausage roll, I noticed how badly bitten his nails were. He was slightly built but had an air of sturdy resolve about him which was very touching. Sausage roll in hand, he gestured towards my coat, from one of the pockets of which my woolly hat in West Ham colours was visible.

'Do you like football?' he asked.

'I do—West Ham's my team. How about you?'

'Arsenal.'

'Ah,' I said in mock horror. 'Arch-rivals.'

He laughed.

'My lot are better than yours,' he said with a swagger, drawing himself up to his full height, in a gesture that was somehow oddly familiar, a likeness I couldn't readily place.

'Fair enough,' I laughed. 'We're at opposite ends of the league table so there's no arguing with that.'

'So do you go to watch the Hammers?'

'Occasionally. I've been going with my friend Luke for years and now he brings his son along as well.'

'I haven't got anyone to go with,' he said, looking slightly downcast.

While I was thinking of a suitable answer, the conductor called everyone to attention.

'Apart from the success of tonight's performance,' he said, 'we have something else to celebrate. A birthday. So please will you join together to sing Happy Birthday to Alex.'

Someone had gone to the upright piano that was tucked in a corner and after they gave a thunderous introductory chord, everyone launched into song. Michael, standing alongside me, joined in with gusto. He sang with a sweet, slightly husky voice and perfect intonation. When it was over there were whoops and cheers and as I stood up to take a bow, I wondered where the years had gone. How could I be fifty-five years old? Was it really twenty-three years since that other birthday concert when I first met Emily?

'So, when were you born?' Michael asked me, as if reading my mind.

'Sixth of December 1951.'

'Sagittarius,' he said, and then frowned as if trying to calculate my age. 'Wow, fifty-five—that's old.'

I laughed.

'So, when were you born?'

'I was born on the thirty-first of October 1993, which makes me a

Scorpio,' he said solemnly. 'I should have been a Sagittarius, but I came two months early.'

He sounded so grown-up and matter of fact, but I felt a lump in my throat as I imagined him as a small and frail premature baby.

It was snowing and as she hurried down St Giles, flurries of sleet were scudding round her feet and beginning to settle on roofs and gateposts. Before long, the streets would disappear under a blanket of white dust. She hoped she would get there in time, that he would not already have left because of the bad weather. Her mind was racing, agitated by her newfound resolve as much as by the waves of memories and fears that were jostling for attention. When she pushed open the front door of the Town Hall, the entrance area was deserted but from the top of the stairs she could hear the tinkle of glasses and the hum of conversation. She took a moment to compose herself, before making her way up to the first floor.

Display screens had been positioned to close off the space for the reception, but by standing alongside one of the partitions, she was able to see into the gathering. She scanned the crowd and saw Mark Summers, the man to whom she'd entrusted her son, deep in conversation with Anna Maxwell. And then she saw her boy, a short distance away from them, talking to Alex who was sitting down, with a walking stick hung over the back of his chair.

Out of the corner of my eye, my attention was caught by Mark pointing at Michael and calling out to someone emerging from behind one of the display screens.

'Lizzie,' he called. 'Michael's over here by the Christmas tree.'

When I looked again, I doubted the evidence of my own eyes.

'Lizzie?' I said to Michael.

'She's my mum,' he said. 'She's come to collect me.'

But surely, this was the woman I had known as Lillian, older now, and with shorter hair, but still recognisably the same person. As she walked towards us, I stood up. Standing behind Michael, she put her hands on his shoulders and over his head, she said, 'Hello Alex.'

She saw my uncertainty and nodded.

'Yes, I am Lillian,' she said quietly. 'Lizzie's the name I called myself when I was learning to talk and couldn't pronounce Lillian. Lizzie stuck and it's what I was known as until I went to college. It's what my family have aways called me, so I'm Lizzie again now.'

Michael had disentangled himself and was looking and listening with interest.

'Why don't you go and chat to Anna and Mark before we leave?' she suggested.

He shrugged but seemed happy to do as he was told.

'What happened to you?' I asked when Michael was out of earshot. 'I wrote to you, I tried to call you. I even went to your flat in Macclesfield. It was as if you vanished without trace.'

I heard the accusatory tone in my voice and saw that she winced.

'There's so much I need to tell you. So much I want to explain.'

'Where do you live now?'

I saw a look of consternation flicker in her eyes.

'Abingdon,' she said quietly. 'We moved there six years ago.'

I stared at her in disbelief. Abingdon was no more than ten miles away.

'Where did you go after Stonehurst?'

'I went where I said I was going—to my parents in Cheadle Hulme. I intended to support them, but in fact I was unwell and needed looking after myself. My poor mother had me and my father on her hands. He died in the August and I was taken into hospital soon after his funeral. I was there for six weeks before Michael was born and for two weeks afterwards. When Michael was well enough to be discharged, we went to live with my mother.'

I was struggling to keep up with what she was saying.

'And Michael?' I asked in growing disquiet. 'Why is his name Michael Manning? Who's his father?'

'Manning is my family name. My maiden name.'

I willed her to go on, to answer the question, but as if she could not stand the intensity of my gaze, she squeezed her eyes shut and shook her head. When at last she opened her eyes, they were glossy with tears.

'You are his father,' she whispered, her voice sounding hoarse and faint. 'He's your son.'

Reckonings

While Lizzie and I stood rooted to the spot, people began to gather up their belongings and say their goodbyes. A member of the security team was moving around the room, urging everyone to make a move. 'It's snowing hard and freezing,' he told us. 'The roads don't look good.'

Anna hugged Michael and when she and Mark brought him over to join us, Lizzie somehow found the words to thank them for looking after him. While Mark shook Michael's hand, Anna rummaged in her bag and produced a card with her address and phone number on it.

'I expect to be in Oxford quite often now,' she said, handing me the card, 'so perhaps we can get together sometime for a drink or a meal?'

'I'd like that,' I said, trying to hide the chaos of my feelings.

'We're going to walk back to Mark's place, but how will you all get home?' she asked us.

'My car is in St Giles,' Lizzie said, 'so I can give you a lift from there, Alex, if that helps. You might struggle to find a taxi now.'

We put on our coats and as I took my woolly hat out of my pocket, Michael, with a gleeful flourish, produced both Arsenal woolly hat and matching gloves which he waved at me before putting them on with a further flourish. I was glad of this playful moment, and we laughed as we made our way down the stairs and out into the snow. It had settled and was still falling steadily as we walked up Cornmarket and past the Martyrs' Memorial. Michael chattered with excitement at the prospect of snowball fights in the school playground the next day, but Lizzie and I said little. The taxi rank in St Giles was indeed deserted and I was glad to be spared the long walk home in what was now a blizzard.

As we drove slowly north up the Banbury Road, the snow began to drift, making it hard to distinguish the road from the pavements or to recognise the turnings to the side streets. The brilliance of the white snow against the darkness of the night was dazzling and Lizzie was struggling to see through the windscreen, the wipers failing to keep up with the volume of snow hitting the glass.

'There's no way you should attempt to drive to Abingdon,' I said, as the car slithered into the turning to Bardwell Road. 'You can stay here for the night—I have a spare room.'

Lizzie looked unconvinced, as if she doubted the sincerity of my offer, but I insisted, and she agreed gratefully, saying she would call her mother to explain where they were.

The flat was warm, and the table lamps I'd left on cast a welcoming glow in the hallway and the sitting room. Michael appeared suddenly overcome by tiredness and I realised it was long past what would be his normal bedtime.

'Would you like a mug of hot milk?' I asked him 'or would you like to go straight to bed?'

'Bed, please,' he said, yawning.

Lizzie was eyeing up the unfamiliar surroundings and looked uncomfortable.

'Let me show you where it is,' I said, leading them to the spare room which was large enough to have a double bed.

'We'll be fine in here,' Lizzie said. 'Michael can share with me—and before you protest, young man, I'm sure you can cope for one night.'

He pulled a face but was too tired to complain.

'I can lend you a T-shirt,' I said to her, 'but I've nothing small enough for Michael.'

'Don't worry. He's wearing a vest so he can sleep in his underwear.'

'I'll get you some towels and I have a new toothbrush somewhere you can have.'

Michael was yawning continually, and I sensed he would soon be asleep. I left them alone and once he was settled, Lizzie joined me in the sitting room, where I was standing looking out of the window.

'A veritable winter wonderland,' I said, without turning round. 'Everything looks different. Nothing looks the same.'

She came and stood next to me.

'What can I get you to drink?' I asked her. 'I need a whiskey.'

'I'll have one, too, thanks.'

I went to pour the drinks and realised that like Freddie, I kept a tray of spirits on a low bookcase, alongside a photograph of Emily and I on our wedding day, at which Lizzie was now staring.

'Come and sit on the sofa,' I said, taking a seat at one end. 'Then you can tell me everything you need to.'

She reddened and I saw fear in her eyes, but she did as I suggested and sat down at the other end of the sofa. I waited but could see she was struggling to know how to begin.

'When did you know you were pregnant?' I asked, hoping this would help her get started.

'Not until after I left Stonehurst when my mother could see there was something wrong. I hadn't been feeling well for a while and she insisted I see a doctor. I don't know how I could have been so obtuse, but it hadn't occurred to me that I might be pregnant.'

I was sceptical about this but then I remembered how often the papers reported stories of women giving birth not knowing they were pregnant.

'I felt unwell throughout my pregnancy,' she went on. 'Nausea, back ache, and overwhelming exhaustion. During *Death in Venice*, I never felt right, but I put it down to the long hours and the stress of the production and I carried on as best I could. After the show ended and I could rest, I felt no better, so it was obvious that something else was going on.'

I knew that my next question would get to the crux of the matter, and I hesitated before asking it, knowing that whatever the answer was, it would not be easy to hear.

'If you knew I was the father, why didn't you tell me?' I asked her at last.

She took a large gulp of whiskey and shifted her position so she could look at me directly.

'I'm not going to try to justify it. I can only tell you that my reasons were complex.'

I'd guessed that.

'Romy was at the heart of it, though of course, I'm not blaming her, but I was terribly jealous because I became convinced that you'd slept with her at some stage during the rehearsals. I was hurt and angry, though I wasn't surprised. All too many times I'd seen leading ladies and their leading men become embroiled and there's no denying that she was very attractive. I'd heard the other men talking about her in more colourful language, and I assumed you were no different. I also wondered if you were in love with her, that it was more than a casual fling and that you might have wanted to pursue a relationship with her after the show was over.'

'No, that was never going to happen. I did find her attractive, but I knew that Gerard, complicated and problematic though their relationship may have been, was the only man she wanted. And I felt bad about betraying you. I am sorry about that.'

She took a moment to take in the apology.

'But then of course Romy died,' she said, 'and it was simply horrible. She should never have died like that and I felt partly to blame.'

'Why on earth did you feel you were to blame?'

'So many reasons. I asked myself why I hadn't spotted the scarf being dropped or seen that a crew member was missing and that Darren was having to manoeuvre the statue alone or realised that Romy was dizzy and disorientated following a clash of heads with Gerard. I tried to rationalise it by saying I had enough to do to follow the score and give the cues, that I couldn't be expected to see any of that. But I was part of a crew that didn't keep her safe and I was afraid you would blame me for that.'

I looked at her aghast.

'But that still doesn't explain why you never told me you were pregnant with my child.'

'I'd liked you from the start, from when we met on *Curlew River*. When we were together again in Brecon, I felt myself falling in love with you. I thought I could overcome my mistrust of love, but then, just a few short weeks later in Stonehurst, I watched you become infatuated with Romy. My hopes that something special could develop between us were dashed and I felt betrayed. Later, when I discovered I was pregnant, I was sure that if you knew you had fathered a child, you would want to do the right thing. But I couldn't bear to be a poor second choice—again—and I thought, better no father than one who might feel trapped and come to resent him.'

'But you denied me the chance to be his father, to know him, to love him,' I cried, feeling real anguish and frustration now.

'I know how wrong I've been and I'm sorry. I'm truly sorry.'

She reached out and touched my arm.

'I want to make it up to you by allowing you to know him now.'

'What does he know?' I asked at last.

She shook her head.

'He knows nothing. He's asked me repeatedly, and I've never told him, but now I know I have to.'

'Why now after all these years?'

She sighed.

'A few weeks ago, he told my mother he was being bullied at school. A new boy had joined his class having just moved into the area. His father's a big-shot businessman and when the boy discovered that Michael didn't have a father, he taunted and mocked him and they got into a fight. The Head and Michael's form teacher have assured me they've addressed it with the boy and his family, but they urged me to open up to Michael, said that by denying him such vital information, I could be storing up problems for the future.'

Poor boy. What stories had he told himself about why his father was absent? My heart ached for him.

'What brought you to Abingdon?'

'That's a good question,' she said with a wry look. 'It was a job, but I've sometimes wondered if I chose to come to Oxfordshire in the hope of seeing you, of being able to make things right between us.'

'What do you do?'

'I work for the Crown Prosecution Service. After Michael was born— well after Stonehurst, really—I didn't want to go back to the theatre world, I'd lost my appetite for it. When Michael was old enough, I worked part-time in a solicitors' office. The work interested me, especially the work of the CPS and I saw a vacancy down here for a Caseworker. I couldn't have even considered it without my mother's support. She was prepared to sell the family home and move down here with me and Michael. She adores Michael but increasingly, she needs our support, too, so it works well. The school is good, and until the recent problems, Michael has thrived, especially in music.'

She smiled. 'He's his father's son, for sure. He loved being in *The Turn of the Screw*—it was good for him—and he was keen to keep in touch with Anna. He asked me several months ago if he could go to the *Messiah* concert, and when I saw that you were singing, I wasn't sure what to do. My work commitment tonight was genuine, and when I mentioned it to Anna, she suggested that Michael could sit with her friend Mark for the concert. So, I agreed that he could go and decided that when I came to collect him, I would try to see you, too... I hadn't envisaged it being like this.'

'Will you tell him now?'

'Yes, I will. Tomorrow.'

I got up to refill my glass and she offered me hers. When I sat down again, she was wiping her eyes.

'I know you must be angry and upset and I know I can't expect you to forgive me, but I am truly repentant, and I hope in time you'll feel able to pardon me.'

The distinction between pardoning and forgiving perplexed me, so I said nothing.

'When I tell Michael that you're his father, can I tell him that you want to be part of his life?'

I was fighting back tears now and at first, I struggled to speak.

'Of course you can. If he wants me to be part of his life, that would be the greatest gift I could wish for.'

I hardly slept and was up early, ready to offer porridge and honey and cups of tea. The snow still lay where it had fallen, with only the slightest sign of a thaw. When Lizzie and Michael appeared, we ate breakfast at my kitchen table.

'Will I be going to school?' Michael asked.

'Not this morning,' Lizzie said, 'but I'll call and ask if they'll be open this afternoon.'

'Can we go for a walk then?' he asked.

'I need to ring my office first to say I won't be in, but yes, we can do that. We have Wellington boots and warm jackets in the car.'

'Do you want to come with us, Alex?' Michael asked.

I guessed that Lizzie would take the opportunity to open up to Michael and she needed to do this alone.

'I'll stay here and have hot drinks and crumpets waiting for when you get back.'

'Yummy,' Michael said, rubbing his hands together.

I watched them go and wondered how Lizzie would explain her decisions to a child too young to understand the myriad causes that might drive even a well-intentioned person to do harm. She had wronged me and wronged her son, but I believed she was genuinely penitent. I hoped she could find a way to help the boy understand all this without him rejecting her; that in time, he would be reconciled to what had happened and could look forward to what might be to come.

I busied myself in the flat, looking for distractions, but before long I gave up and sat at my desk in the window and simply waited for them to come back. Some of the anger I'd felt the previous night had dissipated and now the most powerful emotion was sadness. I grieved for all the experiences I'd missed out on, experiences that were lost for ever, that I could never reclaim. But as I sat there, gazing out at the snowy street, still strangely magical even in the light of day, I asked myself if I could look on Lizzie with compassion, see not only her selfishness but her vulnerability, recognise that she had come to face a reckoning and make atonement. It fell to me to be magnanimous. We could never undo what had been done, but I resolved not to do more harm by nurturing anger and withholding forgiveness.

I could hear that traffic was moving freely on the Banbury Road and tyre tracks on Bardwell Road suggested the side streets were now passable. I could sit still no longer. One of my neighbours upstairs had already dealt with the snow on the pavement and path leading to our front door, so I put on my coat and boots and went out to clear the windows on my car and Lizzie's. When that was done, I walked to the junction with the main road.

I looked to the right, northwards, and watched as a bus pulled up at the stop where I had waited less than twenty-four hours earlier. A commonplace sight in a world now transformed.

I had so much to learn about my son, about the life he had known, about his hopes and fears. He loved football, so we could look forward to matchdays away together, but what else? I was pondering the possibilities when I heard his voice.

'Come on, Mum. Hurry up. I'm cold.'

I turned to my left and I saw them—Lizzie struggling to keep up as Michael pulled her along the slippery pavement. I called out and he stopped and waved, his gloved hands a blur of red and white. After only the slightest hesitation, he came skidding and slithering towards me. Lizzie followed slowly behind and watched on as we contemplated each other as father and son. Michael was breathing hard, his cheeks flushed, his expression diffident and uncertain, as if overcome with shyness. As I leant down to take him in my arms, I couldn't tell if he was shivering or trembling, but I held him close and he clung to me, and for now, that was enough. No words needed.

A child, more than all other gifts
That earth can offer to declining man,
Brings hope with it, and forward-looking thoughts.

William Wordsworth *Michael*
Used by George Eliot as the epigraph to *Silas Marner*

Acknowledgements

I want to thank everyone who helped and encouraged me throughout the writing of this book.

First and foremost, I owe an enormous debt of gratitude to Jan Fortune at Cinnamon Press for her unwavering belief in *The Tenor Man's Story* and her endless support and patience. Jan first broached the idea of me writing a third book for Cinnamon in August 2018. Eventually, an idea began to emerge, but just when I hoped to immerse myself in the world of the new book, events in the real world intruded and for a while, took over, meaning that the process of writing was spasmodic and protracted. Throughout it all, Jan was there—wise, kind, and empathic—and prepared to wait until the book could be finished.

My friends and family were a constant source of love and support, but special thanks go to Angela Richardson for her unstinting encouragement and enthusiasm and for being my first reader, always generous with insightful observations and suggestions; my step-sister, Karen Murphy, for her willingness to share the load of caring responsibilities to ensure I had the space and time to write; Michael Pollock for his review of the musical content and for being the inspiration for Johnny Randall: immaculate accompanist, meticulous and kindly vocal coach, loyal friend; Ian Douglas for his invaluable help in devising the incidents that take place during *Death in Venice* at Stonehurst; and Tim Newman for his equally important legal advice on the narrative relating to those incidents.

I'm grateful to Jan Michaelis and Jennifer Smith for answering a barrage of technical questions when they welcomed me onto their stages at Welsh National Opera and Longborough Festival Opera.

I would also like to thank Heather Mountjoy, Archivist at Glamorgan Archives in Cardiff and Dr Christopher Hilton, Head of Archive and Library at Britten Pears Arts in Aldeburgh for their advice on archiving practises in the 1980s.

I'm indebted to the many books and publications and broadcasts that have informed this novel: Graham Johnson, Trevor Hold, Stephen Banfield and Diana McVeigh for their writings on English song; Claire Tomalin, Ralph Pite and Elizabeth Lowry for their work on Thomas Hardy; Tom Service and Melvyn Bragg for their illuminating discussions on music and literature; and Patrick Cockburn, Daniel J Wilson and Peter Preston for their personal experiences of polio epidemics.

The greatest joy of all this research was listening to the music that features throughout the book. The work of many celebrated tenors helped me develop my protagonist, Alex Ingram, in particular: Mark Padmore, Ian Bostridge, Robert Tear, John Graham Hall, John Mark Ainsley, Peter Pears, Anthony Rolfe Johnson, James Gilchrist, Stuart Burrows, Laurence Dale and Robert Gard. Mention must be made, too, of some wonderful baritones, including Thomas Allen, Benjamin Luxon, Bryn Terfel, Roderick Williams, Simon Keenlyside and Christian Geraher.

Music, when soft voices die, vibrates in the memory!

Milton Keynes UK
Ingram Content Group UK Ltd.
UKHW030628151124
451090UK00014B/133

9 781788 641654